IT WAS [illegible] ER

His hands were soft and gentle. Large and comforting. He moved her. Opened her. Kissed her. She was silent throughout. She took direction well. Her drama coach had always told her she took direction well.

"Now" was all he said. His breathing was even, steady. Then again. "Now."

They were one. There was no beginning or ending. They were joined. Parvati and Shiva. Cupid and Psyche. Dionysus and Ariadne. They were immortal, beyond the human. No longer mere flesh, they were eternal. Two beautiful figures moving under the moonlight on a calm of pillows and coverlets.

They were timeless, fabled. They were what poets sang of. They were complete. They were one.

It was perfect, except for the man lurking in the doorway. . . .

Midnight Sins

Ellin Hall

BANTAM BOOKS
TORONTO • NEW YORK • LONDON • SYDNEY • AUCKLAND

MIDNIGHT SINS
A Bantam Book / January 1989

For information address: Bantam Books.

ISBN 0-553-27542-9

Published simultaneously in the United States and Canada

Bantam Books are published by Bantam Books, a division of Bantam Doubleday Dell Publishing Group, Inc. Its trademark, consisting of the words "Bantam Books" and the portrayal of a rooster, is Registered in U.S. Patent and Trademark Office and in other countries. Marca Registrada. Bantam Books, 666 Fifth Avenue, New York, New York 10103.

PRINTED IN THE UNITED STATES OF AMERICA

KR 0 9 8 7 6 5 4 3 2 1

For Steven,
who refreshes my spirit daily.
Love
without end. And to
beginnings.

And Bob.
I thought your love and friendship
were never ending.
This book is dedicated to the
music
of your soul.

Special thanks to Michael J. Fedak, M.D. and The Lighthouse
for their help and research on blindness.

Midnight Sins

• PROLOGUE •

Isn't that . . .
I can't believe how young she looks.
A child.
She's only twenty.
Did you see her in . . .
Odile! You could die *for her Odile.*
And Giselle*! Balanchine says she was born to dance* Giselle*!*

Olive Kingsley couldn't help but brush by the crowded tables in the "21" Club's posh interior. She tried to smile. Someone asked for an autograph. She graciously accommodated the request, then joined her mother at their table.

As if expecting photographers and a journalist to record the event for posterity, Karen Kingsley rose to greet her, kissed the air on either side of her daughter's cheeks, and sat back down.

Karen was in heaven. She so adored the ambience of "21." Black and white checkered each other on the tables, matched the cushions and the chairs, then gave way to a larger order of gracefulness. Walls intentionally crackled with age to resemble an ancient Roman villa. Flowers were everywhere. Cigar smoke. Famous faces. Ah, this was what Karen had always wanted.

It was 1971 and "21" was the hottest restaurant in New York City. A perfect setting for plastic people and hothouse orchids. It oozed power, insinuated pleasure. Lunching there guaranteed exposure. The food could have been better, but no one seemed to notice.

When Olive asked her mother to meet her at "21" for lunch, it never occurred to Karen to ask why. She didn't have to. It wasn't to celebrate any *one* thing. It was to celebrate *everything*. After all, she knew her daughter like a book.

But this was a chapter Karen hadn't written.

As soon as Olive was seated, Marcos, their waiter, appeared beside their table. The "21" Club's service was just as pretentious as its clientele. At those prices it was expected to be.

"Would you like to hear *les spécialités?*" he asked, pen in hand.

Karen nodded, and he recited the list. Cold lobster salad with cayenne mayonnaise was guaranteed to make one's mouth water. Swordfish braised with caramelized onion, rosemary, and risotto was no less scintillating than Bardot in the flesh. Salmon with saffron noodles was divine, and just the mention of chicken breast sautéed with apple and brandy sauce was an orgiastic experience.

"Shall I give you ladies a minute?" Marcus asked.

Karen turned to Olive, who, in an effort to think better, closed her eyes and wrinkled her nose.

"Don't do that, sweetheart," Karen said lightly. "You'll get wrinkles." At forty Karen didn't have a line on her face. Her skin wouldn't dare.

"I'll have a bacon cheeseburger," Olive said.

"Olive!" Karen's voice had the tone of a finger pointing.

Olive turned toward Marcos. Why was it life seemed to be nothing more than a tapestry of menus these days? she wondered. "You bring me what you think is best." She spoke in her most little girl I'm-starving-to-death voice, which she saved for occasions like these. She knew, of course, that Marcos would bring her exactly what she'd ordered, hiding the bacon beneath the burger.

Karen knew it too. In fact, there wasn't much Karen Kingsley didn't know about her precious Olive. But she decided not to make a fuss. Karen had long ago learned to choose her battles well.

"And I, Marcos," she said, smoothing out the lap of her prized luncheon suit, "I'll just have a large green salad."

"Mother!" Olive knew how much her mother loved the food at "21." "Why aren't you ordering the salmon? You love it so."

"Well, the truth is, Olive darling, I got on the scale this morning and it showed that I had put on four pounds. Four pounds! We know that four pounds is not water weight, Olive."

"But, Mother..."

"Madam," Marcos interrupted, using the reprimanding, demanding voice that customers like this one required. "A green salad is not a meal."

"No?" Now it was Karen's turn to be soft, cute, seductive.

"No."

"He's right, Mother."

"All right. For you, my darling Olive, I'll order the fish." She glanced up at Marcos. "Do bring me the salmon, Marcos, but remember—"

"No butter, madam."

"Yes, and—"

"No dressing on the salad."

He was such a good waiter, Karen thought before turning her attention back to Olive.

"I'm hungry."

"But the cholesterol, Olive dearest." No, age hadn't touched Karen's skin. Just her eyes. They had lost the fervency of youth long ago.

Karen could almost hear Marcos judging her, thinking she was depriving her daughter of pleasure. What if he thought Olive was her meal ticket and she, Karen, was being ungrateful?

"Darling, either a cheeseburger or a baconburger. Not both."

"Now, tell me," she said, gazing at her younger mirror image. "What is the cause for this celebration? And why ever are you playing with your napkin, Olive? Have you been drinking coffee? You know how nervous it makes you." Karen smiled and once again took her daughter's hand. "See that? I go out of town for a few days and you pick up bad habits. I don't know, dear."

"Mother..." Olive had been practicing all morning. No, since last night. No, since yesterday morning, when she'd gotten the report. She let go of the napkin and immediately began toying with her braid, but Karen would complain about that too. The only solution was to sit on her hands.

While she waited for Olive to speak, Karen impatiently brushed a nonexistent speck from her Chanel jacket. It was her one good suit and she wore it everywhere. Accessories make all the difference, she had once told Olive. Not just handbags and gloves, but people too. Always surround yourself with people who bring out the best in you. "If you have something to tell me, Olive, please do so and stop fidgeting. It doesn't become you to fidget."

Olive looked directly at her mother. They were carbon copies of each other. Both inordinately thin. Both inheritors of enviable bone structure, the cheekbones high and pronounced. Black hair, porcelain skin, dark almond-shaped eyes, but most importantly, they exuded elegance. Olive had been born elegant, had come out of the womb that way. Refined, soft-spoken, with a nature that made people want to be with her. She was an authentic masterpiece in a world of artifice. Karen Schultz Kingsley was not. Her elegance was a pretense. Her soft-spokenness was an acting exercise. Karen Kingsley was a fraud, but a fraud of the highest caliber.

Karen reached across the table and placed a perfectly manicured forefinger under Olive's chin. "Now, darling, I'm not an ogre. Just tell me what you need to tell me."

"Mother," Olive began, attempting to hold Karen's gaze. She couldn't. *Say it quickly.* "Mother-I'm-going-to-have-a-baby." *Oh, my God, it's out. I can't believe it's out. Oh, my God.*

Karen's nostrils flared ever so slightly and her face paled. Then, as if it were as easy as applying lipstick, she put her smile back on. "If this is your sense of humor, it's much too bizarre for me."

"Mother! It's true." *Oh, please, don't make it more difficult.*

Karen's nostrils calmed down, but her eyes turned black, scalding, hateful. Obviously her daughter saw fit to pick this moment to torment her. The reason, as yet, was unknown.

"How dare you tell me this in a public place?" It hissed out in a frightful whisper. "I will not discuss this with you here. We will wait until you get home this evening."

"Mother!" Oh, these feelings. At first they had frightened her. Karen had once told her that feelings were for actors, not ballet dancers, and Olive had believed her. But now they rose within her like unwanted bile, anger and hurt and confusion and an appalling vulnerability, and she accepted them. Just as she accepted the life that was growing inside her.

"Mother, please don't make it so hard. As it is, I don't know what to do." She looked away and began playing with her braid. The sweetness was gone. "I thought for once you'd support me in something I wanted."

"Support you?" Karen's mouth tightened. "How dare you suggest I'm not a supportive mother? I sacrificed my life for you, Olive. I gave up *me* for you. Do you know what that means? If it weren't for me we'd be accepting relief."

"A scholarship is not relief, Mother." They had been through this so many times before.

"A scholarship *is* a handout. It's admitting to the world that you can't afford to pay your own way and no one, repeat, no one in the Schultz family accepts a handout."

"Kingsley."

Karen let the interjection go, then spoke softly. "I created you, Olive. Balanchine may have put the dancer together, but I, Karen Schultz, made you great."

She sipped her water, then returned to the attack.

"With all that I've put into you I could have become a designer. Yes, apprenticed with Chanel. Or married a man who would have provided me with a closetful of them. But no, I was Olive Kingsley's mother, first, last, and always. And you . . . you think men don't want me. You think I have to be alone now at forty. I gave it all up. For you, Olive." She stopped and caught her breath. "You're killing me, Olive. Do you know this is killing me?"

Olive, with fingernails bitten to the quick, reached out and touched her mother's soft, lotioned hand. "Mother, you're not alone. You—you have me."

"I have *nothing*," Karen said between clenched teeth. Then she composed herself. "Tell me. Who is the father, Olive?"

Olive blushed pink, as if she had a fever. Her palms began to sweat. "It doesn't matter."

"It certainly does. He's ruined your life. I want his name, Olive. I want his name and I'll have him arrested for statutory rape."

"I'm twenty-one, Mother." She wanted to add that she hadn't been raped, but she decided not to fuel the fire.

"Not for another two weeks you're not." Karen had never felt her heart beat so furiously. Not when Olive tried out for Balanchine's company. Not even when her husband Arthur had died. Not even when Parker Grant had told her . . . Damn this child. She brought it all back.

"Your fish, madam," Marcos said. "And your chopped sirloin with melted cheese, Miss Kingsley."

"Thank you, Marcos," Karen said, dismissing him. She took a few deep breaths, then another sip of water. At last she was calm. "Well, Olive, this *is* an unfortunate turn of events. An abortion could prevent you from attending rehearsals for as long as a week. We'll call Dr. Hardy in the morning and see what he has to say. You want to be ready to leave for Copenhagen on the first of July with the rest of the company, don't you, dear?"

"I . . . don't want an abortion, Mother."

"What do you mean, Olive darling?" The words were uttered with deadly precision.

"I mean . . . I mean I feel something, Mother. For the first time since Daddy died, I feel something."

"You *feeeel* something," Karen said, mimicking her daughter. "It's lucky we're in a public place because if we weren't, you'd *feeeel* the palm of my hand across your face. What do you mean you *feel* something? Don't you *feeeel* something when you dance?"

"Yes, Mother, I do. When I dance I feel pain. I am always in pain. You know that." It was true. The human body was never meant to adapt to such strain as *pointe* or a *grand jeté*. The pain was extraordinary, and while some dancers blurred it with pills or powders, Olive knew better. The pain of the body was easier to bear than the pain of the soul.

"That pain comes from a higher good, Olive. This child—that's a laugh. This *cell* is born from your lower nature."

"How would you know, Mother? Have you ever been in touch with yours?"

Karen let the remark pass. "And who will raise this child, Olive?"

"I will."

"Oh, really." Karen began to play with the rolls on the table. "You don't even know how to keep yourself from getting pregnant and you're going to tell me you can raise a child." She was actually considering putting a roll in her mouth. "Marcos, remove these, please."

"Other girls do it."

"Please, Olive. I'm not interested in your romantic notions of motherhood." Karen's eyes narrowed into slits. "You think you know something about raising a child? No one knows what it is to raise a child except a mother. Had I had any idea—"

"Mother!"

"When I became pregnant with you there were no abortionists. Butchers, maybe, but no abortionists."

Olive's eyes widened, filled with tears.

"Olive." Karen really wasn't an ogre. She didn't want Olive to cry, but . . . "Now don't cry, dear. I'm happy I had you. You've turned out wonderfully. Except . . ."

"But Daddy," Olive said. "Didn't Daddy want me?"

"As much as the father of your child wants it."

Olive didn't understand.

"Arthur Kingsley . . ."

"Father."

"Marcos," Karen said to the nearby waiter. "Please do find me a cigarette. I think I left some when I was here last." Karen never carried cigarettes because it might lead to excess, but allowed herself the occasional indulgence.

"Of course, Mrs. Kingsley."

She turned back to Olive.

"Your father... Do you think I would have married a man like Arthur Kingsley if I hadn't had to?"

"Had to? What are you talking about?"

"Would you like me to spell it out?"

Marcos returned and Karen transformed her glare into a smile. With cultivated grace, she withdrew a cigarette from the pack, allowed Marcos to light it, and thanked him ever so much.

"Arthur was a stand-in, my darling."

Olive still didn't get it.

"He wasn't your father."

Olive wanted to smack her mother. How dare she? "I don't believe you."

"I..." Now it was Karen's turn to stumble. "I foolishly assumed that the man who said he loved me, meant it." Correcting herself and becoming Karen Schultz again, she asked, "Who is it, Olive? One of those fairies you dance with?"

"I'm going to have it, Mother. I will love this child."

Karen smirked. "What do you know about love? You loved the man you called your father and you—you killed him." Yes, she'd show this little snit who was boss. "If it weren't for your arguing with me and insisting on having your way all the time, he wouldn't have had to fight for you. He wouldn't have bought you those skates. He never had a heart condition, Olive. Never. Until you gave him one."

Olive opened her mouth to speak, but no words came out. If only she could die.

Karen looked at Olive and could see she had won. Yes, this had been a battle worth taking on. With a single gesture she dismissed both the problem and the salmon and took a bite of her salad. Actually, she hated greens, but they kept her so nice and slim that she had resigned herself to them a long time ago.

• I •

Karla Kingsley came into the world early on the morning of February fourteenth. Fifteen years later she was keeping the same hours. Early to bed, early to rise. She had inherited her love of daylight from her grandmother. The grandmother she had never met.

For Olive it was a different story entirely. Night was her time. It was when her muse came out. When her body was more pliable, allowing her to move easily and effortlessly in and out of *pas de deux, pliés,* and *grand jetés,* first on the stage and now in the studio in her apartment.

Nighttime, the time of the artist . . . the con artist as well as the performing artist. Nighttime. When the murderers mingle with the muse.

That Tuesday morning, when Olive emerged from the bedroom at nine, Karla had been up for hours. Mixing batter, cooking, cleaning. There was no school today.

"Homemade French toast?" Olive asked, planting a kiss on her daughter's cheek. "Undoubtedly I can expect to find something on your Bloomie's bill this month that shouldn't be there."

"Did you hear that, Bear?" Karla asked, addressing her giant stuffed Gump bear which sat in the high chair that had once been Olive's. "Mommy thinks I have an ulterior motive. Boy, a kid can't do anything right. I hope we don't get that cynical when we grow up."

Olive laughed. She picked up the cup of freshly ground and brewed coffee that Karla had prepared and sat on a leather-covered stool. The stools were Olive's creative touch in Karla's domain, the kitchen. Five years before, Karla had talked Olive into redecorating the apartment that she had once shared with Karen.

"It's ratty looking," Karla had complained, and Olive, looking around, had to agree.

She'd called in her designer friend Walter Edwards and had given him free rein. Walter had taken down the walls and part of the ceiling so that the living room had a twenty-five-foot height. He'd removed all of Karen's choice prints and replaced them with photographs—huge blow-ups of Olive dancing, Nureyev's face, a shot by Mary Ellen Mark of a prostitute in Bombay. All black and white. A perfect juxtaposition with the navy carpeting and gray-flannel furniture.

But the kitchen was Karla's turf and there she had called the shots. Karla, who as early as ten was developing into quite a cook, had demanded stainless-steel appliances and white bathroom tiles. At first Olive had hated it, too anal for an oral place, she'd thought, but it had grown on her. In fact, their kitchen had recently been featured in *Home Restaurant* magazine. The only relief to the antiseptic, industrial setting came from yellow leather-topped stools which squared the center cutting area. They were spots of sunlight.

"There is nothing like the first sip of coffee in the morning," Olive said. "Which brew is this?" Karla had Oren's deliver a variety of coffee beans twice a week.

"Celebese," Karla said, turning over the French toast.

Cradling her cup in her hands, Olive stared at Karla. She loved watching her daughter. She got such pleasure from the girl. Impulsively, she reached over and kissed her on the forehead. "Was I ever as beautiful as you when I was your age?" she asked rhetorically.

"What do you think, Bear?" Karla asked.

"I think she's prettier." Karla answered for Bear in a high, squeaky voice, then feigned insult.

"Well, I never," she said in her own voice.

Actually it was true. The years had given Olive a softness she hadn't had when she was Karla's age. This morning, dressed tidily in her black linen Ralph Lauren slacks and herringbone Mountbatten jacket, she looked particularly girlish.

"I decided," Karla said, "that since we haven't had breakfast together in two weeks, we should today. Right, Bear?"

"Right," said the squeaky voice.

"So how are rehearsals going, Mom? Sugar? Jam?"

"The rehearsals are going beautifully. I'm so pleased."

Karla slid the slice of toast out of the pan, pulled a rose petal off the floral arrangement, and served it to her mother. "Hot chocolate?"

"How about just the French toast?" Olive said, checking herself in the full-length mirror. "As far as I know, Renaissance women are still not the in thing."

Karla, towering over Olive by almost four inches, hugged her mother from behind. "I'd say you have a long way to go before anyone calls you Renaissance."

Karla was right. The only thing that had spread on Olive was her smile. She'd never been happier than she was these past few years. Lonely, yes, but definitely happy.

"How's Becky?" Olive asked, trying to distract her daughter so she could tuck her top in.

"It doesn't go in, Mom," Karla said, pulling it back out. She wanted her turquoise and salmon cowl-neck sweater to lie loose over her skintight mustard-colored leggings. She wanted to show off the fact that her body was not an ounce less than perfect.

As Karla started cooking the second piece of toast the doorbell rang.

"It must be the paper," Olive said, and walked to the door.

She didn't return for several minutes, and the long silence warned Karla that something was wrong.

"What is it, Mom?" she called.

What is it? Olive thought, staring at the lurid, tragic headline. Some would say it's New York. The Big Apple. Sin City. But others would disagree, saying the sin isn't in the city, it's in the people.

"Mom?"

"Another dancer's been killed," she said, gazing at Nina Houston's picture. She remembered the young woman so well. Bright Nina Houston, the up-and-coming star on everyone's list. According to the *Post* it was a sex murder. She had the same cross carved into her inner thigh that the dancer who was killed two weeks earlier had had. "Do you remember meeting her?' she asked Karla as the girl walked into the living room.

"No." Karla looked over her mother's shoulder. "She was pretty, wasn't she?"

"Yes, she was." Suddenly Olive felt very protective of her daughter. Karla spent so much time by herself. She traveled to and from school by herself. Now with the opening of the play, and Olive once again becoming headline material, she wondered if she shouldn't hire a bodyguard for her daughter.

Karla studied her mother as she followed her back to the kitchen. "Mom, why are you so upset?"

"I'm not, darling. I'm not."

"Here, you take a bite of this French toast," Karla said in her perkiest voice. The recipe was from Ratners and it was delicious. The only problem was that Olive had no appetite.

"You don't like my cooking?" Karla asked.

"Since when did you become a Jewish mother?"

"Since you became an undernourished choreographer. You need all your strength to make a dancer out of Ashley Pope, that's for sure." She plucked two apples from the fruit bowl and held them up to her own flat chest, stuck out her fanny, and said, "Know what I mean?"

Olive smiled and tried to sound light. "Gotta run, Miss Know-it-all. What'll it be for dinner?"

"Pizza."

"Karla! We can't eat junk night and day."

"Why not? With all the vitamins we take, our bodies will never know how badly they're being treated."

"I'm picking up a chicken and that's final." Her voice was harsher than she'd intended. *Another dancer's been killed*... She had her hand on the doorknob when Karla stopped her.

"Hello, sweet little umbrella," Karla said, pulling her mother's lace-trimmed collapsible umbrella out of the stand. "Are you going to keep my mama dry?"

"It's raining?" Olive asked, looking vaguely toward the window. She could still see Nina Houston's eyes staring up at her.

"Either that or Sam is washing the sidewalk—and the car roofs, and the awning, and..."

"All right. All right. How did I ever get a comedienne for a daughter? You certainly didn't get it from my side of the family." Why was it that Karla could always make her feel better? "See you later, funny bunny," she said, and kissed Karla good-bye.

But once outside Olive chose not to open the umbrella. She liked the way the fine mist felt on her hair, coating her bangs and her waist-long braid, giving her a halo of sorts. It made her feel like a little girl. That lifted her spirits, as did thinking of Karla. Yes, Karla was the one thing she'd done right.

Olive sighed. *If I die tomorrow I'll have no regrets.*

◆ II ◆

Karen Schultz wasn't born a bitch. She simply had the misfortune of becoming one.

Like every other young girl, she believed in love everlasting, white wedding dresses, and princes on white horses. And then she met Parker Grant, famed neurosurgeon and husband to Kimberly Ambrose Grant. Parker offered her her first job out of high school. Karen, always the opportunist, assumed the job would lead to something. It did. A brief and meaningless affair.

By the time it was over she was out of a job. She was also pregnant. Which is how Karen Schultz, aspiring young beauty, became involved with Arthur-nothing-to-write-home-about Kingsley.

Arthur-nothing-to-write-home-about Kingsley lived down the street from Karen in their mutually unfashionable section of Middle Village. While they may have shared the same address, that was all they shared. Or so Karen thought. But Arthur Kingsley believed they had something in common. He had been asking her out for years. Karen was no dummy, though. Marrying the boy-next-door was definitely not the way to get off the block. So year after year she refused.

After Parker she stopped refusing.

On the first date, Karen permitted Arthur to take her to Mamma Leone's for dinner and to The Rose Tattoo afterward. Coming home on the IND, Arthur took hold of her hand and she begrudgingly allowed it. On the second date, she permitted a good-night kiss, and when, on their third date Arthur-nothing-to-write-home-about Kingsley proposed marriage, she smiled and said, "Arthur darling. Dear Arthur, I would like very much to marry you, but there's something I must tell you."

Whatever it was he didn't care. Nothing could change his feelings toward her, he said. Then, thinking they were friends, he leaned toward her and offered her a shoulder. She didn't take it.

"I'm pregnant," she said, with neither an explanation nor an apology. He didn't need any. Obviously someone had taken advantage of her.

"I will make it mine," he said, his thin lips curving into a smile, giving his too-fleshy face a cherubic quality. "I will make it mine."

I certainly hope not, Karen thought. I certainly hope not.

While Arthur may have been nothing to write home about, he did take very good care of Karen. They married almost immediately and throughout her rather easy pregnancy she designed exquisite clothes for herself. Every month she awaited the newsstand's presentation of Vogue and Harper's Bazaar. Then, with the careful eye of an artist, she imitated patterns and fabrics. By the time Olive was born, Karen had worked up both a mother-and-daughter wardrobe and a new philosophy: Happiness isn't everything. It can't buy money.

When Olive Kingsley came into the world, Karen and Arthur celebrated the event with as much self-congratulatory praise and pomp as an Arab sheik might reserve for the birth of a son. On Karen's side, it was from the need to compensate for the past. On Arthur's side, it was the need to compensate for the fact that he wasn't the real father. Something Karen had reminded him of daily throughout the pregnancy.

Arthur worked all day servicing radiators in public schools—he's an engineer, Karen told anyone rude enough to ask—and at night he sorted mail in the post office. In between, he came home to a hot meal, a clean house, and a freshly made bed.

Not that Karen ever slept in that bed with him. That would have been unthinkable. To actually sleep next to the bulky, barrel-chested man who perspired between his legs and had permanent grease stains under his nails would have been . . . well, low class. Occasionally she allowed him to have sex with her—she had to—but sleep next to him? Never.

Arthur didn't seem to mind. Simply being with his beautiful young wife and child satisfied him for a long time. It filled his need for family. He didn't even mind Karen's devotion to Olive; he had similar feelings. Nor did he argue over the fact that Karen wouldn't bear his child.

But when Olive was six, things began to change. Karen announced that Olive would dance. It was dinnertime and Arthur was slicing the brisket of beef. Not only would she dance, Karen said, but she would dance with Balanchine. Actually, Karen had pulled the great choreographer's name out of a hat. She had no more knowledge of Balanchine's dance technique than she did of Merce Cunningham's or Martha Graham's, but she did like his name. Yes, Balanchine had a nice ring to it. It sounded like money.

"Why Balanchine?" Arthur asked, passing a slice of brisket to his daughter. He had never even heard of Balanchine.

"Why go to the tail, darling, when the head is available?" And that was that.

In order to dance with the head, though, one had to make a few sacrifices. Like food. Like comfort. Like playtime. Like friendships. In a nutshell, childhood. Then, if chosen, if named prima ballerina, the prodigy must give up everything else.

Karen didn't care. She considered it a sacrifice well worth making.

Arthur didn't agree. He criticized Olive's rigorous schedule. He didn't like the fact that Karen fed the girl like a bird or that she had no friends.

"What do you know about such things?" Karen taunted. "You're just a commoner. You've never even been to a ballet."

"I'm not so common," he said, beginning to find his voice. "I married you."

"Yes, and I took a step down."

"Save your fancy airs for your girl friends at the beauty parlor. Don't try to pass them off on me. I know where you came from."

Karen and Arthur began to fight regularly and Olive was always in the middle. They fought over Karen forbidding Olive to go to the movies. She said it took too much time away from dance. Then they fought about Arthur taking her anyway. They fought about Arthur feeding her White Castle hamburgers and sneaking her away to the circus.

There was one thing that even Karen couldn't stop Olive from doing, and that was reading. Late at night, by her tiny clown-shaped night-light, Olive loved to read about Isadora Duncan. She was fascinated by the legendary dancer, this woman who looked nothing like the sticks who danced for Balanchine. Isadora believed that bodies and feet shouldn't be distorted in order to dance properly, and somewhere in the back of Olive's mind a voice told her that Isadora was right. Unfortunately, nothing in her life corroborated that. All of her associations were with other Balanchine dancers—and her mother. They said that distortion in the name of art was beauty.

Olive was also charmed by Isadora's fascination with Russia, and her courage to move there. After all, in the late fifties America was still reverberating from McCarthyism. And then Isadora's two illegitimate children . . . Even as a youngster Olive knew that Isadora Duncan was of a different spirit than most people, and as odd as it seemed, she believed she was of that different spirit too.

When Olive was eleven she announced she wanted to learn to ice-skate.

"No." Karen was adamant. "Definitely not."

"But all the girls skate, dear," Arthur said, turning down the TV.

"She is not 'all the girls,' *Arthur. She is Olive Kingsley, prima ballerina material. Next year she will work directly under Balanchine himself."*

"You're raising your voice, Karen," Arthur said sarcastically.

Karen came up close to Olive. She did love the girl, but it was so hard to get through to her sometimes. Especially with that man around.

"You are not just another pretty face with a pair of long legs, my darling Olive. You are my daughter and I will deliver you to Balanchine just as I delivered you from the womb. In one piece. Is that understood?"

No. It wasn't. So Karen went to a higher authority.

"Injury now," Balanchine said to Olive in his thick Russian accent, "is death for you as dancer. You're too young to take chance with body."

"You will have ice skates," Karen said as Olive persisted, "over my dead body."

Actually, it was over Arthur's dead body.

"An accident," her mother told her. With all the compassion she could muster Karen allowed Olive a week of mourning. And then it was supposed to be over.

It wasn't. One afternoon, when Karen was out at her committee meetings, Olive was home alone. Even alone, she could feel her mother's presence everywhere. Karen was like a constant ache, a splinter under a fingernail. But Olive ventured forth anyway, into her parents' bedroom.

She opened his drawers and found his cuff links and the old tattered sweater that Karen had been after him for months to throw out. The undershirts that he wore until Karen literally ripped them off his back.

She opened the closet and ran her hands over her father's jackets. They weren't sport coats like Karen had wanted him to wear, but zippered club jackets with knit collars and big pockets. As if her daddy were still in the jackets, she brought them close to her face. She hugged them tightly and was surprised to find he had left his scent behind. The discovery delighted her. All she had to do was take the jackets off the hangers, lift them out of the closet, and hold them close to her nose, and Daddy was there. It was heaven. And then she saw the box. At the back of the closet. It was a big, beautiful box, like something you'd get for Christmas.

Olive turned around. Had her mother come in when she wasn't looking? No, she hadn't.

The box was unwrapped in a second. Ice skates! Ice skates! Inside were ice skates.

Mesmerized, Olive sat down in the middle of the bedroom floor, her little fingers running over the white leather tops as if in disbelief. Loving the smell of leather, she brought the skates close to her face and drenched her nose in the aroma of the cowhide. Even the laces were leather. She touched their silken surface, then giggled and fingered the double pompoms on each set of laces. And the blade. How Olive was in awe of that blade. It would balance her as her toes one day would. But on skates she could stand full-footed without cutting through the ice. For the first time since her father had died Olive actually felt happy.

She took off her shoes and maneuvered her foot into the right skate. It was a little too roomy, but she knew heavy socks would fix that. Daddy always thought of everything. Daddy—

"And just what do you think you are doing?" Karen's voice was like an alarm clock going off in the middle of a perfect dream. Seeing Olive with one skate on, she attempted to grab the other one.

"Don't." Olive's tone was one that Karen had never heard before. She froze and stared at her daughter. Then Olive's sweetness returned. "Look what Daddy bought for me." She was excited. She wanted to share this joy with her mother.

"The answer is no," Karen said, again grabbing for the skate.

"Mom, Daddy bought these skates for me. He was going to give them to me for Christmas."

"Your dumb father was going to give them to you now," Karen said, indignant. "And would have if he hadn't died. How I wish that damn attendant weren't so honest."

"What are you talking about?" Olive asked, holding on tightly to the second skate.

"I mean the men's room attendant found them and returned them."

"What men's room attendant? You said Daddy had an accident."

"I lied," Karen said, still eyeing the undone skate. If she could just take it away. "He died... he died on the toilet bowl."

"On the toilet bowl?" Olive was shattered.

"Just like your father to have a heart attack while relieving himself. And he bought you those fool skates. Ridiculous. I don't even know why I allowed them in here."

"You knew," Olive said, not quite believing the deception.

"Of course I knew. Now take them off, darling."

Olive didn't budge.

"Do you hear me? Let me have them."

Olive pushed her mother out of her mind. She would not listen.

"You can't go ice-skating now anyway," Karen said, trying to pull the skate out of her daughter's hands.

"I'm not going ice-skating. I'm just trying them on."

"And then what, Miss Smarty-pants?"

"And then I'm going to stay in my room until it's time to go to sleep," Olive answered in her most smarty-pants voice.

"With the skates on?"

"Yes."

"Take them off, I said."

"I am not taking them off," Olive said defiantly. "I'm going to sleep with them on, and if you try to take them from me, I'll run away. I'll go to Russia like Isadora did and you'll never see me again."

"You little fool," Karen said contemptuously. "It seems as if you've inherited my talent, but you've gotten your father's brains."

"And don't you dare ever say another bad thing about him. Ever."

"Don't you tell me what to do!"

"I'll do whatever I want. I'm going to be a prima ballerina, remember. I'm Olive Kingsley." Just to be mean, she added, "And you're only Karen Kingsley, widow. Be careful, Ma."

Then, clutching the one skate, Olive stomped off, limping, one leg high and one leg low.

Olive had stood up to her mother for the first time. But Karen took neither the loss of the battle nor her daughter's rebellion seriously. In fact, she pretended the incident had never occurred. Certainly she didn't take her daughter skating.

Once Olive went by herself, but it wasn't much fun. It just reminded her of Daddy...and of how alone she was. So ultimately Karen had had her way. Olive never skated.

III

Had Richard Dixon been lucky enough to change his sex, he would have modeled himself after Isadora Duncan. To Richard, Isadora was the personification of all that was female, all that was grace and beauty and creative energy. He wasn't quite that lucky, but still he wanted to dance.

"Plump little brown boys don't dance," his mother had told him, and he believed her. He was too short to dance. His stubbornly stocky body would never make the grade in ballet, and that was the only kind of dance Richard ever wanted to do. He had his mother send him to dance classes anyway, and in the meantime he discovered he could write.

The typewriter didn't care what color he was, or how fat he was. It didn't care if he had a pimple or went prematurely bald. The typewriter loved him regardless. So he wrote and wrote and wrote.

When he was eighteen his first book was published. *Confessions of an Autistic Sailor* was an hysterically funny account of a boy who was afraid to swim and yet joined the navy. At first the critics compared it to *Catcher in the*

Rye, but when they found out Richard was black they changed their tune and called him the new Claude Brown.

In reality, Richard wasn't the new anybody. He was the same old Richard Dixon, but now he had the money to do what he wanted to do. He studied choreography and used it in his writing. Finally, at the ripe old age of thirty-eight, Richard Dixon was making his dream come true and *Isadora, Isadora* was its name.

Isadora would live on Broadway, but who could embody her?

Jessica Bishop was everyone's first choice. She was the brilliant ingenue who turned New York on its spinal cord when she danced for Eliot Feld. She had the body, the diversity of training, the acting ability. Yes, she was everyone's first choice. Everyone except Johnny Green, and Johnny Green was the money man. Johnny was a big Hollywood producer and Johnny had a big thing for Ashley Pope.

Of course, Ashley was no unknown, so it wasn't like he was pushing her down people's throats. Matter of fact, people were pushing themselves down her throat. Which was how she got the name Pope. Folks said she had been on her knees more times than he had. Anyway, she had been breaking box office records in jiggle films, playing sweet, young, sexy things and hard, young, sexy things, for the past half-dozen years. Everyone loved her. She was as American as guilt, as modern as blowjobs, as ditzy as Monroe, and as talented as . . . Well, no one knew for sure, but then no one had asked. Yet.

Ashley Pope, née Frances Rosenbloom, nice Jewish girl from Newark, New Jersey, loved the spotlight from the very beginning. When she was oohed and ahed over in the crib, she knew she'd act. She took center stage in dance class and was every little boy's sweetheart in first grade.

First grade was one thing. Hollywood was another grade entirely. By the time Frannie Rosenbloom quit high school at sixteen and began taking acting classes in New York City, she realized the stage was much larger than the proscenium arch. First thing she did was change her name. Then, she began an exercise regimen that would have intimidated Joe Namath. Next, she got a job as a receptionist in a brokerage house. She figured that way she'd get the proper exposure to guys with big bucks. To guys who could afford to watch the ticker tape at lunchtime. After all, Ashley was no fool. She knew that everything had a price. If God hadn't given it to her, it could be bought. And if she couldn't afford it, she'd find someone who could.

Enter Charlie Eisenberg. Charlie owned a sweater factory in the center of the garment district. On his lunch hours he'd go over to his broker and watch the tape run. There he met Ashley. Sure, he was too old for a girl Ashley's age, but he wasn't too rich. And so a match was made at Merrill Lynch.

Charlie was an easy roll for Ashley. It was easy to put up with his wide ties that covered the belly that peered out from between the buttons on his shirt. She put up with his woven hair, his wife on Long Island, his phony star sapphire pinkie ring. Sure he could afford a real one, but on the real ones you couldn't always see the star, and Charlie didn't see any point in owning a star sapphire if you couldn't see the star.

In exchange for two years of her life, Charlie paid for Ashley's voice and acting classes. He picked up the tab for her exercise classes. He bought her beautiful clothes and kept her in a real hot east side pad. Good old Charlie. It was worth every day of it. Ashley saved all the money she made as a receptionist and started with the tits. By the time she was twenty-one, she had just the body she wanted. As her acting coach Ina Grant once said, "You got it all new, from the nose down."

At twenty-five, the body was holding up perfectly, but Ashley was bored. With the tits. With the ass. Even with Hollywood. So when Johnny received Richard's request to help back *Isadora, Isadora,* the Pope got on her knees and let Johnny know just how much she wanted the role. Johnny, never one to turn away a hungry mouth, called Richard posthaste and agreed to produce his show.

Richard couldn't believe his good luck. I must be doing something right, he thought.

"One little request," Johnny added, as if in afterthought.

"Anything," Richard said, and meant it.

"Do all the union calls you want, but make sure Ashley Pope gets the part."

"Everything has a price," Richard told Benedict, his live-in lover. "Ashley paid hers, I have to pay mine."

"I have a feeling she's getting the better end of the deal," was Benedict's comment.

"Don't be so sure," Richard said. "You've never met Johnny."

Richard began his search for a choreographer. He needed a great talent who loved Isadora as much as he did, could work with Ashley Pope, and put up with a dud like Johnny Green. Olive Kingsley was the first person he called.

"Olive," he said, "I'd like to give you a song and dance about a faaabulous new show I'm doing. . . . Who? Well, Isadora Duncan, darling. That's why I'm calling you."

Richard didn't have to ask twice. Olive jumped at the chance. *Isadora, Isadora* was her dream as well. If she could have brought back any single artist in history, it would have been Isadora Duncan. To Olive, Isadora was still the embodiment of everything free, unconfined, ethereal.

"Your biggest feat," Richard told her, "will be keeping Ashley Pope's back straight."

"Why? Does she have a drinking problem?"

"No, it's just going to be hard to balance those tits."

Two weeks into rehearsals and much to everyone's surprise, Ashley wasn't doing too badly. But *not too badly* wasn't good enough for Olive Kingsley.

The day she learned about Nina Houston's murder, Olive was ten minutes late for rehearsal. She still couldn't get the young dancer's face out of her mind.

"Sorry, guys," she said as she rushed down the aisle. In one second she was in her seat next to Richard.

"Lights," Richard called. They were all ready for business now.

As if heaven-sent, a soft white light enveloped Ashley. It danced around her with brush strokes of yellow, sculpting her, making love to her.

She stood stage left for a few minutes, allowing the heat of the lamps to warm the nape of her neck. She liked the droplets of sweat beading up under her eloquent array of blonde tresses. She liked this feeling. She loved heat.

Slowly, deliberately, she stepped out of her skirt and unbuttoned her blouse. Beneath the clothes she was the antithesis of the Balanchine dancer. Which didn't necessarily mean she was the synthesis of everything Isadora. Isadora's dancers may have been fleshy like Ashley, but they were unselfconscious. Whether Ashley was unbuttoning her blouse or blowing her nose, she was completely aware of the effect she was having on her audience. In other words, Ashley was still playing Hollywood.

The music started. It was Mozart's Concerto no. 20 in D Minor, K. 466. Not necessarily Isadora's first choice. She might have gone for Scriabin or Chopin, but Mozart's Concerto no. 20 was Olive's choice. She thought the piece was perfect for the poignant scene.

"Isadora," Olive said, talking Ashley through the scene, "your lover is walking up the path and you run to meet him. Yes, that's right. On toe, but not on *pointe*." Balanchine would have died had he known of Olive's direction. It would have been much too flatfooted for him. But not for Olive, or Ashley. She took the cue and moved quickly, happily.

"You sense something... Slow down. Good, Isadora. There's a sadness in his face and you... for some reason, you can't ask what's wrong. You wait."

"No, don't stand still. Wait in silence but not in stillness. Yes. Yes. That's right. Lyrical. Now, he tells you. Yes. That's what the music is about. He tells you Deirdre and Patrick are dead. Bum-*bum*. Bum-*bum*. Yes, you clutch yourself. That's right.

"Now, I want that movement *big,* Isadora. The *pain*. We must feel the pain. Yes.

"The joy, music, lightness is all gone. It is dark. Your babies are gone. Yes, run, Isadora. Run, run. Around and around and around like a mother bird who sees her nest is empty. Yes, Isadora. It is setting in.

"Now you stop. Stop." Olive paused.

"Let the music be, Isadora. This is when you let Mozart be the star and you let Isadora die. To the ground. Yes. Tears, Isadora. Sweep the ground with your body. Quiet. Quiet. Now up. Up.

"Okay. Stop the music."

Olive rose from her seat and walked toward the stage. Ashley, drenched in sweat, didn't move. She couldn't move. This was definitely not Hollywood. This was definitely not makeup artists and refreshments served in-between takes. This was work and she loved every smelly minute of it.

"That was terrific," Olive said, approaching her star.

Ashley, panting, began to stand up.

"Stay there," Olive said in the most supportive voice she could find. "Let's do this together."

As the music began to play once more, Olive draped herself over Ashley's body. With a single swift action she curled her fingers around Ashley's and lifted her to the mourning of the music. Gently, slightly. Then back down again. "You are broken, Isadora. You are throbbing with pain."

Again they rose, then dropped. Again. "The pain is born out of your chest," Olive whispered. Over and over they rose and fell until Olive felt they were one. She let go. Ashley, lighter with the weight off her back, rose and fell as Hecuba might have when she learned that Paris was going to go to Helen. She was any mother losing any child.

As Ashley stood, she transcended all of it, gliding across the floor as a symbol. She used the stage as a basis for reality, a visual reminder that she was in the world, but not necessarily of it. She was hypnotic. She was pain and beauty. Ashley Pope was becoming a dancer.

"Uh-oh," Ashley said, taking one look at the guy standing on the other side of her dressing-room door. He was gorgeous, all six feet of him, and he was holding a single white rose.

"For your purity," he said with an innocence more

appropriate to a choirboy than a peer. "I . . . just wanted your autograph."

He sounded sincere, and she gazed at him curiously.

"How did you get in here?" she asked. He looked familiar but she couldn't quite place him.

"I work here," he said.

"Where?" Her voice was a giggle, young and girlish, sparked by the electric current running through her body. She still had on only the cotton tights and filmy tunic she'd worn on stage, and knew how they enhanced her made-to-order sensuality, her centerfold body.

"I'm the lighting designer."

"Robbie Haskins?" she asked. "You're Robbie Haskins?"

"You've heard of me?" Robbie seemed to derive a feeling of power from that.

"You're not serious." A chill suddenly raced through her. The scene with Olive had left her both hot and cold, and Robbie had knocked just when she was about to dry herself. "Everyone's heard of you. You're the best damn lighting designer in the country."

He looked down at the floor. "No. No, I'm not."

"Oh, don't be modest, Robbie. You're the best there is." Had she heard of him? Of course she'd heard of him, and not only as a lighting designer. He also had quite a reputation as a ladies' man. But there was always a cautionary note. He wasn't to be taken seriously. Commitment wasn't his thing. Well, it wasn't hers either.

"Do you know how beautiful you are?" he asked.

"Robbie, I'm cold. Do you mind if I slip into something a little warmer?"

"I'll wait out here."

"Robbie." She put her hand on his forehead. "Are you well? What's the matter with you? You're afraid of being alone with me in my dressing room?"

For the first time he looked closely at her. Not the actress, but the woman, the female, the spiritual incarnation of the Lord's goodness, and he saw that she was good. She was very good.

"You don't mind?" he asked.

"Get in here," she said, taking his hand and practically dragging him inside. "Now, you be a good little boy and sit in that chair. I'll be out in a minute."

As she showered, Robbie looked around for signs of a man, a husband or a lover. He looked for a photograph, a dressing gown, flowers that he might have sent. There was nothing. Ashley had left any trinkets behind in California because she liked traveling empty-handed. It left her lots of room to collect things—like hearts.

"Now that's better," she said as she stepped out of the shower. Even with her hair dripping wet and not a speck of makeup on, she was gorgeous. No pretensions. Just flawless legs, a permanently tight butt, and breasts that seemed filled with helium.

"Ashley, I think I'd better leave."

"Robbie . . ." She moved toward him, moved in for the kill. She knew she and Robbie would reinvent sex together. He didn't seem to know that, though.

"I really think I'd better leave," he said, handing the rose to her. "I must leave."

Ashley took the rose and was about to ask him why the hurry when she felt the sting of the thorn. She let the droplet of blood grow large on her finger before she sucked it away.

• IV •

Olive walked home after rehearsal, and Nina Houston's murder screamed from the headlines of all the papers stacked in front of all the newsstands. Another dancer, the second in two weeks. The first was Ariel Powell from the Lubovitch Dance Troupe. Whoever had a penchant for killing dancers also had a penchant for taking their toes, their big toes. Thus the epithet, Tiptoe Killer.

Murder really isn't such a big deal in the Mad-hattan. In fact, it seems almost as American to eat up pretty young girls in New York as it does to lick your fingers after a good piece of batter-fried chicken. But what bothered the press, and made it headline material, was that both victims were dancers, artists. New York didn't like its artists being killed. Never had.

Nineteen seventy-one hadn't been such a good year for female artists either. Diva-to-be Renata Fracci was stabbed to death in the elevator of the Metropolitan Opera House. Sasha Tobin, cellist for the New York Philharmonic, was killed outside the stage door, and January Stills was raped while coming home from conducting a concert at St. John the Divine. Sweet Jocelyn Gregory was seriously injured when she resisted a rapist inside her dressing room at the State Opera House.

They caught the guy, but not before he gave another sicko a similar idea. This guy was classier. He didn't just drop in on his victims. He sent them notes first. Margot Fonteyn and Judith Jamison each got one. So did Olive Kingsley. The artistic community didn't like their ladies being threatened, and Balanchine called in the cops. The boys in blue had been getting lousy notices for months now, so the NYPD decided to up their image. Olive Kingsley was assigned a bodyguard.

To Olive, Vince Luscardi was a part of the props of the city, like the men selling pretzels in the park or the hansom cabs outside the Plaza Hotel. He would have stayed that way had it not been for the autograph hound who was waiting for her after rehearsal one day.

"Can I have your autograph?" the hound asked.

"Sure," she said, pulling out a pen. He didn't want it in ink, though. He wanted it in blood. He later told the cops that in years to come it would be far more valuable than ink.

He shoved a notebook and knife under Olive's nose. The knife was silver and gleaming and sharp, and for a moment she thought it was a joke. A stunt set up by someone in the publicity department. By the time she realized it was for real, the guy almost had what he wanted. In fact, he would have, had it not been for the bodyguard the NYPD had sent to protect her.

Vince stopped being part of the woodwork then. Olive noticed him, realized he had a name, a life, a sense of justice. Most of all, he was real. Like her father had been. They became a couple. An odd one, but a couple nonetheless. They walked back and forth from rehearsals to the apartment she shared with her mother on Central Park West. They walked and talked about everything from the price of coffee to what makes a Velázquez worth five and a half million dollars. They became friends when Olive needed a friend.

Olive also needed an admirer, a real admirer. Not just a ballet groupie or another dancer who thought that by sleeping with Olive Kingsley he'd have it made. Vince seemed to care about her. He actually thought her body—that frame as narrow as a Giacometti sculpture, as muscular as an athlete's—was sexy. No one had ever told her she was sexy before. She was intrigued. Frightened. Excited.

She listened as he told her about his marriage to Connie. About their childhood in Staten Island, about how he had loved Connie since the second grade. He loved Connie, but not enough to stay home, to be the husband she wanted him to be. Why is it love asks so much of us? he wondered aloud.

Olive didn't know. She was still searching. Oh, she had had her flings. One with one of her Albrechts. Quin Marsden was his name. Beautiful Quin with his square jaw and sapphire-blue eyes. Perfect Quin with his thick honey-colored hair and his quick leaps. His body defied gravity. He seemed to hang in midair. Even Balanchine, who considered male dancers a mere condiment to the female feast, fell in love with Quin. It was as if he had no bones. There was nothing his body could not do.

But Quin was not about love. He was about pleasure. His. Olive Kingsley, who had learned to please Karen and then Balanchine, learned to please Quin.

And then he didn't want to be pleased any longer. There was a younger ingenue who interested him more. He left, but he left something behind within Olive. An awakened sexuality. She didn't tell Vince. She didn't have to. He knew, but he didn't know what to do about it... until the second time Olive screamed.

He was just outside her dressing-room door after a performance when he heard a bloodcurdling shriek. "Olive!" he yelled, ramming in the door with his shoulder.

She was trembling, couldn't speak.

"What?"

"A mouse."

"A mouse?" he repeated. "You're screaming because of a mouse? I almost smashed my shoulder because of a mouse?" Then he smiled. "Olive, I only have two."

They laughed, and when the laughter had stopped, they realized she wasn't wearing any clothes. Unless you count bra and panties.

Vince tried to look away but couldn't. Wrong. Wouldn't.

"I'll be ready in a few minutes," she said in a barely audible voice.

"I'll wait outside."

They walked home in silence, as they had during those weeks before that boy had pulled a knife on her. But this silence had a voice, a strong quiet voice. A voice of wanting.

"I don't feel like going home," she said, turning toward him. For the first time she noticed that his eyes were the color of pale emeralds and that his hair was like the early morning light. She realized his slight stoop made him appear somewhat humble and abbreviated his six-foot-three frame. And then she noticed the way he was looking at her.

"I have a friend who gave me the keys to his apartment," he said. "Would you believe to water his plants?"

No, she didn't believe it. "Yes," she said. "I would believe it."

There were no other words. They walked to the apartment building, let themselves in, and found they were completely at home in each other's arms.

As in her dance, they did not need to talk. Just take quick, tiny movements. Light strokes. Gentle touches. Then the movements became greater. As if she were a porcelain figurine, he unwrapped her, kissed her, fondled her. He ran his hands over the curves of her small breasts. He traced her hipbones with his tongue, kissed her belly button. There was something in him, something almost primitive, that wanted to protect her, this woman, this child, this beauty.

But she was no longer a child and she did not want to be protected. Not here. When he kissed her tenderly she responded in strength, fanning a fire he'd long since forgotten. Yes, there had been women, but for some reason he never felt anything. Hadn't since his fire died for Connie. With Olive it all came back.

She felt it too. Red flames licked their flesh, so hot it hurt. She wanted him to make it stop hurting. Now.

Unsure if the fires would consume him, he rose over her, to enter her, to take her. His gentleness was gone. Then he was inside her and it returned. She called his name. Yes, she said, again and again. Yes, she cried out. The ballet was over. No silence here. Yes, this was what she wanted, had waited for. Yes, she knew of it long before it happened. This was why ballets were written, why music was created, why people loved and married. Yes. Yes. Yes.

Olive glanced at the photograph of Nina Houston's bright shiny face and wondered why she had this horrible feeling that before long her own face might find its way onto the rag's covers. Then she decided to put the notion out of her mind. She was obviously getting paranoid.

This one had a blue face too.

Detective Vince Luscardi, veteran New York City policeman for thirty years, looked into the face of the girl who'd left the love note and couldn't help thinking it was people like her who gave love a bad name. He read the note again.

Dear Danny: I told you I'd do anything for you. Well here's the proof. If I didn't kill me, I'd have to kill you. I'll love you always. Evelyn.

Somebody should have told her that that's not love, Vince thought. Love doesn't make you die. It makes you live.

A lot you know, big guy.

He looked around for foul play, but knew he wouldn't find any. It was a suicide. A rookie could see that. But suicide is murder, so they dusted the place for prints.

As a matter of course, Vince ran his finger over the See Seaman's First Formica coffee table. You can tell a lot about someone by running your finger over her coffee table. Like how often she cleans. What kind of polish she uses. Evelyn's apartment was very clean. Even her dishes were washed and stacked in the drainer. It was a tidy little place inhabited by a tidy little girl who wrote tidy little notes. No doubt she'd wanted to blow her brains out, but then someone would have had to come in and clean up the mess. So she chose pills. It was a lot neater. And a lot more considerate.

What nobody had told her was that when you lie around dead for a few days, fluids build up. Like any other corpse, she'd swelled like a balloon waiting to burst. They'd burst her during the autopsy.

Sorry, Evelyn, Vince thought. If we have to bring Danny in to identify your body, his last impression won't be a pretty one. The human body was amazing. It took nine months to form inside a mother's body and forty-five minutes for a butcher to pull it completely apart. Then just like the nursery rhyme said, All the king's horses and all the king's men couldn't put anyone back together again.

Vince ran his finger over her cold cheek. Too bad. You get dropped into the world from someplace soft and if you're not careful about how you die, you end up in some lousy cabinet filed under nothing.

Funny, he mused. Lots had changed over the years, but morgues . . . morgues were still the same. Same chill. Same lousy smell. Same file drawers. No preferential treatment. Even if you're a cop's kid.

Sixteen years ago, Vince Luscardi had been invited out to California to make an I.D. on his own kid. He'd flown out, gone to the morgue, identified himself to the attendant. The guy took out his key and opened the door to the refrigerated compartments. He did it with as much compassion as a broker showing a prospective buyer an apartment. Vince could have killed him for his crummy bedside manner.

Angelique didn't even get top drawer. No preferential treatment when you're dead. One drawer's as good as any other.

Vince had an urge to talk. Just like when he was a kid waiting on line to get his polio vaccine. Anything for distraction. Anything not to feel the pain. But Vince Luscardi had learned a long time ago that the only way to make the pain go away is to feel it.

He'd seen hundreds, no, thousands of corpses in his career, and they were always just that. Corpses. Dead flesh.

He waited quietly while the attendant opened the drawer. He didn't really have to look. He knew it was Angelique. He'd known that when they phoned him in New York. He could feel it.

The attendant pulled the sheet down. The blue face put him off for a minute. So did the coroner's stitches. The guy would never make it as a plastic surgeon. But then again, he'd never have to. Autopsies weren't supposed to be pretty.

The hair was the giveaway, a dead giveaway. Those wild and wonderful curls. The Almighty had created them black, but Angelique had bleached them colorless, as if in rejection of who she was.

In retrospect it didn't seem all that surprising. Who would want to be part of what he and Connie had? Anger. Name-calling. Silence.

They fought because of his hours. Then they fought because they fought. The more they fought the more overtime he did. When he couldn't get overtime he got laid. That's how it was. No wonder his baby had wanted to escape from all of that.

When her girl friend, Natalie, had invited her to spend the summer at her aunt Celia's house in California, both he and Connie had actually welcomed the departure. They'd work it out, they'd told themselves. Either they'd fix it up or break it up. So they'd kissed her good-bye. Forever.

He kept staring. After all, this was what he'd come to L.A. to see. His angel. And she looked angelic, too, just like her name. Except for the smears of mascara running down her face. Except for those awful fingermarks on her neck. Except for the teeth marks on her nipples. Except for the seams where they'd sewn her back together. Except for all that, she looked just like his little girl.

The attendant saw him staring at the finger marks.

"That's what did it, sir," he said.

"Oh?"

"Strangulation." He waited for a response, but there was none. "They told you about the movie?"

Vince nodded. Yes, they had told him about the movie. "Do you have a copy of the report?" he asked stupidly. Of course, he had the report.

The attendant nodded.

"Can I see it?"

Death by strangulation. Victim had had anal and vaginal intercourse. Teeth marks on breasts and vulva. That must have been some film.

No sign of struggle. She was just like Vince. He hated a struggle, too, even other people's struggles. Maybe that's why he'd become a detective. By the time he was called in it was all over but the burial.

"Did you find anything with the body?" he asked, handing over the report to the bored kid.

"Well, sir, as we told you on the phone, they shipped the body up from Mexico, so we weren't the ones to first discover it. There was just"—he walked over to another, smaller, vault—"her clothes and this medallion."

Connie would die if she ever saw the clothes. She would roll up in a comatose ball and never come out of it. Her baby, her Angelique, whom she'd dressed either in Catholic school uniforms or shirtwaists, had been wearing a skintight leotard and pants so thin her pubic hair—Stop that. Stop thinking that way. *Pants so thin her pubic hair must have shown through. And that medallion. It wasn't his daughter's, but he wasn't going to tell wonder boy that.*

"That's it?" he asked.

"That's it, sir."

"Could you leave us alone for a minute?"

The attendant wasn't supposed to do that, but in giving Vince the once-over he decided the guy was harmless. Plus he had I.D. saying he was the girl's father and a NYPD badge. What could he do? Stick his tongue in her mouth?

"Okay."

Vince wanted to cover her up. He wanted to wrap her in something soft like her down comforter, the one with the hearts and teddy bears on it. Then he wanted to have her take a shower, comb her hair, and dress in something decent. He wanted to take her back to New York. To Connie. Vince wanted to make it all better.

He couldn't, so he told himself to talk to her instead. But he couldn't think of anything to say. Not a surprise really. Once she'd outgrown her undershirts and training bras, he'd never known what to say to her. Why should he be any more comfortable now? Now that she was... Say it, big guy. Say dead. *Vince couldn't bring himself to say it.*

He ran his fingers over her throat. She had been so beautiful as a child. His child. Oh, baby, why didn't you stick around so we could work it out?

Actually Angelique had been right. She was beautiful enough to become a movie star. The problem was she'd picked the wrong kind of movie. But how the hell could she have known that? They didn't teach you about becoming a movie star in Catholic school. Maybe in a few more years she would have been smarter. At seventeen most people make mistakes. Unfortunately, this one had killed her.

Instead of going after horsies like they had in National Velvet, *she'd gone after studs. The kind with two legs, not four. Instead of riding off into the sunset and becoming a star, she'd let someone ride her into the sunset while she saw stars. Yeah, that's how it was for her. The report was cut-and-dried, but Vince had been on the force long enough to know how to read between the lines. She saw stars while some guy played big shot with his dick. But it wasn't his dick that killed her. It was some guy getting his jollies by snuffing out the life of some sweet kid. Yeah, nineteen seventy-one was a very big year for snuff films.*

Vince turned his attention to the medallion. It was expensive, a round piece of gold about the size of a half-dollar. Inside were letters in diamonds. Not chips. Diamonds. The letters read CAL. Short for California? Short for Calvin? Or was it some asshole's initials?

Vince didn't know the answer. Not now anyway. But he knew he'd find out. When or how was irrelevant. He would, if it was the last thing he ever did.

"Anyone have any idea who this Danny character is?" Vince asked the other detective working on the Evelyn Green case.

"Yeah, we got a make on him. Med student. Married. One kid, another on the way."

"Did you get his prints?"

"He says they'll be all over the apartment. They were lovers. He was here all the time. When he wasn't at Columbia or at home. Apparently they'd had a fight three days ago. She'd threatened to kill herself unless he left his wife. It's happened before, he said. Guess she figured he'd come up and find her. That she wouldn't get like this. Maybe she thought he'd even find her before she died. Anyway, he asked us not to tell his wife."

What happens in between marriage and adultery? Vince wondered. That's the real mystery. How many detectives would they have to put on that one to solve it?

"Did this Evelyn have folks?"

"Her last name was Goldstein. There're about five thousand in Manhattan alone. We're looking through her phone book."

"Ask Danny."

"Anything else, Detective Luscardi?"

"Yeah. Start bringing Detective Wilkens in on these girlie deaths. I think I'm getting too old for this stuff."

"Oh, I almost forgot, the captain told me to give this to you."

Vince took the envelope and left.

• V •

The sins of the father rest upon the sons and you, my son, are a sin. A walking, breathing, living sin. You are an abomination to your people. To all people.

Robbie had thought he had cured himself of the voice, but he was wrong. It had returned two weeks ago, living with him as it had in his childhood. Yes, the voice was as much a part of him as the air he breathed.

You are an abomination. A lie.

He had heard the voice just minutes ago in Ashley's dressing room. But no, not Ashley. Even Uncle Earl couldn't get him to hurt Ashley.

Sin is written all over her.

No!

Uncle Earl had once again taken up residence inside Robbie's head and Robbie knew of only one way to exorcise that voice. Joe Allen was as good a place as any to start.

"What'll it be?" the big guy behind the bar asked.

He didn't care. Rye? Hated the stuff. Tasted like warm

piss. Maybe that way he wouldn't drink so much. Warm piss it was.

It's the drink of the white man, boy. Moonshine. Sinful. It eats the soul, Robbie. Takes it and bends it toward the devil. That's right, the devil.

The bartender looked at him funny and Robbie wasn't sure if he heard the voice too. Didn't matter. The guy poured him a shot and set it down in front of him.

It didn't taste like warm piss. Not today. Today it tasted good. Burned. Yeah, it was a good burn. He had two more shots, then looked around to see if any of his friends were there. Fuck. Who was he kidding? He didn't have any friends.

The Lord giveth and the Lord taketh away. You are an abomination of what He giveth, but His mercy can save you.

"Shut up, you."

"Say something, buddy?" The bartender had heard it all right, but he didn't want to get into a fight. Not this early in the day anyway. He still had to get through the supper and after-theater crowd.

Believe in the Lord and ye shall be saved.

"No, nothing," Robbie said. He left three singles on the bar and split.

You are a sinner, my boy. You are your father incarnate. Look at you. Pale as a ghost. A dead man. You are a dead man, Robbie Haskins.

"But it was just a coincidence," Robbie yelled, knowing it was out loud. Real loud. But on Ninth Avenue no one cared or noticed. Or if they did notice, they'd be too scared to say anything. The nut jobs that walk around Ninth and Forty-sixth are deadly.

Robbie slobbered his way down Ninth Avenue. He had to drink. To forget. To prepare. He could feel the voice of the Lord again asking him to do His work.

Another bar. Then another. He was across from the Port Authority Bus Terminal when he thought of Mama. He wanted Mama. That warm, nurturing woman he'd met his first day in New York. She had made it all better for him then and she could make it better now. Her number. Where was her number?

It didn't matter where he began. Just where he ended.

He searched his pockets. Everything fell out, including the number. A warm October breeze transported it into a pile of dog shit. Probably where it belonged, he thought as he picked it up.

Phone after phone was broken. Damn the phone company and their street-smart commercials. Public phones, my ass. Try to find one that works.

Giving up on the street, Robbie walked into the Port Authority. The right clothes would have made him look like Donald Trump's brother, but instead he looked like he was in training to play Mickey Rourke. He stepped over a black kid who was scratching his heroin high. Some young skinny white girl offered him anything he could handle for fifteen bucks. No, he wanted Mama.

She picked up on the second ring.

"You home?" he asked.

"Who is this?"

"This is your boy. Robbie."

"Robbie. For chrissakes. You get your butt right over here. Right now. You hear?"

He heard. And he was moving real fast.

Vince wasn't. You don't catch killers by running after them. Being a cop, a good cop, means patience. Lots of it.

Personally he didn't buy this new upsurge in "female" crime. He had gone through it in the seventies and had allowed for the speculation that feminism was the cause. Women had been angry and had worn their feelings around their necks like thick gold chains, begging to be ripped off. They were. By men, big, strong men who were talking about the new impotence. What was another word for impotence? Death. How do you fight those who are killing you? You kill them first.

Female crime? To Vince, that was a euphemism for male impotence.

He had wondered when women were going to start

catching onto the crime thing. Ninety percent of all violent crime was committed by men—and women were their victims. Men, impotent men, were killing, raping, and mugging, and all those "powerful" women were dying. Female crime was a male disease.

Vince looked inside the envelope the detective had given him and found a note from O'Connor. *"This is a copy of what was found next to Nina Houston's body. We're doing a fingerprint check now."* They sure had his number, Vince thought. Any girlie murder at all and the old man was called in. He unfolded the piece of paper. There were three names. The first one was Ariel Powell. It was crossed out. Then Nina Houston. It, too, was crossed out. Next on the list was Jessica Bishop. That name wasn't crossed out.

"Karla, I'm home."

Olive didn't wait for an answer. Instead she headed directly for the kitchen and put the already prepared and cooked chicken in the oven to warm. She was starved and hoped Karla was too. In any case, the French toast Karla had made in the morning was the last thing she hadn't eaten all day.

Olive moved as if she were a forty-five rpm record being played at seventy-eight. That was how she had been coming home from rehearsals every day now. High. Excited. Alive. God, it had been so long since she'd felt excited and alive. She pulled a package of broccoli from the freezer and remembered she hadn't spoken to Elizabeth Anne for nearly a week. Filling a pot with water using one hand, she picked up the phone with the other.

"You were so wonderful," she heard Karla whisper. "Does everyone know how lucky they are to have you as mayor?"

"Karla? Charles?"

"Olive?" Yes, it was Charles.

"Mother, what are you doing on the phone?" The irritation in Karla's voice was right on the surface.

"Am I interrupting something?" Olive asked, cradling

the phone between her ear and shoulder so she could unwrap the broccoli.

"Don't be silly, Olive," Charles said. "I was just calling to see how you and your beautiful daughter were doing." Olive could see his smile through the phone. He could win an election on that smile alone. "Elizabeth Anne said it had been a while since she's spoken to you. You know we've both been so busy with the election."

"I was just thinking the same thing," Olive said. She heard a click and knew Karla had hung up. "Is Elizabeth Anne there? I'd like to say hello."

"No, Olive. I'm not at home. I'm in the office."

"Oh."

"Karla? Karla?"

"I think she's hung up, Charles." Olive turned around to see her daughter standing in the doorway with her arms crossed before her. "Charles, I'll talk to you later."

"I was on the phone," Karla said, her green eyes growing pale. They always did when she was angry.

"I didn't know, Karla. I'm sorry."

"You always do that."

"I don't *always* do that. Are we going to have a tantrum now, Karla? Is that what you're going to do?"

"We!" Karla said indignantly. "You wouldn't have a tantrum. You're too much the lady. Probably just like Karen." Karla always went right for the jugular. She'd learned that when she was a child. It was how she'd protected herself from the darkness within. The only problem was that when the darkness had left the venom still remained.

Olive turned away from her daughter. She didn't want to involve herself in this discussion, this fight. Or whatever it would turn into.

"Why are you turning your back on me, Mom?"

"Because you're acting like a spoiled brat." She faced Karla and added softly, "Because you're looking for a fight and I'm not."

"I'm not looking for a fight. I'm just looking for a friend and Uncle Charlie's my friend."

"Karla. Karla. Baby." Olive embraced her. She could never understand these outbursts. They were so irrational, so hurtful. Karla began to squirm. "Let me hold you." What she did know was that if it was difficult to lose a father at eleven, it was even more difficult never to have had one. Olive would always feel responsible for that.

She never saw Vince after they made love. The following day another officer was sent to guard her. She asked why and was told personal business had called Vince away. She could accept that, but she couldn't understand why he never called. Being a true Schultz, though, she put the incident behind her. Or tried to. But it wouldn't go away.

And then she realized why. Not only had he touched her soul, he had left a permanent imprint on her body as well. Vince had made her pregnant.

Olive did her best to ignore the fact, yet when her mosquito bites turned into actual mammaries and her tummy became round, Balanchine noticed. He banished her. Karen had already abandoned her a month earlier when she left for Paris.

"I am leaving you the apartment, darling," she had said, kissing the air surrounding her daughter's left, then right cheek. "You may sell it. You may do with it what you'd like." Then fixing her stare on the to-be-swollen area, she'd added, "You have already."

"How will you live, Mother?" Olive had asked coldly, fearful that if she let a feeling in, all control would be lost.

"I am taking the money I've put away from your performances. I do deserve something, do I not?" She'd pulled on her white lace gloves, lifted her somewhat battered leather barrel bag, and left with three suitcases.

At first, not dancing was fun. Olive shopped. She cooked. She read books. She saw every movie in New York. She did what ordinary people did. But Olive Kingsley was not ordinary.

By the fifth week of nothing to do she realized that while her mother may have forced her to dance and Balanchine may have sculpted her into a prima ballerina, she, Olive Kingsley, had lived the dance. It had become her religion, her stage, her altar. At last she discovered something about herself that everyone else seemed to know. Without dance she was a deity without an altar, a servant without a god. All she had was herself, a memory, and a repertoire of strange feelings.

Each time the life inside her kicked, she was reminded to get ready for the big day. But how could a mother be ready without a father? She didn't know. She'd sit up late at night and rock her belly, sending messages of love inside. She'd tell the unborn child that she was enough. That babies didn't need two parents. That it would all work out. Trouble was, Olive really didn't believe it herself.

Once she weakened and called Vince at the precinct. They said he had been transferred out of town. To California. Did she want to leave a message? No, she said.

Karla was born on February fourteenth. The perfect Valentine's Day gift for a girl with no love in her life. Perfect Karla who was warm and pink and laughed all the time. Darling Karla who looked like an angel. Karla, who lit up whenever Olive entered the room. For the first five months Olive truly believed she'd never need anyone else in her life ever again.

Then the feelings came back. They were like the little baby kicks, except these hurt all over. She felt them when she wheeled Karla through Central Park and saw couples with their children, women with their men. Each time it was a reminder that she was alone.

She returned to the barre. It had nothing to do with dance. Her hour of practice turned into two, then three. Sometimes she couldn't stop. But no matter what she did, she could not extinguish the feelings.

And so Olive, former mistress of self-control, returned to the stage. In so doing she became more than just another prima ballerina. She became the idealized mother, the woman who had everything. Fame. Fortune. Beauty. Freedom. She was Balanchine's star. She was the friend of Elizabeth Anne Manchester Long, whose young lawyer husband was being compared to John Lindsay. Dancemagazine *covered her work and* McCall's *covered her life. She was the* Ms. *woman of the year, she was the darling of the* Ladies' Home Journal *set.*

In interviews she talked about taking Karla to her rehearsals. Elizabeth Anne, who had not yet been blessed with a child, would go to performances and sit with Karla, either in the audience or backstage. They became a threesome, Elizabeth Anne, Karla, and Olive.

Then Olive was once again summoned, as she had been when she was nineteen, to dance Swan Lake *at Covent Garden before the Queen of England. Karla was three at the time. Olive was dancing Odette and Odile. Ivan Nicholas was Prince Siegfried. They were new together, young embodiments of perfection.*

It happened during the third act. The prince is yearning for his beautiful Odette, the swan queen. Enter Odile, the queen of the night, the temptress. Prince Siegfried is enchanted by Odile and forgets Odette. He dances with Odile, and it is not like his dance with Odette. This is a dance of arrogance, of pride. To emphasize the brilliance, a light dazzles the stage, highlighting Odile like a shining tiara. Odile who is testing his love. Odile who is deceptive.

She pirouettes across the stage and the spellbound Siegfried lifts her in his arms, showing her off, turning his back on the love of Odette. It is the perfect pas de deux, *perfect in every way. Olive was brilliant. Too brilliant. Something stung her, a current racing through her. She felt it from her toes to her scalp and it didn't stop. Throughout the rest of the performance lightning bolts cut through her.*

After the ballet she found out what had happened.

"Olive!" Elizabeth Anne cried.

"Tell me, Liz. What is it? Is there something wrong with Charles?" Elizabeth Anne shook her head wildly, and Olive could make no sense of her friend.

"Come—come with me," Elizabeth Anne said.

"Of course," Olive said, throwing a raincoat over her costume. They stepped outside to a waiting cab, and then, only then, did she realize . . .

"Karla." At first it was no more than a word that left Olive's lips. But Elizabeth Anne's eyes gave it away.

"What? Tell me!"

Elizabeth Anne was hysterical, babbling. "I looked—looked away just a moment . . ."

Now, Olive, getting emotional doesn't solve anything.

"I know, Mother," Olive said.

"I beg your pardon, Miss Kingsley?"

Dr. Craig Martin, who was attending to Karla at the hospital, couldn't have been kinder. He had just explained that Karla, by sticking her finger in an outlet backstage, was experiencing some sort of blindness. It could very well be temporary but they'd have to proceed with tests.

"I'm sorry, doctor," Olive said. "I was speaking to my mother."

Dr. Martin looked around, thinking perhaps he had overlooked another person. No, it was just he and Miss Kingsley and Mrs. Long.

"It's just that," Olive said in a completely rational tone, "one of us is hysterical. There's no point in two of us . . ." She stopped for a moment. What was she saying? "Liz." She took her friend's hand. "Please, it's going to be all right. Karla will be all right."

Elizabeth Anne looked at Olive and wanted to believe her more than she wanted to believe anything in the whole wide world. She wanted Karla to get well even more than she wanted a child of her own. But she knew Olive was lying. Both to herself and to Elizabeth Anne.

"She will get well," Olive said, pulling on every ounce of Kingsley determination she had within her. "No matter how long it takes I will get her to see again."

And so Olive Kingsley never danced again. She banished herself forever from her own private Eden.

Mama wanted to know where he'd been all these months, told him how good he looked, told him she'd asked around but no one had seen him. Yes, Mama loved him. She really did.

"Mama, Mama," he said, falling to his knees. "Mama, I have sinned. Truly sinned."

"First, boy, let me have a good look at you." She ran her thick fingers over his eyebrows, smoothed back his hair, pierced his eyes with her own. Yes, he passed inspection. "Next time you sin," she said, attempting the impossible task of crossing her arms in front of her bosom, "you ain't gonna find your good ole mama here."

That took Robbie out of himself. "Why not?"

"They're knocking me out. Knocking all of us out. Tearing the building down is what they're doing."

"Who?" Robbie asked, feeling himself get hard. Talking to her, smelling her, excited him, made him feel safe.

"The city, boy."

"It's my fault, Mama."

"Now, how is that your fault, boy?"

"I been bad, Mama. I sinned and because you know me you're bearing the pain for me."

"Is that how it is, boy?"

"Sure is. You know they say Christ died for our sins. Well, you are being punished for mine."

Once again she tried crossing her arms in front of her huge chest. "And just what is your sin, boy?"

"Mama, hold me."

The woman, bulky from having brought eight children into the world and weary from having reared five others, drew him near. Drew him in to the large booming melons that rose from her cotton smock. Oh, how they comforted him.

She sat with her legs spread apart, and his tall lean body lay across hers, his mouth open against her cleavage.

"Sin. This what you talking about?" she asked, pointing at the bulge in his pants. "This what's been making you bad?"

"Mama, I didn't mean it."

She slid her hand down to his crotch and gave him a gentle squeeze.

"Well, I can see you didn't have what to do it with. Not a whole lot there to be bad with."

"Mama." Robbie pouted, standing up. "Don't say that."

"It's the truth. You ain't big enough to be a real sinner."

His minister uncle would heartily disagree.

"Now if it got bigger, maybe I could heal you, boy."

"But it doesn't get any bigger."

"Don't, huh? Well, then, I guess there's no hope. You is a partial sinner and can't get no healing."

"Mama, if I try," he said, placing his hand over his pants. "Maybe if I try I can get it bigger."

She knelt beside him. "I don't know, son."

As he had when he was a little boy, as he had the first time his uncle caught him, he unzipped his fly and took his penis in his hand. He began pulling on it. Maybe it will become longer this time, he thought. Maybe.

Mama was watching. She was close now, real close. He was pulling. Swaying. Pleading with it to grow. Grow so Mama would like it.

"Now that's a good boy," she said. With a quick flick of her tongue she touched the end.

"Mama, please do that again."

"No, son. Because if I do, the Lord will be angry with me and I can't have Him angry."

Robbie continued to pull. His eyes were closed. Then again he felt the flicker of her tongue.

"Is this because I've repented?" he asked.

"It's because you are a beautiful white child and I love my white children." Then she stopped talking and sent her serpent tongue out over him again.

"Mama, if you keep doing that I'm gonna come," the big boy said, holding himself, loving what she was doing.

"You know how Mama feels about that, boy."

"I know, Mama. Please hurry, Mama."

Mama lifted her skirt. Nothing was under it but a pair of rolled-down stockings. She lifted the skirt high, crouched low, and took her fingers to herself. Then real soft she licked the boy. She licked and he pulled and she kept her fingers deep inside herself. Just as she had taught the younguns to do when she watched them. Sure enough, he got bigger, just as they had. As her fingers brought her to rapture her tongue brought him the same. Her tongue, his hand. Yes. And then the finish. That sticky branding of life dripping from her face onto those mounds of flesh.

"Oh, Mama. Am I saved?"

"You are, my son. You are."

* * *

Elizabeth Anne Manchester Long sat in front of the TV like a gleeful child. She had been waiting since the five o'clock news ended for the six o'clock news to begin so she could watch Charles again. Of late it seemed to be the only way she could catch sight of her husband. She flipped through the channels with the same carelessness that people flip through magazines. Terrorist bombings. Sports. Local news. Weather. And then... on location with Mayor Long. Elizabeth Anne relaxed into her chintz-covered couch and became one with her martini.

Roger Grimsby, standing away from the crowds and speaking directly into the microphone, managed to look Elizabeth Anne right in the eye. She liked that, the personal contact. She'd missed it ever since she became The Mayor's Wife. Lots of kids were waving into the camera. She waved back. A few protesters demonstrated. No Charles though. He was probably still inside.

"Many of us wonder what it feels like," Grimsby was saying, "all these years later, to return to one's roots. Or shall we say nonroots? Mayor Long has never tried to hide his childhood. As he likes to say, he grew up when orphans were still called orphans. Now it seems that that word is a dirty one.

"This home which Mayor Long is dedicating this morning is proof of that. Morningside Haven is an attempt to take the stigma away from being an orphan. As well as the trauma.

"Mayor Long, in discussing his own childhood, has said... Oh, oh, here he is. Apparently the dedication is complete. Let's hear what Mayor Long has to say about his own childhood."

Elizabeth Anne slid from the big floral couch to the floor. It never changed for her. She couldn't get close enough to him. She'd loved him from the first second she...

"And tell us, Mayor Long," Grimsby asked, "did this bring back any recollections of what it was like for you?"

Charles flashed that famous quixotic smile. He was so

tall, he had acquired the habit of a slight stoop. It gave him the appearance of humility, a real vote-getter.

"It was many years ago," he answered thoughtfully, "but we all know the effect of childhood. Mine was uneventful, though lonesome."

That was good for fifty votes, Elizabeth Anne thought.

"But some of us never get over it," he went on. "I suppose I was one of the fortunate ones." Again he smiled that charismatic smile. "While I don't recommend being an orphan to anyone"—everyone laughed—"I must say it couldn't have been all that bad. After all, I did end up becoming mayor of the greatest city in all the world." He looked away from the camera and down at the ground.

Elizabeth Anne knew he was shifting his weight from his right foot to his left. That's what he did when he was uncomfortable. Talking about being an orphan always made him uncomfortable. She walked over to the portable bar to fix herself another drink. She didn't need one but he did, and she drank enough for both of them.

"What about these children?" Grimsby asked. "How do you think they'll fare?"

"I think they'll do fine. Morningside Haven is a whole new concept in orphanages. No one is going to be shuffling them around from foster home to foster home. Real people are coming in to care for them. Retired people who themselves have begun to feel useless. It's a wonderful way to bring the old and the young together." Charles paused as if in thought.

"We have commitments from many of the private schools to send their students up here. Dalton is offering course credit. So is Brearley. There's never been anything like it in the world, actually, and I think New York should be proud, very proud, to start such a program."

"What's the ratio of black to white kids?" another reporter asked.

"Seventy–thirty."

"Don't you think that's a little out of balance?"

"Yes, I do." He was unintimidated by the question. "So you might print that the blacks are being given the upper hand. Some of the most forward-looking education is being done up in Harlem and blacks are the main benefactors." Not necessarily the truth, but then politics had less to do with truth than advertising.

"Would you have preferred a situation like this to the one you had?"

Don't you know how uncomfortable this is making him? Elizabeth Anne wanted to scream. Why do you do it?

Charles began sifting his way through the crowd, heading toward his limousine. "I think it was because of the situation I lived through that I can be as helpful as I am."

His bodyguard opened the door of the car.

"Is there any one incident in particular that you can recall that—"

" 'Bye, guys," Charles said, and stepped into the car.

One incident? he thought as the limousine pulled away. How about five? How about ten? How about being six and a fat foster mother fondling you when Hubby went off to work? How about winning a handful of junk rings at the circus and having the school's janitor steal them so he could sell them? How about sleeping with the blanket you were found in until you were too old and it was too tattered, and the nuns still had to tear it from you? How about getting a last name based on the size of your pecker?

No, there was no single incident. He had changed all that by running away from his last foster family. He ended up in California, turned his back on his past, and created a new one.

He told people he was the son of Nancy Remington and Randolph Scott. Randolph was English and unfortunately married. When Nancy was hit by a car and died, Randolph sent Nancy's sisters a check for $100,000 for the care of his ten-year-old son and asked that they please not contact him again.

The truth was that Charles's father had never given him anything. Maybe good genes, but that was it. What Charles did have was an old lady who had taken quite a liking to him. In return for a few hours' pleasure four evenings a week, Charles got free tuition at UCLA, designer clothes, and the freedom to get into the kind of trouble all twenty-year-olds like to get into. As long as he returned to his old lady. Which he always did.

Until he met Elizabeth Anne. By then he had been keeping Sybil happy for close to three years and was ready for something new. Something sweet. Something twenty-one. Something rich.

Elizabeth Anne poured herself another drink. Then another. She waited for the eight o'clock newsbreak, then the ten o'clock news. If Charles wasn't home by eleven she'd watch him again. It wasn't as good as the real thing, but it was better than nothing.

• VI •

While Karen thought she had fallen in love with Paris she had, as the song goes, fallen in love with love. And as everyone knows who has heard the song, falling in love with love was falling for make-believe.

She hadn't been in Paris for more than two weeks when Jean Claude spotted her in Freddy's picking up a bottle of L'Heure Bleue, the only perfume she claimed she ever wore. In truth, she had never heard of it until the flight over when two women who oozed Louis Vuitton happened to mention it. It became her trademark.

It was *presque* Bastille Day and Jean Claude Gobeille had stopped by Freddy's to pick up some presents for the secretaries in his travel agency. One bottle of Joy, one L'Air du Temps, a bottle of Chanel N°5 and then . . . Karen.

"Madame." His tone was reverential, timid but not unmanly. He was, after all, from France, where *liberté* is a word associated with national dogma rather than gender rights.

"Monsieur," she said, part coquette, part Left Bank. Karen had always been a quick read, and in addition to

L'Heure Bleue had also managed to pick up the wealthy expatriate effect on the plane ride over. It was the only way she could separate herself from all the riffraff that had taken that particular July first charter.

Karen examined his clothes first, his gray alpaca suit and the white collar and cuffs on his pale pink, pinstriped shirt. She rather liked the way he wore his glasses on a leather cord around his neck, and that the Gucci insignia on his belt was difficult to detect. When he lifted her hand to kiss it and she noticed the diamond chip in his cuff links, she decided then and there she would marry this man.

"You are American," he said, adding her perfume to his other purchases.

And so it began, as easily and as simply as that. Lunch led to dinner which led to the opera. The opera led to a second date, then a third. When Jean Claude proposed during their second week of courtship, Karen smiled, took his hand so he wouldn't feel rejected, and politely said no.

She permitted him to take her to Cannes for a week, then Monaco. She got busy after that. She told him she needed to go off by herself to Italy. Actually, she only went to Versailles, staying with an old friend of Balanchine's. Then, yes, she agreed to marry him.

Jean Claude introduced Karen to something more than just European grace; he introduced her to passion. She loved it, opening to it as she had opened to "21." She allowed Jean Claude to bring her pleasure, to loose her tight grip on her control, never forgetting that it was her gift, not his. She'd had it all along and he merely brought it out in her. Jean Claude cherished her for that.

And so Karen became part of the Paris high-life. Jean Claude, with his most chi-chi travel agency, jet-setted around the world with her. He had been a sought-after catch, and now that he was married they were a sought-after couple.

Karen dressed and acted the part as if she were to the manor born. There was no more Middle Village, no more Arthur-nothing-to-write-home-about Kingsley. She was Karen Gobeille and the world was her oyster.

"Darling, I adore that emerald pendant," she would say. It went so well with her coloring.

"*Certainement,* my sweet."

"Do you think it is too *cher* to buy this blouse?" she would ask.

"Let me see it on you, my love."

Whether it was the color of the jewel or how the silk melted around her slender frame; whether it was the way her eyes brightened when he said yes... Whatever the reason, Jean Claude could refuse her nothing. Nothing.

But Jean Claude Gobeille was *only* a proprietor of a travel agency. As exclusive as it was, it was *only* a travel agency, not IBM, not Ogilvy & Mather. He was simply a man who, for twenty-five years, had managed to save a tidy sum of money and maintain a rather good income, which he wore well. Karen knew none of this, of course. He wouldn't have been able to bear it if she were unhappy.

When he died, as suddenly as Arthur had, after sixteen years of pampering and love and protection, Karen was left with nothing but a new last name and a few baubles. More than that, she was suddenly an expatriate, a woman newly single who was considered a threat by the other ladies. She was an American in Paris, and a poor one at that.

She returned home.

"Time?" Karla said, looking at the three Swatch watches on her left wrist. "It's three-fifteen, Becky. Why?" The Rudolf Steiner School on East Seventy-ninth Street had just let out and Becky and Karla were making a fast break across the street to Nectar for an order of fries and rice pudding.

"Because you seem nervous," Becky said. She could read her friend perfectly.

Karla tapped her finger on the counter. Becky, not wanting to press the issue, offered up a stingy smile. Becky didn't like smiling. It showed off her braces.

"Let's hit a movie," she said.

"I can't." Karla took their food from George and gave him three dollars. She had to be on the west side in twenty minutes. West Seventy-ninth Street, to be exact. Where was she going to tell her mother she had been? "Listen," she said as she and Becky left Nectar, "if my mother asks, I was with you tonight."

"Karla?" A woman of indeterminate age approached the girl. "Are you Karla Kingsley?"

Of course she was Karla Kingsley. Karen knew that. She had been watching Karla for three days.

On her second day back in New York, Karen had returned to the building where she had lived with Olive. Of course Sam, the doorman, remembered her and of course he was glad to see her. Sixteen years was a long time.

"You must be back for the opening, Mrs. Kingsley," he said.

Karen, still very much the quick read, agreed. After discussing the show—"Oh, yes, Isadora was always a favorite of hers."—they talked about Karla. "Yes, Olive sends me her photo every year. Does she still go to that school? Was it . . . ? Not Dalton. What . . . ?"

"Rudolf Steiner."

"Yes, that's it." Karen got as much information as she could without appearing too ignorant, and asked Sam not to mention to Olive that she'd been there. "I do so want to surprise her."

Karla looked at the woman she had never seen before and somehow felt that she knew her. There was something familiar about her, yet clearly they had not met. She was neither young nor old. Her face, perfectly unlined, wore an unfriendly smile and an aloofness that implied arrogance. It was the throat that spoke of more years than the face had known. When Karla looked at her she felt as if she were looking into the past as well as the future.

"Do I know you?" she asked, handing Becky the rice pudding.

"Why, darling, I'm Karen. Your grandmother."

Becky let out a whistle.

"My grandmother!" Karla looked at Becky, then back at Grandma, then at her three watches. It was three-thirty. "Does Mommy know you're in town?"

"Karla . . ." Karen combed her fingers through her grandchild's hair. How like Olive she looked. Doubles. "Karla, I'm home."

Big fucking deal is what the girl wanted to say, but Karla, very much a Kingsley, smiled and kissed this well-dressed woman on the cheek.

"What are you doing here, Grandma?"

This was theater, Becky thought. Real theater. She wished her father were there to film it.

"Darling, please call me Karen." She touched a tendril of her granddaughter's hair. "Permed hair suits you so well."

She doesn't seem like a bitch to me, Karla thought.

Certainly Olive had never implied that Karen was anything but a perfect mother, but Karla had a sixth sense. What kind of a mother goes away while her daughter is pregnant? she would wonder. What kind of a mother leaves the country when her daughter is so in need of her? Karla herself had written Karen a letter when she was five, when she was still blind. She had so wanted to *see* her grandmother, but Grandma had written back that she was busy and that she hoped all was well.

"Didn't she read what I wrote?" Karla had asked Olive, brokenhearted.

"Certainly, my sweet," Olive had answered, kissing her daughter on the cheek. "She is just so very busy."

That had been their last contact.

"How is your mother doing?" Karen asked. The three were walking down Madison Avenue, the wrong direction for Karla.

"Why didn't you call?" Karla asked, paying no attention to the heads she turned. Her hair so black, the eyes so green, and the legs so long, she had to be either a female basketball player or a model. "Oh, and this is my friend Rebecca Gilbert," she said, munching on a fry.

"How do you do, Rebecca." Karen extended her hand as well as an evaluatory glance. No, this Rebecca would never do. The shoes, Bass's most comfortable, the socks that didn't quite slouch right, the pleated skirt that exaggerated her more-than-one-potato-chip-over-the-limit hips, couldn't have been worse. This child would never do indeed. But Karen said nothing. She had enough on her mind just being back in New York.

"When did you get back, Karen?" Karla asked. It was twenty to four.

"Last week, darling. I've just been so busy I haven't had time to do anything."

A lie, and one which she would have to change. Olive would never believe it. Karen had been back a week, but she wasn't that busy. After finding a room in the Wales and seeking out her granddaughter, she'd spent most of her time familiarizing herself with the new face of the city. Donny Trump had done so much building. The lights on that Helmsley building were divine. And she had discovered Le Cirque. It hadn't been built in 'seventy-one when she left, but now it was here and was exquisite. So much better than "21." Not that she could afford it, but well... she had been through such an ordeal. And all the while she was trying to figure out how to approach Olive. At last, she had decided Karla was the perfect way. "Has your mother married?" she asked tentatively.

Karla looked at her with great distrust. "You know what, guys," she said with a sudden burst of energy. "I gotta run."

"Where to?" Becky asked.

"Gotta see a man about a horse," she said. "Cover for me," she whispered in her best friend's ear, then she leaped into a taxi and yelled, "Karen, I'll tell Mom you're in town."

"Karla!" Karen yelled. Then she softened the tone. "Don't—don't tell your mother just yet."

When Olive found out that Karla was blind, Karen was the first person she tried to contact. But apparently Karen had moved. Either that or the address she had originally sent Olive had never been Karen Kingsley's residence. Olive had no idea where Karen was. The letter that she read to Karla when she was five was completely fictitious.

Alone, Olive took Karla from doctor to doctor. From

ophthalmologist to neurologist and back again. She learned what it felt like to want to kill and what it felt like to want to die. She learned about impotence. She learned that all the will and discipline she had developed over the years didn't mean a damn thing. She tried crackpot cures. She listened to the lady from Omaha who told her if she found a flowering mimosa tree and walked around it three times under the light of a full moon at midnight, the blindness would end. Olive did it. She even hoped for a tumor because a tumor could be removed. But it wasn't a tumor. It wasn't anything. Well, that wasn't true.

Boston's Dr. Eliot Warner explained it perfectly. "She shows the signs of cortical blindness. She's lost all visual sensation and there's no lid reflex. She has maintained retention of pupil constriction to light as well as complete extraocular eye movement."

"What does that mean?" Olive asked with all the control she could muster.

"It means," he said kindly, "that she's blind and the likelihood of her sight returning is minimal."

Olive held on to the word minimal. *And then she held on to Eliot. He helped her get over her feelings of guilt.*

"Had I not been dancing..."

"Bull," he said. "Anyone can have an accident."

She felt secure with him, with his age and his reputation, with the slightly thick body and gentle refinement that is bred into any Harvard Medical School graduate. She fell in love with all of it. Finally, at long last, love.

And so there was a new threesome. The beautiful ballerina who wasn't dancing, the green-eyed child who couldn't see, and Eliot Warner, the famed physician who seemed able to perform miracles.

The only miracle he couldn't perform was to raise himself from the dead.

He wasn't supposed to fly into New York that weekend. He had been booked solid with patients, but Olive had told him she was depressed, told him she couldn't handle Karla. So on that hazy night, he boarded the plane to New York. It crashed right after takeoff, killing everyone aboard.

Olive nearly had a nervous breakdown. It wasn't just because of the death. She had learned long ago to survive a great deal more than that. She had weathered the loss of her father, then her mother, then Vince, and then Karla's eyesight. But what she couldn't survive, what she couldn't live with, was the fear that perhaps her mother had been right. Olive Kingsley somehow was cursed with killing whom she loved the most.

With the innocence of a child, she vowed never to love again. If God would restore her child's sight, she promised not to kill anyone else.

And He did, with agonizing slowness. The doctors couldn't tell if the shadows that Karla had begun to see were permanent or not. Nor could they predict whether total vision would return. Each day, as Karla was better able to distinguish light from dark, shapes and colors, Olive grew stronger. Perhaps the hex was over. She promised never to complain again and to hold true to her vow never to love again.

Had she married? She dared not for fear that something would once again happen to the man she loved.

• VII •

"Johnny?" Ashley said, holding onto her white princess phone with one hand and licking clean the inside of the peanut butter jar with the other. "How come we have such a lousy connection?"

"Because the asshole whose phone I'm using is saving four cents by not using AT&T. Anyway, babes, listen, I'm in L.A."

"Why?" Ashley purred.

"I'm working on a big deal. A real big deal."

"Something I could be in?"

"If you can't I'll get you written in. Listen, baby face, I just want you to be good while I'm away. You know there's lots of diseases going around."

"Johhhhhnny," she said, feigning shock. "How could you even think—"

"Listen, honey, don't try to con a con. I know you ain't after me for my looks."

"Well, you don't exactly drench me in Tiffany diamonds."

"No, but I make sure you make enough so you can drench yourself in them. Besides, you never told me you like diamonds."

"Oh, Johhhhhnny..." She could have gone for another jar of peanut butter, but every lick would show under her leotard tomorrow. She didn't dare. "Baby, I'm with you because I liiike you."

"Yeah, you like what I do for you, doll."

"And what you do for me," she said in a breathy, husky voice that was an imitation of no one but herself. "When you put that perfect tongue of yours inside me it gets me hot, real hot."

"Hey, I'm in some guy's house," he said, looking down at his hard-on. "Why are you doing this to me?"

"Because you get me hot, Johnny. If you were here now and put those fingers of yours inside me you'd know just how hot. I'm as wet as the inside of a ripe peach. I just need someone to suck me out."

"Christ, Ashley."

"If you were here... Here, sweetie, taste this." She ran her finger over the inside of her pussy and kissed the phone with it.

"Oh, shit. Hold on, doll. Let me close the door."

"You remember what I taste like, don't you?"

"And how tight you are."

"Well, I'm rubbing all that on the phone, Johnny. I'm rubbing my taste and my tight all over the phone, honey. Now you gotta rub it too."

"You bitch."

"Come on, Johnny. Rub it. I know you like it that way. Real gentle. In between my tits. Yes, Johnny."

"Ashley!"

"I know you want to come, Johnny. So why are you waiting? It's just you and me, honey. Come. Come all over me. All over my face. Come on, Johnny." Hearing his breathing change she helped him. "Yes, Johnny. I love it. I really love it."

The black man circling the block extending from Columbus to Amsterdam and from Eighty-seventh to Eighty-eighth streets could smell the cops. Their stink was as potent as the smell of urine on the junkies that slept out on the streets. The black man could smell a cop a mile away.

Which was why Jessica Bishop was still alive. The black man wanted Jessica but not at the expense of his own life. He walked around the block and breathed in the cops' stink. Didn't see them though. They might have been one of the drunks on the corner. One of the hookers across the street. Maybe one was even living with Jessica, but the black man knew—because he investigated his ladies before he decided to take them—that she lived with four other dancers. There was no room for anyone else.

He circled the block one more time, then decided that if she was putting up that much resistance to being saved she didn't deserve it. He'd find someone else to save, and he knew just who she'd be.

Madness. Charles knew it was madness, but he felt powerless over his passion. On the one hand he hated it, her, his desire. On the other hand he loved it, her, his desire. From the first taste of her he couldn't get her out of his system. Where the hell was she anyway? He had been waiting for her all afternoon. Why was this feeling so intense?

Something in that damn orphanage yesterday had set it off, made it worse. So much so that he had called her at home, something he never did, and asked her to come today.

Morningside Haven. What a euphemism. What a joke. Some haven.

Haven from what? From the sickos who need to get their jollies by taking advantage of kids? Not a chance. From people who themselves led loveless, lonely lives?

Everyone wanted a haven, a refuge from life. But Charles knew it was impossible. One way or another, life came in and hit you right between the eyes, no matter how protected you were. Some didn't get their first smack until high school or college. Charles got smacked at birth. First by killing the tit that fed him, then again when he was five and some bitch decided she didn't want to take care of him anymore.

Charles Andrew Long came into this world at the expense of his mother. She died on the table. His father didn't go for that. He moved away but sent his sister Bea money to raise Charles. That lasted a few years, but then the money stopped. The contact stopped. Bea, who was nobody's fool, took him to an orphanage. Damned if she was going to get stuck raising someone else's kid—and paying for it.

The Sisters of Mercy rented him out, so to speak. Foster families took him in and there he found his pleasure. With fat old women whose husbands hadn't touched them in years, with fat daughters and pimply-faced girls who wanted to have what their mothers were having. All women ever wanted to do with Charles was please him.

When he met Elizabeth Anne, who never knew such things existed, who wouldn't spread her legs on the first, second, or fifth date, who spoke softly even when she was angry, who was kind to everyone, he fell in love. Or he called it that. It worked for a while. She was sweet and innocent like a child. But she too became one of them, one of the women who wanted too much—and who was willing to give too much. But he had married her, if not for better or for worse, certainly for political office. Elizabeth Anne was a Manchester, an influence to be reckoned with. A name in a world where names counted. Keeping his pecker in his pants didn't seem too high a price to pay for that connection.

Maybe if this were the sixties and he were a Kennedy, maybe then it would be different. But it wasn't. This was the eighties, when any reporter who suspected that you did anything from drugs to adultery could buy his way into your private life.

So Charles Long continued to opt for the limelight rather than the bedroom light. When he did have an indiscretion it was with someone who had more to lose than he did, like the wife of someone big.

Then he came home one day and found Karla swimming in his pool.

It was innocent enough. The daughter of a friend. But she wasn't there as a friend's daughter. She was there as a seductress. He could tell as she walked toward him, playing with the fringes on her watercolored bikini. She polished her toenails right in front of him, bending over just enough to show the beginning-to-bud breasts. Yes, it was clearly a setup. From the touch of gloss on her lips to the edges of fur peeking out at her inner thighs, he knew he was being set up.

"I'm all grown-up now," she said, gazing at him.

"Yes, you are, Karla. Yes, you are."

"Show me what grown-ups do, Uncle Charlie." Her eyes held the promise of ecstasy.

And so he showed her, that very afternoon, in the bed he shared with Elizabeth Anne. Karla was like most sweet things. Once had, they are only desired more. Just thinking of her got him hard.

The car drove up. His car. His driver. Bringing his little girl-mistress to his weekend home on the Hudson.

"I couldn't believe it when Mom picked up the phone yesterday," Karla said rushing in, breathless. It was all new to her. She couldn't wait. She wanted it. She was unwrapping herself. "See," she said, showing him her nakedness. "I took all the understuff off in the car."

"In the car!" He was moving in, like a tiger. She was his prey. Oh, don't ask him to give it up.

"Don't worry. Arnie didn't see."

That's what you think, Charles thought. Arnie sees and hears everything. That's what I pay him for. But he plays dumb real good.

"Let me do it," Charles said when she fumbled with her shirt buttons. Unbuttoning her shirt excited him. Touching her skin excited him. Smelling her hair was incredible. *Control yourself.* No, there's no control. Stop feigning it. She doesn't care. She likes it this way. Wants it this way.

She saw that he was ready and wanted it, too. She wanted him. She wanted it all. She went for it.

"Karla." He groaned deep in his throat. All week he'd been like this. Aching for her.

"Please let me."

"Let me close the shades," he said, trying to move away from her. But not touching her was unbearable. He couldn't let go.

"No," she said. "We're so beautiful. So very beautiful." He was already half undressed. She ran her hands over his chest, watching as he tore off his trousers, his underpants. Then there he was. Huge. Oh, she loved how huge. He had thought the first time might be a problem, she being a virgin. But no. She was able to take him. With pleasure.

He struggled with himself, then gave in. First in kisses, lots of kisses. Her face. Her ears. Her neck. Her hair. She was weak from him. He loved that. He loved it all. He lifted her and carried her to the bed. She lay atop the coverlet; he lay on top of her. She giggled.

She wanted only to be kissed. She loved that the most. So he kissed her, everywhere. That throat. It was flawless. He could kiss it forever. Then her breasts. Buds. That's all they were, buds. Her stomach. Flat, long, lean. Perfect. She stopped him from going any lower. She wanted more of his mouth on hers. He felt his penis rub over her soft down. It wasn't what he wanted to feel. It excited him too much. He moved away. No. No. Not now. He thought he murmured it, but she didn't hear. She was guiding him. No. No.

He lifted himself, touched her. She was wet. Oh, God, young girls got so wet so quickly. He remembered what it was like back then. He always remembered. It was so good. So very good.

She called out his name.

He lowered himself. He had to taste her. He had to. He knew it embarrassed her. She loved it, but it embarrassed her. That excited him more. After a few moments it excited her too.

"Kiss me," she cried out. "Kiss me."

Her mouth. Yes, he'd have her mouth. She was all things. She was everything he had ever wanted. This was insane. He knew it. He didn't care.

"Please," she begged.

"No, I must taste you again."

"Please."

He gave it to her. He couldn't refuse her anything. This was his haven. This and nothing else. That's how it was for him. He was giving it to her. To him. To both of them. He was giving it to her. Oh, God, he was giving it to her.

♦ VIII ♦

Jack Gilbert thought it ironic that he was a photographer, a goddamn fucking film-maker right in the middle of La La Land—possibly the best-lit place in the whole fucking country if not in the whole fucking world—and here he was shooting indoors. It was nuts. But then so was everything else in California.

Originally he had made the move to Venice because of the light. Not the one from above but the one from below. The boys. The mindless, beautiful boys who did drugs all night and weights all day. But he didn't even dig the light boys anymore.

He wondered if Erica Jong had tried zipless fucks or just fantasized about them. It had taken him ten years to get tired of them. For the last three he'd been operating on memory and maybes. Jack Gilbert was bored. Bored with the beautiful Barbie dolls that seemed to thrive on Venice's sandy beaches and crystal-clear waters. Bored with his own smart-ass remarks like, "The only one who makes more dolls than Venice is Mattel—but theirs are smarter and probably last longer too." Jack was bored with being the intellectual among primitives. He was even bored with sex. Which was what worried him the most.

Take Mike the Mule. Jack could have had Mike just for letting him play in the film. It would have been easy. But Jack didn't want him. Now watching him act this scene with Nick, he knew why.

Mike was too quick on the draw. It was the third time in a week that he had covered Nasty Nick's pecs with his own sticky brand of love, ten minutes too soon. A definite no-no in porn. A definite no-no in life.

Jack ran his fingers through his weighty mane of auburn hair and counted to ten. That in itself was an accomplishment for anyone from Venice. Well, maybe that was an exaggeration. The dolls Jack had gotten to know could count. Some could even get as high as twelve—if it involved dick.

Keep it cool, he told himself. "All right. Let's reverse it." He shook loose the elastic band that held his short ponytail in place. "Mike"—sigh—"bend over for rear entry."

"Now, don't pout, honey," Nick called down from the set. He and Jack were lovers and Nick felt that he not only had rights over Jack's sex, he had rights over his emotions. "You know how upset I get when you pout." He walked over to Jack and gave him a big hug.

Yeah, Jack knew. In fact, he knew everything there was to know about Nick. Two fucking years. To a Scorpio that was a lifetime. Jack tightened his shoulders. It kept him from saying what was on his mind.

Call it love, he'd always told himself, and you end up making promises that no man can keep. Call it love and you think you're capable of doing the impossible. Call it "finished" and you've got a pain in the ass on your hands. Especially if you're finishing it with Nasty Nick.

Do unto others, the Scriptures said. Well, that was Nick's adage too. Abandon Nasty Nick and he'll do it right back—but one better. Twenty-three and already he had had two guys blown away. Or so they said on the street.

Jack had heard all the rumors but had gotten involved with him anyway. Couldn't resist his California tan, his

Steve Reeves body, his Tyrone Power face. He'd never expected to get tired of the kid. He figured if anyone lost interest it would be Nick. After all, Jack was forty-five and Nick only half that.

But Jack had been wrong.

"In Manhattan. The number for R. Haskins."

"Is that a residence or business?"

At half past midnight it's a residence, you asshole. "Residence, operator."

An electronic pleasantry announced, *"The number is . . . 555-6969."*

"Figures," Ashley said as she dialed. "Two sixty-nines in his number."

"Hello," a groggy voice answered.

"Robbie?"

"Who's this?"

"Ashley. Ashley Pope. The girl in the play."

"Ashley." Suddenly the voice was awake, alive. "Is something wrong?"

"Yeah." I got a fire going on and I thought you might want to bring over some ice."

"Ice?"

"Ice, as in maybe you can put out the fire?"

"Where is the fire?" he asked with genuine concern.

"What are you, a fireman?"

"Well, if you want my extinguisher. . ."

"With all the foam you've got."

"Don't we have rehearsals tomorrow?"

"At ten."

"Won't you be tired?"

"Are you taking a survey or playing fireman?"

"I'll be right over."

"Bend over!" Jack screamed.

"But that wasn't the arrangement my agent made for me," Mike whined.

"And just what did your agent say?" Jack was unkind, sarcastic, fed up.

"He said I'd come before dinner and I'd get rammed after."

"You'll come before dinner! My, my," Jack said, imitating a drag queen. "How about we feed you? Now."

"But it's only five o'clock." Mike had that Christopher Street whine. Always sounded like he was on the rag.

"Bend over," Nick ordered the inept stud. He was pretty pushy, but then again he was Jack Gilbert's lover. Anyone who tried to put him in his place was reminded of that immediately.

"But..."

"Shut up, bitch," Nick said, giving him a shove.

"Oh, I love it when you talk dirty," Mike said.

Nick was working on the beginnings of a hard-on. "Suck it," he said. "I'll tell you," he called over to Jack. "He can suck off real good."

"This is not a blowjob we're shooting, remember?" Don't let it get to you, Jack. It's not worth it. "Get your cock out of his mouth. Now."

"Sorry," Nick said. "I forgot."

"Yeah, I bet you did."

"Aw, come on," Mike said with a saccharine-sweet smile on his face. "You were young once."

Wrong. Jack Gilbert had never been young. He had been Jake, Jakele. He had been a kid but he had never been young. He was once innocent enough not to understand his yearnings for young men. Or why all the other kids wanted to leave their mothers and he wanted to be with his. That was when fagele *didn't mean gay. It just meant Jewish. Yes, maybe Jack was young once, but he got over it.*

When he was ten Jakele did what all the other kids on Division Street, in lower Manhattan, did. He became a tough guy, a hoodlum of sorts. He hated it at first, but so what. His mother hated being a seamstress. His father hated delivering seltzer bottles. Jake Gilbert learned early on that life was not a bowl of cherries.

He started to steal. He'd cut school and grab ladies' handbags. Rich ladies who shopped downtown for pretty clothes, for soft underthings with lace on them. Stuff that his mother wouldn't be caught dead in. Lizard bags that came from Spain. Sweaters that had been made on machines and had lots of colors in them. He stole from very modern, very rich ladies.

If he caught them before they shopped, he could make a killing. Fifty, maybe a hundred bucks. But if he got them afterward, well, he could pull in six, eight dollars a day that way. Not bad for a ten-year-old during the Eisenhower years.

Then one of the kids got him wise to going uptown. He'd take the bus up Madison Avenue to Fifty-seventh Street and just walk around. After a few weeks of that, he caught on to the Plaza Hotel. Lots of rich tourists stayed there. He'd watch his victims carefully, very carefully. Then when they least suspected it—pow—he'd grab their bags and run.

But what Jake noticed more than the matrons were the cars and the apartments and the doormen. The people that got respect. Even kids. While the doormen chased away the downtown kids, they were real nice to the little kids with loafers and white socks. Or the ones who wore saddle shoes and corduroys with a crease. Jake Gilbert was not one of them.

He would watch them come home from school with their nannies. He would watch fathers arrive at six o'clock looking fresh and newly shaved. He'd watch families go out to dinner. None of the wives looked like they had been sitting over a sewing machine all day long. Not one wore stockings rolled down around her knees.

That year was an important one for Jake. He learned something it sometimes takes others a lifetime to learn. He learned that no matter what anybody says, money is everything. Not prayer or keeping the laws of kashruth or studying the Torah. It was money. With money you could do all of that. Without it you could only be poor. So that's why Jake vowed to leave Division Street. Get out of the Gilbert family and away from poverty. He vowed that when he grew up he'd never be poor again. Jake really began to grow up then.

Jack looked out onto his Venice, California, seascape. Everything was in order. His translucent glasshouse straddled a fifty-foot swimming pool. The deck faced the

Pacific. Plants grew in his living room and the tennis courts were being repaved. He even managed to give his daughter a respectable life in New York City. Yes, Jack Gilbert had made it. Money ran through his fingers like water and there seemed to be a never-ending supply of it. His life was his own. And he planned on keeping it that way.

Before Jake got rich, he got transplanted. He was caught stealing handbags. Once. Twice. Three times. On the fourth collar the authorities decided to send him to reform school. His mother screamed and cried. He'd never seen her that upset before.

Ruchel didn't mind that they wanted to send Jake to reform school. She felt the discipline would do him good. She and Heimie certainly couldn't give it to him. What killed her was that it would be a goyish penitentiary. Sausages. Ham. Butter on his bread when he'd be eating chicken. Such habits he'd learn. It was bad enough he was a crook, but to be a goy on top of it . . . She begged and pleaded with the authorities that they grant him one more reprieve. Let him go to California and stay with her brother Sol and his wife Leah, her Orthodox kin. If anyone could straighten Jake out it was Ruchel's brother.

Sol certainly did try. Sidelocks and all, he was a pretty rough guy. When he wasn't praying three times a day or eating kosher, he was coaching boxers. Anyone who laughed at Sol could expect one of his fighters to bash him. But Jake wasn't cut out to be either a yeshiva boy or a fighter. He was made to have money.

Days he studied the Torah and nights he went out looking for trouble. He found rich kids. No sidelocks, no prayers. Just convertibles, cologne, and girls. He loved everything but the latter. The girls loved him though. He looked like a young Burt Lancaster. Eventually one of the girls got him in the sack. It wasn't so bad. But it wasn't so good either.

The girl didn't get pregnant, but she wanted him to marry her just the same. He refused. She went to Sol, who was furious at both of them. He politely apologized to the girl for Jake's unforgivable behavior and told her to get lost. Then he married Jake off to a cow named Chana Lifshitz. Chana reminded Jake so much of his mother he hated looking at her.

She couldn't get pregnant no matter what she did. He didn't help any. He never wanted to touch her. She got blessing after blessing. The doctor said there was nothing wrong with her, or with him. The Rebbe said it must be God's will. Finally, just when he was ready to leave her, she got pregnant. With Rivka. Sweet darling Rivka. Then when Rivka was six, Chana choked on a chicken bone and died.

Jack didn't know what to do with the girl, so he let Sol and Leah have her. After a few years, though, he decided he didn't like what was happening to her. She was beginning to look like what he had run away from on Division Street. She was a ten-year-old matron.

Jack knew he had to get Rivka away from Sol and Leah. She had a voice like a nightingale and he would be damned if she were going to be raised in an environment where it was considered a sin for a girl to sing. So in the middle of the night he stole her away. Sol and Leah tried to get her back. They took him to court saying his movies invalidated him as a father, but the judge didn't agree. Satisfied, Jack stayed in L.A. and sent Rivka to New York. She first attended Dalton, then The Rudolf Steiner School. She stayed with respected dowagers and came home during semester breaks. Rivka became Rebecca, and then Becky.

Nasty Nick was coming. It was long and sweet and the camera was getting it all. So was Mike. Jack? He wasn't getting much of anything lately. Just aggravation and a record two-year relationship with some guy who was beginning to bore the shit out of him.

"Good show, guys," he said. "It's a print."

Now if only he could find a way to get rid of the kid without becoming the third lover to be blown away.

Vince woke up in a sweat. Heat. He never remembered it being this hot in early October before. He could even smell his body. Janice slept beside him. Should he wake her? No, it wasn't that kind of heat. It couldn't be quieted by decency, by promises. This was a dirty kind of hot, stemming from old longings, old feelings. And from a premonition. Death.

Should he wake her? *No!*

"Janice," he said, rubbing up against her. Life. He thought of that Evelyn girl. He wanted life. Did that mean Janice? Not necessarily. But she didn't seem to care. She loved him, she said. Just like that Evelyn girl loved that married med student. Sloppy seconds. That was what it was about. Seconds. Vince let his hard-on press against her ass. Janice was awake instantly.

His need was her need, even in her sleep. Mumbling, she turned to him and said something about love. It wasn't love he was feeling, but he muttered something back. What he wanted was to get rid of the heat. He had to quench the fire.

He always said the right words and she always woke up wet. He sometimes wondered if she slept in anticipation. No foreplay was needed for these late-night intermissions. Just two fleshy components finding satisfaction.

Janice embraced him, burying her face in his neck. She hated to be kissed without brushing her teeth. Hated it. He didn't force it.

One. Two. Three strokes.

Their bodies shook. She mumbled something about love again and dozed off. He didn't. The fire had only gotten worse.

IX

"Karla, where were you last night?" Olive, exhausted from the rehearsals, had fallen asleep early. She hadn't even heard Karla come in.

"I was with Becky."

"Oh. Where did you go?" Olive hoped that was casual enough as she took a Granny Smith apple from the fridge.

Karla didn't think it was so casual. "What is this, the third degree?"

"Karla, what is the matter with you? You're a mass of nerves lately."

Karla walked away. She had no time for this. Did her mother think she was a baby or something?

"Karla."

"I'm sorry." Her tone said she wasn't. "We went to see *River's Edge*."

Olive bit into the apple. "Was it any good?"

"Great! Now stop the questions. Why are mothers such a pain in the ass?" Then she added softly, sneakily, "Becky is so lucky not to have one." Shit, she didn't mean that and was about to apologize when the doorbell rang.

"All right, Sam," Olive said into the intercom. "I'll come down and get it." She turned back to Karla. Her voice was cool. "It's a letter. I'm leaving for rehearsal now. We'll talk later."

"Hear that, Bear? Mom wants to have a summit meeting. Okay. We'll talk later."

Olive took the elevator down to the lobby. Sam was waiting with the envelope. "Who brought this, Sam?"

"No one I ever saw before, Miss Kingsley. I think he was a messenger."

Olive walked out into the daytime. Summer lingered in the air like a woman's perfume and Olive liked it. She began her short walk from the apartment to the Longacre and opened the letter. It was the crazy writing that got to her first. Then the words:

Isadora got her due.
And so will you
If you Star Ashley Pope
In Your Broadway Stew.

At first she simply stared at it in disbelief. But it didn't go away, this message, this threat. Why now? Why when things seemed to be going so well?

She crumpled the note, as if by hiding it the message would go away. Her pace quickened. But with each step Nina Houston's face became brighter, clearer. For the first time in ten years she wanted her mommy.

Elizabeth Anne decided that the problem was children. Or the lack of them. A man couldn't be expected to remain childless forever, no matter what he said. It was only natural to want to pass on a name, one's genes.

She was afraid that by the time Charles realized all of this it would be too late. Not for him, for her. He, the male, could make them forever. She, the female, could not. After all, she *was* thirty-seven.

The Mayor's Wife had awakened late. Later than Charles.

He was gone when she got up, had told her he would be. Business, he'd said.

Alone, without her husband's disapproving eye, Elizabeth Anne felt free to stick her bedside thermometer under her tongue. When Charles was there she didn't have that freedom. He frowned on her preoccupation with pregnancy.

She read the numbers carefully. Her normal 97.2 was up to 97.6. Wanting to make sure she was right, she turned on the light. Yes, yes, yes. She was ovulating. Today was the day. She charted the temperature on her graph and began the business of being The Mayor's Wife. The business of pretending.

She knew she was the envy of all the socialites. She had the husband, the looks, the money, the power. They even envied her her childlessness. Well, they might envy her but she hated it, despised it. All of it.

So why was she attending all of these luncheons? Why had she agreed to meet the press? So he could get reelected and she could spend another four years imprisoned by his title? And then? While he never spoke of it, she knew he was after the presidency. Truth was they'd had much more fun before he was elected. But who was interested in truth?

Elizabeth Anne wouldn't have minded nearly so much if she had something to do, something meaningful. While she loved reading to the blind and visiting the children's wards in hospitals, she wanted a child of her own.

Charles may have been an orphan but she was not. The Manchesters, after all, did come over on the Mayflower. The goddamn Mayflower. Didn't she owe them something? Or the world? Didn't she owe everyone another generation of Manchesters? Didn't she owe it to herself?

Where was her husband anyway?

With another woman.

No.

Yes.

Their sex life had been an on-again, off-again thing for the past year now, and if there was one thing she knew about Charles it was that he *loved* sex. Adored it. So where was he getting it?

Another woman.

Elizabeth Anne, the only child of Millicent and Carter Manchester, had been visiting her friend Tulee Benson in San Diego when she met Charles Long.

There had been a party. Tulee's father, Emmett Benson, had recently acquired Betty Crocker and the family was having a cake-bake to celebrate. Tiffany Diamond was there. Tiffany's father, while not known for any singular acquisition, was well known as the most serious Monopoly player on Fifth Avenue. This was, of course, pre–Donald Trump. And then there was Garth Buckley III, whose family owned all of Arizona. Well, ninety percent of it anyway. Alexander Yarborough was there. His mother owned oil wells in Texas. His daddy owned a football team.

Charles wasn't invited. Charles wasn't heard of—not by this crowd, anyway. He wouldn't have even been noticed had Elizabeth Anne not practically fallen over herself when he walked through the door. Charles Andrew Long was the delivery boy assigned to bring in their buffet dinner. Elizabeth Anne took one look at him and it was over for her. Totally.

Her friends said it would pass, called it a fling. They said she and Charles had nothing in common. But they were wrong. They had lots in common. They both appreciated the good life—she out of breeding, he out of aspiration. Oh, and one other thing. They both loved Charles.

She took him home to New York. Her parents were not amused. He obviously had good genes. They quite liked his sharp bone structure, cornflower-blue eyes, and combed-back ashen hair. He fit the picture. From the top of his pastel turtleneck down to his well-pressed white ducks, Charles looked very much like a son-in-law should look. But to the Manchesters of Tuxedo Park, looks aren't everything.

The Manchesters would never allow their daughter to

marry just anyone and Charles Long was worse than just anyone. He was no one.

Time healed none of it. Their hearts were still closed to him. He was a poor relation, even now. Even after his election they still preferred to see her alone. Still preferred to believe he didn't exist. They never spoke of grandchildren, never spoke of the future.

Elizabeth Anne didn't care about any of it. She needed a child. Wanted a child. She didn't care that her parents said it would be a mongrel. If it was a mongrel, so be it. She needed somebody to love, somebody to care for. Obviously neither her parents nor her husband felt any great love or commitment toward her.

But until she became pregnant she needed something. Something to make all the loneliness go away.

Vodka!

But it's only ten-thirty in the morning.

So what!

The plainclothesman who walked into the Longacre Theatre had lost none of his contradictions—the humble stoop, the serious jawline that rarely yielded a smile, the eyes that seemed to laugh constantly. It was all there, packaged in a fit body, a well-lined yet handsome face, and hair that had turned a dignified gray.

Olive sat tenth row center watching Richard direct Ashley when a tap on the shoulder almost sent her through the ceiling.

"I'm sorry for startling you, Olive."

"Vince?" She felt as if someone had slid her through a time machine, but in a moment she managed to compose herself. "I'm so sorry. Detective Luscardi, how are you?" She extended her hand.

"You were right the first time. It's Vince." He took her hand, but not to shake it, merely holding it the way one would hold the hand of an old friend.

"Richard, Detective Luscardi and I will be in the back."

Richard nodded, sensing something was up.

Vince studied her as they walked up the aisle. Over the years, Olive's name had cropped up in the tabloids. A benefit here, an opening there. She had been curator of over a dozen exhibits on the dance around the country. She was often invited to be a guest speaker at dance lectures. She attended as many dance openings as she could. Every once in a great while she performed in special recitals. Yet with all the publicity she was never linked with anyone.

He looked for signs of love in her. A comfort that might have added extra flesh around her jaw or exaggerated her hips. He found none of it. Instead he saw a sweet but unreal smile, as if she'd penciled it on that morning with her lipstick. Her eyes did not sparkle, but instead were filled with critical evaluation. Intimidation. Exotica made severe by hair pulled back too tight, by a body too thin. Still, she was beautiful. Gorgeous in an ephemeral way. Even vulnerable. But it was all frozen in time, some other time. Vince took one look at her and knew he wanted nothing more than to thaw the ice.

"They told you about the note," she said. It was still crumpled up in her pocket.

"May I see it?" he asked.

Like a young child showing her daddy her report card, she took it out and handed it to him.

"Olive, let's sit down." The rich cranberry-colored damask seats were heavily cushioned, and Vince was grateful to sit in one. What with the two dance murders and all the other girlie killings he was checking out, he felt as if he hadn't sat down in days. "My captain told me you didn't want anyone to know about this, Olive. Why is that?"

"I don't want to alarm anyone." She sat tall, facing him as if she were a complete adult, something she didn't feel at all. "And mostly, I don't want my daughter to find out."

He remembered reading something about Olive having a daughter, but the recollection was vague. That time had been so confusing for him.

After Angelique had been killed, Connie almost had a

breakdown. The psychiatrist who helped her suggested they have another child. Vince, who really had no feeling other than compassion for his wife, agreed. Yes, he'd make a go of it. Connie became pregnant shortly after Angelique's death. The child could have kept them together had it lived, but it hadn't. Connie gave birth to a stillborn. Three years later he left.

Vince looked at the note. "It didn't come in an envelope?"

"Yes," she said, realizing she had done something wrong. "I threw it away. I guess I was so upset." She paused, then asked hesitantly, "Am I in any danger?"

"I'll have this checked by our handwriting analyst." He knew damn well it was the same person who'd written out the list they found by Nina Houston's body. When he looked up, Ashley was sweeping across the stage. "She's good," he said.

Olive looked toward Ashley. She was bathed in the whitest light, washing out what little coloring she had.

"Robbie," she called up to the lighting director. "That's too much light." Nothing happened. "Robbie?" Still no change. She'd speak to him later. To Vince she said, "You didn't answer my question."

"What's that?"

"Am I in any danger?"

"Is that Ashley Pope?" he asked.

"Yes, it is."

"Why wouldn't someone want her to star in your play?" Vince was trained to ask questions rather than to answer them. "Is there someone else who wanted the part?"

She hadn't thought about that. "That's a good question."

"Is there any chance you can use someone else?"

"Isn't that like giving in to the terrorists? They take your hostages and you meet their demands."

"In other words, the answer is no."

"Detective Luscardi," she said with a slight smile, "we are *all* replaceable."

"Well, if you won't choose another Isadora, then have you considered a bodyguard?"

"I still can't get a straight answer from you, can I?" she

asked, standing up. "I think it's time for me to get back to work. Thank you for stopping by."

"Olive," he said, but she had turned her back on him. "Olive." He touched her shoulder. It was a spontaneous gesture. "I'm going to assign someone to watch over you."

"A bodyguard?" she asked, meeting his eyes.

He nodded. "Yes."

X

"Grandma, what are you doing here?" Karla asked.

Karen had been waiting outside The Rudolf Steiner School for at least half an hour watching the students come and go. They ranged in size and age from children to young adults, and as she watched them, Karen realized for the first time what her exile had cost her.

"Are you free this afternoon, Karla?" she asked, reaching out to stroke her granddaughter's cheek. Karla looked heaven sent in a black on white polka-dot circle skirt and a slinky leotard.

Karla was free.

"What if we just walk around?" Karen asked. "Perhaps do a little shopping. How does that sound, darling?"

Karen had said the magic word. Shopping. Karla loved clothes. Leather was her passion this month. A nice denim-looking leather skirt and a jacket to match would be perfect.

"Let's go to Fiorucci," she said, suddenly animated.

"Who?" Karen asked, turning up a well-turned nose.

"Grandma . . ."

"Darling, it's Karen."

"Karen. Fiorucci. Believe me, it's great."

Karen looked at Karla with a kind of detached freedom that she had never had with her own daughter and agreed. "Yes, darling, let's go to Fiorucci."

Olive wasn't in the house five minutes when she headed for the barre. It was her only defense. Against what? Against life. No, against love. Against need. Against despair.

She returned to the familiar, to the pain of *pointe*, to stretched-to-the-max hamstrings, to building quadriceps as strong as any football player's. It was still less painful than feeling vulnerable. That had been true for Olive sixteen years ago and it was true now.

With the same single-mindedness that an addict has in finding her fix, Olive slipped out of her comfortable jumpsuit and sought relief at the barre. She felt her hamstrings lengthen. Stretch. Point. Exteeeend. Stretch. Point. Exteeeend. Painful, yes, but familiar. She was sure that if someone were to place his ear against hers, he'd hear Balanchine saying stretch, point, exteeeend.

She wanted to make it go away. Reality. Life.

Out, Vince Luscardi. Out.

For the first time she was grateful for the tape playing inside her head, the tape of Balanchine and her mother.

But where is Olive?

She didn't care. She did *pliés* until she was ready to drop, *port de bras* until her arms couldn't extend anymore. Then *tendus*. One hundred and twenty-eight on each side. "Feet are like moles," Balanchine always said. "They have no eyes and they still know exactly where to go."

Stretch, two, three, four. Stretch, two, three, four. Extend that muscle. Slooowly extend. She continued mindlessly. But for some reason it didn't help. Like Brick in *Cat On a Hot Tin Roof,* she couldn't get the click.

Karla, feeling pleased with Karen's gift to her from Fiorucci, stood by the door and watched her mother. Olive's frustration was as tactile as the sweat on her brow. It had been a long, long time since Karla had seen her mother work at the barre with such resolve. Something was very wrong.

Olive moved away from the barre. In the center of the floor she executed a *grande jeté,* then another and another. Without thought. With visual ease. Like a doll atop a jewelry box.

Vince Luscardi, who invited you back, dammit?

She lifted. She pointed. She did a series of *jetés,* that movement where you spring from one foot to the other. First from fifth to second, front and back. Then a series of half-turns. They bored her. She went on to a *brisé volé.* These were far more difficult, requiring that a body tilt in midair. It was what she did best in *Sleeping Beauty.* Over and over again she danced the steps. Over and over again until the pain obscured the memory of the man and the desire she felt for him.

"You need a boyfriend, Mom," Karla said from the doorway.

"A what?" Olive was startled, and then grateful for being taken out of the trance she was in.

Karla entered the room and hugged her. "A boyfriend."

Olive let go of the hug. "Shouldn't I be saying that to you?"

"No one should be alone as much as you are."

"Is this what I need to hear? A lecture from my daughter about the birds and the bees?"

"Who said anything about birds or bees? I said a boyfriend. They're great."

"Oh, really. And just what does my precious Karla know about boyfriends?" Olive grabbed the towel from the barre and dried herself off.

"Mom."

"I'm serious, Karla." And she was. The afternoon was forgotten. Was her daughter dating? "Is that where you were last night?"

"Listen to her, Bear. Already she's accusing me of being a liar." Even after Karla had regained her eyesight she was able to maintain the look of blindness, a blank, deadpan stare.

"Well?"

"I told you I was with Becky."

Olive was about to continue with the cross-examination when the phone rang. Karla made a mad dash for it.

"It's for you, Mom." Then softer, away from the mouthpiece, "It's a man!"

Charles came home early on Thursday. The campaign trail gave him a perfect excuse for keeping long hours, but he came home early anyway. Because of last night. And because though he really didn't want to be there, he knew he needed Elizabeth Anne, the image, the name. She gave him the past he'd never had.

He found her sitting up in bed. Her soft brown hair, cut in a sleek pageboy, was mussed, and her big blue eyes were overly bright.

"My temperature's up." Her voice was lilting, tipsy. Yes, this was the time. She had even called her astrologer, and Rona had confirmed that for Elizabeth Anne, a Pisces with Saturn in the fifth house and Capricorn rising, it was an excellent time to conceive.

"I thought I told you to stop that," he said, watching her pore over her charts from Rona. He hated it. No, hated himself.

"Stop what?" she asked, nervously gathering up the papers and charts and notes.

"Charting your goddamn temperature and organizing our sex life around it, that's what." He could still feel Karla's body under his. Still taste her. No matter how hard he tried he couldn't wash her away.

Elizabeth Anne's eyes clouded over. The tiny lines in her forehead became more pronounced. She put the charts away, so as not to disturb him.

"I'm sorry, Charles. But I . . ."

"I know. You want a baby." He sighed. "Can't you get it into your brain that maybe sex should just be enjoyed?"

There was a time when, in response, she would have slipped out of her cashmere robe and seduced him with her nakedness. She had a good body. The kind of good that comes from never having had breasts large enough to sag, from playing tennis, riding horses, and swimming regularly. The kind of body that's good because it's been pampered and powdered to perfection.

There was a time when she would have taken his hand and placed it on the soft mound between her thighs. Then she would have lifted her head to catch his kiss. Maybe she'd nip his lips, even draw blood, just for the sting of it. It had been that way between them once. Hot and young and sweet. But when he stopped coming to her nightly she began to lose confidence. She became afraid that by asking for too much he'd resent her. So she asked for nothing. And that's exactly what she got. Nothing.

Elizabeth Anne sat there all squirrelly eyed and frightened and allowed her husband to reprimand her.

He wanted her to scream back at him. Why was she so afraid? He hated her for it. No, he hated himself. Why? *They* had finally gotten to him.

They. Women. They pursued and pursued and pursued him. No matter that he was married. No matter that he was a public official with an image to maintain. No matter at all. They sniffed around him like bitches in heat.

One woman, a star reporter interviewing him for the *Times,* uncrossed her legs in the middle of the interview. Sitting across from her it wasn't difficult for Charles to see that she wasn't wearing panties.

A Park Avenue hostess giving a party for Charles and his wife offered him use of the bedroom... if he used it with her in it.

A White House press secretary, while showing him the presidential quarters, made him an offer he found almost impossible to refuse.

But he did refuse. He refused them all. So then what happened?

Karla was what happened. Karla got to him, with her youth, with her sweet tastes, with her radiance. So in trying to temper his passions he withdrew them. Not from Karla but from his wife. How could he make love to

Elizabeth Anne Manchester while he was getting it on with a fifteen-year-old?

"Charles?"

"Yes?" He tried to look at her kindly.

She was about to approach him, to take the chance. But the expression in his eyes . . . pity, pure pity. She had never seen it before. That look, that pity. She had become a stray animal to him, to be taken in and sheltered. He was offering her shelter, but where was the love?

"What is it, Elizabeth Anne?"

"Can I get you a drink?"

"Vince," Olive said in a hushed tone. "Where did you get my number?"

"Listen, kid. I'm not just another dumb flatfoot."

"Oh, really. And here that's what I've been telling people about you all along."

"Look, Olive, enough of the jokes. I think we should meet. There are some things I have to tell you about this case."

"Well, that's fine, Vince," she said, realizing she hadn't worked him out of her system at all. "Just come to the theater tomorrow."

"No, that's no good. I think we should speak tonight."

"I'm in danger?"

"In a manner of speaking, yes."

"And you think something could happen to me tonight?"

If he had anything to do with it, yes. "No."

"Then let's meet tomorrow at the theater."

"Dinner."

She had to laugh at his persistence. "All right, Vince. Tomorrow at seven."

"Seven it is."

"Vince?"

"Yes, Olive?"

"Nothing. Tomorrow at seven."

Karla had overheard it all. Her mother didn't fool her a bit. She had met someone.

"Mommy has a date. Mommy has a date," Karla yelled,

jumping around the room like a jackrabbit. "Mommy has a date. Mommy has a date." Then she stopped. She stood in the middle of the living room, placed her hand on her hip, and asked in an accent straight out of a Yiddish theater troupe, "So who is he?"

"It's a long story," Olive said, smiling. "And it's been a long day. Let's have dinner."

"Don't you ever sleep?" Ashley asked. She'd opened her eyes and found Robbie staring at her. It was 2:00 A.M. and he was lying in bed staring at her. She didn't regret his coming by last night or tonight. He was everything he was cracked up to be. As gorgeous in the flesh as he was in his clothes. And gentle. She had a thing for gentle men. But she did need her sleep.

"You're a wonderful lover, Robbie," she said softly, sweetly, losing all that tough sexiness that she used as part of her routine.

"You make me want to be a wonderful lover."

"Robbie . . ." She propped herself up on one elbow and ran her finger down the center of his chest.

Before she could finish the thought he hushed her with his lips. He wanted her sweetness all over again. He wanted to feel the fullness of her hips between his hands. He wanted to devour her.

"Do you really like the way I make love?" he asked. The street lamps sent in a beam of light and it ran silken over her hair. It gave him a new way to see her. He would use it tomorrow.

"I love it," she said. "I love what you do to me off stage as well as on."

"This is just the beginning," he promised. "Just the beginning."

• XI •

"Don't tell me Daddy prepared this all by himself," Nick said, not feeling nasty at all.

He sat back and fingered the crystal stemware that sat in Early American pewter coasters. He fingered the vase, as striking and slender as his most prized body part, which held a single yellow rose. If he could have, he would have fingered the whole outdoors alongside Jack's fifty-foot pool. He wanted to touch it all. Perhaps then he'd become part of it, part of the beauty, part of the California full moon, part of the *Architectural Digest* cover look.

"All what?" Jack called back from the kitchen. "There's nothing out yet."

"The artichokes in vinaigrette are out. And who designed this silver for you, Picasso?" After two years, Nick had just begun to feel comfortable with Jack. Trusting him, he allowed himself to be the child, the uneducated wop from the wrong side of the tracks. He allowed Jack to teach him.

"Maybe he did. I bought it at an auction. Cost plenty,

too." Jack emerged from the kitchen with two endive and arugula salads that he'd smothered in melted goat cheese and olive oil.

"Where's Juanita?"

"I gave her the night off."

"So you did prepare this."

Jack pinched Nick's cheek. "I only let her cook for the masses. For the film crew, the black-tie dinners. Anything that makes me nuts. You know that, Nick."

The film was over. Jack could relax. Or he should be able to anyway. But he couldn't. There was a gnawing feeling inside his stomach that told him he had much to do before he slept.

"What's so funny?" he asked. Nick's face had suddenly begun to beam.

"When I get old enough to look for a husband you're going to be my first choice," Nick answered coyly.

Husband. It struck Jack like the back of his mother's hand and he quickly shook it away.

"Listen, sweetie," he said. "You're only half my age, which means that neither of us are kids anymore."

"Looking for younger stuff?"

Jack paused a little too long.

"Daddy?"

"Nah," Jack said, putting on his TV voice. "I think I'll keep you."

But the pause was real and pushed Nick's buttons, of which he had many. His motherfucker attitude was never too far away. *Better believe you'll keep me,* he thought. *And God help you if you decide not to.*

When he spoke his voice was sweet, soft, as unassuming as possible. "So tell me, what have you decided for your next film? Any projects in mind?"

The dinner was a ritual. After the completion of every film they had a little dinner and discussed new projects. Or that's how Nick saw this dinner. Jack just wanted out.

"I think the steak is almost ready," he said, clearing away their salad plates. "It'll be a few minutes. Why don't you put on some music?"

Nick wasn't in the mood for music. He was in the mood for a flick. Something good. One of his.

Jack Gilbert loved toys. He'd never had any as a child. When he finally made it big and built this house, he had it equipped with every technological device under the sun. And even more under the moon.

The pool was his Seine. It ran right through the center of his home. Traversing it was an open-air portico that ran seaside to roadside. The kitchen was glass-enclosed on one side, the living room on the other. Controls released a large viewing screen that seemed to descend from the stars. The projector popped out and, presto, you had a movie.

Nick riffled through the stacks of films.

"Hey, what are these?"

"I can't hear you." Jack was turning over the porterhouse.

They were old. Nick could see that. Old sixteen-millimeter movies. They looked turn-of-the-century. He set one up, then returned to the table to savor the food.

"Where's the music?" Jack asked, slicing through the double thick steak.

"I decided to get kinky. Start early. It'll inspire us."

"Is that a complaint?" Like Jack really gave a shit. The steak was perfect. Singed black on the outside, Beaujolais-colored on the inside.

"Insecure?" Nick teased.

"Should I be?"

The film began. No title. No credits.

"When the hell did you make this? During the Korean War?"

"Jesus, this is old. Nineteen seventy or thereabouts."

A pretty blonde girl lay on her stomach, spread-eagled and naked on rumpled sheets. She was sucking on her finger, obviously waiting for something more exciting to put in her mouth. She turned toward the camera. Someone was giving her directions. Finger out of the mouth. A guy came over and set up a reflector. Finger back in her mouth. Buns up.

"Not bad," Nick said.

Jack was too into his food to notice. "What's not bad?"

"Those buns. Not bad for a girl."

"Are you getting strange on me now?"

"Why didn't you edit—Jesus Christ."

"Now what?"

"Look at the size of him. He's got me beat by an inch."

Jack looked up. Squinted. Forty-five was not kind to the eyesight.

"Oh, I remember this. I shot this down in Tijuana. Never did anything with it. Never had to. The next year I came out with *Cherry Vanilla*."

Cherry Vanilla *had been pure luck for Jack. The first porno flick with a plot, a comedy of sorts. It was about a sweet young girl with a passion for cherry vanilla ice cream. She couldn't get enough of it. The kids even called her Cherry Vanilla. It was her obsession.*

The guys in class had other ideas, but no one could get near her. Then one day a guy got smart and bribed her with cherry vanilla ice cream. He dipped his dick in it and got her to suck him. Then he covered his stomach with it. Then he stuck it up her ass. She fell in love with the guy and it turned out he couldn't keep up with her. She changed all that passion for ice cream into passion for him. But because he had an ego as big as his dick he couldn't tell her she was wearing him out. The poor sucker died from love, leaving the chick looking for a new sucker.

Cherry Vanilla *made so much money for Jack he was still counting it. After the movie, he decided to come out. He said he'd never make a straight porno flick again and didn't.*

He also said he'd leave Chana.

That endeavor wasn't quite as successful. She was already pregnant with Becky. Ten fucking years she couldn't conceive and suddenly... Well, that was life. Every year he planned on leaving and every year something came up. Then Becky was six and Chana was dead.

"Do you see who the fuck that is?" Nick couldn't believe his eyes. "Is that...?"

"Yeah, it's him." Jack was blasé.

"You have Charlie Long on film fucking a broad and... Jack, do you know what this is worth?"

"Yeah." The steak was good, real good.

"And it's just sitting there. Like any ordinary film."

"It *is* an ordinary film. Less than ordinary, as a matter of fact." The discussion was beginning to annoy him. He got up and shut off the movie.

"Why did you do that?"

"Because it's part of the past and I only live in the future."

"Just as long as I'm a part of it, Daddy, we'll never have any problems."

Unfortunately for Becky she had inherited none of her father's good looks. Neither the taupe of his eyes, nor the fabulous cheekbones. Not the aquiline nose nor the wavy auburn hair. Rebecca Gilbert was a walking portrait of her mother. And what had made Chana so unappealing—the boneless cheeks, the frizzy, mouse-colored hair, the nose that looked as if it had been fashioned out of Silly Putty—did the same for Becky.

Fortunately she had not inherited her mother's shyness. If she had she would have died by now. At times she seemed frightened of people, but she wasn't. She was cautious, tentative, because of her looks. She had learned early that people want to surround themselves with attractive people.

Boys could be ungainly or rough looking, but girls had to be pretty. Becky... *Meese* was the way she once heard herself described by an aunt. *Meese*. In Yiddish it meant homely. In any language it wasn't a compliment.

So Becky was flattered when, of all the girls in the tenth grade, Karla Kingsley picked her to be her best friend. For Becky it was the greatest compliment. For Karla, at the beginning she needed a friend. If there was one thing Rebecca Gilbert knew how to be, it was a friend. But as time wore on Karla learned to appreciate Becky. She honestly grew to like her.

"Come on, slowpoke!" she yelled as she raced ahead of

Becky on her horse, Nijinsky. When she was ten years old, after it was established that she would not follow in her mother's toe shoes, after it was established that she could risk a fall, could have a normal childhood, Balanchine had bought her Nijinsky. "Come on, Becky. Stop dragging your ass."

If she had an ass like Karla's, Becky thought, it wouldn't drag. But her ass dragged.

"There are too many trees," she said. "And Nelson is frightened."

"What are you talking about?" Karla asked, pulling in on the reins. Nijinsky could stop on a dime. "There are the same amount of trees we have every week."

"Don't you know how many trees there are in the Black Forest?"

"Is food all you think about?" Karla asked, kidding her.

Becky had to laugh. Karla was almost as funny as she was.

"Where did we go last week?" Karla asked, beginning to play the game.

"Last week we were in Jamaica. Don't you remember? We were together and that big wave came in and almost toppled you over."

Yes, Karla liked Becky. She was serious and fun all at the same time. She made up lots of stories, fun stories. Whatever she didn't have she created. Except for a boyfriend. Karla had never heard Becky talk about boys.

Not being pretty had to be worse than anything in the whole world, Karla thought. She couldn't even imagine what it was like. Not that she'd ever have to. Karla had been given storybook eyes, skin that looked as if it had just been powdered dry, perfectly straight white teeth, and a body that had to work to collect weight.

Alas, the same could not be said for her best friend. By Becky's fifteenth birthday it was obvious her baby fat was going to be a companion for life. But that wasn't the problem, Karla thought. It was the face. When Karla had told Chip Johnson that she and Becky went riding every

Friday afternoon, he had asked her how she knew which horse to mount. She hadn't spoken to him since.

"Come on, Becky. Let's go."

"Okay."

Becky let loose. She gave Nelson a kick and let him see the whip. He took off like a bat out of hell. As long as there were no crowds around he was fine. Claremont Riding Academy guaranteed that. Put him in a crowd and he just might throw you. Nelson had been a police horse but he'd failed crowd control. Becky didn't make that up. It was true.

The two girls galloped through the October air. It was getting cooler, finally. Everyone was happy to see summer make its exit. Especially Becky. She could stop wearing all those cut-out clothes that showed off her fat.

But the cooler season also brought with it shorter days. She and Karla would have to change their riding schedule. While not religious, Becky still kept some of the traditions her mother had raised her with. Lighting candles on Friday at sundown was one of them. It was the only way she knew how to keep Chana alive.

Lately, Chana Gilbert had begun to appear to Becky in dreams. In them, Becky could almost smell Chana. She could smell the pungent odor that her mother's body emitted after she had been cooking all day. She could smell her hair after it was set free from the kerchief that had covered it. She could also see her mother light the *Shabbos* candles. It was mystical, magical, as if she were actually breathing in the smell of the Sabbath.

Yes, Chana had come back. And Becky knew why too. She was straying. Not only had she begun to eat foods that were forbidden, she was thinking about boys. Real boys, not make-believe ones. Gentile boys. Boys who did bad things. Boys she wanted to do bad things to her.

"Earth to Becky. Earth to Becky. Come back, Becky. We need you."

"Did you say something?"

"Yeah. So did the guy who came out of the bushes and opened his coat."

"You're kidding." Becky was astonished. She slowed her horse to a walk, and Karla did the same.

"You didn't see?"

"No. Did I miss anything?"

"Miss anything? You missed the biggest you-know-what I've ever seen in my whole life."

"Oh, really. And just how many have you seen, hot-shot?"

"Enough to know big."

Shit. Becky was really disappointed. Not too many opportunities like this came along in a fat girl's life.

"Is your mystery lover big?" she asked.

Karla looked into Becky's earth-brown eyes and wished she could tell her. She needed to tell someone. But she couldn't. He'd kill her.

"He's big," she said. "And don't ask me anything else. I can't tell."

Becky was disappointed. "Does he love you?" she asked in all innocence.

"Of course, you silly," Karla said, annoyed. "Otherwise we wouldn't do . . . well, you know, those things."

Olive tried telling herself it was silly to be so nervous. She was just meeting with a detective who was taking her out on official business.

Bull.

Why couldn't she find the perfect outfit? She tried on an Armani, a Vittadini, then her closetful of unknowns. Everything looked wonderful on her. Finally she chose something simple. A cotton pullover and a long skirt to match. The important piece, the belt, was a spectacular hand's width of lizard joined by a silver buckle made by Paloma Picasso herself. Stunning. Perfect. Just like the lizard boots that matched.

But why the excitement? Olive asked herself. It's business. All business. Don't you remember? He's the man who carries a gun but leaves his heart at home.

He's the father of your child.

"Mom?" Karla had just come in from riding.

"Karla?" Olive ran out of her bedroom like a lunatic. "Where have you been? You know I can't get dressed without you."

"Whoa, he must really be something." She walked into the bathroom to wash her hands. Nijinsky's smell would stay on her until she showered. "Mom?" she called when Olive was silent.

No, he wasn't something, Olive was thinking. He was only Vince Luscardi, a memory, an afternoon spent in passion.

"How do I look?" she asked. Karla came close to her and she smelled the deep earthy aroma of the stables. "You've been riding."

"Yes, Mom. It's great. You really ought to take—"

The doorman's buzz interrupted her.

"Oh my God, he's here already."

"Then he'll just have to wait." Evaluating the outfit she asked, "Where's that choker Eliot gave you?"

"Choker? Choker?" Olive repeated the word as if her daughter were speaking a foreign language.

"You know, that thick silver-link choker."

"Oh." Olive hurried back into her bedroom and rummaged through her top bureau drawer. "I haven't worn this in years."

The doorman buzzed again.

"Karla."

"I'll tell Mario to have him wait. Try it on."

It looked stunning. Karla had such an eye for things like this, Olive thought. She must have gotten it from her grandmother.

"Is it all right now?" she asked when Karla returned. She felt like a girl going out on her first date.

"Just one more thing," Karla said.

"What's that?"

With a single swift motion Karla cut the elastic that held her mother's braid together.

"Karla!" Olive screamed.

"Just stand still." In no more than a minute, with Karla's

coaxing, fluffing, and reorganizing, Olive had an elaborate array of black curls around her face.

"Now look what you've done. I look terrible and I don't have time to fix it."

"You don't look terrible. You look beautiful. Doesn't she, Bear?"

"Sure does."

"I just hope he's worth it," Karla said.

XII

"I didn't mean to snap at you last night, Liz," Charles said. He sipped cognac from the crystal goblet. It was Courvoisier, the only cognac he drank. "It's just that I've been under such pressure lately, darling." He got up from the dressing table and sat next to her on the bed.

"I understand, Charles." Oh, just to have him close again. "Charles . . ." She reached out and touched him. He was warm, so very warm.

"All right, Sunshine. Let's talk about a baby," he said, rubbing her neck like he used to. Like he did in the old days when it meant they'd make love. It would serve him well to have a child now, he thought. It would prepare him properly for the White House. One child now, then another in three years. In four years, after he'd served his second term as mayor, he'd run for the presidency.

"Charles, are you thinking . . ." She was anxious, excited. Another chance. He was giving her another chance.

Suddenly she seemed young to him again. She wasn't the frightened, squirrelly eyed, dependent female whose every smile he felt responsible for. At the moment he didn't know whether to feel sorry for her or love her. He'd try the latter.

"I'm sure I ovulated yesterday," she said. "That means we're still good today. We could have a child if we . . . made love. Now." Her voice dropped to a whisper. "Tonight."

"Oh, really." He kind of enjoyed this, playing her like a violin. Why were women so damn easy? he wondered as he stroked her hair.

"Are you interested?" she asked.

"I sure am." She looked so cute tonight, much like the young girl he had met so many years before. He got up to set his snifter on the dressing table and turned back to her. "I'll tell you what. I was thinking."

Elizabeth Anne felt young, alive. She followed him across the room. Oh, to stand close felt so good.

"Do you realize we're going to be married fifteen years next month?" he asked.

"Well, yes, Charles. I know."

"Let's celebrate. I mean, really celebrate."

She looked toward their king-size bed.

"Listen, Sunshine. How about a party?"

"A party?"

"Yes, a bash."

She hated parties. Hated all those famous people she'd have to invite. They terrified her, absolutely terrified her.

"No," she said.

"No? Why not?"

"Oh, Charles, I'm so busy with the play. Going to rehearsals." Yes, that was a good reason, if not necessarily true. Next to Johnny Green she was the major backer of *Isadora, Isadora*. "And I want to redecorate Gracie Mansion. We'll be here for another four years."

"Hogwash. We're married fifteen years and I think it should be celebrated in style. Grand style."

Long ago, when Charles decided to opt for public life, he put a wall between himself and his libido, hiding it away as if it were dirty laundry. He saved his passions for his public, and they responded in kind. But, he knew one could keep the flood back for just so long.

The obvious questions were when, where, and with whom. The when? It took longer than most people would have thought. The where? New York was as good a town as any. As far as with whom . . . The not so obvious answer was Karla. Yes, she was a perfect choice. She was his buddy, his friend, a secret sharer of sorts.

From the moment Karla was born, she, Olive, Elizabeth Anne, and Charles were a team. Four eccentrics committed to life and youth and everything fresh. Life felt clean, like newly brushed breath. The dancer, the politician, the child, and the auntie. They all seemed to feel that life was their oyster.

Then the trouble started. Elizabeth Anne couldn't conceive. She insisted on having a child, on becoming a mother. She wasn't raised for a career, she said. Maybe volunteer work, but motherhood was what she wanted.

Next was Karla's blindness. During that time, Charles and Karla grew particularly close. He'd come over to the apartment and read her stories. She'd place her fingers over his lips, trying to "see" the words. She'd put her mouth on his, too, forming the words with him, saying them with him.

Every word had a color. Kite was blue and dance was red. Pretty was yellow. Happiness was also yellow, and so it was. Sad was green. The Farberware pots were silver, like the lining inside clouds. But blind was black.

Blind. Olive forbade anyone even to say the word. Her daughter was not blind, she had a temporary vision impairment. But sometimes it slipped out. Karla would fall over a piece of furniture that had been moved. When they were on a bus together, someone would whisper, "That child is blind." Old people would get up and give Olive a seat on the subway because she had a blind child with her. Whenever Karla heard the word she'd say it was black. Actually Karla adapted to her condition much better than Olive. Karla picked up Braille very easily and she was equally content learning French or Spanish, or simply sitting in her room playing with her dolls. All the while Olive ran around looking for answers.

In a strange way, Charles mused, they were happier when

Karla was blind. Not because of it, but because they were all young and spirited, and the blindness gave them a reason to rally, to fight. There was meaning. They were a family.

When Karla regained her sight their raison d'être was gone. The family was divided. So in a way, Charles thought, his affair with Karla was bringing the two camps together again. But he needed more than camp. He wanted adult reality, adult success.

His voice got lower, sexier. He was as sexy as they came, especially when he wanted to be. "Come up with a list of guests and I'll have my secretary send out the invitations. And listen, I want your astrologer there."

"You do? Why?"

"Because everytime we go to Marylou's parties she has a fortune-teller. So we'll have an astrologer." He was, of course, referring to Marylou Vanderbilt Whitney, whom *Town & Country* listed as one of New York's top twenty partygivers.

"And we'll make a baby, too?"

He leaned over and kissed her. Very slowly he untied the cashmere belt on her robe.

"Yes, Miss One-Track Mind. We'll make a baby."

In a single movement he eased her down onto their softly cushioned bed.

Vince had chosen a little restaurant called The Chart out in Dobbs Ferry. It wasn't elegant but he didn't want elegance. He wanted a fireplace, comfort, and good food. The fireplace was going summer and winter, and The Chart had the best bleu-cheese dressing this side of the Hudson.

"I love being on the water," Olive said, looking out across the brightly lit waterway.

"I remember you once telling me how much you loved water. I made them promise they'd save me this table. Look at those lights. That's New Jersey over there."

"And that way?" She pointed to a window at the opposite end of the restaurant.

"I believe that's the ladies' room."

She was grateful for the humor. "You can still make me laugh." Abruptly, she drew back. It was the word "still." Where had it come from? It wasn't yesterday, it was sixteen years ago. She felt that she had given too much away. "Vince, just how much danger am I in?"

Her eyes were suddenly filled with fear, and he hated seeing that.

He decided to keep it light. "At this moment, your very being is threatened. In fact, I don't think I can resist you for another moment." He took her hands in his and held on tightly. She was lovely. He had never seen her look so young. Her hair was actually buoyant, her smile radiant. She had used the softest blush on her cheeks and a gloss on her lips. "You're beautiful," he said impetuously. "You are."

"Thank you," she said, turning away. It embarrassed her to have him look at her that way.

A waitress asked if they'd like anything to drink and he ordered champagne.

"What are we celebrating?" Olive asked, knowing the answer. They were celebrating them.

"Olive."

"Please." She removed her hands from his. It actually hurt her to let go. "You said this was strictly business."

"I lied." He wanted to tell her of the years he'd thought about her. He wanted to tell her of his losses, his loneliness. Instead he put on his business voice and said, "Okay. The man who wrote your note was the same man who killed Nina Houston and Ariel Powell."

"Vince!" she said, visibly shaken.

He took her hand again, and this time the gesture was natural, filled with compassion. He wanted to make her feel better. "I don't think you really have to be concerned. We've had... Look, when Nina Houston's body was found, a note was beside it. I don't believe we were supposed to find it. The killer had listed three names. The first two belonged to Nina Houston and Ariel Powell. The third name I can't tell you."

"Was it mine?"

"No, it wasn't." As he spoke his lips touched her fingers, again to comfort. "A handwriting analyst identified both specimens, your note and the one found in Nina Houston's apartment, as being of the same origin."

"What happened to the third woman?"

"Nothing yet. Which could be a good sign."

"How so?"

"Perhaps the killer has stopped." He didn't believe that, but there was no law against lying. "That will make him more difficult to find because the only clues we have are the ones he left."

"And in what way isn't it a good sign?"

He let go of her hand and looked at the tablecloth. Then he realized the waiter had placed the champagne in an ice bucket beside him.

"Vince?"

He didn't look at her as he spoke. "It could mean that the killer decided to let girl three live and take you instead."

"But why?" It seemed so irrational. Why would someone want to kill her because Ashley Pope was playing Isadora?

"Do you know anyone who has a vendetta against dancers?" he asked, pouring the champagne.

She took a glass from him. "No."

"Well, we have to find out who does. Because that's the guy we want."

"Is there anything else?"

"He's rather ghoulish."

"In what way?"

"You know, Olive," he said, stroking her arm, "dead is dead. And if I were you that's all I'd be concerned about." He paused for a minute. How was it, he wondered, that such sickness could live side by side with beauty, that ugliness could reign in a world where ecstasy could thrive?

"Olive, I told you I was going to assign someone to cover you, but I'd like it to be me. If you don't mind."

At some point they had ordered their dinner. Olive looked down at her plate and realized she had no appetite.

"I have a daughter, Vince."

"Yes." Again he took her hand. "I believe I read once, shortly after I returned from California, that you had a child. Her name?"

"Karla." Somehow Karla made it all real, her daughter made it all matter. "Vince, if I die there's no one to take care of her. Vince . . ." The tears in her throat stopped her. Dammit.

"Olive, it's all right." He was up and sitting next to her, holding her. "Nothing is going to happen to you." All he wanted to do was make her feel better.

She struggled to pull herself together, embarrassed to admit her fears. "Once, a long time ago, when . . . well, when things weren't going well, I asked my friend Liz to take Karla if anything happened to me. But that was so long ago."

"And what did she say?" He was kissing her fingertips.

"She said yes. But . . ."

"And your mother?"

"Mother's been in France since I became pregnant with Karla."

"Karla's father?"

She shook her head.

"So you're all alone."

"No, I have Karla. Please, Vince. I can't die. Not just yet."

"Olive." What was even more dangerous than the case was his feeling for Olive. If he were really professional he'd replace himself on this case. But he wasn't. "You won't die. Not if I have anything to do with it."

After Johnny made his nightly check-in call to Ashley, she got in a cab and headed straight for Robbie's. Sex was what she liked best. More than food. More than booze. Drugs weren't even on the list. Sex made her feel all those things she was supposed to touch on stage. Sex made her feel safe and whole and loved. It was where she did her best—and it wasn't an act either. It really was her best.

"We make the kind of love books are written about," she told Robbie hours later. They were fragrant with the scent of their lovemaking.

"Or movies." His kisses were laced with her perfume.

"Or both."

Love, he thought. She had said the word love. He'd heard it but let it go because he had to think about it. Love. So many women had loved him, or had claimed to, but they were trash. Ashley was different.

She was so different he allowed her to sleep in his apartment. He'd never permitted that before. He always slept in the woman's apartment. It was easier that way. When you wanted to leave, you left. If you wanted to stay, you stayed. And that way you could keep the contamination out. *Stray cats bring in stray diseases*. That's what Uncle Earl had said. That's what Robbie remembered.

What would Uncle Earl say if he saw Ashley? Would he know who she was?

"The Lord come but once," his uncle told him. "And when He did, He gave His Son, His only Son. Gave Him to us and we killed Him. That Boy died for our sins."

"Who done it, Uncle?"

"Some say the Jews did it 'cause Jesus was one of them and they was angry that He found a new way. Some say it was the Romans. But, boy . . ."

"Yes, sir."

"Make no difference. The Lord, He gave His only Son to die for our sins."

Robbie had always wondered how come if Jesus was the Savior He could die. How does a god die? And how come if He was God He yelled out from the cross, "Why hast thou forsaken me?"

"Boy, don't ask so many questions," his uncle Earl said, serving himself a second helping of potatoes and gravy. "Dangerous to ask so many questions."

Robbie had wondered about that for a long time. Tried to figure out the mess the world was in. Tried to figure out how he was going to make it better. Eventually he thought maybe he wouldn't have to, especially since Uncle Earl's voice stopped.

But it had started again, real loud and real clear. He got scared. Then he met Ashley and he understood the voice.

He watched his goddess sleep, putting his face close to hers, listening to her breathe. She was so quiet, he wondered if she could have died without his noticing. No, she must never die. God had allowed His first child to die because the people hadn't loved Him enough. It would be different with Ashley. Robbie would keep it safe for her. And clean.

He stared at her for a few more minutes, then got up to clean. He cleaned to make it holy, to surround her with perfection. He took out his bottle of Top Job and scrubbed around the waterfall that he'd built in the corner of his bedroom. Ashley had loved the waterfall. Soon he would tell her it was his altar. An altar that he prayed to every night. Prayed for salvation for him and the rest of the world. And now he knew his prayers had been answered.

So he cleaned and cleaned and cleaned some more.

"Are you sure I can't offer you a drink?" Vince asked on the way home. "We're right near my place."

"If you want to go by way of Oshkosh," Olive said, laughing. The champagne had filled her with happiness and laughter. "But I did have such a good time, Vince."

"I'd like to see you again."

"But what about Connie?"

"Connie?" He was surprised to hear his ex-wife's name leave Olive's lips. She wore the name as incongruously as a polyester skirt. "We divorced long ago."

Instead of sobering her up, it made her giggle. All this time she'd thought they were still married. "No more babies?"

"No more babies." He should have added not yet. That was one reason why he'd decided to marry Janice. He wanted to leave this world with something other than a list of solved crimes and a few unsolved ones. But life was growing very confusing, and his decision to marry Janice no longer seemed as certain.

He pulled to the side of the road and took Olive in his arms. She turned to him as if it were the most natural thing in all the world, as if everything she'd waited for was in this moment. She wanted to speak, to tell him what she felt, but instead his lips met hers like a whisper.

"Vince," she said, not wanting to withdraw from the warmth of his arms but pulling away nonetheless.

"Don't say it, Olive." He kissed her eyelids, her cheeks, her mouth. How could he have forgotten the sweetness of that mouth?

"Vince. We're going to be seeing a lot of each other in the next few weeks. Please don't think I'm being insensitive, but I think it's best that we're not intimate."

"Is there someone else?"

She let go of his hands and looked at the darkened landscape. She felt like it, dark and peculiarly alone. The way she'd felt after Karen had left, before Karla was born.

"Olive?"

"No."

Vince had planned on going home and had told Janice not to expect him. But it seemed that ever since Olive Kingsley had walked back into his life everything was topsy-turvy. Should he go home or see Janice? Couldn't decide. First he'd stop off at a bar. That would help. Some cheap joint with watered-down booze for seventy-five cents a glass. It would take him twice as long to get drunk, but he didn't care. Fuck it.

Then he went to Janice.

The rattle of the doorknob woke her. "Vince?"

"I can't open the damn lock."

She thought he was joking, playing around, until she opened the door and he practically fell on top of her. He reeked of alcohol and cigarettes. His clothes and hair smelled of old smoke.

"Vince! Are you all right?" She wanted to help him but was overpowered by the dead weight of his drunkenness.

This was ridiculous. He never had more than a few glasses of wine with dinner. He didn't even like hard liquor. It made him sick. "Darling, did something happen?"

If something did, Vince didn't answer.

"Let's get you to bed. We'll talk about this tomorrow." All she managed to get off were his shoes. Probably one of his cronies had taken him out either to celebrate or mourn the end of his bachelor days. She hoped he wasn't going to make a habit of this because if he was, by the time they married he'd be an old sot.

She watched him sleep and thought he looked more like a little boy than an old sot. She wrapped her arms around him and snuggled into the warmth of his chest. God, she loved him. She stroked his chest, and when she did he mumbled something. She couldn't quite hear it. Then he mumbled it again. It was somebody's name. "Olive," he said. "Olive. Olive. Olive."

• XIII •

Karen sat in Sarabeth's Kitchen, a restaurant on Madison Avenue, with a bowl of carrot soup and a zucchini muffin, reading the *Post*. Karen Kingsley would never publicly admit to reading the *Post*, much less liking it, but in truth she loved it. It was a vein into the intestines of the city, and having been away for so long, she needed a mainline. She needed to familiarize herself with the names, the places, and the parties that were going on. Babs's column was one of the easiest ways to work her way in. Babs knew it all. And better yet, she talked about it.

> ***Babs says:*** This season's most coveted invitation is not Brooke Astor's, Annette Reed's, or Dixon Boardman's. Our own Golden Couple is celebrating their fifteenth wedding anniversary and the event couldn't be more gala. Peter Duchin will be playing piano, and while Elizabeth Anne won't say who is doing the catering, we all know her cook Paulette is possibly the best in town. Elizabeth Anne Manchester Long, the darling of the artistic set, has not yet released the guest list,

but we expect the list to be top-heavy with *l'esprit des artistes*. It seems that the event of the season, if not the year, will be held at Gracie Mansion three nights before the election. In anticipation of the expected landslide no doubt. Don't some women just have it all!!!

Elizabeth Anne Manchester, Karen mused. Wasn't that Olive's friend from school? Yes, attending that party would be a perfect way to reintroduce herself into New York society.

It was Vince's first hangover since his sixteenth birthday and his response was much the same as it had been then. He'd spent much of the night intimately involved with the toilet bowl, and when he awoke his head weighed a ton and throbbed uncontrollably. Even his hair hurt.

"Good morning, old sot," Janice chirped as she handed him a cup of her freshly brewed coffee. Normally he would salivate at its smell, but today it made him nauseous.

"Sweetheart, you look positively awful," she said. "Although that color green isn't half bad for a sweater."

"I don't want a description of how I look. I feel . . . I feel . . ." He couldn't get the words out, just the food. He couldn't believe he had any left. He didn't. Dry heaves. God, this was awful.

"Are you all right?" Janice asked, waiting outside the bathroom door.

Yes, he was all right. He felt much better now. "I could use some of your delicious coffee."

"Whatever made you drink so much?"

He paused. "Remember Bill Donnelly? You met him last Christmas at Richie's house. He became a grandpa yesterday for the thirteenth time. This time it was a boy. Half the precinct must be hung over today."

"Was Olive there?" Janice asked, handing him the cup of coffee.

"Who?" The gulp of coffee was too large and he almost choked on it.

"Olive. You called out the name Olive in your sleep last night."

"Olive? She's my latest case."

"Oh." Janice immediately felt better. She never interfered in Vince's work.

"Thanks, honey." He set the empty coffee cup down. "Just a bite of your cheesecake and I'll be a completely mended man."

Janice smiled at the pleasure of taking care of him. It was all she ever wanted to do for the rest of her life.

"Don't forget Tuesday night, darling," she said. "And, darling, please try not to upset yourself with this case, whatever it is."

"Aye, aye, boss." With a kiss on her nose he left.

Jack wasn't so sure he wanted Nick to star in his next film. Six films in two years. It reminded him of marriage. Which reminded him of girls. Which reminded him of his mother. Which made him feel guilty.

He thought of all those times his mother had had to open her legs for Heimie, small, fragile Heimie. He remembered all the miscarriages she'd had, the sister that had died and the six that hadn't. Truth was, he didn't know who was better off. Those who lived or those who died.

Jack put the thought out of his mind, looked down at his racing form and circled Calendar Man for the second. Hollywood Park had some good horses running today.

"Who do you like in the second?"

Jack looked up and into the eyes of a young man who had probably never seen the inside of a temple or tasted the likes of chicken soup in his life. And those eyes were hungry. The question was for what?

"I like Calendar Man. But then Green Clover isn't bad, either."

"Which one is better?"

"Racing new to you?" Jack asked, trying to be serious. He knew when he was being cruised.

"Yeah," the kid said. "But it's not new to you, is it?"

"No," Jack said, still not cracking a smile. "I'm an old hand at this."

"I'll bet you are."

"So which one are you gonna go with?"

"I was hoping to go with you."

Well now, Jack thought. That was quite an offer. Not bad from an eighteen-year-old with muscles the size of cantaloupes and a bulge in his pants to match.

"Where?"

"Here."

"In front of all these people?" Jack was finally smiling. In all his years with men this had never happened before.

The kid smiled back. "Why not?"

Clubhouse bathrooms were a lot cleaner than the bathrooms in the stands, but not nearly as safe. Jack Gilbert didn't feel like getting caught. It would look silly. Even more, this kid might still be jailbait.

The kid could read his mind. "Scared?"

"Yeah."

"Don't be. I know the maitre d'."

Jack tried to tell if he was lying, but couldn't. He was a gambler. What the hell.

"Lead the way, buddy."

"How did you know my name?"

"Is it? Nice name."

On the way into the clubhouse, Buddy winked at the maitre d'. Christ, Jack thought, this kid could be an undercover cop. But so what? There was a first time for everything. Besides he liked the kid's style. And his ass. Jack had a thing for muscle-bound boys. It was so far removed from Division Street it didn't seem wrong.

"It has to be quick," he said, walking into a stall.

"It's your time clock." Buddy put his hand over Jack's crotch and felt the instant erection. "Nice," he murmured. Nothing girlish about him, Jack mused. Friendly but not femme. He liked that. "How do you want it?" Buddy asked.

"You call it. As long as it's safe."

"Safer than it's ever been," Buddy said, undoing Jack's belt and zipper. "Mmm. Can I have a little lick first?"

This was getting Jack very hot. Very fucking hot.

"It's my pleasure," he said huskily.

Buddy liked that. He loved hot men. And older men. Men with class. Jack seemed to have class.

He lowered himself and took Jack in his mouth. Good. It was real good, but he felt like fucking him. Right then. Standing up.

"Bend over," he said.

Just what Jack loved. He turned around and found himself peering into an open toilet bowl that some pig had forgotten to flush. Not at all scatological in his tastes, Jack closed the lid.

Buddy could tell this guy was ripe. Ready. Just a lubricated rubber and he could slip it in. Right in.

Jack sighed.

"Good?"

"Love it." And he did. Just that way. Hard and fast. Hard and fast. He really did love it.

"Yeah." Buddy had taken himself in hand. Jack didn't need to. He was already swollen. Almost beyond waiting. Didn't have to. Buddy pumped, holding himself the whole time.

"Shoot it!" Buddy screamed. "Shoot it out!"

If this guy was an undercover cop, Jack sure did like his methods of investigation.

"I don't think he's going to go after her," Vince told O'Connor.

"Why?" O'Connor was a big Irish brogue of a cop. A cop from the old school. Tired from too much overtime, honest as the day is long. And kind. Too kind. "It's only been a week. That Houston girl got it two weeks after that first one."

"Gut feeling."

O'Connor looked at Vince over the top of his reading glasses. He felt about Luscardi the way he would about a brother. They'd been together for twenty years now and he'd seen Vince through the death of a child, the loss of another one at birth, a divorce, and now an engagement. But something was wrong, and what made it worse was that Vince wouldn't talk about it.

"We can't call the surveillance off just because you got a gut feeling."

Vince stirred his coffee. He liked it so sweet that the sugar never quite got around to dissolving. He took a sip. "This is mean coffee."

"You're working for the city," O'Connor said. "Not Chock Full O'Nuts."

"Why do you think this guy wants Olive?" Vince asked casually.

So that's it, O'Connor thought. It's that Kingsley woman again. He remembered the relationship the first time around. He'd thought it was a terrible thing that pulled them apart, the death of Vince's little girl, but was happy it had ended. It couldn't have worked out. Vince would have been hurt. Classy girls who liked tough guys were a dime a dozen. Liked 'em until it came to finding out how much they made and how little they were around. Cops could fuck good, but they had to put in a lot of overtime to pay those bills. Wouldn't have lasted.

"Don't know why he wants her," O'Connor said. "What do you think?"

Vince took another sip of the coffee. It was brutal, even with all that sugar. "Is that Ashley Pope seeing anyone?"

"Don't know."

"For a cop," Vince said, adding some more milk, "you don't know a hell of a lot."

"Hey, man," O'Connor said. "Ain't my job to be smart. Just my job to catch 'em."

"I want to put a tail on Ashley Pope. Got it?"

"You don't need to say another word."

• XIV •

The Longacre Theatre was dead, inside as well as out. That was what was upsetting Richard Dixon the most. He had been working with Ashley Pope for three weeks now—more than one half the allotted rehearsal time—and he couldn't get her to bring Isadora alive. You don't have to be Flo Ziegfeld to know that without a live character you have a dark house. Richard Dixon couldn't afford a dark house.

He had put everything he had into this play. His career was on the line. So was his color. Richard knew perfectly well that when a black becomes a star he's suddenly the exception. When he fails, he's the rule. Richard didn't want to become another rule. He wanted to be the star, the exception who appeared on the cover of *People* and *Us* and *Vanity Fair*. But before the recognition came the work. If Ashley couldn't bring Isadora alive it was his failure, not hers. It was his job to direct and hers to become one with the director.

The problem wasn't movement. She moved just fine. She was fluid and beautiful and theatrical.

"I don't know what the hell you want!" she screeched at him one day.

"I don't want Hollywood's version of Ashley Pope!" he screeched back. "I want Broadway's Isadora and I want her every night and twice on Saturdays and Wednesdays." So far he couldn't even get her once.

"Then maybe I'm wrong for it." Ashley didn't mean it. It was fear speaking. Had Johnny not gotten the part for her, she would have gotten it herself. She would have given her eyeteeth for the part. She'd have given anything to play Isadora Duncan on Broadway. Who was she kidding? If anyone tried to take this part away from her, she'd kill him. Really kill him.

Richard, too, knew he hadn't chosen the wrong actress. But something was holding Ashley back, and that something was her. The problem was he didn't know what the problem was, nor was it his business. He had to walk a double-edged sword. He had to get to the person to bring the character to life without discussing what was keeping the person closed, shut off. It was a bitch. So he set up a closed rehearsal. No Olive. No actors. Just Ashley and himself.

As far as Ashley was concerned she was giving all she had. She had left Hollywood and come to New York against everyone's advice. Tits and ass don't go quite as far in the Big Apple, her friend Peora had told her. Not true, Ashley thought as she stood backstage. Across the street, tits and ass were selling like crazy. For a quarter a peek.

So what's your problem, girl?

Her problem was that she didn't want to know what her problem was. What bothered her more than anything was that she couldn't even remember her goddamn lines. It was that goddamn trunk. It had something to do with that trunk.

She walked on stage. It was quiet, too quiet. The only thing that spoke to her was the trunk. Richard had it set up that way. The trunk was lit by an ominous blue light. The rest of the stage was soft, in shadow. Stage left was totally dark. Richard instinctively knew she'd need a place to run to for solace. You learn about people when you direct them. You learn what they need so that they can live on the space known as the stage.

"Ashley," he called to her.

The lights blinded her. She created a visor with her hand. "Where are you?"

"Fifth row center."

She searched him out and felt better for it.

"Ashley, let's just take the scene without words."

She nodded and waited for him to continue.

"Ashley, now listen to me. You're in the country. You're getting over the death of your third child. It died two months ago, hours after its birth. A few years after Deirdre and Patrick died. You never talk about it, but they are with you. Spiritually."

He continued very slowly. "It's getting cold out and you've sent to France or to England—it doesn't matter—for a trunk of your sweaters. They arrived this morning. Now, Isadora." Richard spoke more softly. "You've had a cup of coffee and asked the maid to pour a second one. Isadora, take the cup."

She held the invisible cup away from her so as not to spill.

"You walk up the stairs with the second cup of coffee in your hand. You go to your bedroom and close the door. Now. There's a sweater you want. You don't know if it's in this trunk or not, but you're going to look for it."

"All right." She was still standing stage center and Robbie put the hot light on her. All actors loved the hot light. It made anyone standing under it feel like a star. In Ashley's case it merely reiterated the point.

Richard's voice came from somewhere far away. "Isadora, what color is the sweater?"

"Color? Why, it's red."

"Fine. Walk over to the trunk and open the top."

"Now?"

"Now."

Robbie had a white light follow her across the stage, creating a ghostlike effect, an ephemeral white trail behind her. She moved hesitantly. Then, as if something told her to hurry, she quickened her pace. Without any hesitation she opened the trunk. She stepped back.

"What's in there?" Richard asked. There was no response. "Isadora?"

"Children's things."

"Fine. Tell me what you see?"

"I see . . . I see little baby clothes. Infant's clothes. And some things that look a little larger."

"Is that all?"

"I see a doll."

"Tell me what you feel when you see the contents of the trunk."

"I feel shock."

"Do you want to stay in the room with it? Do you want to call someone in and have them remove it? What do you want to do?"

"Well, I sort of feel stunned more than shocked. I'm almost anesthetized."

"Would you want to pick up the doll?" Richard asked with the utmost kindness. "Or would you pick up the clothes?" He waited and watched. She stood there staring. Indeed she was stunned.

"I think I'd walk away and then come back to it screaming what are you doing here?"

"How long would you stay away?"

"Not very long."

"Okay. So now you've returned. Do you want to look at anything else in the trunk?"

Her gaze was riveted to the open trunk, as if she were hypnotized. Then slowly, almost dreamily, she turned toward him. The direct light bleached her as if she were a ghost in a photograph. The expression in her eyes was haunted, but no one was close enough to see that.

"I do want to look," she said, "but I can't right now."

"What are you feeling right now? What do you want?"

Air. Memory. Stark white light.

"It's a question of exploring," Richard continued, "of

investigating what's inside the trunk in order to get to what's inside of you."

"Yes." It fell from her lips, not from her heart.

Richard walked to the stage, took off his pullover, and threw it at her. "You knitted that for Deirdre, Isadora. It's the first thing you ever knitted. Touch it. Hold it. Do you remember how you felt knitting it?"

"I knitted this for Deirdre." Ashley repeated the words as she rubbed the soft sweater against her cheeks.

"That's right," he said, resuming his seat. "Remember how you hugged and kissed her when you dressed her in it the very first time?"

Ashley traveled with the memory and Richard watched her as she did so, watched her move inward.

"I want you to go offstage for a few seconds," he said in his softest voice. "When you enter you will be in your own bedroom. The trunk will be there. It will be closed. Open it when you're ready, Isadora. Allow yourself to let whatever happens, happen. Take your time. Don't think you have to make anything happen. I don't want any dialogue, only what comes organically from you. The words can come later."

Richard lit his hundredth cigarette of the day. He felt like an expectant father, pacing the floor.

All she has to do is let it all go. That's your job, to help her let it go.

Yeah, but who's going to help me?

No answers came and so he waited, taking a long drag of the cigarette. It didn't help.

Ashley walked back on stage. The trunk was there and she was prepared to confront it. No, she wasn't. She left.

Then back again, this time with less fear. He could feel it. She sat down on the bed, lit a cigarette. Who had left the cigarettes for her? he wondered, but it didn't matter. Ashley Pope didn't smoke but Isadora did.

Isadora took off her shoes because she had to lie down and didn't want to mess the bed. Maybe a nap. Eyes closed, then open. The trunk. She needed to put her sweaters away. Yes, fall was near and she had to give them air. She got up from the bed and walked over to the trunk. She opened it and then stared, disbelieving.

They were not her sweaters. They were her babies' clothes. Her dead angels' sweaters, dolls, and rattles. Baby things without the babies. Pain. Unbearable pain. She slammed the trunk shut as if to obliterate the memory, but nothing obliterates memory. Not drugs, not drink. Nothing. Perhaps death, but some people say...

Isadora didn't know what to make of it. Again she opened the trunk. There was a doll.

Don't touch it.

"Your sweet babies are dead," Richard whispered. "All of them. You'll never have any more babies, Isadora. Now pick up the dolly."

But Ashley had gotten in Isadora's way. No, she couldn't, wouldn't pick up the dolly.

"Do you know any nursery rhymes, Isadora?"

Ashley nodded.

"Which one?"

"'Jack and Jill.'"

"Can you pick the doll up and recite the rhyme to her?"

It took a moment. Richard was afraid she wouldn't do it, that she'd go back to the darkness. At last she picked up the doll and in a little-girl voice recited, "Jack and Jill... went up the hill to fetch a pail of water. Jack fell down... and broke his crown... and Jill came tumbling after."

"Where's Deirdre now, Isadora?"

"In the ground."

"Do you ever think about her?"

"All the time."

"Do you miss her?"

Ashley turned away.

"Do you miss her?"

The house was full. There was a hush. The audience was waiting for this moment. It was what would give her rave reviews. The tears. The show of emotion. But these were real tears and they didn't want to stop.

"You see what you feel," Richard said. "This is what you have to come into the scene with."

"My babies. My babies are gone." She rocked back and forth on her heels, holding the doll as if she were her own, her Deirdre. No, *her* baby, Ashley's baby. The baby she never... would never... Ashley ran offstage.

Richard let her. She had given him what he wanted and now she could have anything... anything at all.

Olive had caught the tail end. She had seen Ashley erupting with feelings, then running off the stage like a frightened child. From whom was she running? Herself, of course. Can we ever escape ourselves?

There was a time when Olive believed she could, when she knew if she cried, Daddy would be there to pick her up, to help her out. But then Daddy wasn't there anymore. And the pain got worse.

Somehow Vince made it better on that long afternoon so long ago. And with Eliot she thought nothing bad could ever happen again. Even Karla's blindness seemed tolerable. Then he wasn't there anymore. That was the worst thing about being an adult, she thought. The realization that you'll never be rescued. That life, with its moments of joy and beauty, was just that, moments. But the moments of sadness were just that too. Moments.

That Saturday afternoon Janice Alison Canfield was waiting downstairs when the mailman arrived. If she didn't have a job she'd be waiting there every day to greet him, like a child. When she saw the powder-pink RSVP envelope emerge from his satchel she practically ripped it out of his hands. It was her first RSVP. To the wedding. To her wedding to Vince. Someone was actually answering.

Of course, someone is answering, she thought. Everyone would answer. This response was from her college roommate, Pamela Lehman Forbes. Pamela had checked off the box that said "yes." And she had added that she and Chester would be happy to fly in from Houston to attend the wedding. Written in larger letters was: "You bet your ass I'll be there." Janice laughed. PDC. People don't change— even if they do marry investment bankers whose incomes weigh heavily into the six-figure bracket.

"Bless you," Janice said under her breath.

"Good news?" the mailman asked.

"Great news."

Yes, Pamela was coming. And her sister had called from Australia to say that she and Stuart would be there. The doorman handed her a package from UPS, and she glanced at the label. It must be the towels she'd ordered from Bergdorf.

Back in her apartment Janice tore off the brown paper. Inside the box were gray velour towels with a yellow monogram. She raised a towel to her cheek. So soft. But it wasn't the cotton that excited her, it was the monogram that sent chills down her spine. JLC.

In six weeks Janice Alison Canfield would be Mrs. Janice Luscardi. Now it was her turn for joy. For love. It had taken her thirty-nine years and she was going to have it. And wear it. She'd wear his name as proudly as she wore the pearl engagement ring he had given her.

She would be Mrs. Vince Luscardi and they would build a life together. Maybe even bring another life into the world. With Vince all things were possible.

Seeing Ashley cry like that was more than Robbie could bear. He hated seeing a woman cry. It reminded him of his ma.

Robbie's ma would weep long into the night. Then she'd seek out comfort, sin, in all the wrong places. In the arms of the wrong man. No, men. There were many. Sometimes Robbie would try to comfort her, hold her, to say it would change, but she would push him away. So when he went to Ashley and she did the same thing, he split.

The flicks always made him feel better. A couple of Ed Wood movies were playing up at the Thalia. Robbie liked Wood. Wood and he agreed that the medium wasn't the message at all, the message was the message. So Wood made bad movies with good Christian messages. Going to an Ed Wood flick was like going to church, except there was a plot.

The Thalia was dark. Not empty, but very dark. As if to give the weirdos a public opportunity to be weird in private. The crowd was mostly male. Fat men. Bag men. Some men together. A couple of guys were with girls. One girl was alone. She sat close to the front.

Robbie walked down the lopsided theater aisle and sat two seats away from the girl. He didn't want to frighten her. He just wanted to be near her. She turned toward him, saw that he was white and wore his shirt tucked in, and decided he was harmless. She returned her gaze to the screen. He saw that she was pretty. Too pretty to be alone. Maybe she was looking for a trick. Why else would a pretty girl be alone? Probably a slut.

Reruns, that's what the Thalia was about. Rerun sluts. Rerun tricks. Rerun movies. Yeah, he had seen them all before.

Sinister Urge was the best. Some guy named Deke gets off from watching porno pictures, hunts out the stars, and murders them. Robbie saw him as the hero but the cops didn't agree. It didn't matter. Robbie had learned a long time ago that people didn't have to agree with you for you to be right. His uncle had taught him that.

Uncle Earl was responsible for Robbie growing up. They had lived down South with the cornfields and the dairy farms and the Baptist churches. Uncle Earl told him he was a good boy but that his blood was bad. That's what his uncle Earl said and his uncle Earl was a man of God. He'd never lie. Bad blood. It ran on both sides of his family. His mama was a whore. She gave it away and his daddy took it. His mama told him who his daddy was, but his daddy didn't seem to agree.

"Know what they say," his daddy once said to him. "Mama baby, papa maybe."

Well, maybe Ben wasn't his daddy but Robbie sure did look like him. He had the same mustard-colored hair and ebony eyes. He had Ben's big build too. Strapping, they called him. Good on the outside, his preacher uncle reminded him, but lousy on the inside.

His mama had been a tramp. Any guy with two bucks could

get up her dress. She was always that way, his uncle Earl told him. Ever since she was a youngster. Which was when she had Robbie. She was thirteen. But that wasn't so unusual in the South in those days.

What was unusual was that she and her girl friends danced in the dance halls. Nobody did that then. Nobody but tramps. They'd all come home just when the sun was rising and wake him up. They'd lay with him and hold him and hug him. His mama's friend, Alabaster White, kept promising Robbie he was going to be her boyfriend when he got older. She'd tell him that when she fingered his sex, when she put her mouth on it. When she made it grow big, sinfully big.

But she lied. Just like Eve tempted Adam and brought evil into the world, Alabaster White tempted Robbie. Then she found herself another guy.

When Robbie got to be twelve or so he sprang up like a blade of grass. Alabaster White took a liking to him again. She came back one night without his mama. When Robbie was alone, when Robbie could learn her secrets about what she and his mama did with men. How she'd sit on a man and put his sex inside her. He had never felt anything like it before. It was warm and safe. It felt even better than her mouth. Then she moved. Up and down. Up and down. He felt himself getting bigger and bigger... bigger and bigger until... God, he had never felt anything like that. He loved it. But he hated that his mother did it too.

Alabaster White taught him about women. About what whores they were.

When he was fifteen he came home from school and there was his mama doing what Alabaster White let Robbie do to her.

He watched them for a moment. Watched his mama and the man on top of her, grunting and pushing into her as if he were a drill and she a maple tree. Grunting and grinding and his poor mama sighing. All for two bucks. He couldn't stand seeing it. He took out his fishing knife and stood over the man. Then he hesitated. He who hesitates is lost, Uncle Earl always said. He hesitated and his mama screamed. He moved, but so did the man. Robbie got his mama instead of the man, high up in the thigh, near her sex.

Robbie didn't kill her. Well, he didn't think so anyway. But the blood... Robbie never did like blood. He saw the blood and ran. He never went back. Never even sent her a Mother's Day card. Just saw the blood and ran.

Robbie thought of himself as a hero. But the cops probably wouldn't have agreed. They indicted Deke Andrews in Sinister Urge *and they'd probably indict Robbie. If they ever found him. Well, they wouldn't. They hadn't found him all this time and they sure wouldn't now. Now was the time to repent. The question was how.*

Make an honest woman out of that whore, his uncle Earl said. You do what your daddy never did with your mama.

Of course. Why hadn't he thought of that? He'd marry Ashley. That way he wouldn't have to kill her.

"You really take me for granted, don't you?" Ashley said to Robbie later that afternoon, opening the door to her spacious apartment.

"No, baby." His voice was deep. Husky. Sexy. "I don't want to take you for granted, I want to take you to Scarlatti's. But first..." First he would undo his shirt and tie, slip off his loafers.

"First what?" she asked in her ditziest-blonde voice.

"First I'm gonna kiss you where the sun don't shine, baby doll."

The sun was definitely shining down on Jack and Buddy. Shining as if to give them its blessing. Jack was just beginning to awaken. The newness of the affair was what was making him open his eyes, as well as his mouth.

He liked Buddy's youth. He liked Buddy's smell. Most of all he liked Buddy's newness. They were just rolling over when the phone rang. Jack didn't like that. It probably meant trouble. Why else would somebody call him at seven o'clock in the morning?

"Yeah?" His voice was gruff and angry, but when he

heard Becky on the other end he put the anger away. "No, baby. I wasn't sleeping. Just getting up. What's going on?"

"I want a horse, Daddy. One of my own so I don't have to rent one."

"Is there something wrong with the ones you rent?" Jack asked through a yawn.

Yes, Becky thought. She'd decided that while Nelson and Cinnamon and Avenger were fine, they were rejects. Just like her. She wanted something perfect, like Karla had. But she didn't say any of that.

"I want my own. That's all."

"Well, if that's what you want, then that's what you shall have. But why did you have to call me at seven in the morning to ask me? Oh, right. I forgot you're three hours ahead. No, I was just teasing. I simply didn't know I had such an impetuous little girl on my hands."

He stifled a second yawn and asked her how she was. She told him fine, but knowing his daughter he asked again. He could never get a straight answer from Becky. If anything was wrong she'd never tell him. It was the martyr in her.

"Grades good, Becky?"

"I'm doing great. And I have a new friend. Karla Kingsley. She's Olive Kingsley's daughter. You've heard of her, haven't you?"

"She's that filly who runs at the Meadowlands, right?"

"Daddy, stop teasing me."

Jack laughed. He loved to tease.

So did Buddy. He threw a limp arm over Jack's chest. The heat of his young flesh was contagious. Jack again grew thick and hard. Buddy, playing Sleeping Beauty, lolled about on his lover's chest for a while, then decided he needed more heat. He headed south.

"And how's the singing?" Jack asked his daughter.

"Fine, Daddy. They're going to let me sing Mimi in *La Bohème.*"

"Are you talking dirty? Is my little Rivka talking dirty?"

"Daddy," she squealed, again feigning exasperation. "Daddy, when can I have my horse?"

"Well, what kind would you like?"

"An Appaloosa."

"An Appah . . . ah." Buddy traveled fast. His moist mouth opened wide and took in Jack's full length. "An Appaloosa. Well, sure."

"I can?" Becky was surprised he had given in so quickly. Not that her father was cheap, but Appaloosas cost a lot of money. Five thousand dollars. To Becky that was a lot of money. For a horse anyway.

Buddy had the rhythm down pat. First soft and slow, then fast and rough. Then on to the balls. Oh, this kid may not have been around very long, but he sure was a quick learner.

"Daddy?"

"Yes, darling."

"Karla's mother is working on a play about Isadora Duncan. It's opening at the end of October. The twenty-ninth. It's a Sunday. Will you come?"

"If I'm not filming." Jesus, this was too good. Stop. No, don't stop. Buddy was daring him and Jack was taking the dare.

"Will you let me know?" Becky asked.

"Certainly. Listen, baby, someone's at the door. I'll get back to you later."

"Thanks, Dad."

Thanks Dad. Thanks Dad. That was the rhythm. Yeah, you got it, Buddy-boy. You got it. Thanks. Oh, yes. Nothing was as good as a morning blowjob. Nothing. But how the hell was he going to tell Nick?

• XV •

On Tuesday, Karen met Karla after school as she had done every day for a week. Karla was actually beginning to like her. She thought she was real interesting with her stories about Paris, her funny way of talking, her clothes that were new but old. Karla decided Karen looked like a painting in a museum.

Karen spent lots of money on Karla. She took her to Rumpelmayer's for an ice-cream sundae and told her about how much Olive loved ice cream and how she'd never let her have it. Karla liked it best when Karen told stories about Olive, about how Balanchine had loved her, about how crazy her father had been about her. She even told Karla stories about Olive's performances.

That afternoon, just before the temperature fell, they went up to Karen's hotel room and Karen showed her the scrapbook she had kept all these years.

"My mother was beautiful, wasn't she?" Karla said.

"I would think she still is," Karen said, quite surprised at her defensiveness.

Karla, staring intently at a photograph, scarcely heard

her grandmother's response. "We look alike, don't we?" Karla looked up. "All three of us."

It wasn't that Karla hadn't seen pictures of her mother before. Olive had kept her own scrapbook. Her picture was always included in anthologies on dance. It was just that there was no one else who had known Olive when she was young.

"We do look very similar," Karen said, pushing Karla's hair away from her face. She had hated it when her own daughter wore her hair down, but for some reason with Karla she liked it, thought it quite flattering. "Except for your eyes."

Karla put the picture of the young Olive down on the table. "Karen?"

"Yes, darling?" Karen neatly placed the picture back in the book that had held it safely all these years.

"Whose are they?"

"I don't know what you mean, Karla." Karen laid the large book in the bottom of her long portable wooden closet.

"Whose eyes are these?"

Karen stopped. She understood exactly what Karla meant and was stunned by the directness of the question.

"What has your mother told you, Karla dear?"

"Ah," Karla said, smiling broadly. "Another politician. My mother told me the following. She fell in love with a man who gave her an afternoon of pleasure and a lifetime of joy. How does that sound?"

"Just like my daughter."

"Is it true?"

Karen evaluated her grandchild for the very first time. Not just the clothes, which today were Benetton, or the attitude, which was strong. She took in this adult child, this exquisite creature whom she had deprived herself of for fifteen years. For the first time ever, Karen Kingsley felt maternal. "Come here, darling. Let me hold you."

Karla let her, and that's when Karen told her to call her Grandma.

* * *

"Olive?"

Olive couldn't recognize the voice over the phone. It was deep and husky and sounded like someone was playing a part, the part of a stud. "Who is this?"

"You don't know?" This time there was a bit of laughter, just a hint.

"No, I don't," she said, telling herself she shouldn't feel frightened. Why should she feel frightened? This was silly.

"It's Robbie. Robbie Haskins."

"Robbie." Right, Robbie. "Oh, Robbie, I'm sorry, but I can't talk right now. I'm meeting a friend for dinner. And my daughter's supposed to join us and I don't know where she is..." She stopped herself. Why was Robbie Haskins calling her? "Is everything okay?"

"Yes, Olive. Is everything all right with you?"

"Yes, Robbie, of course."

"I had an idea, Olive, a fabulous idea, and I thought I might come over and discuss it with you."

"Now?" Olive looked at the wall clock. It was seven. She had to meet Elizabeth Anne in an hour. "It can't wait until tomorrow?"

"I'd like to try it tomorrow, Olive. It's about the lighting and I'd like to try it tomorrow."

"I'm meeting a friend at Joe Allen in an hour. I'm really rushed. Why don't we take a moment to discuss it on the phone?"

There was no response. "Robbie?"

"You know what, Olive? I'll try it out tomorrow and then we can discuss it. It just had to do with the dance Ashley's dancing, but really I'll give it a try. We still have enough rehearsal time to experiment, don't we?"

"I guess we have some time," Olive said, amused. Naturally, she knew about their little liaison. Everyone did. Not that it mattered. Actually, it seemed as if Ashley's dancing had improved as a result. "Robbie?"

"Sorry, Olive. It's a bad connection. I'll see you tomorrow."

Janice was wearing Vince's favorite perfume, L'Air du Temps, and it mingled well with the fragrance of curry in the air. They both loved Indian food, but Janice rarely enjoyed cooking. Tonight she didn't have to. Akbar, the Park Avenue Indian restaurant, delivered.

"What's the occasion?" Vince asked. In truth he knew damn well what the occasion was, but he decided he'd let Janice say it. She had sprinkled fresh rose petals everywhere, in the Baccarat bowls, in the Lalique stemware. She'd even lined the windowsills with petals. Small platefuls of fruit and curried hors d'oeuvres were strategically placed around her Gramercy Park co-op.

Janice was one of those women who came from money. Not trust-fund money like the Manchesters, but small-business money invested properly. Large-home-in-the-suburbs-without-a-swimming-pool money. Private-school money without the European vacations.

When her father died she had inherited a small trust fund and invested it wisely. Then, when her building went co-op, she bought her apartment at an insider's price. By the time she retired from her job as a book editor she would be living very nicely.

"The occasion, my darling," she said, unwrapping her arms from around his neck, "is our anniversary. Two years. You haven't forgotten, have you?"

"Of course not." From his inside pocket he took out a brooch. He had bought it for her before he'd seen Olive again.

She squealed. She loved it, and jumped up and down over it. For a classy girl she was very theatrical. In private, of course. In public, Janice Alison Canfield was always the lady.

"And what's the latest countdown?" he asked, winding his arm in hers.

"By my calendar we're just five weeks, four days, five hours, and eight minutes away from being Mr. and Mrs. Give or take a few seconds."

He laughed. Vince enjoyed Janice. Her enthusiasm, her taste, her love of him. "Aren't you afraid you'll turn me off by being too eager?"

"Am I too eager?" she asked flirtatiously.

His kiss was the answer.

"It seems that instead of turning you off, I'm turning you on."

"As a matter of fact, I was going to ask if we could have dessert first."

"For you, darling . . ."

He didn't wait for the rest of the sentence. He simply took her by the hand and led her through the living room, past the overstated candelabras set off by understated grays, past the perfect touch of cream here and splash of eggplant there. Flowers dotted the room and a large oil painting hung on one wall. Her apartment looked like her, understated and refined. It all made Vince feel very comfortable. He turned toward the bathroom.

"A shower?" she asked. It wasn't a refusal, just an inquiry. Janice would never refuse Vince anything. She loved him madly. Her eyes loved him. Her mouth loved him. Her whole being loved him. Had he wanted to do it in the kitchen sink she would have acquiesced.

Even before they reached the bathroom door he began undressing her, unbuttoning her silk sheath. The silk felt good under his fingers, like skin.

Olive's.

He ignored the voice, but it didn't go away. He could feel it waiting, wanting to speak up, speak out. It had always been a question of what happens between marriage and adultery. Now he sensed the question was what happens between adultery and marriage.

Olive. In both cases, Olive.

With Janice it will work, he told himself. At fifty-two you don't outgrow people. You get married for forever.

She had a beautiful body, this woman who loved him. Her breasts were full and round, like her buttocks. He liked her slender waist. He also liked her modesty. It had taken him months to get her to open up sexually with him. He liked that, too. It was very Old World.

The shower was cold. Against its chill they held each other. Then they kissed. He soaped her. Loved her squeaky clean. His hands explored the already explored territory.

Nothing new, but it was exciting nonetheless. How was it, he wondered, that the flesh can hold us and then suddenly turn us away?

He was already hard and she soaped his hardness. Happy with it, the hardness, thinking it meant he loved her. He took the lather from his body and draped her thighs in it, then her stomach. He turned her around. He liked that the best. That tight little hole that she never allowed him to enter. Except maybe with his finger. Sometimes, if she drank enough. But in the end it always excited her. He knew that. Still she shied away from it.

"Please," she whispered as he began the penetration with his finger. "You know I don't like that."

He knew she loved it. She loved it if he could distract her with his tongue. He redirected the water, made it warm, and sat her on the side of the tub. Yes, she liked that. She slid forward. Now they could both have it. Hers and his. Why did that turn him on so? Because it was forbidden. She had told him she thought it was dirty. That excited him.

He carried her into the bedroom. Wet. Kissing her. Finger where he wanted it. She held him around the neck. Yes, this was good between them, this passion. Funny to have it with a woman like Janice. She was so proper, and yet there it was. Passion.

The sheets were cold. They bundled under her blankets like two children. He was directing himself into her. No more games. He wanted her and she him. She touched his hair. His face. Sought out his lips. Then guided him, guided him in.

"I love you, Vince." She had said it so many times before. So many times holding him, wanting him, having him. And he? Well, he hadn't called it love. Not yet. He had proposed. That was love by implication, wasn't it? He had taken her to his daughter's grave. That was love, wasn't it? He had promised it would be good together. Forever. And Janice knew he would call her name out soon, in love. And he did . . . almost.

"I love you," he said. "I love you." It was a whisper first, then louder. Unmistakable. "I love you." He said it as he came. He said, "I love you, Olive."

Her whole body contorted as if in orgasm. But it wasn't orgasm. It was pain. For the first time since she'd known him she sought safety, away from him. Pulling herself back she got out of bed. She turned on the lights. She had to see the eyes of the man who was killing her.

"Janice." Oh, God, he hadn't meant to say that. "No, Janice. I'm sorry." But his words didn't stop her tears. They left her like blood, as if she were a maimed animal.

"Who is she?" she asked. The question was born out of torment. "Tell me."

He told her. Yes, he had told the truth the first time. Olive Kingsley was his latest case. But they had known each other before.

"Were you married then?"

"Yes, I was." He saw what she was getting at. "But our marriage was over. Janice, I love you." That was the only salve he could put on the wound.

"How often do you see her?"

"I'm in charge of the investigation," he said, unsure of his feelings about Olive, knowing he wasn't ready to risk his whole relationship with Janice now.

"Well, what's the charge? Why is she being investigated?"

"Janice sweetheart, you know I can't tell you that. I would like to but I can't."

She couldn't accept that, but she had to. "Vince," she said, drawing near. "I do love you so."

"Janice." He warmed her body with his own. "Does that mean I get another chance?"

"I don't know," she said, sobbing. "I don't know."

The well-bred half of New York's Golden Couple extended the toe of her Charles Jourdan shoe and attempted to touch ground. Deciding it was too daring a move, she withdrew the lime-green pump and color-coordinated ankle and calf back into the limousine and waited for help.

It seemed that Joe Allen was slightly lopsided today, not an altogether new experience for Elizabeth Anne. Fortunately for her, the solution was rather easy. Her chauffeur, as he had in the past, would set it straight.

When the door to the restaurant opened, the waiter, Ramon, took over. The care of the very rich goes far beyond hair and nails.

"Oh, by the way, Mrs. Long," Ramon said respectfully. "Miss Kingsley called to say she'd be a few minutes late."

"Oh." What to do? "Ramon?" She spoke his name slowly. That way it wouldn't be mispronounced. Control. Yes, that's what it was about for Elizabeth Anne. Control. "Ramon darling, tell Olive to . . ." Now, what was it she wanted Ramon to tell Olive? Oh, yes. ". . . to meet me . . . in the . . . ladies' . . . room."

"Certainly." He changed direction and deposited her outside the rather ratty-looking ladies' room door.

Once inside, she sat on a toilet. A resting place. Yes, she needed a rest. A long rest. Olive, where are you? You will know what to do. She looked up at the ceiling. It desperately needed paint. Oh, God, so would the mansion once Charles was reelected. How she didn't want him to be reelected.

"Liz, are you in there?"

The voice, which eked its way through the closed door, was small and unsteady. "Olive? Yes, darling. I'm in here."

Not good, Olive thought.

"Please come in," Elizabeth Anne said. She extended the invitation as if she were asking her friend into her parlor.

Olive opened the door tentatively. "Liz?"

Elizabeth Anne had been crying. Long mascara tears made a clown of her otherwise perfectly powdered face. Olive bent over and took her best friend's hand.

"Olive," Elizabeth Anne said, trying to look Olive in the eye. It was an effort to keep her head up. Her spine couldn't seem to straighten out. The words didn't want to come out straight either. No matter. It was only Olive.

"Are you not feeling well?" Olive asked.

Liz shook her head. No, she wasn't feeling well. Cotton inside. That's what it was. Someone had put cotton inside her head when she wasn't looking. And her eyes hurt.

"Well, perhaps I should take you home," Olive said.

"No!" It came out much louder than Liz had planned. "No." That sounded better. "Talk. We must talk."

Olive bent over to listen.

"He's all I have," Liz said.

"Who?" Olive asked, knowing full well she was speaking of Charles.

Liz ignored the question. "Mother was right. He—he is a mutt. No breeding."

"Charles?"

"Shh." Liz put her finger on her lips. "Someone might hear. Election."

Olive nodded.

"Woman. He has a woman." The words were undisciplined, falling out like spittle.

Olive didn't want to hear. But Olive didn't have a choice.

"The other night..." She stopped so she could gather the strength to finish. "He took me to bed...." Tears stopped the speech. Then she quieted herself. Control. The Longs had no control but the Manchesters were riddled with it. "He couldn't get an erection, Olive." The words came out precise and exacting, like blows from a hammer.

"Maybe we should go, Liz."

"Don't. Let's—let's just stay... here."

"You're probably wrong."

"He lies. Don't you lie." She waited for Olive to come back with something, but Olive said nothing. "Have I ever told you about our sex life?"

"Liz."

"No. I must tell you. Our sex life..." Her gaze moved from her feet to Olive's face. She spoke as if she had been struck stone-cold sober. "Our sex life was what fairy tales are made of. We made love for hours. Hours and hours. He—he could never get enough, Olive. I thought it was me, but..." Suddenly she felt as if her tongue were held captive by a jar of honey. The words just wouldn't come out.

"Liz."

"No!" This time it was loud on purpose. "But it wasn't me. It was just that he couldn't get enough. Then for the past year . . ."

"He's so busy, Liz. Do you know what kind of energy it takes to be a mayor and campaign for an election at the same time? And now this party."

"Damn this party," Elizabeth Anne said. "It's a funeral. Death of a . . . death of a marriage is what it is. Not a celebration." And then she was back to her original thought. The love of her life and the lack of love in their life. "Energy? Charles Long has more energy than Balanchine ever had. Did you know that? Sex? Could never not get hard. He was like a machine. A fucking machine." Realizing the unintended pun she laughed. Laughed and laughed and laughed, and Olive, fearful she would get hysterical, took her hand and rubbed it as if to wake her up.

"Listen, Liz. Let's say there is another woman. Let's just say."

Liz nodded.

"Then there's probably been a woman for a while. Right? You say it's a year."

Liz nodded.

"Then why now?"

Liz looked hopeful. "What do you mean?"

"I mean that if there was another woman this would have happened before. It would have had to. I think it's tension. What did he say?"

"I—I didn't ask." She was feeling better. She had to pee though. "Olive."

"Yes, sweetheart?"

"Have to pee."

"Oh." She got up to leave the stall.

"No. Stay." She slipped her pantyhose down around her ankles. Olive had never seen anything like it in her life. Had it not been so pitiful she would have laughed. Her friend looked perfectly ridiculous; and yet through all of it she was still elegant. Well, that's breeding for you.

Liz wiped herself and pulled up the pantyhose. "Should I leave him?"

"Liz."

"Where would I go?"

Someone came in, saw the two women holding hands in the stall, shrugged, and locked herself in the next one.

"Stop speaking foolishly," Olive whispered. "You can't leave." With a finger over her lips she added, "And we can't talk here. Too many spies."

"Easy for you to say," Liz muttered. "You have . . . it all. You . . ." The liquor had transformed her sometime-envy into contempt. Olive had never heard it before and couldn't believe it.

"What are you saying?"

"Balanchine. You were the best. You have a beautiful child. You have everything. Even . . . after the tragedy . . . with Karla. And your mother . . . You've triumphed like a phoenix." She stopped, burped. "Phoenix. That's that bird, right?"

No, Olive thought, she couldn't let Liz get away with this. Even though she was drunk. "And you have the husband of the decade, the drop-dead enviable position of being Mrs. Mayor and no kids to worry about. You have it all."

Elizabeth Anne made sure of her balance by bracing one hand against the wall, and stood up. She teetered, sat down, then stood up again. "I do?"

"You love him, don't you?"

Elizabeth Anne had to think for a minute. Love. Of course she loved him. She nodded. Yes, she loved him. Oh God, how she loved him.

"Olive?"

"Yes, Liz?"

"Did you love Karla's father?"

She did not have to stop for a minute to think. "Yes," she said. "Yes."

Elizabeth Anne nodded again. With envy. With admiration. Olive had a love child. But she didn't say it, because Olive might get angry again. Instead . . . "Dinner. Let's have dinner. We can't stay in here," Elizabeth Anne whispered. "Someone might hear." She looked in the mirror. A few strands of dark hair had attached themselves to the corners of her mouth, creating lines on her cheeks. Her eyes were ringed with mascara. The well-bred half of the Golden Couple looked like a rag. She pulled out a comb and attempted to repair the damage. "Give me a few minutes to get myself ready to meet my public. You go in first."

"You have reached Olive Kingsley's residence." Olive's voice mingled with a few chords of Tchaikovsky's *Sleeping Beauty.* "Miss Kingsley and her daughter Karla are not in at the moment. Won't you please leave a message so that one of us can return your call?"

Vince was relieved she wasn't home. What would he have said to her?

He was glad she wasn't there. Glad he didn't have to speak. But still, he was also glad he had heard her voice. Yes, that's all he wanted. To hear her voice.

Damn you, Luscardi.

Despite himself he picked up the phone and redialed her number.

Just when Olive was about to go back and find out if anything was wrong, Elizabeth Anne emerged from the ladies' room looking like the Grand Duchess Anastasia. Her makeup, which twenty minutes earlier was everywhere but on, looked as if Way Bandy had risen from the grave to do it.

Well, Olive thought, as Karen had often said, feel if you must, just don't get sloppy about it. Elizabeth Anne wouldn't have disappointed her.

"The fish is divine," Ramon said as soon as Elizabeth Anne was seated. "Monkfish."

"Give us a few minutes," Elizabeth Anne said. She turned to Olive. "How are rehearsals going?"

Olive knew the game they were playing. It was let's pretend. Let's pretend the ladies' room never happened. Actually she preferred pretend herself.

"Fine, Liz. It's quite interesting watching someone like

Ashley Pope emerge. I feel as if I'm watching a butterfly come out of a cocoon."

"Is it wonderful?"

"Yes, it's wonderful." Olive felt better speaking about the play than about Charles's possible indiscretion. "You know she has a thing with Robbie Haskins."

"Really! Is that new?" Elizabeth Anne was growing fidgety. She wanted another drink.

"I think so," Olive said.

"Tell me about it." Should she order vodka or whiskey?

"He stops by her dressing room after rehearsals." Olive giggled. "I think the panting can probably be heard at the Shubert."

Elizabeth Anne smiled. Maybe tequila for a change.

"You know how she got her name, don't you?"

"Ashley?"

"No, Pope."

"How?"

"They say she's been on her knees more times than he has."

"Oh, Olive," Elizabeth Anne squealed. "You're so bad."

"Maybe. But at least you're smiling again."

"And look who's not."

Olive turned to see Karla stomp in.

"You said we were dining alone," was Karla's greeting to her mother.

"You might say hello to Aunt Liz."

"Hello, Aunt Liz." The enemy, Karla thought. She was the one keeping Uncle Charlie from her. And she was bombed for a change.

"How are you, Karla, my sweet?" Elizabeth Anne stood to kiss her. "Why are you so perturbed, Karla?"

"Why? I just wanted to have dinner with my mother alone, that's all. Since she's working on this damn play—"

"Karla!" Elizabeth Anne said, taking her friend's defense.

"She has time for everything and everyone except me."

"That's not true. You're the most important person in your mother's life."

"Maybe I should get blind again." It was a poisonous dig, meant to hurt. It did.

"Karla!" Olive wasn't going to let her daughter get away with that one. "I apologize for not telling you Elizabeth Anne was coming, but it was a last minute decision. When you left this morning I didn't know. It's not like she's a stranger so stop this tantrum right now. I won't have it."

"I'm always sharing you. It's either the play or Elizabeth Anne or... I'll bet as bad as Grandma was, she gave you all of her attention."

"Stop it, you two," Elizabeth Anne said. "Olive, why don't you take her home? We can have dinner another time."

Karla got up to leave.

"What made you bring up Grandma?" Olive asked coolly. "Sit down, Karla. You've never called her Grandma before."

Karla raised her chin, her hair sweeping across her shoulders. She had started doing that when she was blind. A definite attempt to shrug off discomfort. While it looked arrogant and could have driven somebody else crazy, it broke Olive's heart. Karla's vulnerability was still there. She reached out and touched her daughter's hand.

"Karla." Her voice was neither soft nor loud. It was simply gentle. "What brought Karen to mind?"

Karla felt guilty. Her mother was being nice even though she had been a bitch. And Karen had been so nice and she had promised not to tell. "She's in town."

"What!" It was a sobering shriek, from both Olive and Elizabeth Anne.

"And you didn't tell me," Olive said. "You little stinker. You..." She got up and began tickling her daughter. "Keeping secrets? I'll get you."

"Mom." Karla, being the most ticklish person in the world next to Olive, was hysterical. "Stop. Besides," she whispered, "people are watching."

"She's right," Elizabeth Anne said, not looking for any publicity in her present condition.

"Tell all," Olive said, playing big sister.

Karla did. She told her mother that Karen wasn't so bad after all. She had been buying things for Karla, they had gone for walks in the park, Karen had shown her Olive's pictures.

"And you say she's not too bad?"

"No, Mom, honestly."

"Then why the hell is she hiding?" Elizabeth Anne asked.

"Yes, why?" Karla asked.

For Olive to explain that, she'd have to explain many cruelties, many unanswered letters, many feelings of abandonment, and she had no intention of doing that. She may have been deprived of a nurturing mother, but that didn't mean she wanted her daughter to be deprived of a nurturing grandmother.

"Listen," Elizabeth Anne said with a new burst of energy.

"What?" Karla asked. Everything was all right between them now, and Karla even felt happy that Aunt Liz was there. If only she weren't married to Uncle Charlie.

"I was just telling your mother, Karla, that Charles and I are having a gala anniversary party. It's our fifteenth, you know."

"Is it going to be formal?" Karla asked, feeling her mood come up and trying to keep it out of her voice.

"Well, yes, it is," Elizabeth Anne answered. "Why?"

"Because," she said in her most dramatic tone. Another sweep of the black hair. "I'm going to come dressed like Madonna."

"The singer?"

"No, the virgin."

"Oh," Olive and Elizabeth Anne said together, not sure if she was being serious. "And how are you going to do that?" Olive asked.

"White lace," Karla said. Her excitement was uncontainable. "And I know just the dress. I saw it, Mother. A Zandra Rhodes. Oh, Mother, it's fabulous."

"Well, that solves one problem," Elizabeth Anne said. "Neither of us could figure out what to wear, but now we won't have to. Nobody will notice us with our young green-eyed beauty done up in white lace."

Karla smiled. So did Olive. Liz was back to her old self.

Ramon walked over to the table, pencil and order book in hand. "Well, are you ladies going to have dinner or what?"

After Janice asked him to leave and he called Olive and everything turned up empty, Vince did the next best thing. He went out and bought himself a pack of Marlboros and stalked the streets. Had the stores been open, he probably would have stalked Saks or Hermès, but everything was shut down for the night. Even in New York things close down. All that was left at eleven o'clock was his old standby—cigarettes and checking out the nightlife. Jessica Bishop's place looked quiet. It was still on the stakeout and would be until this nut job struck again. But Vince had a hunch. Something was going to happen—to Olive.

He walked down from Eighty-seventh and Amsterdam to Sixty-second and Central Park West. He really didn't think much about where he was going. When you have a direction in mind you don't have to think about it. You just go. Was he going to see Olive or just to check out the neighborhood? Now that was a good one, one he couldn't answer.

The black man could. He was sitting on the bench across the street from Olive Kingsley's apartment building. He didn't mean anything by it. He was just sitting. Watching. Waiting. Thinking.

He watched while Olive and her daughter walked up Central Park West and Vince walked down. Unrelated figures in the night, surrounded by blackness, innocent victims of the times, the black man thought.

Vince was staring down at the toes of his shoes and breathing hard when Olive saw him. She slowed down, almost stopped.

"What's up, Mom?"

Olive looked at her daughter and realized she was going

to come face-to-face with her father. Please God, Olive prayed, don't let her feel it. Olive couldn't handle that yet.

"That's an old friend of mine, Karla," she said, and just as she did, Vince looked up and smiled. Oh, it was Karla's smile all right.

"He's the guy you went out with the other night, right?"

"Right."

"Olive." Vince had quickened his pace. He was delighted to see her. "And who's this?" he asked, knowing full well it must be her daughter.

"Karla," she said, taking her daughter's hand. "This is Vince Luscardi. He was . . . well, he was a big help to me once a long time ago."

"And I'd be the same again if your mother would just let me," Vince said, not at all ashamed of his enthusiasm.

"Uh-oh," Karla said. "This sounds like it's too much for me. I better leave you two guys alone."

"No," Olive said.

"Yes, Mom." Karla kissed her mother on the cheek, then whispered, "Not bad, Mom. Not bad."

As Karla stepped inside the apartment building nobody noticed the black man leave the bench.

• XVI •

After lunch with the boys—those politicos who can make or break a career—and after faking a good laugh over Babs's latest column mocking Liz's public drinking, Mayor Long walked the few blocks over to the Longacre Theatre.

The house was full, of guests and of cast. Of old friends and new enemies.

Olive had not been liking what she was seeing, either on stage or off. Ashley seemed distracted. Liz, sitting to Olive's right, definitely was. When she thought Olive wasn't looking she'd slip out the small Evian bottle she carried in her purse and take a nip. You didn't have to be a detective to know it was filled with vodka.

Karla, because she had the day off, had decided to have a look-see too. What she was seeing was Ashley drenched in white light and white gauze and looking exquisite, ethereal. Her untrained eye didn't catch the uneven rhythm, the detachment from the self.

And Vince was there, way in back, doing his job and wanting to do much more than his job.

Charles walking in carrying the rag completed the social

picture in a newsy sort of way. He had every intention of taking his wife off to the side, reprimanding her, and leaving. He had every intention of being charming and smooth. But he never had any intention of being so entranced by Ashley Pope. Truth was, when Karla had opened the Pandora's box that held his passion, she'd opened all the other wormy compartments as well. If adultery with one was good, adultery with two was better.

Charles Andrew Long, impeccably done up on the outside, was completely undone on the inside by the blonde bombshell on stage. Big tits, big vulnerability, big acting ability. That's what he saw and that's what he wanted.

Naturally, Vince caught it all. He watched Elizabeth Anne fly toward her husband as if he were a god. He watched Karla, not quite a woman, no longer a child, demand of Charles something he didn't really want to give. He watched Olive smile demurely and kiss the mayor warmly on the cheek.

Then he watched Ashley Pope leave the stage and walk up the aisle, languidly, erotically. Charles embraced Elizabeth Anne, Karla, and Olive without ever taking his eyes off Ashley. The twenty feet between the star and the mayor meant nothing. They were touching. It was foreplay, obvious and intentional. Ashley walked slowly, her hips swaying as if they were being massaged. Every part of her moved except her eyes. Charles was helpless, a child. She extended her hand and he his. They came together.

Elizabeth Anne tried to talk to him. Why was he here? Charles handed her the column. All very smooth, all very right. But Vince saw something else. He saw a love affair in the making.

"Have you seen Babs's newest tidbit?"

"No." Elizabeth Anne liked the word *no*. She could say it without a slur. "No, less see." Ah, now that was one more thing. She had to remember not to say any words with t's in them.

Babs says: It seems that the Golden Couple is personally caring for the city in their own individual and idiosyncratic ways. Downtown it looked like Tatiana Penn, world-famous photographer, had had it. And she would have, had our own Mayor Long not been dining in La Colonna. Tatiana must have been thinking of another scene entirely when she attempted to swallow a too big bite of La Colonna's scrumptious sirloin smothered in peppercorns and red-pepper puree. Tatiana began to choke, but before you could say *Heimlich*, Mayor Long came to her rescue. Out came the morsel. Thanks were extended and business continued as usual. Well, Charles, we've heard that girls lose their breath over you, but this is ridiculous. Seriously, Tatiana thanks you and so do we all. Oh, by the way, Tatiana had the remaining portion sent home in a doggie bag.

Uptown, much laughter was heard by our very own Elizabeth Anne when she and party of two—that wonderful Olive Kingsley and her raven-haired beauty of a daughter—apparently had one bubble too many and got real silly. Everyone loved it though. Liz, as intimates call her, has a great laugh.

When Charles had walked into the Longacre, it was the last line he objected to. By the time he'd undressed Ashley Pope with his eyes he'd forgotten he was even carrying a newspaper. Sex was happening right there in the aisle of the theater, and no one saw it but Vince... and Robbie. He saw it too. Vince could tell by the way the guy strutted. Not only did he know, but he objected.

Who was he, Vince wondered, this guy with big shoulders, a *GQ* face, and blonde hair? Oh, that's right, he was the lighting designer. Vince had done a make on him. Nothing showed up. Robbie Haskins didn't even have a driving ticket.

"I'm Robbie Haskins, how do you do?" Robbie said, extending his hand to the mayor.

"Mr. Haskins, pleased to meet you," Charles said.

Robbie shook Charles's hand while stroking Ashley's. She was his property. Yes, that's what she was, property. The question was, did she know? Vince doubted it very much.

"So what do you think?" Ashley asked.

"I think you've got a hit on your hands," Charles said. He turned his attention back to Robbie. "You look very familiar."

"Do I?" Robbie's arm was around Ashley, his woman, his goddess, his possession. "I spent most of my life in California. Hollywood, in particular. Ever spend much time in Hollywood?"

"Hollywood, huh?"

The memory of Hollywood brought a smile to Charles's face. The memory was of youth, pre–Elizabeth Anne. Hollywood was a memory of abandonment, sweet innocence, and noncommitment. "I spent some time out in California. That was when I had visions of becoming a star."

"I bet you could have too," Ashley said quickly. "You've got the looks." Vince noticed that neither Elizabeth Anne nor Mr. Sex Almighty appreciated her candid appraisal.

"Well, that was a long time ago," Charles said. His attention was still on Robbie. "Do you think we could have met out there?"

"I don't think so. Did you hang out at Anna's?"

"Anna's?"

"Restaurant in West L.A. She makes the best tortellini on the coast, and when there's lobster Fra Diavolo on the menu . . . mama mia. They drive in from San Francisco sometimes. Nothing like it."

"No, before that. Maybe fifteen, twenty years ago."

"Could be. But I really don't think so. I have a feeling we ran in different crowds. Before I became respectable I was—"

"Unrespectable," Ashley finished.

Robbie continued. "And I'm sure that other than your

well-publicized anonymous background, you're about as respectable as they come." He smiled. "Am I right?"

"Yes, I suppose you are," Charles said musingly. "I suppose you are."

Vince watched. Vince listened. Vince took notes. He liked this. He liked this a lot.

Nasty Nick never took notes. He never had to. For Nick life was real simple. Maybe it was so simple because he was limited to two emotions: love and hate. When he loved you, he ate you alive. When he hated you, he got even. In either case you were dead.

Anyone thinking of getting involved with Nasty Nick was warned to think otherwise. He was still young enough to be beautiful, sane enough to be manipulative. By the time you found out who he was, how he got the epithet Nasty, it was too late.

When Jack hadn't made it his business to stop by after their dinner together, Nick got to feeling real nasty. He plotted and planned and was hateful and mean, but did nothing. He'd wait. He was a boy in love, so he'd wait.

At first Jack played coward. He would have preferred avoiding the issue, but he couldn't. He would have preferred sending a note, but you don't end a two-year affair with a Hallmark greeting card. He wrote a check instead. He decided to get Nick the perfect gift. Something a twenty-three-year-old would find irresistible. Something that might make the rejection slightly more palatable. A '53 Thunderbird in mint condition fit the bill just fine. In Jack's opinion anyway. He took Wednesday afternoon off and drove it over to Nick's house.

Nick was still waiting. The longer he waited the more he steamed. For five days Jack had left him sitting by himself, in the sun, getting hotter and hotter. Who the fuck did he think he was? Even more, who did he think Nick wasn't?

"It's for you," Jack said, stepping out of the T-bird. He looked so California. Tanned, tennis shorts, and La Coste shirt. The only thing missing was the Mercedes, but that was in his garage.

Nick smiled his satanic smile. "A fuck-off gift?"

"Come here, you," Jack said, embracing him. "It's not fuck off. I just want to use a different lead. This once."

Nick felt the steam rise. Not from his toes but from his cock. That's where most things began with Nasty Nick. But he smiled anyway.

"Just this once, huh. Why now?"

"It's the part. It calls for a muscle-bound moron. You know. An Italian-Stallion type."

"If I'm not Italian, then who is?"

"Well, it's sure not me," Jack said, trying to make light of the situation. "But it's just for this one film."

Yeah, and my mother has balls. "Where did you meet him?"

Jack was surprised at Nick's acquiescence. Very surprised. "At Hollywood Racetrack."

"A trick?"

Jack smiled. "You think I have to go to tricks?"

I think you will when I get through with you. "Just asking."

"No."

"An actor?"

"The truth is I don't know that much about him." Nick's eyebrows went up. "Really I don't."

"Can I come down and watch?"

"Watch what?" Jack's eyes twinkled.

"The shoot."

Jack wasn't sure it was such a good idea. Oh, well, what the hell?

"Sure. We'll be starting in about a week. Give him a few days to get used to the set. I don't think he's acted before. Let me break him in. I don't want him to be nervous."

Nasty Nick nodded and walked Jack out front.

"How about giving me a lift back?" Jack asked. "I figured I'd leave it with you."

"I'll tell you what," Nick said, patting Jack on the

back. "I'll call you a cab. I have some business to take care of."

Charles left the theater. Elizabeth Anne was pleased he had stopped by, but was just as happy when he was gone. She was afraid she'd slur again.

Olive went back to choreographing. Richard went back to directing. Vince went back to observing, wondering how come a nobody like Charles could end up being mayor of the greatest city in the world while a prize like himself was still stuck on the beat. He laughed. Them's the breaks.

Robbie wondered the same thing about Charles, but not with the same easiness.

Karla knew why Charles was mayor. She knew it every time she saw him, touched him, felt him inside her. He was perfect, just perfect. Her only question was when she was going to be with him next. She decided to take matters into her own hands. She went home, put on her roller skates, and skated down to city hall.

Miss Hearly was not happy to see her.

"Miss Kingsley," she said in that deep resonant voice that made people who called the mayor's office mistake her for a man. "Did you go on the subway that way?"

"No, Miss Hearly. I came down on skates."

"From where?" Miss Hearly was trying to sort some papers that sat disorganized on her desk. Her blouse, as usual, was buttoned up to her chin, exaggerating her overly endowed matron's bosom. The suit jacket, a wool blended with polyester, was neatly closed right below her cleavage. She wore, as she always did, a circular pin of pearls on her lapel and slightly too much perfume. Always Arpège.

"I skated down from my apartment."

"Are you serious?"

"I do it all the time."

"And you stay in one piece?" Joanne Hearly scanned the tall figure clad only in leotard, leggings, and tutu, and it did not go unnoticed by Karla that it was not without a touch of desire.

In her most adorable voice Karla asked, "Where is he?"

"Miss Kingsley, the mayor is a very busy man. He's—"

"Right here, Joanne. Right here. What seems to be the problem?" He turned and saw Karla. "Karla, what on earth are you doing here?" Oh, that body. "There's nothing wrong, is there?" Joanne was watching them carefully. "With your mother? Or Elizabeth Anne?"

Karla said no and asked if she could see him privately.

He glanced at Joanne who picked up on it right away. "You have a three o'clock with Carol Bellamy. Dwight Davis is coming at four."

"Who's Dwight Davis?"

"*Vanity Fair.* Story on the politician-as-celebrity."

"Right. What else?"

"Jonathan Herman from the *Daily News* is stopping in at five-thirty."

"It's only two-forty," Karla said. "Can I have the twenty minutes?"

Joanne Hearly raised her eyebrows.

"Come right in," Charles said, overdoing the geniality. "I like to think of myself as available to all of my citizens. Even those not old enough to vote."

He shut the door behind them.

"Now, Karla, what is it?"

"This," she said, and kissed him.

"Karla!"

"And this! And this! And this!" Each one was a kiss. "And this!" The last was her taking his hand and placing it on her crotch. "Look, there are snaps and they undo. We could have a quickie."

"Karla." He was shocked. Sort of. Not so much that he didn't have an immediate erection. "This is an office."

"Offices are for fucking," she said in her sweetest voice.

"Karla, what's gotten into you?"

"You." She walked over to his desk and stood near his

chair. "Just stand in front of me. No one will see." With her roller skates on she was only two inches shorter than he. A perfect match. With one hand she unsnapped her crotch, with the other she caressed the front of his slacks.

Decorum, Charles.

Fuck decorum.

That's exactly what you're going to do. Fuck decorum.

As if she were a part of the woodwork he pushed up inside her and polished her dry.

Ashley had nothing to worry about. She'd learned a long time ago it takes one to know one, and one thing Ashley Pope knew was that beneath that made-to-order suit and wing-tip shoes, Charles Long was anything but respectable.

Ashley's barometer? Her panties. Total gentlemen never, ever got her panties wet. With Charles it was instant creamy crotch.

Did the fact that he was married bother her? Not if it didn't bother him.

Ashley decided to call his office and test her theory. She left a message with his secretary and was told the mayor was very, very busy; probably wouldn't be able to get back to her. Ashley knew that was ridiculous. Of course he'd get back to her. And he did. As soon as Karla left.

"I didn't exactly expect you to be free this evening," she told him on the phone, "but I thought you might want to get together some other night."

What goes on between your legs is not the most important business in life, Charles told himself. *Haven't you learned that yet?*

No.

Had she not called him he probably would have contacted her. But he didn't have to. It had always been that way with Charles. If he couldn't get to the Pope, the Pope would come to him. And he was sure that this one could come and come and come.

No.

Yes.

"Ashley," he said with a sigh. "I'd love to. You have no idea. But I am"—*married, already having an affair*—"very busy with the election. It's only a matter of weeks now."

"You mean you don't need any assistance? Or better yet, inspiration?"

Need? No. Want? You bet.

"Can I take a rain check?" he asked politely.

"Certainly," she said, not at all put off. He'd come around sooner or later. And if Ashley knew her men, it would be sooner rather than later.

• XVII •

The Wales is a European-style hotel at the upper edge of Madison Avenue's fashionable east side. The neighborhood, just the right blend of old rich and old poor, can truly qualify as the *real* New York. Foreigners love it, though it's not trendy enough to be appreciated by natives. But Karen Kingsley was no longer a native. As far as she was concerned, the Wales held just the right kind of casual snobbery she had grown used to in Paris. When Karla told Olive that Karen had taken up residence at the Wales, Olive wasn't surprised. She knew two things: Her mother hadn't changed a bit and Karen still wasn't rich enough to stay at the Carlyle.

Olive didn't call to tell her mother she was coming. She didn't even know if Karen would be there when she arrived, but she did know she had to surprise her, catch her off guard. Olive felt that would give her the upper hand.

"Mrs. Kingsley, please." She announced her mother's name to the desk clerk as if it were gentry, as if it were only natural that he would have heard of it. Then, realizing that the name was no longer Kingsley, she began to correct herself. But the clerk was already answering. Five-oh-one.

Five-oh-one. Five-oh-one. Five-oh-one.

"Who is it?" Karen called when she heard the knock. Olive couldn't say a word. Again Karen asked the question, but this time on the word *it* she opened the door.

Robbie called from the doorman's phone in the lobby. "How about dinner, Ashley?"

She looked in the mirror. She was decent enough. Why not? "I'll be down in five minutes."

It was obvious to Robbie that the Lord was on his side. The ease with which Ashley slid into his life proved that. He was clearly meant to protect her, watch over her. Then she could save him. Not only did he have to protect her from herself, from all those evil inclinations, now he had to protect her from the inclinations of others, like the mayor.

Robbie had felt the chemistry between Ashley and the mayor. Evil inclinations... Yes, that's what they were. What if Ashley gave in? That would make her a whore like all the others. And if that happened, then Ashley couldn't save anybody, not even herself.

"Has anyone ever told you, you look like an angel?" he asked as she entered the lobby.

Ashley had discovered Chelsea Designers, a wonderful shop on Twenty-third Street near Seventh Avenue. Everything in it was made to flow, to stream behind the wearer. Everything was made for bodies that oozed *femme*. This evening she wore a mint-green silk tee and olive-green silk pants. Over it, she draped a pistachio-green coat.

"You do look like an angel," he repeated.

"And you look like a choir boy."

"No, I'm serious."

"So am I," she said, lighting a cigarette. "Would you like one?"

"Don't smoke. You're too pretty to sit around with a cigarette dangling out of your mouth." He took the cigarette from her and opened the door to the taxi. She kind of liked the way he took charge.

Was she really flesh and blood? Robbie wondered. She

seemed no more than light. Pure light. "Ashley, do you believe in God?"

She kissed him. "Is this a test?"

"No, I'm serious. Do you believe that God gave His only Son to us to die for our sins?"

How sweet, she thought. He wants to have a serious discussion. But she was tired and really didn't want to answer. "You know, Robbie," she said as gently as possible, "I don't discuss God on Wednesdays."

"You don't?" It was Satan trying to come between them. "Why not?"

"Just my personal preference."

"When do you talk about God?"

"On Tuesdays and Saturdays." She moved closer to him. Their faces were just inches apart and he could feel the softness of her skin without even touching her. He could smell her. Oh, how he could smell her.

"Then what do you talk about on Wednesdays?"

The cab pulled in front of Ferrara's in Little Italy.

"I talk about chocolate mousse and napoleons and..." She ran her tongue over her lips; her fingers found her breasts. "I speak about pleasure."

"Mother?" Olive said.

"Olive... what are you doing here?" Karen straightened up. Her voice became stern. "I see Karla broke our little confidence."

"Mother, Mother." Olive opened her arms and Karen flew into them. "Mother, why didn't you call? I don't understand."

Karen held onto Olive as if she had finally found home. As if the time apart was meaningless. And it was, she thought. There was only the present, and the future.

"Olive," she said, pulling away, needing to look at her from a distance. Without thinking she smoothed imaginary hair from her daughter's brow. "You're still beautiful. And slim." She caught her lip quivering and stopped it.

"Mother, why didn't you call me?"

Karen breathed an unsteady sigh, one that betrayed

emotions like sadness and regret. "I suppose I felt you'd be angry."

Olive squeezed her mother's hand. "Let's sit down on the couch."

As if she were a child, Karen allowed herself to be led. They sat, and Olive studied her mother, as if seeing her for the very first time. It frightened her. Karen Kingsley was getting old and vulnerable.

"I *was* angry, Mother. You left me alone with an unborn child, with an unrealized career. You left me alone."

"I had to have my own life. You had disappointed me so."

"Shhh, let me finish." It wasn't said with any temper. "You left me when I needed you most. But when you left me, you left me with something. You left me with dignity. A great deal of dignity." Tears came to her eyes and she didn't try to hide them. "Mother, all of that training really helped me. I suppose I didn't like it at the time, and really, if I had my druthers, I would have wanted more love."

"I always loved you, Olive. Always. Oh, Olive, I'm so sorry. Seeing Karla..." Karen's tears came now, flowing down her cheeks, smearing the mascara and lining the foundation on her face, but she didn't try to stop them. "I was such a fool. Oh, Olive." She embraced her daughter, perhaps for the first time in her life with real love. "I missed you so much. Jean Claude would have returned with me had I asked him, but I was having such a good time. I felt as if I had been deprived, as if I had been locked away all those years. My childhood, the years with Arthur, and even..." Karen really didn't want to say it but Olive understood. "When he died..."

"He died?" Olive asked. "I'm so sorry. When?"

"A few months ago."

"From what?"

"His heart."

"I'm so sorry, Mother."

"I know, Olive. I believe you are. But when he died I realized those people weren't my friends. For fifteen years I shared my life with them. They came to my home and I went to theirs. We traveled together... But when he died there was no one. No one."

"Oh, Mother." Olive stroked her mother's hair, kissed her cheeks. "I'm here. And so is Karla."

"Now, now, Robbie," Ashley said with a little more wine to her words than Robbie would have preferred. "This man is my pubic, I mean public." She turned to the creep standing beside their table at Ferrara's. "Aren't you, sir?"

"Yeah. Hey, how about that autograph?"

Ashley spread out her napkin. "Who shall I make it out to? Or is that, to whom shall I make it out?"

"Don't get smart with me," the guy said. "Just write to Jimmy Cognito. Love, Ashley."

Guys like him made her want to get married real fast. "That's a funny name, Mr. Cognito."

"It's a family name," he said, winking. "Know what I mean?"

She didn't, but she signed him off anyway.

"That guy was part of the mob," Robbie said after he left.

"Then he ought to buy himself a new face. He sure was ugly."

They laughed as if she'd said the funniest thing in the world. But it was true, Ashley thought. If a woman had a face like that she'd stay home and get fat. She'd never come out. But this jerk thought he looked good enough to approach her, the Pope.

Then some other guy wanted her autograph.

"Hey, you must get this all the time," Robbie said.

She was surprised by his comment. "This isn't Hollywood where every other person is a star," she said, laughing. "Of course I get it all the time." She pinched his cheek. "But right now I want to get it on... with you."

It turned him on. Her fame. Her comfort with herself. Her silken skin. It turned him on and off at the same time.

"Your place or mine?" he asked, once they got inside the taxi.

"Here."

He didn't need an explanation. His lips covered hers, wetting them, wanting them, melting into them. Then he sought out the hollow of her throat. Her earlobes. Her hair. He covered it all with shivery kisses. She had no defense. She didn't need one.

"Ashley."

"Hey buddy, where to?" the taxi driver asked.

"Just drive," Robbie answered hoarsely.

"Can we do it here?" she asked softly.

Robbie's response was his tongue along her lips, his hand along her thighs. His hand skimmed them, then up to her hips. Oh, and then . . . Yes, there was her honeypot. Nothing like it in the world. She sighed, relaxing back into his arms, opening herself to him. His fingers crept beneath the panties.

Could they do it here? he wondered. Why not? She was Ashley Pope and he was Robbie Haskins. They could do it anywhere.

His hand moved in and out of her moistness, in and out of the joy.

"Robbie." It was not a question, nor a request. "Robbie."

Again he took her lips, sucking in her breath as if it were her life. Nothing pleased him more than pleasing her. She was pleasure itself. She placed her hand over his, guiding him. Not because he was doing it wrong, but because it excited him. They were doing it together. He liked that. Yes, he liked that a lot. He could have come. Without touching himself he could have come. That's how hot he was. But he wouldn't. He'd save it for later.

"Hey, you two." It was the driver again. Robbie would have belted him if he didn't see the badge first. The guy stopped the taxi.

"I'm an undercover cop and you're both under arrest."

"Shouldn't you be out catching criminals," Ashley asked, "instead of bothering innocent people like us?"

"You are criminals. You're committing an indecent sex act."

"Actually, I thought it was pretty decent until you butted in."

He recognized her. "Say, aren't you Ashley Pope?"

"In the flesh." God, she wanted to finish it. Have it. Jesus, would this guy mind? "Would you mind?"

"What?"

"Just turn around for a minute."

He stammered. This big cop actually stammered. "Sure, Miss Pope."

"Robbie," she whispered. "Here, right here." She was touching the spot. He looked at her and smiled. He loved his women with balls.

"Here . . . or here?"

"Anywhere. Yes. Like that." Ooh, that was good. But she couldn't come. Piss. Might as well deal with this cop.

"You gonna arrest us?"

"Well, considering the publicity might not be so good . . ."

"Actually, the publicity would be great. Ashley Pope, star of Hollywood and Broadway's new hit *Isadora, Isadora*, arrested for attempted orgasm in backseat of a taxi. Then they'd go to Robbie here and ask him to shed some light on the situation."

The cop didn't get it.

"He's a lighting designer."

"Oh."

"Listen, I live on East Fifty-seventh. Do you think you could drive us home?"

"Well, I really should arrest you."

"How about if I give you a couple of house seats?"

He smiled. "If you add your autograph to it, you've got a deal."

As if she did it every day of the week, Ashley took off her panties, asked the guy for his pen, and signed her name on the cotton crotch. Guys! Ashley could read them like they were transparent. Children, each and every one. So no, she was not surprised when Charles called her back that night.

"How does 'Sunday in the Country with Charles' sound?" he asked.

"Like the title of a play," she answered in hushed tones.

"Did I wake you?"

"Well, it *is* twelve-thirty."

"I'm sorry. It's just that I called you back and you weren't home, and then I started working and totally lost track of the time. I'm so sorry." Charles was really apologetic.

"Don't worry about it," she said.

"Who is it?" Robbie asked.

"Nobody. Go back to sleep." Then to Charles, "It's just that I have an early rehearsal tomorrow."

"Okay. Sunday then. I'll have my driver Arnie pick you up around eight. Is that all right?"

"Fine. But don't you want to come along for the ride?"

"Sorry, I can't. He'll take you and I'll meet you there. You'll be coming to my country house. You're perfectly safe."

"Oh, I know that. I just thought it would be fun to go up with you. Not to worry. It'll be fine." And then with wishes of pleasant dreams they bid each other adieu.

"Who was that?" Robbie asked as soon as she hung up.

"Just a friend."

Robbie believed that one like he believed the earth was flat.

• XVIII •

The plans for the anniversary party were well under way and the columnists vacillated between oohing and ahhing and digging up dirt. Everyone loved it—except for the party girl herself. She hated it. Despised it. The only way she could get through making all the arrangements was with the help of an afternoon cocktail.

Well fortified, she called Renny about the flowers. She wanted calla lilies and orchids. "Long slender displays," she told the master florist. "I'm using eggshell and lavender." Yes, it would be lovely. "But the lavender is very subtle. Sprays here and there. Everything very delicate."

"Fine, Mrs. Long," Renny said. "We'll call you when we have something for you to look at."

Then to check on her gown.

"Quintaro, love. How is my dress? Is it fabulous?"

"Darling, it is divine. Just divine." He asked tentatively, "You definitely don't want even an *itch* of color? I think black is—"

"Quintaro." Her tone was one of an adult reprimanding a small child for even thinking such a thought.

"Whatever you say, darling. Just the beads."

She had not chosen black because it looked better on her than any other color. The truth was, her patrician features and snow-white skin looked good in anything. She picked black because it suited her mood.

And the gown *was* divine. Of the finest crepe de chine, it had extended shoulders and puffed taffeta sleeves. The skirt, pleated at the waist, fell into a flood of fabric once it reached the floor. Quintaro was touching up the sleeves with bugle beads. Black of course. Elizabeth Anne would add the color—an emerald necklace from her grandmother. Five rows of them punctuated by carat-size diamonds. The Manchesters were marvelous at punctuation.

Despite Babs's praises, Elizabeth Anne had decided against using Paulette for the food. Instead she chose Mr. Chester. He had catered Bill Paley's last party and the food was heavenly. Not that Elizabeth Anne had bothered to taste any of it, but the reviews were superb. Yes, Mr. Chester would do just fine.

The toughest job was paring down the guest list of four hundred to two hundred and fifty of their closest friends. Babs had called it right. It would be *the* party of the year. Everyone from artists to politicians to socialites were being invited. Beverly Sills. Fran Liebowitz. Judith Jamison. Danilova. Martha Graham. Merce Cunningham. Wendy Gell. Art Buchwald. Bill Blass. The Buckleys. Jimmy Breslin. Eizo Ninomiya. It would be wonderful. For the guests.

Do you think you've invited her?

Who?

The other woman.

Elizabeth Anne ignored the voice inside her head and looked at the two swatches of fabric she held in her hand. One was eggshell piped in lavender, the other eggshell with a lavender silk checkerboard pattern running through it. Tablecloths and curtains. Which should be which?

She finished her seven-and-seven and walked over to Charles's office. He was working at home today. Dare she enter without knocking? No.

"Come in," he called.

"Charles?"

The prize was on the phone.

"Mario," he was saying, holding one finger up to her for quiet. "I understand what you're saying, but I think... Naturally I understand about the tax reform. Mario, wait a minute." He covered the mouthpiece. "Elizabeth Anne, what is it?"

"I need your help on colors."

"For chrissakes, I'm on the phone with the governor. Can't it wait?"

"No."

"Well then make the decision yourself. Sorry, Mario. Yes. Of course." He shooed her out, but she wouldn't leave. She sat herself down on the couch, in fact. Had he ever had one of his women here? she wondered. Was there more than one? That had never occurred to her before. It was possible, wasn't it?

Anything was possible.

"New York is getting the short end of the stick," Charles went on. "I told you that the last time I was in Albany." As he listened to Mario's response, he glared at his wife. This was not at all like her.

"All right. Around four." He hung up and said to Elizabeth Anne, "What the hell is this all about?"

"I have to decide which should be the curtains and which the tablecloths. I thought the obvious selection is to go with the solid for the cloths, with that touch of lavender around the edge." She pointed to the solid swatch. "But it might be more interesting—"

"Have you lost your mind?" He stood up and for a moment, just a moment, she was terrified. She thought he might hit her. But then the whiskey came to her rescue.

"What makes you say that, Charles?" she asked sweetly and demurely.

"You are coming to me to ask me what color to use. Are you out of your mind? I'm running a city here. And I'm running for office."

"And I'm running a household. And I'm making a party for you."

"For us."

"For you." She was fortified, she could say it. "It seems that *we* aren't anymore. It's you, you, you. And more of you."

"Elizabeth Anne." He walked around the desk and took her hands.

"Don't try to placate me."

"I don't understand what's gotten into you."

"You wouldn't. I want to know who she is."

Charles couldn't stop himself from flushing. She read it as an admission.

"What do you mean?" he asked.

"Last week—"

There was a knock on the door.

"Maybe that's her," Elizabeth Anne said.

"Come in." Charles felt as if he had just been saved.

"Hello . . . Aunt Liz. Uncle Charlie."

"Karla," Elizabeth Anne said. Seeing the girl raised her spirits. "What are you doing here?"

Karla looked from Liz to Charles and back to Liz again.

"I—I was looking for you and your secretary said you were in here so I . . ."

"Isn't she sweet, Charles? Visiting us like this in the middle of the afternoon. Come, darling, Charles is very busy. The governor is calling him soon and he has to get some reports done. We'll visit with him later."

Elizabeth Anne led Karla out of the room. On the way Karla turned and blew Charles a kiss. He did not reciprocate.

Karla had been hoping to tell Charles the news, but Liz had intercepted her attempt. Yet what was the news? One day the test read one thing, the next it read something else. *He made me pregnant. He made me not.* It was scary. It was exciting. It was wonderful. Charles would love it. Karla was able to do what Elizabeth Anne hadn't been able to do all these years. So on the one hand it was real scary, but it was going to be real wonderful. Now he could show the world how much he loved her.

Karla left Gracie Mansion, went home, and opened her

fourth in-home pregnancy test kit. The first test had registered positive. The second negative, the third positive. She opened the fourth package and took the test again.

This time the test showed she was not pregnant.

After thirty years on the force Vince Luscardi felt he had earned the right to be comfortable. He sat with a glass of Drambuie and a pack of Marlboros in an easy chair in the comfort of his own home and began to unravel the tiptoe killer.

Fact: Nina Houston. Age 19. Dancer with Eliot Feld. Left Opera Espresso on October seventh with an unidentified male. The next morning she did not show up for rehearsals. The day after, members in her company had the super open the door to her apartment and found her dead.

Fact: Dead meant partially propped up on pillows in bed, arms crossed over chest over white lilies. Six burnt candles surrounded the body.

Fact: She had had sex, probably with her killer. She had not been raped.

Fact: She died as a result of a pillow over her face. Afterward, he sliced a cross into her upper thigh and removed the big toe of her right foot.

Conclusion: Sex crime.

Fact: Ariel Powell. Dancer with Lar Lubovitch. September twenty-third left the Giselle Pub with an unidentified male. The next morning she did not show up for rehearsals. That afternoon a roommate who had spent the night elsewhere came in and found her dead.

Fact: Dead meant partially propped up on pillows in bed, arms crossed over chest over white lilies. Six burnt candles surrounded the body.

Fact: She had had sex and had not been raped.

Fact: She died as a result of a pillow held over her face. Afterward, he sliced a cross into her upper thigh and removed the big toe of her right foot.

Conclusion: Sex crime.

Friends had been questioned. The descriptions of the men differed. Both were tall, both had sandy-brown hair.

But a few people thought the guy was Mexican while someone said Indian.

An Indian with brown hair? Not possible.

Vince's train of thought was interrupted by the phone.

"Vince, it's O'Connor. They found out that neither of those girls ever wore a cross."

"What?"

"Whoever snuffed them out gave them the crosses they were wearing."

"Gee, he must have been a real nice guy, giving gifts like that. Were they gold?"

"Plated."

"Put it in the stew."

"Got it."

Snuff. The word brought him right back to Angelique. He wondered where Olive was.

The guy who had brought Nick out was a debonair forty-year-old who headed an ad agency owned by his father-in-law. The guy, Garrison Sommers, was a happily married well-to-do suburbanite with two-point-two kids. Jeslyn was nine, Smythie was four, and Stormie was on the way.

One of the reasons Garrison Sommers stayed so happy was because he had learned how to have it all. Girls and boys. Little boys, big girls. By the time he met Nick, Nick wasn't so little anymore. In fact he was big, very, very big.

It was the summer of eighty-four and Nick was a halfhearted college student working as an intern in Sommers's agency. Nothing prestigious—just a mailboy. Nick didn't mind. He liked being around the kind of people who worked in ad agencies. He thought they were smart and well-dressed. He thought it might rub off on him.

Garrison had the same thought about rubbing off. He asked Nick to work late one night, said he had a special mailing to get out. Nick was innocent. He didn't know the impact his overgrown body and petulant face would have on a covert queen like Garrison. But as innocent as he was, he sensed something exciting and excited about his boss.

"Have you ever made it with a guy?" Garrison asked him flat out.

"No," Nick said, knowing Sommers would be the first.

"Would you like to?"

Nick cocked his head to one side, then lowered his eyes as a young virgin might. But then again, Nick was a young virgin. "Sure. Why not?"

Garrison made his move and embraced Nick passionately. Nick mistook the passion for love, an error he would continue to make throughout his life. He began to undo his pants.

"No, not here." Garrison's voice was deep with desire.

He led the young virgin into the conference room, turned off the lights, and introduced Nick to himself. When the summer was over Sommers figured the affair was too. "I do have a wife," he told Nick. Nick interpreted that as, "I'm looking for new blood." Of course Nick was right. Garrison hadn't wanted to marry Nick. He had just wanted to fuck him.

Which pissed Nick off.

Nick had learned a long time ago, when his dad left his mom, that getting angry never did any good. But getting even did. He arranged for an intimate going-away party for himself. He invited Little Benjie and J.M. Little Benjie was a fourteen-year-old who loved to suck cock. He told Nick he must have been a vacuum cleaner in a previous life. J.M. loved to watch. Then just because he was sentimental, Nick set it up in the conference room.

He invited the family, Garrison's family. The pregnant wife, the in-laws, the two kids. He told them they should come out from behind the one-way mirror and yell surprise when the cake was cut.

Which is exactly what they did. But before that Nick gave them an eyeful, a nice ménage à quatre. Everyone was really surprised. Especially Sommers's father-in-law who fired him on the spot.

Poor boy. He lost his wife, his partnership, and his two-point-two kids. A year later he lost his life. Slit his wrists. Poor thing.

It wasn't that Nick wanted to be nasty. It was just that any time someone tried to get rid of him, he was reminded of what his father had done to his mom. Nick had been a baby *then and couldn't do anything about it. But he could sure do something about it now.*

So he earned his reputation. They called him nasty. What the hell did he care? As long as he wasn't abandoned.

Nick did just as Jack asked. He let the film go a few days, then paid them all a little visit. Just to say hi. He had to admit it. Buddy was a nice piece. Real nice.

"I decided to get into P.R.," he told Jack who was concentrating on the action on the set.

"Yeah, that's nice."

"Maybe I can do something for you."

"Maybe."

"Got any stills of this guy?"

"I don't know. Gino, we got any stills?"

Gino did.

"Thanks, Jack. Good luck with it."

Nice boy, Jack thought. That Nick was a nice boy. "How's the T-bird?"

"Fine. Everything's just fine."

♦ XIX ♦

Robbie ran his tongue over the spot in the small of Ashley's back. Next to her clit she claimed this was the most sensitive spot on her body. So after she came with his mouth on her he would trail his tongue up over that narrow piece of skin that connected back and front, over the separation that separated right from left, just a bit farther to her waist and then that spot, that delicious spot. They lay on the carpeted floor in her not-so-glamorous dressing room and he was making her come all over again.

"Ashley?" he asked when the vibrations stopped. "When did you decide to become a dancer?"

Shit, she thought. She wasn't ready for a serious discussion. She had three more orgasms left. "Robbie," she said, reaching up for his mouth.

"Seriously." He wished he had X-ray vision so he could read the answer inside her brain.

"I—"

"Hey, Pope!" It was a loud, blaring voice. Fleshy and wanton. Ulysses returning home.

"Oh, no," she said, squirming like a worm that had one end caught under a rock. "That's Johnny."

"Who's Johnny?" Robbie's jaw was set tight. He didn't like this. Not at all.

"My main squeeze," she said, standing up and trying to throw some clothes on.

"Hey." Johnny opened the door without knocking. He had obviously not read Emily Post, but then neither had Ashley.

Johnny saw Robbie. "You fucking whore!" His voice was booming, uncontrolled. He went to hit her, but Robbie got in the way. He smashed Johnny's face in with a fist the size of a grapefruit. The fat guy was down on the carpeting.

"Anybody for a threesome?" Ashley muttered.

"Who is this joker?" Johnny asked, rubbing his jaw.

"He's a toy, Johnny."

You're a ghost, boy.

"A toy." She was oohing and ahhing all over Johnny, swearing she was sorry. No one believed her, but Johnny made like he did because he didn't want to have to give up that pussy. Robbie knew there was pussy just as good around. It was her soul he hated to sacrifice.

"That looks like a pretty big toy to me."

"Robbie, put your pants on," Ashley said, sounding more like Mother Teresa than the hottest piece of ass on both coasts.

"Like hell I will," he said, pulling her to him.

"Robbie, you're acting like a lunatic."

"What's the matter with you?" Johnny screamed.

What's the matter with you, boy? You hear me?

"You hear me!" Johnny was yelling. "I'm the producer of this show! I'll have it closed down!"

"You have it closed down," Robbie said, "and I'll have you closed down."

"Olive," Karen asked, spearing a broccoli floret, "who was the father of your child?"

"Just like that." Olive took a tiny bite of her chocolate

mousse praline cake. "After being away sixteen years you want to know who the father is?"

"Well, I asked at the time but you were so secretive."

"Mother, let's not discuss it. Let's talk about my work. I am working on the most wonderful show."

"You said it was about Isadora. You were always fascinated with her, darling. Actually, I've thought it was her influence that led to Karla." While Karen had developed a new softness to her manner, she still held the same prejudices. "But then, I must admit, if that's the case, I can't really dislike her so much. Karla is a lovely child. I must congratulate you on having done such a wonderful job, Olive."

Olive, unused to receiving compliments from her mother, blushed.

"It's just that I think she should have a father."

"Mother."

"All right, Olive," she said, taking her daughter's hand. "Tell me about the play."

"This is a dream. Isadora was an innovator, the mother of dance. Do you realize that eighty years ago she was exposing her body on stage when bodies were completely hidden?"

"And you, my darling," Karen said with that inimitable effect of hers, "exposed your soul." She paused for a moment. "Tell me, darling, was it Balanchine?"

"Balanchine who?" Olive asked, plunging her fork into the cake.

"The father."

"The father?" Olive repeated, then laughed hysterically. "Balanchine. Mother, you have some imagination."

"I'm telling you I'm going to close down the whole fucking show!" Johnny yelled at Richard Dixon.

"What happened?" Richard asked. When he heard, he thought he should be so lucky. Leave it to him to be out of the theater during the newsiest lunch hour on Broadway.

"Is this the way theater people conduct themselves?" Johnny continued to sputter.

"Mr. Green," Richard said, trying to quiet him. "Please, you're getting yourself upset."

"Damn right I'm upset. He's *shtooping* my girl."

"Johnny," Ashley said. "You're going to make yourself sick."

"You're the one making me sick. You know you stink from him."

Robbie clenched his fists. "One more remark, fatso . . ."

"It's Johnny, you pig. Who the fuck are you anyway?"

Robbie pulled himself up tall. "I am Robbie Haskins."

"Big fucking deal. Who the hell ever heard of Robbie Haskins? What do you do on this show?"

"I create light," Robbie said with a strength that would have made Uncle Earl proud.

"Oh, give me a break."

"Johnny, baby. Let me undo your tie."

"Get your hands off of me. I want him out of the show. Either he goes or I do."

"Johhhhnny." She cooed it in the same way she cooed on the phone.

"Him or me."

Actually it wasn't such a bad idea, Ashley thought, not having Robbie around so much. He was getting heavy. Discussing marriage, religion. Philosophy was something you talked about when you got old.

"I'm not leaving," Robbie said.

"Over my dead body you're not leaving."

Robbie looked at him, then through him. Through this fat guy with pungent-smelling breath and greasy hair. He looked at him and envisioned him in darkness. He saw him with his eyes closed. Saw him lying flat on the ground, feet turned out. No light. No light at all.

Johnny screamed. He felt the thump, an excruciating twist around his heart, and pulled at his neck. Air. He needed air. He fell to the ground.

"Johnny!" Ashley yelled. Olive heard it from out front. She and Karen were just coming back. "Johnny!" Big crocodile tears ran down her face. "Johnny, don't die."

The fat guy opened his eyes for one last look at Ashley.

Shit, he was going to miss that pussy. Robbie saw the look and brought the darkness closer. Pussy was the last word Johnny Green ever thought.

Babs says: Lots of excitement on Liz Anne's new venture. What with Johnny Green out of the picture it's her baby now. Would she let it die? Never, says Liz, longtime friend of Olive Kingsley, choreographer of *Isadora, Isadora*. But insiders say that what goes on backstage at the Longacre is more interesting than what goes on up front. Well, we'll find out, folks. Just one more week 'til opening. Services for Johnny Green will be held today, Saturday, at Campbell Funeral Home on Madison Avenue and Eighty-second Street.

The Lord giveth and the Lord taketh away. Satan had come there to destroy Ashley, but the Lord had won. That was how it had been with Robbie all his life. Satan was always waiting in the wings, but the Lord weighed heavier on stage.

The Lord forgives, so Robbie found it in his heart to forgive too. While Johnny lay in wait to meet his Maker Robbie paid his final respects. Ashley sat like a bride in back, filled with grief. She was pissed off at Robbie, so Robbie was left on his own.

Johnny Green had touched a lot of people's lives. He was a big man with a big heart. He liked to do good. Especially when the payment was a piece of ass. Granted, Ashley was the best he'd had, but still every now and then he had needed something else. Like Jessica Bishop, a sweet young morsel Johnny had helped out a few years before.

"How did you know him?" Robbie asked, turning to the woman who was standing behind him in line.

She just smiled, sniffled, and didn't answer. "And you?"

"We were working on a show together. It's really an awful thing. I was talking to him one minute and he was lying dead on the ground the next."

"Did you know him well?" Jessica asked, her huge eyes brimming over with nothing in particular.

"No, and you?"

"No."

With nothing else to say Robbie suggested they take a walk.

Outside they talked about the arts, death, what dance she was doing. How she liked New York, what he did in California. Eventually they reached her apartment building. It was the middle of the afternoon.

"Do you want to come up for a soda?" she asked. It was a normal question. A warm afternoon. Emotional. Quiet.

"Yes," he said. "Yes, I think I'd like that."

Vince looked around the room of the funeral home and sensed the killer's presence.

"Olive." He placed his hand firmly on her shoulder. The sound of his voice, the touch of his hand left the hair on the back of her neck standing up. Despite herself she placed her hand over his.

"Are you free for dinner?"

She turned around and looked into his eyes. Dinner? For a moment she didn't even know what the word meant. "Yes," she said. Dinner. She composed herself. "Do you remember my mother, Vince?"

Vince forced his gaze away from Olive. There were so many things he wanted to say, but this was not the place.

"Mrs. Kingsley." He extended his hand and took Karen's. It was cold. "Are you all right, Mrs. Kingsley?"

"I remember now," she said with instant recognition. "You were the young man who was my daughter's bodyguard. You were..."

"Yes, he was, Mother," Olive said with a look in her eye that was nothing short of murderous. Nothing else was said.

"Where are your roommates?" Robbie asked Jessica.

"How do you know I have roommates?" Jessica asked, placing a chipped cup with herbal tea before him. "Honey?"

"I beg your pardon. I just assumed." She had joined him on the couch. Sitting so close he saw she wasn't as young as she had looked initially. That tall, slim dancer's body gave her a childlike aura, but those crow's-feet around the eyes told him she wasn't a child.

"They're away." She picked up a cube of sugar, placed it between her teeth, and let the tea wash over it. "I know it's bad for my teeth," she said as if she and Robbie were discussing her manner of drinking tea. "It's something I picked up from my grandpa. He said that's how they drank tea in Russia. I kind of like it."

Robbie thought she had large hands. Not unattractively so, but large. They, like the crow's-feet, removed the sense of youthfulness that at first he'd thought she possessed.

"Did you know Johnny well?" she asked.

"No," he said, sipping the horrid brew. "I just met him the day he died. As I said..." But Robbie really couldn't continue. The smell bothered him, the smell of cops. It ran up his nostrils like a line of coke. He wondered if one were hiding in the closet.

"Robbie Haskins. That's a nice name," she said. "Where are you from originally?"

Brown eyes, he thought. The other two had blue. Ashley had brown eyes. He wondered what color eyes Jesus had.

"I'm from Louisiana," he said. "Where we all spec layk thees." It was slow and melodious and Jessica smiled.

"You do that real well."

He thought perhaps it was a come-on, the way she said that, and decided to take her hand.

"I didn't invite you up here for that," she said.

"Then what did you invite me up here for?"

"Just to talk. I...it's been real hard for me. I can't go out. I can't have people in." She told him about the surveillance. How the cops were always around. How she had no privacy and neither did her roommates, which was why they weren't there. "Sometimes I just crave company," she said in the sweetest tone Robbie had heard in a very long time. "I..."

He took her other hand and kissed them both. Something in her melted.

There ain't no better way to show the Lord how much you

love Him than to die for Him, boy. The Lord gave His only Son for our sins.

Robbie knew if he took her now he would be walking in the footsteps of Jesus. He knew that and felt no fear.

Yea, though I walk through the valley of the shadow of death, I will fear no evil, for Thou art with me; Thy rod and Thy staff, they comfort me.

Robbie walked with the Lord.

"I could please you," he said, and again she smiled that young smile, the smile that took away the lines. She was a child when she smiled.

"I would like that," she said. "But not now. Not here. Maybe at your place."

Robbie let go of her hands as if they were burning embers.

"What's the matter?"

No one went there but Ashley. Did this woman think she was in the same category as the Pope?

"Some other time then," he said, and got up and left. Jessica Bishop would have to be saved by someone else.

• XX •

Olive waited for evening as if it would bring with it the messianic promise. By the time it arrived, in leaps of pink and blue across the mid-October skies, she almost felt feverish.

Her first inclination was to hide in something dark or frilly. Her second inclination was not to. The second inclination won out.

By the time evening fell, striating the sky with a lush, tropical weave of colors, she had grown used to the feeling and wanted to reflect it. The simplicity, even the uncomplicated longing that she felt, no longer seemed foreign. She owned it.

It was a little early in the season for a salmon-colored cable-knit angora sweater-dress, but she wore it anyway. "Only you can wear such a high turtleneck," Vince would say later in the evening, brushing his hand through her upswept hair. But that would be later. After his surprise. After dinner. After their walk home.

She chose no ornaments, not even a pattern in her stockings. She even removed the large hoop earrings she loved. She considered the new pearl drops that her mother had given her, but decided against them. While beautiful, they no longer fit her personality. So she decided not to wear anything.

Karen had bought three tickets for *Les Misérables*. When Olive informed her she had a date with Vince, Karen had lifted an eyebrow, turned to her granddaughter, and said, "Darling, why don't you invite that friend of yours to come along? The one I met the other day." That was just fine with Karla, who said something about dinner and Karen added that to the agenda, too.

That was hours ago. Since then Olive had tried to make herself look calm, as if someone were watching. She leafed through the latest *New York Woman*, hemmed a skirt, drank a bottle of Evian. When the doorman rang and said her chariot had arrived, she left her apartment in a state of excitation normally limited to fifteen-year-olds. When she got downstairs and saw that Vince had actually ordered a chariot in the form of a hansom cab, she practically swooned.

"How did you know?" she asked with such ingenuousness that he smiled.

"You look like a little girl," he said, taking her hand and helping her into the cab.

"I thought we'd go skating," he said tentatively. She had told him, all those years earlier, what it had meant to her. He wasn't sure if it was too soon to share that intimacy. "Or would you just prefer dinner? Are you very hungry?"

"Skating," she said in a voice far louder than the rhythmic clip-clop of the horse's hooves. "Skating." She repeated it as if she couldn't believe it. "Oh, Vince."

"You know, Olive, it feels as if we've never been apart. Do you feel that too?" He spoke completely out of character, giving it all away.

She smiled. Yes, it seemed as if they'd never been apart, and in a way they hadn't been. Karla had kept them bound eternally together.

"I thought about it all day," he said, and she didn't know

what he was talking about. "That we're together, I mean." Again all she did was smile.

Vince Luscardi wasn't the only one who had the idea to visit Rockefeller Center. Hundreds of people were milling about, cruising the night, the rink, and the statues, as well as each other. Neither Vince nor Olive cared. It was even questionable as to whether or not they were aware of anyone but themselves.

"I didn't know you knew how to skate," she said in a sudden burst of talk. He sensed it was a cover, but he didn't know for what.

"I started skating about fourteen years ago," he said. "Soon after my daughter died. Soon after Connie miscarried." He waited for a response but there was none. "I remember after his brother was assassinated, Robert Kennedy took to daredevil sports. Riding the rapids, climbing mountains. As if to defy the gods. As if to prove he were immortal." Amused at the analogy, he laughed. "Not that ice skating is the same thing. But I did take up sky diving as well. Anyway, it was about immortality."

Impetuously, she kissed him on the cheek.

"What did I say?" Vince asked with a smile. "Because I'd like to say it again." Leading her to the bottom of the stairs he bowed. "Your size, madam?"

"Eight," she answered with a curtsy.

And so the night began, he in black skates, she in white. Her dress didn't inhibit her a bit. He, in jeans with an exquisite turquoise belt from Billy Martin and an old flannel shirt, was dressed perfectly for the part of knight in shining armor. His jacket was Ralph Lauren, but who was reading labels?

Paparazzi were interested in the faces. They caught the beautiful Olive Kingsley, her hair flying in the October air, a handsome stranger accompanying her in no less gallant a fashion than James Stewart might have accompanied Grace Kelly.

Flashbulbs went off but neither one saw them. They were transfixed with each other.

Dinner wasn't touched. If asked, neither could tell where

they'd been, what they ate, what they saw, or who saw them. He walked her uptown slowly, savoring their conversation, telling her about his life for the past sixteen years. What it was like with Connie after Angelique died—the near breakdown, the psychiatrist who suggested they have another child, the stillbirth, and how he finally couldn't take it anymore and had to leave.

She told him nothing.

He asked how long she had been divorced, why her mother had left, and if she had ever thought of him.

She smiled and glanced over her right shoulder. It was partly an attempt to throw off the nervousness, partly to delay the answer. The presence of a man so close behind her startled her and she held Vince's hand all the more tightly.

"You're afraid," he said after the man passed them.

"Yes."

He wanted to tell her there was nothing to be frightened of, but didn't. It wasn't true.

As slow as the walk was it wasn't slow enough. Her building appeared all too suddenly.

"Has my daughter come home?" she asked the doorman.

"No, Miss Kingsley. Not yet. But someone was asking for you and left a note."

"Vince?" She knew what was in the envelope without even looking.

"What, my sweet?" He didn't, but sensed her discomfort. He ran his fingers through her hair, telling her that only she could wear such a high turtleneck and still have her throat show. He told her how beautiful she was.

"Vince!" She hesitated, then handed him the paper. The script was mean, like the first time.

Coppers are floppers.
Warnings a waste.
Hang up your ballet shoes baby
'Cause you a corpse making haste.

Vince was calm. All business now. His arm around her shoulder was supportive and professional.

"Who delivered this?" he asked the doorman, keeping his voice low. For all he knew the doorman wrote it.

"I don't know. I wasn't on duty."

"Great. I'll question the other man tomorrow." He turned to Olive, who was shuddering like a cold puppy. "Let's go upstairs. We'll talk about it there."

Louie the Lip called Nick back as soon as he got his message. He liked Nick. He liked guys who were straight with him, who never lied, who never told tales. Hard to find that in the world of smut. The only problem with this little puppy was that he never liked to be left alone. So the way to avoid that problem was not to get involved. Too bad. Nick had a rep for dynamite blowjobs.

"His name is Buddy," Nick said. "What do you have on him?"

"Buddy who?" The Lip asked, lighting a Lucky. He always had one dangling from his mouth, as if it were carved out of his lip. He didn't smoke them. He just dangled them. That's how he got his name.

"If I knew, I'd tell you."

"Come on, Nick. I'm a source, not a mind reader. There's Buddy Terraro, Buddy Harris, Buddy the Buzz, Buddy One-Shot." Everyone knew why they called him one-shot.

"He's about eighteen. Muscles like he was trying out for the circus. Lots of curls. Funny eyes."

"How funny?"

"I don't know. For a big guy he has awfully little eyes."

"Jack probably isn't interested in his eyes."

"Yeah, I know."

"Get a last name on him."

Her machine had three hang-ups and one message from Karla. With shaking hands she dialed her mother's number.

"How was it?" Karla asked.

"How was what?" It was as if Olive couldn't even remember her name. Vince stood behind her with his hand on her shoulder.

"The date, you nerd," Karla said. "Come on. Let's hear the dirt."

"It was wonderful, Karla." She turned and looked at Vince, eternally grateful that she hadn't come home alone to that note.

"Is that it? Oh, I get it. He's still there."

"Right."

"Whoa, Mom. Listen, do you mind if I stay at Gram's? It might actually work to your advantage."

"Karla!"

"Okay. Can't you take a yoke?"

"Is there enough room, Karla?" Olive remembered how her mother had always required so much space around her. She had even made her father sleep in another bed.

"Yeah. There're two beds here. Oh, please, Mom. I haven't stayed in a hotel since you used to dance. Please. It'll be like going away."

What Olive wanted more than anything in the world was to have Karla next to her, to hold her. There was something about physical contact with her daughter that made her feel secure, invulnerable. But she knew it was a lie. There was no such thing as security, as invulnerability.

"Of course, Karla. Enjoy yourselves. Tomorrow?"

"Tomorrow we'll go out for brunch and then I'll call you in the afternoon."

"Fine." But it wasn't. Not at all.

"I'll stay with you," Vince said after she'd hung up, but she said no.

"Olive, I know what you're thinking, but please, I'll sleep on the couch if you like."

Not on the couch, she thought. In the bed. That's where she wanted him. In the bed.

"I'll be fine," she said, holding his hand as tightly as she could. "Really I will."

"Are you sure? I don't think it's such a good idea for you to be alone now."

"I'll be just fine," she said, and walked him to the door.

It was about readying one's self. Robbie knew that. Anyone familiar with the way of the Lord knew that. And so Robbie readied himself. For the baptism into the Holy Kingdom. For the final judgment.

Robbie realized when he came home that night that he hadn't been to church in a dog's age. It was time. Time to visit the Lord in the Lord's home.

Once Uncle Earl had said, "God is beyond time and place, boy," and Robbie in innocence had asked, "So how come we have to get up early on Sundays and go someplace else to pray to Him? Can't we just carry Him around in our hearts and pray at home?"

Robbie was a boy at the time, but his reverend uncle took neither age nor innocence into consideration. Learn them young, learn them right was his motto. So he smacked Robbie, smacked him hard. He made his lip bleed. That was nothing new. It had happened before. It would happen again. It was just a matter of time before Robbie learned not to ask questions.

When Robbie moved to New York he felt right at home. If anyplace was beyond time and place it was New York. Rooted in the physical, it was as sinful as Sodom and Gomorrah, as competitive as Cain and Abel, and as up-to-date as Tofutti.

Robbie decided to visit the Lord this Sunday. But tonight he would get his own house in order.

He began his ritual with the crucifix he'd picked up in a curio shop in New Orleans. He laid it in front of the black lacquer box that held his greatest work of art. He covered it with palm leaves and a sprinkle of rose petals, white for purity. Then the wafer. Then the blood. He didn't use wine. He thought that would be cheating the Lord. He pricked his finger to show God how much he loved Him. He'd bleed for the Lord just like his mother had bled for him.

Yes, he would show the Lord his appreciation for sending an angel like Ashley, an angel who could remove his sinister urges. Without question, Ashley was angelic, white light incarnate, and she could transfer that light to make him pure. Yes, Ashley Pope would remove the blackness from his soul and bring him everlasting light.

It wasn't that he was unaware of her failings. Like Mary Magdalene she was the vehicle for both salvation and sin. Yes, Ashley had sinned, but so had Mary Magdalene. And as Jesus had said unto the world, let he who is without sin cast the first stone, so Robbie would do the same.

Afterward? He'd marry her, of course. It was quite simple really.

In preparation for the wedding he cleaned the altar. You must always be ready to meet your Maker, his uncle said time and time again. So Robbie readied himself.

First he dusted. The question was whether to use Pledge or Endust. Since Endust had come out with a lemon-smelling cleaner, Robbie had begun to deviate from his favored Pledge. Then he decided to take turns. One week Pledge, the next Endust. Some weeks he liked spraying the polish onto a rag. Other weeks he preferred spraying it directly onto the furniture. Such were the decisions Robbie had to make this Saturday night when salvation was in the air.

Somewhere in the distance a church bell chimed three times and Olive awoke in a cold sweat. The house was black. She waited for the feeling to pass, the fear, all of it. But nothing passed except time. Three-fifteen. Three-thirty. She got up and began moving around. Where was Karla? Right. With her mother.

For a moment she considered calling them, joining them. All she wanted to do was to curl up between the two of them. But no, that was silly.

She turned on the lights, each and every one. Then she went to the kitchen. Karla had left some of her extraordinary tomato sauce in the freezer, but there was no spaghetti. That's what she'd do. Defrost the sauce and cook some spaghetti.

As she waited for the water to boil, she put the sauce in

the microwave. Karla had the ability to transform an ordinary tomato into manna from heaven. She dropped the spaghetti in the water and stirred it. She was beginning to feel better. This reminded her of Karla, of warmth, of home.

A noise in the outer hallway startled her. She thought at first it was a neighbor. But no, the other two tenants on the floor were away. And the doorman hadn't buzzed her.

She walked toward the door, terrified. It had been silly to tell Vince to leave. Silly. Why was she such a fool? As she got closer to the door she heard a louder stirring. And then a voice, a small voice, saying, "Food, food, food."

She looked through the peephole but it was dark. Someone had his hand over the hole. Then suddenly there was light and she saw Vince's face.

"What are you doing here?" she asked, opening the door.

"You didn't think I'd leave you, did you, Olive?"

She had never been so happy to see someone in all her life.

"Vince, it's really you." He was rumpled, his hair falling over his forehead. "Vince."

"I parked myself outside your door, and then all of a sudden I smelt marinara sauce. *Marinara* sauce." He said it with the same sense of drama that Karla did. Why hadn't she ever put that together before? "My childhood came back to me. You know. . . my elegant upbringing on Staten Island. It all came back to me."

He was really there. Someone was there for her. "Vince," she said, all aglow again. "I think you're wonderful. I really do. Oh, please come in. Let's eat."

♦ XXI ♦

Charles had Arnie pick up Ashley early that Sunday morning. By eleven they were making brownies in the luxurious Croton-on-Hudson house.

"And what did you say after he said at eighteen, blonde, and with big tits you were perfect for movies?" Charles wiped his chocolate-covered fingers clean on his apron.

"Got any nuts?"

He raised an eyebrow.

"You know what I mean," Ashley said, beating the brownie mix to a pulp.

"Slow down. That's not whipped cream, you know. You'll take all the moistness out of it." He opened the cabinets one by one.

"Not only do you have time to go to the movies, you also know how to make brownies. I'm very impressed." She slowed down the speed on the electric mixer.

"Here they are." Charles reached up and took down a bag of walnut halves.

"Okay, let's mash 'em up."

"Aye, aye, ma'am. So tell me. What did you say after that?"

"I said that I was nineteen."

Charles dropped the walnuts in the blender, set it on chop, and waited until they were broken into bite-size pieces. "Here, is this all right?"

"Perfect. And then he tweaked my breast. Can you imagine? He tweaked my breast and said 'I'll never tell.'"

"Have you ever thought of doing stand-up comedy?" Charles asked, leaning against the Formica work area. "You're very funny."

"No. Only acting," she answered, her tone turning serious. "I wanted to be an actress from the moment I left the womb."

Ashley looked like anything but an actress today, Charles thought. Maybe a cheerleader or an out-of-town waif trying to impress the city kin, but not the soon-to-be Broadway star that she was. And it suited her, both the ingenuousness and the natural charm.

He would have told her that she certainly had the lungs for stagework, but thought better of it. Ashley Pope didn't deserve a crack like that. She'd had too many of those already in her life. But he still couldn't help staring. What amazed him more than anything else was the unlikeliness of the two hottest libidos in Manhattan being locked away for an entire hour and remaining fully clothed.

"Any marshmallows?" she asked.

"Are you expecting someone that I don't know about?" he asked.

"No. Why?"

"Because from what I see you've made enough brownies to feed all of Croton-on-Hudson."

"Where I grew up there was no such thing as too much food. When my mother made a meal, it was like a bar mitzvah."

"You're Jewish?"

"Frannie Rosenbloom. Why?" she asked, hand on hip. "Damn, I got my jeans full of chocolate. Why?"

"It's just that you don't look it."

"Talk about stereotypes. Can you open the oven?"

"Did you turn it on?"

"Did I turn it on? All I had to do was touch it and it almost exploded."

"All right," he said, amused. "Just put the brownies in and cut the schmaltz."

"Schmaltz," she squealed. "So you know a little Yiddish."

"How could I avoid it being mayor of New York?"

Now it was her turn to ask questions. "Did you always want to be mayor?"

"Sorry. I don't give interviews on Sunday."

"Not fair." She set the pan of brownies inside the oven. "I've told you all my deep dark secrets. Tell me one of yours."

Perfect opening to tell her you're the big bad wolf.

"I'm an orphan."

"That's no secret. The whole world knows that."

"Do they now?" He had to admit she was cute. Not just gorgeous and sexy but cute. Sweet. Not intimidating like he thought she'd be.

"Well, maybe not the whole world," she said. "Hey, I didn't see the rest of the house. Don't you think since I made the trip all the way up here—without you I might add . . ."

"Is that supposed to provoke guilt?"

"Does it?"

"A little."

"Good. If I came all the way up here I think you should at least play tour guide for me."

"Is that a new movie? Like *Play Misty For Me*?"

"You got it."

"All right, madam. Consider the tour begun."

Morning was an unwelcome intruder in the Kingsley residence. It entered surreptitiously through the bottom slit of the blinds, like a thief stealing sleep from the needy. It found its two victims huddled together on one end of the couch, as if some invisible guests were holding the other end hostage. Morning moved in, removing the shadows of night, leaving new shadows, new lines, new wrinkles yet to be smoothed.

Vince awoke calling her name as if there had never been any other name to call. As if her truth was the one truth he knew. When she heard her name, the afternoon they had shared so many years ago returned. In memory. In reality.

Again there were no words.

At first, he was afraid to touch her, afraid that if he frightened her she might send him away, or worse yet, fly away herself. He lifted his hand to her cheek and brushed her hair back, then kissed the sleepy lids until they opened. When they did it was as if she too opened. As if she had never closed.

He sought her mouth and she sought his. It was as if neither had ever known a kiss before, a mouth before. Rodin must have known this, Olive thought. He must have had this and then sculpted *The Kiss*.

The phone rang and she remembered Karla. He understood. Together they went to the phone in her bedroom. The machine answered and they listened to her daughter's voice; his daughter's voice.

"Mom, listen. Karen, I mean Grandma and I are going down to SoHo. She's never been there and I wanted to take her to the Spring Street Bar. She's really hip, Ma. I'll either come home this afternoon to pick up my clothes for the dance tonight, but if you don't see me it means Grams bought me something." She whispered, "I'm hoping for something *faaa*bulous." Then back to normal. "Have a great day. Maybe you and Vince can do something nice. The weather's great. If you want to meet us in SoHo come down to Spring Street. Love you."

It was as if they had permission.

With lips never leaving each other, they undressed. Clutching, pulling. Wild. It couldn't be fast enough. Once they were naked, it couldn't be slow enough. He touched her. She was not real to him. Not now, not all these years later. What had he done to deserve her return?

But she was impatient. She wanted him. The last time?

She couldn't remember. Somehow Eliot came to mind and yes, she recalled the last time with Eliot. Too many years before.

He rose over her. "Olive."

She murmured.

"Open your eyes, Olive."

She didn't want to. It was a dream. What if opening her eyes made it go away?

"Olive."

She opened them and he saw the tears.

He stroked her face, kissing the sadness away. "I want to make love to you, Olive. Do you understand that? When you feel me inside you, know that I . . . I am loving you."

It only made her cry more. She was so hungry for those words, they were almost unbearable.

"Olive?"

She couldn't speak. Gently, she lifted herself, turning him over. She sat on his chest, leaned down, and kissed him. She would possess him, she thought, the way she had always wanted a man to possess her. The way she thought Vince had, so many years ago. The way Eliot had. But now it was her turn to possess.

"No promises, Vince," she said softly, believing she meant it. "No promises." She mounted him, drawing him up to her. She wanted him to feel her power. His power. Their power.

"I want you to fuck me, Vince. Vince?" She was breathing heavily now. The word excited her. She had never said it before. Not like this. Not in bed. Not in love.

And he said, "No, no, I won't fuck you. I'll love you, Olive. I'll love you like I've never loved anyone else before."

She believed him. As he lifted himself she took him, rode him, as if he were the animal and she the master. She rode him and together, in the name of love, they cried out promises of eternity.

Karla had played her grandmother right. SoHo was as much for Karen as it was for Karla. It reminded her of the little shops Jean Claude had introduced her to on Paris's Left Bank. It had an intimacy that Karen craved. It was a new craving and she yearned to satisfy it.

While Karla begged and pleaded for the leather-trimmed pajamas with rhinestone pockets, Karen suggested something more conservative, something younger.

"That outfit is more for your mother than you, darling," she told Karla.

"Then let's get it for her," Karla said, already eyeing a rough and tough brown denim dress with rodeo fringes hanging from the sleeves.

"Maybe I will."

Karla ended up with the brown denim, and thanks to her American Express Card she was able to get boots to match. Now she had something to wear to the dance that night.

You can't have an altar without a goddess. Everyone knew that, especially Robbie. But Ashley was nowhere to be found. Oh, Robbie knew where she was. With Charles, of course. He was her temptation. Just like Jessica Bishop had been his temptation. Even Christ had temptations. The difference was that Christ didn't give in. And neither had Robbie.

Robbie prayed that Ashley wouldn't. Hoped it with all his heart and all his soul. He knew if she did it wouldn't be her fault. It would be Olive's. Olive who had given her this chance to dance. Everyone knew that dance was the devil's work. Yes, if Ashley sinned it would be Olive who would have to pay.

Robbie Haskins would rid the world of sinners. And with that thought he turned to the lacquer box for yet another solution.

Ugh! The dance. How creepy.

While the DJ was playing "At the Hop" and the dance floor was definitely hopping, Karla stood stark-still. The idea of anyone other than Charles touching her made her sick. S-I-C-K, sick. Becky, on the other hand, yearned to be touched. But since no one was offering, she had attached herself to the brownies and peanuts that The Rudolf Steiner School was kind enough to supply to wallflowers like Rebecca Gilbert.

About ten guys had asked Karla to dance. No one had asked Becky.

Karla felt really awful about that. She wished Becky would learn how to dress. She had chosen very baggy khakis and a black turtleneck. Simple but nice. It was just that her two greatest assets, those big boobs and her small waist, were lost under the bigness of it all. Plus, she didn't have the neck for a turtle. It sort of squashed her all together.

Chip Johnson came over. It was pitiful. Becky got all gaga and googoo-eyed and he only saw Karla.

"Dance?" he asked, real cool.

"No thanks."

"You really think you're hot shit, don't you?"

"Don't think it, know it," Karla said, looking down at her yellow fingernails.

"How about you, Becky? You think you're hot shit too?"

"Me? No." Becky glanced at Karla and rubbed the peanut salt off her fingers onto her khakis.

"Dance?"

"Okay." Becky's voice was high. She was frightened. She'd never danced before. Well, once. With her father.

Poor Becky, Karla thought. She has no idea that jerk thought she had a face like a horse. Well, it was only a dance.

Becky didn't look like a horse anymore, though. In Chip's arms she looked like she had been transported to heaven. They made an odd couple. He was over six feet tall and Becky was barely five-four. He was blonde all over, perfect except for the braces. She . . . well, she was Rivka Gilbert. He held her close, and even though Karla knew he was faking it, she was kind of happy for Becky. No one ever paid any attention to her. So what if it was only make-believe? Not everyone could have something real like she had with Charles.

Just the thought of him sent tingles up her spine.

"Dance?"

"No, thank you." Danno Roth was another one. Thought he was God's gift.

"Aren't you dancing at all?" he asked.

"No," she said, very nonchalant.

"Then why did you come here?"

"To be with Becky."

Danno glanced at Becky who looked as contented as a cow. "You're not doing a very good job of it."

"What do you mean?"

"Well, you're alone and she's not."

She danced with him. He tried to hold her close but she kept putting distance between them. Lots of it. When they danced close she could feel his hard-on and she knew what that was all about. She didn't like it, not one single bit.

In the process of dancing to a few songs she lost Becky. She knew the girl wouldn't leave without her. She was annoyed, and concerned. Where the hell was she?

During the wait, she accepted dances with three other boys. None of them thrilled her, but what was she going to do? Where was Becky? And Chip?

Karla was just about ready to leave when Becky came rushing out from where the bathrooms were. Jesus Christ, Karla thought.

"Where were you?" she asked.

"Let's go outside," Becky whispered.

"What happened?" Karla asked, walking her outside. She noticed that Becky looked great, flushed and warm and happy. Her clothes weren't quite as neat as they had been, but she made an interesting picture.

"Chip let me touch his thing. You know, like you and your mystery lover."

"Uh-oh."

"What's the matter, Karla? You do it."

"But we love each other. I mean he loves me."

"You don't think Chip... Oh, Karla, he was so sweet."

Karla looked in Becky's eyes and saw absolute innocence. Total naïveté. The girl was dense, real dense.

"Let's go for a hot chocolate, Becky. Okay?"

"Sure."

• XXII •

Karla was the closest Charles had ever come to making a pass at a woman since he'd married. He had reached for her. He had embraced her. He had wanted her in much the same way a child wants a confection in a dessert shop. But she, Karla Kingsley, had made it happen. It was the way she had rubbed against him. The way she had walked around practically naked. The way she had licked her lips when she spoke to him. He had made the overture, but she conducted the symphony.

Ashley had done none of that. The sex goddess was quite happy baking brownies and admiring all the *objets trouvé* that Charles and Elizabeth Anne had collected on their tours of Europe. She seemed quite content listening to war stories. Ashley Pope was the first woman who did not seem to want him only for his body.

That made him feel good, confident. Not that he didn't desire her. Oh yes indeed, desire was the key to Charles's psyche. But for some reason with Ashley he was able to put it away. He knew where it was and could call on it at a moment's notice. In a way, for the first time in his life, he was totally at ease with a woman.

When the evening ended, it just ended. No painful words of love and make-believe promises like he had with Karla. Nothing like the interrogation that Elizabeth Anne put him through. It simply ended.

The next day Charles had Arnie send her flowers.

"Two dozen daisies, one dozen white roses, two dozen lilies of the valley, and a handful of babies' breath. And sign it *Thank you, CAL.*" Then he thought for a moment. "Have them add calla lilies to that too."

Arnie nodded. He didn't have to be told that under no circumstances should the bouquet be able to be traced back to Charles. Arnie knew the rules, and was generously rewarded for following them.

With opening night just a week away, Robbie had to work quickly. The first thing they had to agree upon was the church. He had been raised Baptist but didn't much care for their brand of Christianity. He'd rather go for Pentecostal. Yes, Pentecostal would be good. But Ashley had to agree. After all, she was the light, the descendent of the covenant.

He arrived at Ashley's apartment Monday morning in hot pursuit of some answers. The doorman, who was used to Robbie's nocturnal visits and early morning departures, thought nothing of this reversal. In fact, he told Robbie that Ashley hadn't even called down for her morning dose of cappuccino yet. He smiled at Robbie. "So you know we give preferential treatment to our stars. I just ordered a cup for her."

"You want me to bring it up?" Robbie asked, winking and slipping the guy a ten.

"Sure," the doorman said. "But do me a favor."

"Sure. What do you want?"

"Take these flowers up for me."

"You've got it," Robbie said, beginning to understand why God had brought him there that morning. Obviously the Lord was on his side, showing him that someone else was after Ashley too. Someone who signed his name CAL.

"Who's there?" Ashley asked when he rang the bell.

"Messenger."

That's who Ashley was expecting when she opened the door. Not Robbie Haskins.

"Am I disturbing you?" he asked courteously.

"Well..." She didn't know what to say. "No." She looked at the flowers and thought they were from him. "For me?"

"Yes. They were downstairs."

"And the doorman gave them to you?" She'd have to speak to that doorman.

"He knew I wouldn't run off with them."

"Robbie, I just got up." She didn't dare open the card in his presence, fearful he might have the same response he'd had to that creep who wanted her autograph in Little Italy.

"Ashley," he said, bending over to kiss her.

"Robbie, I'm so beat." She unwrapped the flowers. They were breathtaking. "God, aren't these gorgeous?"

"They are. Who are they from?"

"I don't know."

"Why don't you look?"

At first she couldn't. She knew how jealous he was. But then she changed her mind. She wasn't going to let him frighten her. These flowers were for her. She read the note and smiled.

"A friend?" he asked.

"Yes, a friend."

"Ashley," he said, sitting down and making himself comfortable, "I was thinking about the wedding."

She looked at him blankly.

"How do you feel about a Pentecostal ceremony? There's that beautiful church on Fifth Avenue."

"Marriage? Are you nuts?"

"Ashley..."

"Robbie," she said, sitting down next to him. "Do you read lips? Marriage is a serious endeavor. It has to do with lots more than what goes on between our legs." She giggled. "Although what is going on between our legs is just great."

"Did you fuck him?"

"Who?"

"Cal."

"Look, Robbie, I'm playing Isadora, remember? Broadway." She fell back on her ditzy routine. "I can't get married now, babes."

"When?"

She sighed and it seemed he read her mind.

"Never," he said petulantly. "You don't ever plan on marrying me, do you?" He saw the light leave her. That's what had happened, he realized. This whole thing with the play was dedeifying her.

She sighed again.

Always tell the truth, boy. There is redemption in the truth.

"Who is he?" he asked as if he didn't know.

"Who?" She played innocent.

"The cocksucker who sent you the flowers. That new guy. That's what it is, isn't it? This new guy has stolen you from me."

"Robbie," she cooed. If anyone knew how to make things right it was the Pope. "Robbie." She came close to him and tried to kiss him. For the first time he saw her darkness. "No one has stolen me from you, Robbie. You're still one of my very favorite people in the whole world." That made him feel a little better. But he saw through her.

Redeem yourself, woman. So many times Uncle Earl had begged his mama to seek salvation, but his mama was stubborn. Just like Ashley. Maybe they were all evil, these women.

"You don't understand, do you?" he said.

The look in his eyes frightened her. "No."

"You will," he said, and left.

"I'm back." Janice's voice was up and bright and happy. Ecstatic, even.

"Hi," Vince said, not quite as ecstatic. "Did you have a good time?"

Yes, she'd had a good time. Time to think over her decision. Time to decide not to be rash. Time to recommit her love.

"Yes, and I think we should celebrate with dinner."

"Good. Let me take you out." He hoped she couldn't hear that the words were sticking in his throat. "There's a great new place in NoHo." Taking her out would make him feel better. Less guilty. Less intimate.

"Uh-uh," she said, refusing the offer. "Mom gave me a new recipe for lasagna."

"Janice, please let me take you out."

"Lasagna. My place. Eight."

"Eight it is."

When Charles asked Karla if she was on the pill, she lied. Not that she wanted to get pregnant. It was just that Karla Kingsley never really considered that she could get pregnant. At fifteen, reality isn't a very big priority.

But now it was.

Reality, whether acknowledged or not, always surfaced. She had gone down to the lab for a test, to see if she and her beloved had actually made a baby, and found out, proof positive, that she was about to become a mother.

The doctor's office had called Monday afternoon to tell her the news. Five minutes later the doorman rang to tell her that Becky was in the lobby.

♦ XXIII ♦

Olive was like a child, a little girl at Christmas. For the first time in years she was allowing herself to dream, to feel excited, to be in love. Vince had brought it all back, and it was distracting her dreadfully.

She had had trouble concentrating all day, partly because of her dreaming, partly because of reality. The lighting was so bad. She and Richard had both asked Robbie to correct the lights a few times, but he didn't seem to pay any attention. She was about to ask again when Vince came up to her, tapped her gently on the shoulder.

"Oh, Vince." Just seeing him made everything all right. "Richard, give me a second."

"You got it."

"Tell me what time." Her eyes were bright, joyous. He wanted only to kiss her, to touch her, but not here, not now.

"I have to work tonight, darling."

Immediately the light in her eyes dimmed. "Work?" She didn't understand. His work at this moment had to do with her. "Where?"

"Some more evidence has come in and..."

"Will there be someone else?"

He thought she meant Janice. How did she know?

"At the house?" she explained. "To stand guard." Why was he so slow on the uptake?

He took her hand. "Of course, darling. Of course."

"What's up?" Karla asked when she opened the door to Becky's bright, shiny face.

"Got the new Sting album," Becky said, entering the plush apartment. As usual, Becky presented herself like a neat package, as if her mother were still dressing her. "Thought you might like to hear it."

"Okay." Karla said. She was grateful for the company, yet not quite sure how to show it. "Let's take it into the bedroom."

"Don't you think Chip Johnson looks just like Sting?" Becky asked, handing Karla the album. Actually Karla was not interested in adolescent conversation. She couldn't care less about Chip Johnson or Sting or even Becky at that moment. She was carrying a baby and wasn't sure whether or not to be happy about it.

"Karla?"

"I think Chip looks as much like Sting as I do."

"What did I say wrong?" Becky was hurt. She just wanted Karla's opinion.

"For chrissakes, Becky, what do you see in him?" Her expression and voice were brutal, uncompromising. Becky had never seen Karla like that before.

"He's the most beautiful man I've ever seen."

"He's a dork," Karla said, in between cracks of gum.

"He is not. He said I made him feel good."

"Chip is a conceited jerk who just uses people. He doesn't care about anyone but himself."

"Are you saying he doesn't like me?"

Karla stopped cracking her gum. She couldn't believe how juvenile Becky was being. For a moment she was about to tell her the truth, how Chip had asked her once how she knew which horse to mount, but Karla didn't have the heart. Becky would have to learn the hard way.

"Karla?"

"He acts as if he likes you, but, Becky, all the girls in school like him."

"So, I'm not asking him to go steady."

"Becky, can we drop this for a moment?"

"Okay."

"Becky."

"What?"

Karla sat up straight on her bed and took the tired piece of gum from her mouth. "Becky..." She put on a smile. Maybe if she smiled she'd be as happy as she thought she was supposed to be. "I'm going to have a baby, Becky. Isn't that the most exciting thing you've ever heard in your life?"

"What do you mean, you're going to have a baby?"

"What do you mean, what do I mean? Read my lips. I . . . am . . . going . . . to . . . have . . . a . . . baby. You know. One of these." She made a cradle with her arms.

"Your mother will kill you."

"Who cares about my mother?" Karla popped a new piece of gum into her mouth. "It's—it's him I want to make happy."

"Who's him?" Becky asked, half expecting the answer to be Chip Johnson.

"Swear you won't tell anyone?"

Becky nodded, feeling sick and scared at the same time.

"Charles Long, the mayor."

"The mayor! He's . . . he's old enough to be your father."

"So?"

"Will he marry you?" Becky knew Karla was in trouble even if she didn't.

"Of course he'll marry me. He loves me."

"But isn't he already married?" Good old practical Becky.

"So what? People get divorced."

"But what if he doesn't want to?"

"I told you," Karla said, feeling frightened for the first time. "He loves me."

"Well, what did he say when you told him?"

Karla bit her lip. "I haven't told him."

"Why?"

"He's very bushed, Becky. The elections are coming up." Becky was not smiling, which bothered Karla a lot. "You're not smiling, Becky. What's the matter? Why aren't you happy for me?"

What Becky felt was nightmarish. How come Karla seemed unfazed by it? "What about school? And college?"

"I—I haven't thought about it." Karla was getting nervous. She began fingering the curtains, then reached into her night table and took out another stick of gum.

"What will your mother say?"

"Becky, stop asking me about my goddamn mother. I don't care about college and I don't care about what my mother says. Don't you understand? The most wonderful man in the world loves me and I'm going to have his baby."

"But he's married and—and you're just a kid."

She wasn't a kid, Karla thought. Becky was. Which was why Becky couldn't understand. Becky had never had love. What did she know? "The only reason you don't understand is because you've never had a man love you the way Charles loves me."

"You're right, Karla, I haven't." Karla had made her angry. Insulted her. "But I will. I'm only fifteen. And so are you." She spoke with natural practicality. "And besides I don't need an old man to love me. I have my father."

No, Karla would not tolerate this. Calling Charles old. Suggesting he might not want to divorce Aunt Liz. She wouldn't tolerate this at all.

"Get out of here!" she yelled. "I thought you'd be screaming with joy for me and instead you've done nothing but ask a bunch of stupid questions. I know what's wrong with you. You're jealous. You're just jealous because you don't have anyone. Not even jerky Chip Johnson."

Becky's expression became tearful.

"You know what he said?" Karla was beyond reason now. "He told me you had a face like a horse. He wanted to be with me at that dance, but I wouldn't go out with such an asshole. He's just using you to get what he wants."

Becky's lower lip quivered and the tears started. "Give me my album," she said. Karla would never be her friend again. Never, ever, ever. She'd never let her. Even if she apologized. She grabbed the album and ran out of the apartment, ran out of the building.

Karla? Karla had nowhere to go.

It would have been so much easier, Vince thought, if Janice had allowed him to take her out to dinner. That way they wouldn't be in the environment they had shared together. But she didn't make it easy. She didn't know it was over.

For the first time in two years he knocked.

"Did you forget your key, darling?" she asked, opening the door. She didn't give him a chance to answer. "Miss me?" She held on tightly.

"Of course," he said, and it was the truth. How could he not miss her? They had been a part of each other for two years.

She took his hand and led him over to the couch. "I thought and thought and thought."

"And?" He was tired. Worn. He had been thinking too.

"And I decided that I'm glad you met her. It was a way to clear up the past."

He was silent.

"Vince?"

"Yes, sweetheart."

"We still have a date in four weeks, don't we?"

He hesitated.

"Vince?"

"Janice... Janice, I need time."

"Tell me the truth," she said, not meaning a word of it. "Have you seen Olive?"

"Yes, Janice. I have."

The air didn't move. Nothing in the room moved.

"On the case," he added. "Yes. And then personally."

The last admission stopped her like a blow.

"Do—do you love her?" she asked.

"I don't know."

That more than stopped her. It ate away her heart. She got up from the couch. She needed to move.

"Vince," she said, walking over to a table. "I bought us something when I was away. No big thing, but I thought they were fun. Matching sweatshirts." They were oversized and the message on the front read Don't Postpone Joy. "Would you like yours?" Maybe if she didn't talk about it, if she didn't push it . . .

He stood up and faced her. He didn't want to hurt her, but this was worse. "Janice."

"What, darling?"

"It won't work. I think we shouldn't postpone pain either. Janice . . ."

In a silent protest she pressed her finger against his mouth.

"Please," she said, using all her control not to cry. "Give it some thought."

He didn't need any thought. Not after yesterday morning.

"Vince?"

"What is it, sweetheart?"

"Let's not discuss it. Just wait. And know that I love you, really love you."

Elizabeth Anne sat quietly. Very, very quietly. Maybe if she didn't move or didn't make a sound no one would notice.

But they do. Especially when you don't show up.

She pulled out Babs's column and reread it.

> ***Babs says:*** Trouble in Paradise? While all predictions anticipate a landslide in the upcoming mayoral election, one must remember that not everyone can keep up the pace. Yours truly, Joan Kennedy, and, of course, the courageous Betty Ford included. Some might also include Elizabeth Anne Manchester Long in that group.
>
> Apparently the mayor's wife missed an appearance as guest of honor at "21" yesterday. No call either. Elizabeth Anne's social secretary said the telephone lines to the famed restaurant were busy and she

couldn't get through to cancel. She added that Mrs. Long had caught a bug and wanted to save her strength for the upcoming events. She was referring, of course, to Liz Anne's pet project—the opening of *Isadora, Isadora*—and her gala anniversary party. Well, we hope her staggering schedule won't lead to a more staggering swagger, which is how some observers have seen her of late. Not to worry. Dr. Babs suggests a day in bed with a good book.

Actually Elizabeth Anne was quite pleased with the column.

It should make him lose, she thought. Yes, lose. Then this would all go away. She got up from the bed and mixed herself another drink.

She was bombed and didn't care two figs. It was nighttime. Liquor was the only pleasure she had left. She was about to go downstairs to open the package that had arrived earlier, but then she heard the car. His car.

Please let it be his.

She looked outside just in time to see a premature blast of winter whipping its way around the trees. And then Charles. Tall and slim. Movie-star handsome. Yes, the prize. He was definitely the prize.

She heard him take the stairs two at a time. That loud thumping was almost like a teenage boy's. He was still young. Would always be young. Virile. She? She was a rag. What good was breeding now?

Dare she speak? She must. Another drink would help her speak. He came into the bedroom and began to undress, this husband, this god. He started with his tie and she watched him with longing.

"Time was you'd let me do that," she said, no longer able to contain herself.

"Do what?" He was tired. Yesterday with Ashley. Today with the press. Tomorrow with Cuomo. All the time fending off Karla's calls, Karla's needs, his desires. God, he was tired.

"Undress you."

"I'm tired, Elizabeth Anne." He tried to be gentle. She was sick.

She reached over the edge of the bed for the short fat glass of whiskey and soda sitting on the carpet and sipped a little. It was just the ice cube she really wanted. To suck on. She was dry. Why didn't whiskey ever quench her thirst?

"You saw Babs's column today?" he asked matter-of-factly.

Why wasn't he yelling at her? It was a confirmation that there was another woman.

"Yes."

"What happened?"

She shrugged and sipped some more.

With frightening control he took the glass from her. There was no violence in it. He just took it, her only pleasure.

"Don't . . . do . . . that," she said, trying to contain the rage. Why did she always have to be the one to contain it? "Is she younger than me? Is that what it is?"

Charles gave her back the glass, then put his hands on her shoulders. That look. He had that look again. Pity.

"No!" she screamed. "Don't look at me that way!"

"Elizabeth Anne, please. Sunshine." He was begging. He didn't want a scene. Not now. It was almost midnight. "Sunshine, please."

She was back in California and he was telling her that her presence outshone everything else. That she was sunshine. How many years ago was it? How could she recapture them?

"I'm sorry, Sunshine. You have a right to be angry." He spoke with a sigh. Yes, he'd give her up. Karla. He had to. But now Ashley, Ashley . . . "I was with Jed. The budget meeting was canceled. We had to go over the last month of campaigning." It was the truth.

Lies, she thought. She couldn't bear them. He thought she was a fool.

"Charles . . . I know."

"Dammit," he said, cursing her tears. "What do you know? That I work twice as many hours as any other man?

That you live better than any other woman? So much better that when you're asked to do something, like a luncheon, you can't even do that?" He was yelling now. "You knew what you were getting into when we got married!"

She had gone too far this time. She knew it. Why had she confronted him? Didn't she know better? She had breeding. He had none. He was excused. She was not. Now he would leave her.

He had gone too far. He knew it. He shouldn't have thrown it up in her face. Fucking press. They drag your life through the gutter. No privacy. What if they found out he was screwing a fifteen-year-old? What if they found out that he wanted to, planned to make it with a superstar? What if they found out . . .

"I still love you, Charles. I just want to know what I did wrong." She spoke as if she were sucking on ice cubes. Her mouth was twisted, distorted with pain, with liquor. "Please tell me what I did wrong."

"Let me tuck you in, Sunshine."

"You're not sleepy?"

Exhausted. "It's early, Sunshine. Maybe a little food and then I'll come upstairs. Do we have any milk? I'd like to get a glass of milk."

Elizabeth Anne smiled a wide smile which pleased him. He hated seeing her so sad, so lost.

"What's making you smile?" he asked.

"You're just like an overgrown kid," she said, and the tears started again "I know it's not your fault. It's just that you're still a kid and I'm ready to be a grown-up."

He looked at her and for a moment was transported back in time, too. To California. To sunshine. To when they were both kids.

"I know what you think," he said, embracing her. "I know. But you must believe you're very dear to me. So very dear."

"Then why do you hurt me so much?" She hadn't meant to say it. It just spilled out. It didn't matter. He was already halfway downstairs.

Charles reached the vestibule and saw a package that had been left for him. There was no postmark. It was probably delivered by a messenger. He ripped the brown wrapping off and looked for a note.

Nothing. Just a cardboard box. Inside was a video. Apparently someone wanted him to watch a movie.

It wasn't that Charles had forgotten the film. One never forgets the triumphs and indiscretions of youth. Especially not Charles Andrew Long who had received his last name from the length of his sex. But Charles, in becoming politic, knew the advantages of keeping such indiscretions hidden. So when he'd transformed himself from stud to politician, he moved this trophy to the back of his closet, expecting to take it out like an old photograph when he became incontinent, impotent, ready for the grave. He would call on it to remind him that there *had* been a past, that life *had* been lived. That indeed it wasn't just a dream.

But Charles was neither impotent nor old. Nor was he defeated. He was planning on the presidency. This could change everything. The past could annihilate his future. The film was not a surprise. The surprise was the moment. Why now? And why was there no note?

He watched, knowing exactly what to expect, knowing exactly what he'd see.

There was that girl. That sweet bleached-blonde who was so angry at the world that all she wanted to do was fuck it and everyone in it. Charles was merely an instrument.

He watched, recalling it all. She was naked. He was not. She undressed him. Someone ordered her to suck him. She did, quite terribly, he remembered. Much too rough, as if she had the tongue of a cat. Funny how all that came back to him. It could have been yesterday. That's how life was, either yesterday or tomorrow.

On the screen he played with the blonde, touched her, put his mouth on her sex. Then they wanted her to turn over. He remembered it was the first time he ever came that way, from behind. He remembered it all. It had been haunting him all these years. Not the event, but that he had allowed it to be captured on celluloid.

Then it stopped being memory. The film went on longer than he recalled. He didn't remember his dick pumping away while his hand held tightly to her throat. The director cut to his cock, to her torso, to her face. Then to his hands. Then . . . oh, my God. She was dead. The angry young blonde was dead.

He stared in disbelief, utter disbelief. He wanted to go up to the screen and yell that it couldn't be true, but he didn't. He couldn't. But somehow it was wrong.

How many other people had seen this print? And what did they want of him? This wasn't just a matter of winning the election. It was a matter of . . . Christ.

Charles began to do what anyone in his position would do. He played reruns in his mind of all the people who hated him. There hadn't been all that many really.

♦ XXIV ♦

Janice cried. She cried and talked to her friends, then she cried some more. They told her to wait, to give him a few days. Yes, that's what she'd do. Give him a few days. In the meantime, she'd think of other things, distract herself. And she would have been able to had it not been for the *Post* on Friday. She read Babs's column, then looked at the pictures.

> ***Babs says:*** Backstage, *Isadora, Isadora* gets more interesting every day. Between producers dying, a real-life love affair between the star and the lighting designer, what more icing could we ask for than Olive Kingsley, who hasn't been linked with anyone since ill-fated Eliot Warner, having a new man? Look to the right and you'll catch our prima ballerina skating with a tall, gray-haired, mystery man. Oh, some girls have all the luck. (Didn't I say that last week?)

Alongside the column was a picture with the caption: Stunning Olive doing a perfect *pas de deux* with a handsome stranger.

Janice couldn't believe her eyes. Her stomach knotted painfully as if to remind her that part of her was dead. Nevermore. *I'll fix her.*

She went into her bedroom, took out a wedding invitation, and addressed it to Olive Kingsley/Longacre Theatre/West Forty-eighth Street.

Don't do it.

Yes, that was what she'd do. She'd hurt Olive as Olive had hurt her.

You'll be sorry.

No, she wouldn't send it. She'd deliver it herself.

"Previdi. That's his last name." Louie the Lip laughed.

"What's so funny?" Nick asked nastylike. He didn't take kindly to jokes that he wasn't in on.

"He's not a porn star."

"No? Then what is he?"

"The don's son."

"The don? Which one?"

"Previdi, you asshole. Certainly not Giambelli."

Suddenly Nick felt on top of the world. "Whenever you need something you come to me, Lou. You understand?"

"Sure, kid."

Elizabeth Anne's mother called them the Blue Meanies. It was her name for a woman's period. Like mother, like daughter. From the start Elizabeth Anne had suffered from the same pain, the same cramps, the same blues that her mother had. Even after all these years, when her period came, she still felt very blue and very, very mean.

Not even martinis could make her feel better. That was how serious it was.

The only one who could make her feel better was Charles. But he wasn't there. Even when he was there, he wasn't. So she sat alone. Watching out the window. Filing her nails. Washing her hair. Drinking. Waiting.

Then she remembered the package that had been delivered that morning. It looked like the one Charles had received earlier in the week. She wondered what was in it. A gift from his mistress? She considered taking a peek, but didn't dare.

Another martini and there wasn't even a question.

It wasn't from his mistress. Inside the brown paper was a box. Inside that was a videotape. She had some entertainment for the night, she thought. Great. Quickly, excitedly, she took it into the study. Time was short and her husband could return any minute.

At first she couldn't believe it, and then when she did she felt nauseated. It wasn't watching Charles having sex with a young girl that made her sick, it was being carried back in time. Back to when they were happy, before he became a goddamn celeb. That's what made her sick. Lately she had begun to think it had been an illusion, their earlier life together. He'd looked like that when the two of them were happy, hopeful. And they'd still be that way if it weren't for this damn public persona she had to wear.

Yes, it made her sick, so after five minutes she turned it off, methodically placed the tape back in its case, and reloaded the first one into the VCR. She stared at the tape for a minute, and then elation flooded through her. She had found the way to keep Charles from being reelected. She had found the way to return to a normal life, a life of love and privacy.

Feeling quite pleased with herself, Elizabeth Anne placed the tape in the bottom of a small Tiffany shopping bag and wrote her favorite newscaster's name on it. She'd have a messenger deliver it the next day. Then for the first time that day Elizabeth Anne smiled. The Blue Meanies were lifting. A bubble bath should make them go away completely.

Karla was so excited when she got home Friday afternoon and Sam handed her a package, she opened it up right there in front of him.

"It's a teddy bear!" she screamed. "He sent me a teddy bear. A real teddy bear."

She was so excited she didn't wait to hear Sam tell her it wasn't a he at all. Her sweet, slightly plump girl friend had left it for her about an hour ago. Karla practically flew up in the elevator all ready to call him and thank him. But when she got in the phone was ringing.

"Did you get it?" Becky asked.

"How did you know?"

"Because I left it. I bought it for you."

"You?" Karla couldn't hide her disappointment. "Oh, I thought it was from . . ."

"Charles?"

"Yes. We had a date last night and he broke it and I thought this was to make up."

"Oh, well he's busy with the election." Becky tried to sound sincere. "He'll probably call you tomorrow."

"I told him I had a surprise for him," Karla said, feeling dazed.

"I bet he'll be really happy, Karla."

"You think so, Becky?"

No, she didn't, but she also hated being without a friend. "Of course."

"Oh, Becky, you're back. I missed you. It was hell without you. Come over. Please."

"Fab," Becky squealed. It was good to have a best friend again.

"And Becky?"

"Yes?"

"I'm sorry I said all those things. None of them were true."

Becky didn't believe that either, but she was happy to hear it anyway.

Vince had been dreaming of Olive all day. Having told Janice about her made him feel cleaner, better. He still didn't know how to end it, but . . . Well, he didn't want to worry about that now. He wanted Olive. He hadn't been able to think of anything else since their morning of love. She went everywhere with him. He felt her, tasted her, craved her, couldn't have been more thrilled when he saw her emerge from the stage door.

"Perfect timing, wouldn't you say?" He was about to

kiss her on her nose, but she walked right past him. She didn't even say hello.

"Olive?" Maybe rehearsals had upset her.

She didn't stop, and he chased after her like a lovesick boy. "Hey, slow down."

Then he saw the envelope she was carrying. He recognized the stationery that he and Janice had picked out together, but he still didn't get it. It didn't register that Olive Kingsley should not be holding an invitation to his wedding. Stupidly he ran in front of her. He expected her to kiss him but instead she handed him the pretty pink envelope. And then he understood.

Morbid curiosity made him open it up anyway. Just as they had for her, the words reverberated in his brain.

Janice Alison Canfield and Vincent James Luscardi invite you to . . .

"Olive, wait, I can explain." But it was too late. She was getting into a taxi, leaving him. Well, he would do the same. He hailed a taxi. Following Olive was not his objective, though. Going to Janice's apartment was.

The wait was driving Charles mad. Every day he expected a letter, a phone call, something.

Nothing.

He went over all the possibilities. While Harv Monroe, his opponent in the mayoral election, didn't hate him, he would certainly benefit from exposing Charles to the world as a porn star. But that was ridiculous. If Monroe wanted to eliminate Charles from the election, all he'd have to do is release the film to the press. So it couldn't be Monroe.

Women? He thought back to Sybil, the woman he had left for Elizabeth Anne. She had found a new guy immediately. No, it wasn't Sybil.

He considered the cast in the film, the director. Jack had had sixteen years to blackmail him. Why now? The girl? Unless they were faking it, she was dead. Who else was there? No crew really. A cameraman, a stylist. But again, why now? And why no note?

Charles watched the film over and over again. He knew

how it was done. Some sicko had gone in after the filming was over, reshot the last scene, and changed the ending. That's how all snuff films were done. Just the victim and the murderer present. That way there could be no witnesses. But whoever did it needed access to the original. Who was it? And why now? That was the question. Why now?

It was becoming an obsession. An obsession as powerful as drugs or booze or sex. And the results were the same. It took the life right out of him.

One thing was for sure, regardless of what the law said, Charles Andrew Long would be guilty until proven innocent. Just like in the old days.

The nuns moved Charles around as if he were a piece of furniture in a decorating scheme. They sent him from family to family, year in and year out. When he was seventeen it was the Livingstons. Grace Livingston was sweet and motherly, a real homemaker. A meat and potatos kind of gal. On her it showed. On Charles it didn't. He was lean and tall, like her husband John. Grace called him Daddy.

Every day Daddy went out to the phone company to climb up poles. Every day Grace went into Charles's room and tried to climb on him.

Charles didn't mind, as long as she paid him. One dollar to give him a blowjob, two for a fuck, and four if she wanted him to do it to her.

One day Daddy came home early. He found Charles with lipstick on his cock and Grace begging for more. Daddy picked up a baseball bat, but Charles was fast. He just took the money and ran. Right back to the orphanage.

He met Arnie there. They were two overage orphans who had had it with orders and nuns and frustrated housewives. So they hitched out to California.

Charles met a hooker who took a liking to him. Arnie decided to go for the big time, boxing. He had nothing to lose. Certainly he was no beauty. Charles was too pretty to fight. But they stayed in touch. They were both survivors from the same prison.

While Arnie learned to fight, Charles learned to love. When he became an expert he moved on to Sybil. She was no hooker, but she was rich and she liked to share. She paid his rent, sent him to college, bought him clothes and jewelry.

But Charles had a taste for the kinky. It seemed to be in his blood. When he met Jack Gilbert and Jack asked him if he'd like to star in a movie for five hundred bucks, Charles asked him what he'd have to do.

"Screw a blonde."

"Hell, yes."

"Can you travel?"

"Do bears shit in the woods?"

"Tijuana?"

"Sure. Why not?"

Well, now he found out why not.

"Arnie?"

"What's up, Charlie?" Arnie was the only one ever permitted to call Charles Charlie.

"I want you to see something."

Arnie, his faithful driver, came up to the mansion, sat down in the study, and loosened his collar.

"This is very important to me, Arnie. Someone is trying to blackmail me."

Arnie didn't like that. Let him find the guy who was trying to screw up Charles's success and he'd kill him. It would be easy, and quiet. No one would know.

"Now I want you to watch this movie and I'll explain what's happening. And why."

"Okay, boss."

Charles turned on the tape and when they got to the end he explained how he didn't do it. How he was being set up. How terrified he was.

Arnie nodded as if he understood, but he didn't. It really didn't make any sense to him why Charles was lying, and to him of all people. He didn't care. It didn't matter to Arnie if Charles murdered ten broads. Or if it happened twenty years ago or last week. He owed this man his life, his respectability. The fact that he could take good care of his wife and kids was all due to Charles. He owed this man everything.

But for some reason Charles wanted Arnie to believe that he was innocent, so Arnie went along with it. He nodded and smiled and yessed him a lot. And Charles understood just how much trouble he was in. He knew that if Arnie didn't believe him, no one would.

Wrong. Ashley Pope would.

This time Vince didn't knock. He walked in, just as in the old days. He found Janice curled up in a chair. He wondered how she'd gotten out of it to deliver the invitation.

"Vince!" He was life to her. She started to get up, then remembered the message. "Don called and said that you should call him immediately. Vince, it's great to see you in the middle of the afternoon like this."

He didn't respond. He picked up the phone and called Don.

"Vince?"

"What's up, Don?"

"You free tonight? There's something I'd like you to take a look at."

"What?"

"Big. Can't talk about it on the phone."

"How about eight? You want me to meet you at your television station?" Janice had gotten up and was wrapping herself around him, as if he were a Maypole.

"Yeah, eight is fine."

Newsmen like to have friends in the law and vice versa. It's a way of getting leaks, of getting an inside scoop. But with Don Green and Vince Luscardi it was more than that. They were buddies. It was part fatherly but mostly friendly. Vince liked the newsman's style. It was human, nonplastic. Don deserved the exposure and accolades he was finally getting.

Hanging up and having two hands free, Vince unwrapped Janice as easily and as naturally as if she were a minor inconvenience he had entangled himself with. Then he held up the invitation. It felt glued to his fingers, as it had been to Olive's.

"Vince?"

"Why did you do it?"

"Why? Why?" She opened the top drawer of the breakfront and took out the *Post* clipping. "This is why," she said, handing him the picture.

He took it from her and saw Olive's innocent eyes staring into his. Olive. Yes, it was Olive he wanted.

"You never looked at me that way," Janice said. "Never."

"Why didn't you come to me with this? Why did you have to hurt her in this way?"

"I couldn't," she said. "I . . . suppose I stopped trusting you. And I had to find out what she really meant to you."

Whatever guilt he may have felt about Janice was gone. Rage took over, pure animal rage.

"You want to know what she meant to me?" he yelled. "Well, since you went to so much trouble to find out, I'll tell you. In one word, everything. Every-fucking-thing." The envelope was no longer stuck. He ripped the invitation into a dozen tiny pieces, and with it he ripped Janice's heart in two.

"I can't marry you." He spoke softly now. "It wouldn't be fair to either of us." His voice was hollow, empty. There was nothing for her, only emptiness. Barrenness. Nothing.

"I can't live without you." It made her sick but it was true. Her hands shook, her stomach was in turmoil. "I love you."

"You do?" He walked over to her and the look in his eyes made her flinch.

"Vince?"

Without a word he slipped her key into her hand and wrapped her fingers around it. "You can leave my clothes . . ." She hugged herself tightly as she watched him walk toward the door. ". . . downstairs. I . . ." There was nothing. She was nothing. ". . . won't be back." He slammed the door behind him.

* * *

Robbie knew snakes wore many suits. Tonight Charles wore Daniel Hechter.

Charles had Arnie drive him and Ashley around. Charles needed her, her advice, her street-smarts, her comfort. They talked for more than an hour, then Arnie parked across the street from Ashley's apartment building. The limousine's tinted windows prevented anyone from looking in.

"I'd like to kiss you," Charles said.

"Yes," Ashley said.

Cupping her chin in his hand, he tilted her face upward. At first it was a mere brushing of the lips. Then—then there was that exquisite thrill that accompanies the perfect kiss. She wanted more, much more. And she knew she'd have it.

Yes, the devil wears many suits, but Robbie recognized them all. Patience. No one had more patience than Robbie. He stood in a doorway three buildings down and watched the mayor's limousine pull away. It was obvious his work was cut out for him.

• XXV •

Saying that the Previdis controlled L.A. was a nice way of saying that everyone was on the take. The cops. The clubs. The unions. Everyone.

Saying that the Giambellis were second in command was like naming the runner-up in a Miss America contest. So what? Unless Numero Uno is caught doing a threesome in *Playboy*, number two is just another also-ran. So the Giambellis got to play bully to any action not big enough for the Previdis to protect one hundred percent. Which pissed Carlos Giambelli off. After all, why the hell should Previdi take the biggest share? And who the fuck was Previdi anyway?

Periodically there were wars. But the eighties were peaceful times. No bloodbaths in L.A. Still Carlos Giambelli never really forgave his *paisano*, Sam, for owning it all. For getting the territory, the girl, the money, the family. God had even blessed him with five sons.

Oh, Giambelli got a girl, but not *the* girl. Money? Yes, but less of it. Sons? No. Daughters? He had six of them. So there wasn't even a chance of one of his offspring getting the number one spot. Well, maybe if the girls married the right boys. But they didn't. And Giambelli's grandchildren were all girls, too. No fucking luck.

So when Carlos Giambelli got the picture of Buddy Previdi sucking a guy's dick he was elated. For the first time in years he considered himself lucky. He may not have had sons, but he didn't have pansies either. It gave him a chuckle to know Previdi's youngest son was a *coulitoni*, an honest-to-goodness *finòcchio*.

Carlos made a copy of the picture for himself and had his man drive the original over to the Previdi estate. Let Sam put that in his pipe and smoke it.

"So what am I looking at?" Vince asked Don.

"You're going to tell me."

"Why? Is it so difficult to figure out?" Vince lit a Lucky and put his feet up on the desk.

"No. As a matter of fact, it's simple. So simple it's eerie. And before I do anything about it I need an opinion."

"You got it."

Don inserted the video. The colors displayed themselves and then the action began.

"Does that guy look familiar to you?" Don asked. "The guy mounting the broad."

Vince said nothing.

"Does that not look like the honorable Charles Andrew Long?"

Vince continued to puff away.

"Vince?"

Ever spend much time in Hollywood?

Vince watched. Yeah, it was Long all right. And he was pumping it to his Angelique. Vince puffed and watched, watched and waited. Waited until Charles put his hand around Angelique's neck and snuffed out her life.

"Vince, what do we do?"

What do we do? We hang him by his balls. We fucking kill him. Cut his heart out. But Vince Luscardi was a professional. He kept quiet.

"I'll call you tomorrow. Don't let that film out of your sight."

"Where are you going?" Don asked, but the phone rang before he could get his answer.

Good question, Vince thought. Where was he going? He drove around like a wild man, then finally went to the only place he could go. To the only woman who would understand all of this.

Connie was surprised to see him. Vince never just dropped in on her. Sometimes he called. Sometimes after a really bad girlie murder, if Tommy wasn't home, he'd come over and she would make him lasagna. Tommy had replaced Vince as husband and had even given her the children she wanted. He wouldn't have liked Vince just dropping by like this.

"What's wrong?" she asked. He looked terrible. His face was washed out, bleached pale like Angelique's hair. Expressionless, as if he were in shock.

He didn't wait to be invited in. He simply entered. "I found her."

She knew. "Angelique."

He nodded. "I saw the film."

"Vince, sit down."

He didn't hear. He told her what he saw. That the film was sent to Don. What was in it. Well, he edited it some. She knew that, and it was okay. She didn't want the truth and nothing but the truth. This was her daughter. Their daughter. And he'd seen her die.

"Should I see it?" she asked, shaking her head. She wasn't sure she could withstand seeing the horror that shone in his eyes.

"No." He spoke loudly. But why was his vision clouded? Oh, the tears. They were running down his cheeks. Quietly. Painlessly. She was coming toward him to hold him. "It was awful." His voice was gruff, hoarse. Angry. "But I saw him. The killer."

"Why?"

"What do you mean, why?" His tears were nowhere near stopping.

"Why did they send this to the television station and not the police?"

"I—I don't know. Hadn't thought about it." Not like Vince Luscardi not to think about something like that. It meant he was too close. He wasn't observing it. He was in it.

"Who is the killer anyway?" Connie's face was dribbled with blue and black streaks from her eyes. As Angelique's had been the last time he saw her.

"Can't tell... you." His tears were stopping, the sobs were slowing down a bit.

"Vince..."

He looked at her. She was the rational one, the logician, the fighter. Sometimes he thought she would have made a better detective than he.

"He's famous. Too famous. That's why I can't tell."

"Well, then, if he's famous, why didn't they go to him? Perhaps to blackmail him. Why send a film to the news without a note? What do you think they hoped would happen?" She always felt better when she could ask questions. She thought that meant she was figuring things out, making sense of it all.

There wasn't any sense. "Don't know," he said. "One of two things could have happened. One was that they'd call in the police. But because it was me and not the local cops there's a chance that the investigation could be quiet. The other is that T.V. could let it leak to the press which would force the T.V. station to perhaps air part of the movie. That's unlikely."

"Why?"

"Because when you're dealing with someone well known you don't just expose them. You have to get in touch with them first. If the public were to get hold of something like that they'd indict him in a second."

"Vince."

"Hold me," he said.

She stroked his face, her eyes not leaving his. There were

crow's-feet she hadn't noticed before. New strands of gray, frown lines that had become a permanent accessory. A slight puffiness around his eyes, puffiness she'd never seen before.

"Vince?"

"What, Connie?"

"Promise me that you'll call."

He pulled away. "What do you mean?"

"After this is over you'll call. I mean every few months."

Now it was his turn to stroke her. "Why do you say that? Of course I'll call."

"There won't be any girlie murders, but you'll come over for lasagna?" It was a plea, an acknowledgment that it was, finally and completely, over for them. The search was over.

"Connie, of course."

"Promise."

"I promise."

"Where are you going now?" she asked.

"To him."

"No. You don't go to him. You go to your captain and he will go with you. I don't want you to go to this man alone."

"Afraid I'll kill him?"

"I certainly am. I certainly am." She sighed a deep, poignant sigh. "And then you'll never get to keep your promise."

Olive had been at the barre for three hours. The first time Karla opened the door and found her mother doing warm-ups was six o'clock. At seven the music from the ballet Balanchine had choreographed especially for Olive, was blasting through the walls and Olive was dancing it as if the house were full, as if she were unaware of being alone. Karla watched, shook her head, tried to make a joke, and left. Silence brought her back the third time. She opened the door and found Olive sprawled across the floor like a discarded towel.

"Mom?"

Olive didn't move.

"Well, Bear. Look at this. She must be getting old. What do you think, Bear?"

"I think she's just tired," Bear answered. "There must be lots of things on her mind."

Olive still didn't move. Not a hair, not a cell. Nothing.

"Mom." She approached Olive slowly. The droplets of sweat were drying and Olive had goose bumps all over her.

"Mom?"

Karla's light touch broke Olive. Tears flooded from her.

"Mom, what's the matter?"

The sobs were too strong. She couldn't talk, wouldn't talk.

Karla let her sit in the middle of the floor and cry. But when half an hour went by and Olive still hadn't stopped, she called Karen.

"She was right, your wife," Captain O'Connor told him. O'Connor still thought of Connie as his wife. "I don't even think we should keep you on this case."

"You've got to. I've been on it for sixteen years. You know that. And no matter what, I can't give up now." Vince was smoking nonstop. His skin had yellowed, exaggerating the circles under his eyes. He looked terrible.

"Well, before we do anything I want to see it. The film, I mean. We have plenty of time to question him. Does he know Don has this?"

Vince shrugged.

"He's not going anywhere and we have the evidence. Will Don let you have the film?"

Vince nodded.

"Fine. Then you get a copy made and bring it up to me tomorrow night. I want to give this some thought."

Sam Previdi was more enraged over the fact that Giambelli got the picture before him than that Buddy was a fag. He could straighten out his son. Giambelli he wasn't so sure about.

He looked at the snapshot again. It was his Buddy, all right. His boy. But who the hell was the other guy? The note read, "If you want to catch the act yourself stop by 15 Malibu Drive. Any night."

Nice note. Nice way to have your son repay you for all you've done for him. Sam Previdi picked up the phone.

"Vito, I got to talk to you."

"What's up, Pop?"

A dick up somebody's ass. A cock being sucked off by your baby brother. Vito wouldn't like it any more than Sam did.

Vito was the eldest of Sam's sons. Not Sam's favorite but certainly his most efficient. He wasn't smart like Gino, or charming like Buddy. But he was very good at bashing people's heads in. That's exactly what Sam needed, a bashed-in skull. If Buddy looked so good on film maybe they should fix it so he wouldn't look so good. If that didn't work, if he was still pretty enough for the flicks, maybe they'd have to cut him.

"What's the matter, Olive darling?" Karen asked, walking into her daughter's studio.

"Mother, please go away. I . . . it's nothing."

"Nothing!" Karen carefully leaned her purse against the mirror. "It looks to me like it's something." She knelt down and, as if her daughter were a little girl, tucked her finger under Olive's chin. "Please tell your mother what's bothering you."

Olive looked up at Karen and indeed felt like a child, maybe for the first time since Arthur had died.

Karen saw that and had compassion for it. "Come, darling. You're not too big to be held, you know. Now tell me what happened."

"Mom, oh, Mom." And again she wept. She wept for all the years she had spent alone, for all the time when there was no one to hold her, for all the hopes that she now knew were dreams never to be realized. She wept for all the years she'd never wept. "He said he loved me, Mom. He said it and I believed him and he..." She was so ashamed.

"He what, darling?" Karen stroked her daughter's hair.

Olive saw her reflection in the mirror. "I'm ugly. Look at me."

"Stop it, Olive. Please finish the sentence. He what?"

"He's getting married."

"Who, Olive?" Karen smoothed her daughter's hair away from her face. "Tell me who."

"Vince. Vince."

"Karla's father?"

"No. The other night..."

"You're seeing him again."

"Mom, stop trying to find out."

"All right, darling. Just tell me what you want me to know."

"He said he loved me and..."

"Olive," Karen said, her voice stern.

The tears stopped. "What, Mother?"

"Look at me, darling."

Olive obeyed.

"You are a Kingsley, my dear. Better, a Schultz. No man can ever reject you. Just remember that. Any man who doesn't see..."

"But I love him."

"...who you are is blind. You were Balanchine's prima ballerina, were you not?"

Olive nodded, listening as if the tale were being told about someone else.

"And you were your daddy's best little girl, were you not?"

Again she nodded.

"Arthur loved you very, very much. Remember how he'd sneak you into a movie? Remember that, Olive?"

"Yes, Mom."

"And I love you, Olive. I missed you so much when I was with Jean Claude. I told him all about you, you know."

"You did?"

"Yes, darling, I did."

"But you left."

"But I'm back. And look at Karla. Look at the job you've done."

Olive was beginning to feel better. Not much, but a little better.

"And you're choreographing a play based on your favorite dancer's life. You're opening up a whole new career for yourself, Olive." She kissed her daughter on the forehead. "And I'll never leave you again, my darling. I promise."

• XXVI •

Olive really thought he'd call. She thought there would be an explanation, even a poor one. Even just an apology. So she slept that kind of touch-and-go sleep that a doctor or a cop sleeps when on duty.

When morning finally came she had to acknowledge it was over. She thought maybe he'd be at the theater, but no. He sent one of his cronies. All in all, as mornings went, this one ranked at the bottom.

"Ashley," she called up to the stage. She was sitting next to Richard nursing her fourth cup of coffee. "You're playing Isadora, not a pregnant elephant."

"Olive," Richard said, trying to calm her. She had been relentless all morning. "Do you want to go for a walk or—"

"I don't need a goddamn walk!" She caught Richard's shocked glance. Nobody had ever heard her curse before. This was about him, she thought, angry at herself. "I don't need a goddamn walk," she repeated, a little softer. "I need an actress who can act. And dance. Look at her. Doesn't she know that that combination starts on the left foot?" She turned back to Ashley. "You should know your left side from the right by now." She didn't want to deal with this. It was blocking. All that was required was simply moving from place to place. No acting. No dancing. Ashley couldn't do it. Wouldn't do it.

Why now? Why was it so awful?

"Ashley, I've asked you before to remember that your hands are connected to your body. For chrissakes, you're going on tomorrow night."

Ashley tried to correct her movements but it was hopeless. Was it nerves? She doubted it. It was simply that she was terrible.

"That movement has meaning," Olive persisted. "Would you care to tell me what it is?"

She didn't give Ashley a chance to answer. She rose from her seat and headed toward the stage. Ashley, frightened, practiced discipline.

"I'm going to demonstrate the combination for you for the millionth time, Ashley dear. Now do try to pay attention."

Ashley tried to pay attention, wanted to, but instead of walking it through, Olive began to dance. To dance! Her feet barely touched the floor. Her arms had a life all their own. She soared through the air as if... as if she were Isadora. The movements were lyrical and sensuous and fully alive, and so much more, Ashley knew, than she could ever achieve. She would not tolerate it.

"Get off my stage, cunt."

Lost in the dance, Olive barely heard her. "What?"

"Get off my stage, cunt!"

Olive stopped dead, all rhythm gone. Then she turned and smacked Ashley hard across the face.

Ashley slapped her back.

"Don't you call me a cunt, you cunt!" Olive yelled, pulling Ashley's hair.

Ashley tore herself free. "So you can talk dirty. Bet if you did it once in a while you wouldn't be so fucking bitchy all the time. Fucking ice queen." She kicked Olive in the shins.

Olive kicked back. "I don't have to do it," she said. "You

fuck enough for both of us. For all of New York, you goddamn tramp."

The crew tried to pull them apart but it was too late. They were on the floor fighting, rolling on top of each other, cursing each other, killing each other. Then suddenly Ashley sat on top of Olive and began tickling her. Olive started to laugh hysterically, and so did Ashley.

"Hey," Richard said. "Is this a private party or can anyone play?"

"Dad, are you coming?"

"Huh?"

"Dad, are you coming to the opening?"

Jack scratched his head. There was something amiss here. He hadn't the foggiest idea what his daughter was talking about.

"The opening of *Isadora, Isadora*. Don't you remember? I told you about it."

No, he didn't remember, but that was okay. He seemed to be forgetting more and more lately. The movie was totally absorbing him and whatever he had leftover Buddy was taking. That boy sure could love. Jack could never remember being so taken by a boy before.

"Darling, I'm sorry. Will you tell me about it again?"

"I told you my friend Karla Kingsley's mother is choreographing a play on Broadway. Ashley Pope is starring in it. You said you'd see if you could fly in."

"Oh shit, I forgot."

"Dad, can't you just fly in tonight and go back tomorrow night after the show? I want everyone to meet you. Please."

Hearing his daughter beg weakened him, made him feel guilty. "I'm getting you the Appaloosa."

"You are! What color?"

"Well, you said your friend had a white one with black dots. How would you like a black one with white dots?"

"Neat, Dad. That's real neat. Oh, thanks."

"Does that mean I'm forgiven for not coming in?"

"Of course," she said, feigning disgust. "But next time . . ."

"Next time I promise, baby. When are you coming home, honey?"

"Semester break. Daddy?"

"What, Rivka sweet?"

"Love you."

"Love you too, sweet pea."

Vince stood under the hot shower. He made himself soapy all over all at once, from head to toe. But he still felt dirty, like Lady Macbeth. There were no bloody hands, though, just a feeling of slime.

The phone rang and he strode into the living room soapy and naked.

"Vince?"

"That you, Mike?" Vince recognized Captain O'Connor's voice immediately.

"Tomorrow night."

"Tomorrow night what?" He wasn't up for guessing games.

"You're going to bring him in for questioning."

"Why not during the day?"

"It'll be too obvious. We don't want the media to get hold of this. Tomorrow night is that opening. You're going with that Kingsley woman, right?"

"No."

"Why not?"

"It's personal."

"Okay, okay. Look, you and Philips go down and bring him in. Quiet. I want this very quiet. No one will notice if you play it right. Got that, Vince?"

Vince took a little too long to answer.

"If you think you can't handle it..."

"I can handle it. I'll see you tomorrow."

"Miss Hearly?" Karla asked.

"Yes, dear."

"Is he back yet?" Third call that morning.

"No, Karla. I know it's important that you get in touch with him, but he's so busy. Forgive him, won't you?"

"Well, tell him if he doesn't call back soon I'm going to pay him a surprise visit."

"Karla." Miss Hearly's voice suddenly got sharp. "I don't think that's a very good idea. Really I don't. He has little more than a week until the election and he's really going mad with all the arrangements."

"All right, Miss Hearly," Karla said obediently.

Robbie ran his fingers over the blade as if it were a sexual organ. A cold sexual organ, smooth and seductive. He felt the need to use it. That would happen soon. Very soon.

"What kind do they use for circumcisions?" he asked the quiet-looking man behind the counter of the surgical supply store.

"Circumcisions? No particular kind really. Can't be too long, of course, because it becomes unwieldy. As long as it's sharp."

All the blades were sharp. Perfect. Just what he was looking for.

"Have you ever used one?" he asked. The man seemed to be watching him carefully.

"Me? No, I'm not a doctor. Are you a doctor?"

"No," Robbie said, suddenly feeling like talking. "But I have doctors in my family. A long time ago we had a doctor. Before we came to America."

"Oh? Where are you from originally?"

"France," he lied.

"What part?"

"Are you familiar with France?"

"Yes, I've been there a number of times. I like the countryside."

"My mother said we came from Versailles."

"Beautiful area. *Parlez-vous français?*"

"No," Robbie answered. The man was getting too close. "May I think about it?"

"Certainly."

Robbie couldn't decide whether to use a knife or nettles. His uncle Earl would have known which one to choose.

Uncle Earl once told him that women like his mama should have been taken care of at birth. Never would have gotten like she had if they did what they were supposed to do. Female pleasure—either cut it out or cauterize it. Then a ceremony. Ashes and bat droppings mixed with honey to stop the bleeding.

That's how they treated girls in the old country, his uncle Earl said. Like messengers from the devil.

"See what happens when a woman experiences pleasure?" Uncle Earl said. "They get sick with it. Like power. The female doesn't have a strong enough mind to control those urges. Shouldn't have to. Should be fixed. Like dogs."

That was Ashley's problem, Robbie thought. Pleasure. She even said it herself. Preferred pleasure over speaking about the Lord.

For the first time in years, Robbie actually missed his uncle Earl. Missed the stories he'd tell, stories about the old country.

Like his mama, Uncle Earl had been born in the United States. But Robbie's great-grandma had come from Africa. She, like Uncle Earl, had been black, like the dark heart of that continent. But not Robbie. Robbie favored his daddy. One of the many men his mama took on. Robbie had the same pale eyes, nut-colored hair, fine nose. White like his daddy. A ghost, his uncle said. A portrait of sin. Yes, that's what he was. A portrait of sin.

Now he wanted to go home, to his people. And he wanted Ashley to come with him. To cleanse him. To die for his sins. She was like Jesus, was like white light. An angel. But she was also a pleasure seeker. One way to change that was to take the pleasure away. Then she would die for both of their sins.

He had liked the way the blades felt under his fingers. They'd be kind to the flesh. Lifting away the skin would be easy. Probably not painful. Perfect to get to the core. But then he thought of nettles . . . brambles. Perhaps they would be good enough. Decisions, decisions. Afterward he could apply the salve of animal droppings, honey, and ashes.

Then he'd take her home. To Mama. To Uncle Earl. Yes, then Robbie could go home again.

Robbie stood in darkness and light at the same time. Like his mother. Like his heart. Like his black thumb which allowed no living thing to grow. But no more. No more.

"Charles?"

Ashley said his name so softly he didn't recognize her voice.

"Who is this?"

"Ashley."

"Ashley. What's wrong?"

"Charles, I'm so frightened."

"Why? What happened?"

"We had dress rehearsal today. I couldn't remember any of my lines. I couldn't even remember where I belonged on stage. Charles, I was terrible."

He had a date with Karla. "You want me to come by?"

"Would you? I promise I'll never do this again. Call you at home like this, but . . ." Her voice cracked and she didn't go on.

"Look, it will be difficult. I'll have Arnie use his own car, but you can expect me in an hour or so." He heard her sigh. "All right?"

"Thank you. A thousand times thank you."

Karla was having trouble concentrating. In school. Out of school. Everywhere. She didn't want to read about Romeo and Juliet, she wanted to live it. Without the tragic ending, of course. She wanted to tell Charles about the baby, have him lift her in his arms and tell her how happy he was. Then she'd wear her Zandra Rhodes dress for her wedding. That's what Karla wanted.

But that's not what Karla was getting. Three broken dates spelled despair, real despair. She was lost without her Charles. But tonight they had a date. He promised he'd keep it. Why was it that she didn't believe him anymore? Where was her self-confidence? Probably in the bottle of turquoise nail polish she was applying for their date.

The phone rang. It was Charles. He called her angel. She knew. She heard it in his voice. Another broken date.

"But what about my surprise?" she asked.

"Karla, please." He felt awful. But not awful enough to keep the date. "Something important has come up. Something very important."

"But my surprise."

"Baby?"

"Yes?"

"Tomorrow night. I'll see you at the opening. You can show me your surprise then."

"Promise?"

"Cross my heart and hope to die."

"I love you," she whispered, and hung up.

"Ashley."

"Hi, Robbie. What's up?" As if she didn't know.

"I thought I'd come by. Tomorrow's opening and I thought you might be nervous." *Last chance, Ashley.*

"Me nervous?" she said, playing the role well. "What I need most is a good night's sleep."

"Sure?" *Say yes and you'll be redeemed.*

"Sure, baby. Why don't you get some sleep too?"

"Okay, Ashley. Whatever you say."

Whores, boy. They're all whores.

Well, Uncle Earl, then we'll just cut out her sin and save her.

"Olive?"

No, she wasn't going to answer him. She had had her tantrum. Everything had subsided. Everything was all right, and now he thought he could just walk in like this.

Vince had called five times and five times she had hung up. He decided not to call again. This time he'd shown the doorman his badge and gone up.

"What are you doing here?" she asked.

She looked terrible, he thought, deep circles around her eyes. She looked sad, tired. "Olive, I have to talk to you."

"I have nothing to say." She turned, started to close the door, but he stopped it with his foot.

"Olive, you must listen to me."

"Go to Janice Alison Canfield. She's your fiancée."

"Mom!" Karla called. She was getting ready to go out and visit Becky.

"Yes, Karla?"

"I . . . Oh. Hi, Vince." She took one look at the two of them and decided to spend the night at Karen's. She told her mother that.

"No, I want you here," Olive said.

Turning to Karla, Vince put his hands together in prayer and mouthed, "Please." Karla got the message and split.

"We have to talk," Vince said to Olive, and pushed his way in.

Ashley was naked, emotionally undressed. She was a little girl. A seductress. A woman. All things. She was terrified and needed him. He saw it, knew it. And oddly enough he didn't want to turn from it. Ashley Pope's neediness made him feel important, not burdened as he felt with Elizabeth Anne.

Ashley was different. She was no stranger to him. He seemed to know her. They were one and the same. Both strangers to the world, oddities. Successes perhaps, but aberrants nonetheless.

He was on the verge of losing his success, the life he'd worked so hard to create. And so was she. Tomorrow Ashley Pope would open herself to the world and no longer be able to control the results. Tomorrow the world would take over. The critics. Oh, how he knew about critics—the expected trial of joining the public domain.

And so Ashley stood there, fully garbed and naked. She was wide-eyed and sweet. She wanted to be held but didn't know how to ask for that. Instead she was going to ask him to make love to her. It was easier than saying, "Please hold me." But he knew her. He knew what she wanted and so he stopped her. Yes, he wanted her, but he didn't want it taken away from him, the experience of making her his.

He hushed her with his finger. She understood. Yes, she understood him. From the first moment.

It was not like it was with Karla. Insane, rushed, wanting more and more. Nor was it like when he was with Elizabeth Anne, naughty and nice.

It was different. Different than it had ever been before. This was Ashley Pope. Larger than life and still a little girl. And he was going to have her.

He savored her, as the audience would tomorrow night. Evaluating her gifts as the critics would. It was a prelude.

"You know, they used to call me fat Frannie with the big fanny."

He didn't answer. He didn't have to. He just ran his hands over the perfect derriere. Perfect, like her breasts, like her thighs.

"Please undress," she said to him.

Yes. He took off his uniform. The suit. The tie. The black socks. The wing tips. Out of uniform he was exquisite. Perfect.

Together they were exquisite. Perfect.

There was nothing sweeter than this woman. Her skin was softer than spring air. Her lips were ripe, yearning, new. It was new. Newer than Karla.

She knew what he wanted. He wanted to take her. He didn't want to be guided, requested, seduced. He wanted to direct it, her. And so she yielded. It was easy to yield. To be silent. To listen to her heart. Good. It was good.

His hands were soft and gentle, large and comforting. He moved her. Opened her. Kissed her. She was silent throughout. She took direction well. Ina had always told her she took direction well.

"Now," was all he said. His breathing was even, steady. Then again. "Now."

He was inside her and they were one. There was no beginning or ending. They were joined. Parvati and Shiva. Cupid and Psyche. Dionysus and Ariadne. They were immortal, beyond the human. No longer mere flesh, they were eternal. Two beautiful figures moving under the moonlight on a calm of pillows and coverlets.

They were timeless, fabled. They were what poets sang of. They were complete. They were one.

It was perfect, except for the man lurking in the doorway. But had it not been for Robbie and Arnie, no one would have known of their rapture.

"Olive, you must listen to me."

"You lied to me, Vince. Why?"

"Because I love you."

"That's love?"

"Olive." He took her hand. "You must understand. I did plan on marrying Janice, but after I met you..."

"Why didn't you tell me?"

"I was afraid of losing you."

"Losing me!" She was shocked. "Losing me! You never had me to lose. What you had was an afternoon with me sixteen years ago. And then you left." Compassion made her reach out and touch his hand. "Vince, I know why you left, but sixteen years. Surely in all that time... And now again. You didn't even have the courtesy to show up at the theater today and explain." She pulled away from him.

"Don't let go of my hand, Olive." There were tears in his eyes and they softened her.

"What's the matter?" she asked, wanting somehow to make it better.

"I saw the film."

She was confused. "What film?"

"The film where Angelique was murdered."

"Oh, Vince." She had to touch him now. She had to, yet...

"It's a long story, Olive, but I know who the murderer is."

"Who?"

"I can't tell you. It would be very unprofessional."

"I understand." She paused. "Why did you lie to me, Vince?"

"Is that all you care about?"

"No," she said softly. "It's not all I care about. But the truth is, I can't do anything about the film or the fact that your daughter was horribly brutalized. It's terrible. But if you want to be a part of my life then I need to know why you lied. The wedding is barely a month away. When were you planning on telling her, or me? Did you actually plan on marrying her and seeing me on the side? Is that it?"

"You think I'm that devious?" How could she? All he wanted to do was love her. "Aren't you being a little self-centered? I've been looking for my daughter's killer for sixteen years and I think I finally may have found him, and you're worried about your pride."

"My pride! My pride!" She stood up. "You came into my bedroom and promised me love while another woman was believing you'd marry her, when I believed..."

"You said no promises."

"I... believed I meant it."

This wasn't working. He had to leave. Otherwise he'd say the wrong thing. "I'll call you in a few days, Olive."

"Don't bother," she said, and slammed the door behind him.

Maybe falling in love with love *is* falling for make-believe, but Jack didn't care. It still felt good. And isn't that what everything was about? Feeling good. Looking good. Eating good.

Tomorrow night he would prepare Italian. Sicilian, specifically. Spaghetti with tuna caviar. Grilled Cornish hens garnished with fried grape leaves and thick onion slices.

Dessert would be tortoni. Wine—Mouton Rothschild '64. Perfect.

Then the bedroom. Neither of them had an aversion to sex on a full stomach. Neither of them would eat enough to slow them down.

It would be good. Real good.

♦ XXVII ♦

Mornings. Ashley loved them. She opened the window and let in New York, inhaling its sounds and its smells, letting them wash over her like a favorite cologne. This was her big day. What she had worked for, planned for, lived for. When the doorman brought up her morning cappuccino from Oren's, she savored it. This was the day she'd been waiting for all her life.

For weeks now she'd been bumping into notes plastered to the walls of her low-ceiling, high-rent apartment on East fifty-seventh Street. Think Isadora. Feel Isadora. Move Isadora. Breathe Isadora. Be Isadora. A friend left one in the bathroom that said Pee Isadora.

Well, today she could pull the notes down. Either she was or was not Isadora Duncan. And it wasn't hers to decide.

"Half an hour to curtain, Miss Pope."

Her stomach was somewhere in her throat. She had forgotten all of her lines. Every single dance step. Olive was outside the dressing room. So was Richard. "Break a leg," they whispered through the closed door.

Flowers. The room looked like a wake. But nothing from Charles. Where was he?

Olive had lived through opening nights in all the capitals of the civilized world—and some that were not so civilized—and she had never felt this churning, these butterflies, the fear that she felt tonight. All those moments of self-exposure were nothing compared to this. Before, she always had the Balanchine name behind her. But now it was she, Olive Kingsley, who had to make it work . . . or not.

The house was full. Ashley could hear the chattering. It broke her concentration. Shit. Who was she kidding? There was no concentration.

"Ina." Her acting coach, Ina Grant, had flown in for the opening.

"What, baby?"

"I can't do it."

"Ashley."

Ashley's eyes were tearing.

"Ashley, no tears." They got worse. Ina's voice grew harsh. "Now I want none of this. No tears. You'll destroy the makeup. There's nothing to be afraid of."

"Do you think I can do it, Ina?"

"Did I tell you you could do it in Hollywood?"

Ashley nodded.

"And when you came to New York?"

Ashley nodded.

"And didn't I tell you you'd get the part?"

Ashley nodded.

"Five minutes to curtain."

"I never lied to you, Ashley," Ina said.

"Present for you, Miss Pope," a voice outside the door said.

She opened the door, grateful for the distraction, and the boy gave her a small package. Inside was a brownie and a note. *Not nearly as sweet as you, but I had to find something to tide me over until after the show. How about it?* No signature. No incriminating evidence.

How about it? You got it, Charles.

Olive waited for the curtain, and she waited for Vince. For flowers, an apology, anything. There was nothing.

"Olive?"

"Mom." She reached over and touched Karen's hand.

"Remember how we'd wait like this when you were dancing? But you'd be moving, warming up. Tell me, are you nervous? Like you were then?"

"Much more, Mother. Much more."

Ina gave Ashley a big hug and it was over. All the support. All the training. All the rehearsals. It was Ashley and only Ashley. Orchestra. Curtain. Silence. No applause when she entered. This was New York. They loved you until they hated you and they were always ready to hate you.

And then there was nothing. No memory. No Ashley. No Charles. No Olive. Only Isadora. It was Isadora who moved across the stage, who spoke and danced and held the children. It was Isadora who lost her children. Isadora who was bereft. Isadora who opened the trunk and cried. It was Isadora who brought the house down. Ashley had transcended it all.

"Was I wonderful?" she asked Richard.

"You were *fucking* wonderful," he said.

"Fabulous," Ina said, not letting go of her.

"It was perfect," Karen said, meaning it. "Perfect."

"Olive?" Ashley asked.

Olive was simply staring at her.

"Olive, how was I?"

"You *were* Isadora," Richard said.

"Olive? Tell me the truth, Olive."

Olive reached out. She reached out to the star. Yes, Ashley Pope was a star.

"Ashley." Her eyes filled with tears. "Ashley, you were

everything I've ever wanted to be. You were sensuous and erotic and ethereal, all at the same time. You were words to a poem. You were beyond flesh and blood." She paused for a moment to catch her breath. "Now I understand what the critics were saying about me for so long. Now I understand it. You were all of those things that they said I was and I could never see in me." She embraced Ashley. "And because you made me see, I shall be eternally grateful. You were beautiful, Ashley. Just beautiful."

And they had themselves a well-deserved cry.

The critics agreed that Ashley Pope was everything Olive had said she was.

Charles was waiting for Ashley at Sardi's, but Vince wasn't waiting for Olive. Everyone else was.

Telephone calls with offers. Telegrams with offers. Tomorrow, Olive said. Tomorrow. Now she wanted magic. She wanted Vince. Where was he? Earlier she had broken down and called his house. No answer. No machine. Nothing.

"Charles." Karla was able to corner him for a moment. "Look what I bought you."

It was a beautiful buckle. Not his taste but exquisite. "You shouldn't have, Karla. Is this my surprise?"

"I have another," she said, but Charles didn't stick around to hear what it was. The crowd around Ashley parted and he caught her eye. He patted Karla on the shoulder. "Just a minute, dear. I must congratulate the star. It would be so rude of me not to."

"But my surprise!"

Charles bent over and dismissed her with a kiss on the cheek. Karla Kingsley did not like being dismissed with a kiss on the cheek by the man she loved. She didn't like it one single bit.

Elizabeth Anne had been watching it all and realized the culprit was Ashley. Realized he'd probably been having an affair with the blonde bombshell all along. She attempted to console Karla and therefore console herself. Elizabeth

Anne decided her husband would never be alone in the same room with Ashley again.

From that moment on she literally stood between the two of them. Charles wanted to take Ashley home, but Elizabeth Anne's constant presence prevented it. He knew his wife would cause a scene. She had started on the booze earlier and he didn't want to provoke her.

Ashley saw the problem and understood.

So did Robbie.

"Can I take you home?" he asked.

Ashley looked at Charles, saw he couldn't get away. "Yes, of course," she said.

XXVIII

Nick's information wasn't one hundred percent correct. Buddy wasn't spending every night with Jack. Vito waited alone in the dark for three nights. But when Buddy did show up on Sunday, he made it worth Vito's while.

Vito let them dine in leisure, surrounded by the perfect California breeze. In fact, he really didn't believe it. He didn't believe his brother was a faggot. How could little Buddy, the kid who loved basketball, won swimming medals in junior high, was the heartthrob of all the girls in Laurel Canyon, be a faggot? But Vito waited, sincerely hoping they were no more than just two guys having dinner.

As soon as they left the table, though, and ascended the spiral staircase, Vito knew it was true. They had linked pinky fingers. It made him sick. It made him so sick he wanted to leave, but he knew his father would beat the shit out of him if he did. So he waited another twenty minutes, figuring fifteen would get them into whatever they wanted to get into. Half an hour might be too much. Twenty should be just right.

It was. The door was unlocked, so there was no problem walking in on them. This time Buddy wasn't sucking cock. It was the other way around. Vito thought it was disgusting, sinful.

Buddy saw the expression on his brother's face as soon as he walked in, but he couldn't stop. Vito saw that and being a gentleman he let Buddy have his orgasm. Then he really let him have it, a fist in the gut. First thing the kid did was anoint his brother's six-hundred-dollar suit with Jack's fabulous dinner. Vito didn't care. There were plenty of dry cleaners in L.A. and the Previdi family collected from all of them.

Vito smacked the kid around some more, then he took him outside. Jack was horrified.

He shouldn't have been. The show was just beginning.

Vince arrived at Sardi's and watched all the celebrating for a minute. Then he walked up to Olive and congratulated her. He wanted to embrace her but couldn't. She wanted to reply, to ask, to speak, to wonder aloud why he left her to go to Charles, but he didn't give her a chance to do that.

"Is something wrong?" Elizabeth Anne asked Vince after he told Charles they'd have to go down to the station house.

"We just have to ask him a few questions."

"What about?"

"I'll be fine, Sunshine," Charles said. He knew, and he didn't want anyone else to know.

"Vince!" Olive called out in dismay. He had no idea how to explain, so he just turned and left.

Ashley couldn't imagine why she had consented to Robbie taking her home. Just because that bitch wouldn't let her near her husband didn't mean she had to leave. And even if she wanted to leave, why Robbie?

Ashley, you're dumb.

"We have to discuss the wedding," Robbie said, taking her hand in the taxi.

"What wedding?" she asked in her most ditzy, tizzy voice.

"Ashley." He kissed her fingers.

"I am not Ashley." Ah, the voice was sexy, tough, strong. Like Isadora playing Ashley. "I am the great Duncan and the great Duncan never marries."

The kissing stopped. Robbie didn't like the message. "You think you're too good for me now, don't you." It was a statement, an accusation. "Because you're a star now. You think you're too good for me."

"I came to Europe to bring about a renaissance of religion through dance," she said, holding true to her role. "To bring the knowledge of the beauty and holiness of the human body through its expression of movements to the masses." She was paraphrasing Duncan. No, she would not drop it. She would live out the role. She had to. She was a star.

"Ashley, stop it. You're not on stage."

"Life is but a stage."

"Ashley."

The taxi driver pulled up in front of her building and Ashley, intoxicated with her new stardom, jumped out of the cab in an elaborate theatrical gesture. " 'Good night, good night! parting is such sweet sorrow...' "

"Aren't you getting your playwrights mixed up?"

"Good night, Robbie," she said, giving him a sweeping kiss on the cheek. Then she ran. She felt his disease. How the hell, she wondered, running inside her building, had she allowed him to escort her home? But once inside, feeling safe and sound, she forgot about Robbie completely. It was Charles she thought about. Charles and how he was going to get away from Elizabeth Anne in order to be with her.

" 'Parting is such sweet sorrow,' " Robbie whispered, " 'that I shall say good night till it be morrow.' "

"You know why we picked you up, don't you?" Vince asked it cool. He couldn't say it any other way. He was so fucking hot under the collar, he could have killed this guy.

"I think I should get legal counsel," Charles answered.

"After you explain this medallion." *Cool, Vince. Cool.*

"I didn't do it."

"Do what?"

"Kill her."

"Kill who?"

"The girl."

"How do you know she was dead? And what about the film? What was your mug doing in the film? And this medallion. How do you explain the medallion?"

Charles, with his legal background, had all the answers. Everything was based on circumstantial evidence. There was even a question of the statute of limitations. But Charles knew it was all bullshit. If this leaked out to the press he was dead. Politically anyway.

Vince grabbed Charles by his collar, by his neat, perfect Windsor knot. Fuck being cool. "Answer me, you mother-fucker."

"When I left her she was alive." The words raced out. "She was just a trick that the director brought in. It was straight sex, that's all."

"Which director?" Vince let go of the knot. It was no longer perfect.

"A guy named Jake. Jake or Jack. Gilbert was his last name."

"So how did she die?"

"I don't know."

"What do you know?"

Charles had to tell him. It was a matter of survival. Charles Andrew Long, who'd brought himself up by his bootstraps, was damned if some cop was going to take it away from him. And so Charles told him. He told him about making the film, and then about receiving the copy a week ago. He told him because he knew that in another week he'd still be mayor and this jerk would still be nothing but a high-class cop.

Vince listened. He listened and hoped the desire to kill Long would leave. It didn't. So Long didn't do it. Big fucking deal. It didn't really matter. He had still fucked her.

Screwed her on film for all the world to see. He could have killed him for that.

"I'm going to let you go," Vince said, turning his back on Charles. He couldn't look at him. "I don't have to tell you that if you try to leave town you're finished. Your career, your bar certification, everything is over."

Charles nodded as he got up. "One question."

"Yeah?" Vince was already dialing the L.A. police.

"How did you get that medallion? I lost it a long time ago."

"And I found it a long time ago."

"How?"

It was none of his fucking business but he liked scaring this guy, this guy he'd seen screwing his daughter on film.

"I found it when they asked me to go out and identify the body. I'm her father."

Suddenly Charles got scared all over again.

Actually, what with Robbie going back to Sardi's to look for Charles, the mayor was much safer in the hands of the police.

"He left early," Elizabeth Anne explained when Robbie asked her where her husband was.

"Without you?" So the mayor was sideswiping everyone. Going back to Ashley after all.

"Business," Elizabeth Anne said, knowing she had to save face. Then to Olive, "I must leave now."

"No, Liz. Don't go home alone." Olive felt as lost as Liz. "Please don't. Stay with me. Come on. We'll make a night of it."

Some night. "May I?" Elizabeth Anne asked.

"And what about you, Mother?" Olive asked. "How are you getting home?"

"Well, I'll probably take a taxi, darling." Karen was feeling good, triumphant. Olive's triumph was really her triumph. Had always been her triumph. God, it was good to be home.

"You shouldn't have to go home alone, Mrs. Kingsley," Robbie said, finishing his whiskey. "Let me escort you."

Karen gave him the onceover and decided he was harmless enough. Certainly it was better than going home alone.

"Well, thank you, young man. Chivalry is not dead."

"Are you sure, Mother? Because it's no problem for me to drop you off."

"Don't be silly, darling. You and Karla and Liz have a lovely evening."

Ashley wasn't in her apartment five minutes when she started to primp. To clean thoroughly, inside and out. To make herself beautiful all over again. For Charles. And the way she looked the most beautiful was *au naturel*. That's how he liked it, so that's how he'd get it, and get it he would. An hour and a half later the doorman rang.

"Mr. Long is here, Miss Pope."

"Send him up."

"Do you want your cappuccino tomorrow morning?"

"But of course," Ashley said, reapplying her lipstick.

The guy laughed when Jack asked him who he was and where they were going. The guy laughed and Jack got angry. The guy didn't like angry men, especially angry faggots. He stopped laughing and shoved Jack to make him walk faster. Jack went to slug him. The guy threw him on the ground and kicked him in the face. It wasn't the pain that made Jack not slug him again, but fear. Fear of messing up his face.

It didn't matter. The guy liked kicking Jack so he did it again, and again. This was how it worked. In Previdi's world, the Babylonian edict of an eye for an eye, a tooth for a tooth prevailed. Killing brings killing. Robbery brings about a retrieval of goods.

The way Previdi figured it, Jack was guilty of robbery and murder. By imprinting Buddy's sexual preference on celluloid, Jack had captured Buddy as a faggot for all to see.

So Previdi decided an eye for an eye, a tooth for a tooth.

Jack took a little beating en route to the warehouse in the center of L.A. where three guys were waiting for him.

He wanted to ask what the hell they thought they were doing, but he could still taste the sole of the first guy's shoe. He kept quiet. They liked that. It made tying him up and taping his mouth even easier.

"What happened?" Ashley asked Charles as she undid the once-again-perfect Windsor knot. "Tell me." But her lips were close, much too close for him to answer. He started to speak but the sweetness of her breath intoxicated him. Like a heavy cordial, like a snifter of Drambuie.

She was undoing his belt, the expensive alligator belt he had meticulously chosen for himself. It was the image he was after more than the leather. But where was his image now?

"Ashley."

"Did you do it for me?" He was down to his briefs now and she was holding him. Grabbing him. Oh, she wanted that length deep inside her.

"Do what?"

"Have Vince take you down there. So we could be together. Was it a setup?"

Her eyes were closed. She was waiting for his lips and before he gave them to her he looked at her, amused, tired, yearning. Ah, the ego. Yes, the almighty ego. He thought of telling her the truth. He knew she could take it. But he was, after all, a politician. So he ran his fingers through her hair and lied.

Elizabeth Anne had been hoping Charles would arrive home, be upset by her not being there, and telephone her at Olive's. She was wrong. Very wrong.

He never called and she never slept. She hit Olive's bar, which was inadequate. Olive wasn't a drinker, so the selection wasn't great. It did provide some solace. Then, because she couldn't stand it anymore, she went home. To the mansion. To the palace. To the prison.

Vince wasn't asking permission this time. He had to take Charles at face value. If he called the LAPD and had them investigate, there would be reams of red tape. If he asked O'Connor, O'Connor would forbid it, telling him you can't go barging in on a guy sixteen years after the fact.

He couldn't call Olive and say he was leaving because O'Connor might call her to find out if she'd heard from Vince. Then she'd be in a position of having to lie for him. He just left.

♦ XXIX ♦

"How was she?" Elizabeth Anne asked.

"What are you talking about?" Charles was in no mood for guessing games.

"Ashley Pope. That's where you were, wasn't it?" Her voice was slightly slurred.

"You know I was down at the police station." He was disgusted.

"They said they released you late last night."

"Who said that?" He undid his tie. He felt awful. Wonderful but awful. The interrogation still covered him like a layer of scum.

"Whoever answered the phone."

He was tired of her. Weary of his life, the sham.

"Elizabeth Anne, there's something I have to tell you."

Gone too far, she thought. He was going to tell her he was leaving. She got up and walked over to the window. She wanted another drink but knew that would aggravate him.

Too bad.

Right. She poured herself a glass of vermouth.

He watched. No comment.

"There's this movie," he said. "You'll probably find out about it sooner or later, so I might as well tell you."

"I know about it." She didn't look at him as she spoke.

"You do?" He was surprised, curious, then began to think. He walked over to her. "How do you know?"

"I saw it." She tried to look innocent, pitiful. Yes, now was when she needed his pity.

"When?" No pity. Just suspicion.

"They sent you a copy." She sipped the vermouth. She was frightened.

"I know. I got it."

"One after that."

"What?" His hands clamped on her shoulders. "When?"

She put down the drink. "The other night. When you were with her. I waited up for you and you didn't come."

"And what happened?"

"I saw it. Part of it. It disgusted me to see you doing that with another woman. Knowing you were doing that then. With her. With someone."

"And what did you do?"

"I sent it to—to Don Lindt, the television newsman."

He was shaking her now, disbelieving. No. Believing all too well. "You're crazy! Didn't you know that could ruin me?"

It was time for the truth. "Yes."

"You fucking brat! Why?"

"I wanted you back."

He smacked her hard. She bounced against the wall. It startled her. And him. "You fucking brat!" he shouted. "Everything's been handed to you. You've never worked a day in your life. I worked my balls off to get where I am and now you want to take it away."

She stared at him. No tears, no defense.

"You saw that movie and you sent it to a reporter?"

"I only watched about five minutes." She spoke quietly, then something in her snapped. "I hated seeing you with that girl!" she screamed.

"But that was before us."

"I don't care."

"You didn't see the end?" He came close. She could feel his breath.

"No."

"Then let me tell you about it, you bitch. Right after I stuck my dick in her, just the way you like me to stick it in you."

She couldn't bear it. She covered her ears. He took her hands away.

"There's a shot of me killing her. *Me.*"

She stared at him horrified.

"No, I didn't do it, but they have me on screen killing a girl. If they don't find out who did kill her I'm going to be put away for a long, long time."

"No. I couldn't bear losing you."

"You already have," he said, and left.

This was how the world would end, Robbie thought, recalling T.S. Eliot's poem "The Hollow Men." Not with a bang but a whimper. Yes, Ashley would scream out in orgasm, then when she realized pleasure was to be hers no more, she would whimper.

He directed his energies inward, in order to be worthy. Then he reviewed his life. It was all in the cans, the many reels that made up his life after leaving Louisiana. After leaving Uncle Earl. He watched it all roll by and prayed for redemption. That's what Robbie Haskins did the day after Ashley's biggest night. He prayed and cleaned and prayed and heard God tell him to let her have one more night. One more night of pleasure.

"Jack Gilbert. Sure we know him," the captain said with a smirk. "He's a respected member of the gay porno circuit."

"What about before he shot gay films?" Vince asked.

"He made his millions off a straight film. *Cherry Vanilla.* Remember that?"

"Vaguely. Where can I find him?"

Captain Duvall called in Sergeant O'Rourke. "Drive Detective Luscardi over to Gilbert's place."

"Yes, sir."

"Don't never say we didn't make it sweet for you," Bennie said, looking down at Jack. "I heard how you like it real sweet."

Jack would have told him thanks but no thanks, but he couldn't say anything. His mouth was still taped.

"Now, don't you be frightened," Bennie said as he poured some topolino honey over the well-known movie director.

Jack *was* frightened. He had already shat twice. But that was nothing compared to the feeling he had when they left him alone, covered in honey. Well, almost alone. Except for the rats that came out of the corners of the cellar to make a tidy dessert of Jack Gilbert.

Funny what you think about at the last minute of life. If forced to guess, Jack Gilbert would have never thought that the *Sh'ma*, the prayer of Israel, would have been the last recording that went off in his mind before he left this plane.

"Do you think he was expecting me?" Vince asked Sergeant O'Rourke.

"What makes you ask that?"

"Well, for one, he's not home. Secondly, the projector's set up."

"Maybe we should check the hospitals," Officer James said as he descended the spiral staircase.

"Why?" Vince asked, turning on the projector.

"Someone puked their brains out upstairs."

Vince wasn't interested. What did interest him was the film on the reel. It began exactly where Nick had turned it off that night that he and Jack had watched a bit of it. It was Angelique again. Vince felt like puking himself, but watched anyhow. He was glad he did. His daughter didn't die in this one. Apparently Charles was telling the truth.

Plus there was another difference. This one was uncut. A stylist and cameraman were included.

Vince ran through it again, putting the pieces together. More than likely one of the other two people killed his daughter. Or else a stranger. But Vince was gonna gamble on that not being the case.

"Know these guys?" he asked O'Rourke.

"One of 'em I do," the sergeant said.

"Which one?"

"The guy on the left."

"Who is he?"

"Who *was* he, you mean. Big in porn. Started off as a stylist. Graduated to director. Then graduated to cocaine. Died from an overdose three years ago."

"The other guy?" Vince asked.

"Never saw him before, but I'll run a check on him."

• XXX •

First Robbie watched the movie. He sat quietly with his head shaved watching his past, present, and future. He watched Charles and the girl have their pleasures, commit their sins. He watched and tried to stifle the stirrings in his loins. Tried but could not. Then he watched his magic, his craft with the camera, with the lights. He watched as he mounted the girl and took her. Yes, it was in the taking that Robbie felt the most.

The Lord giveth and the Lord taketh away.

So this was how the Lord felt, Robbie thought. Giving and taking. And there was no more appropriate night than tonight, All Hallows' Eve, Halloween, in which to give. And take.

Uncle Earl referred to All Hallows' Eve as The Night of the Living Dead. *These folks ain't alive. They're ghosts, can't you see that, boy?*

If Robbie didn't answer quickly enough he'd get smacked around the ears.

Yes, sir.

They're colorless figments of God's imagination. God's evil inclination. The white folks is sin incarnate. Just like you, boy. Just like you.

As luck would have it there was nothing on the second guy, the one who was still alive. All that was left to do was draw up a current-day composite on him.

Funny, something about the composite rang a bell for Vince, but he didn't know why or where he could have seen the guy.

"I think I should stick around," he told O'Connor when he phoned his New York precinct.

"Really?" O'Connor said. "You want to pull a seventy-one to seventy-two?"

"What's that? A new code number?"

"No, it's your history. Remember? You stayed out there when Angelique was first killed."

He remembered all too well. He'd lost a wife as well as a daughter. And Olive.

Olive. He couldn't believe it. He had actually gone for a full day without even thinking of her. Olive.

"I'll be back later tonight or tomorrow."

Too late. Tomorrow never exists except in our minds. There was no tomorrow. For Jack. For Angelique. Or for Ashley Pope. Especially for Ashley Pope. After all, hadn't Robbie given her two nights to redeem herself? And hadn't she missed both opportunities?

"Rebecca?" The man's voice was kind, very kind.

"Yes?" Becky said, somewhat distracted. She had a chemistry test tomorrow and chemistry was her worst subject.

"Rebecca, I don't know how to tell you this." The voice showed genuine concern. It made her sit up and take notice.

"Who is this?"

"I'm a friend of your father's, dear. My name is Nick. Nick Dalsass."

"Is he sick?"

"He's—he's dead, Rebecca. He had an accident. I'm so sorry, dear. I'll miss him too. We were very close."

"Karla?"

"Hi, Becky. You must really be studying for that chemistry test. It's late."

"Karla . . ." Becky was sobbing. "Please come out to California with me. My father . . . Karla, my father is dead. I'm all alone."

"Becky!"

Becky's voice was tight, holding back hysteria. "Karla, come with me. Please."

"Let me ask my mother. Yes, I'm sure she'll say it's all right."

Olive wanted to say no. She didn't want to be left alone. But Karla was right. Of course Olive would let her go. She even rode with them to the airport.

Ashley had been prowling the apartment like a hungry cat. Opening and closing cabinets, the refrigerator, as if something new had grown there in the past two hours.

Success is a bitch.

So she'd transcended Hollywood. That's what reviewers were saying anyway. Movie offers galore. Everyone wanted her. Including Robbie Haskins. As far as she was concerned he was history. Nice while it lasted but . . . not as nice as with Charles. So she bored easily. So sue her. She was headed for the phone to call in an order to the Chinese restaurant when it rang.

"Isadora?"

"Daaahling. I've been awaiting your call all evening."

"You received the flowers?"

"All ten bunches, you precious lawmaker, lawkeeper, and Lawd knows what else."

"You're free?"

"Well, now that I'm such a big deal I don't have to charge anymore."

"I'll be by in an hour."

"And I'll be ready, willing, and naked."

* * *

After shaving the hair off his body Robbie painted himself black. One application of base, then another, and another. Only after he was the same color as Uncle Earl, which was practically the color of his mother, did he dress. Actually, even if he walked out carrying a cross he wouldn't have looked strange. It was Halloween.

When he got to Ashley's building a new doorman was on duty.

"Whom would you like to see?" he asked.

"The Pope."

"I beg your pardon?"

"The Pope," Robbie repeated, straightfaced.

"Oh, you must mean Miss Pope." The doorman liked the allusion. "And whom shall I say is calling?"

"God."

Assuming it was Charles, Ashley told the doorman to send him up.

"What are you doing here, Robbie?" She was not thrilled to see him. Not at all.

"What's the matter?"

"For starters, it's almost midnight and I have to do an interview first thing in the morning. For finishers, I'm tired."

"But Charles could come up?" he asked, trying to set the salvation scene in his mind.

"You didn't say you were Charles. You said you were God." Then giving him the once-over she whistled. "And I daresay, you're not."

"But you were expecting someone," Robbie insisted.

She ignored the pressure. "What the hell are you dressed up for? A Halloweeen party?"

"Forgive them, for they know not what they say." He extended his hand in benediction.

"Robbie, you know you get scary when you talk like that."

He crossed himself.

"Where's your hair?"

"Shaved it off."

"That must have been one hell of a Halloween party."

"Ashley..."

"I know. You want to marry me."

"No, I don't."

His face was blank. She didn't know if he was serious or not. Didn't know if, in fact, she liked the fact that he didn't want to marry her.

"Well, then. Maybe we do have something to talk about." She moved toward him, hoping that she could soft-soap him and he would leave. But he didn't. He simply thought back to the Bible, the First Testament, the only testament. Before Christ. When Eve came to Adam. And like Eve, Ashley was under the influence of Satan.

He moved in toward her. In for the killing. "Let's make love," he said.

"Actually," Ashley said, stepping back, "you're a bit much for me now. If you don't mind I like you better with hair."

"And white."

"And white."

"A little love," he said, going to her, taking her in his arms.

She figured it would be easier to get rid of him that way, after the sex. He figured she wanted to be saved, knew it was the only way.

So he lay with her, held her. Yes, he would cleanse away her sins. He'd cleanse the area of pleasure with his tongue. He could make it quick. He didn't want her to suffer. She must be one with God quickly. She resisted at first but resistance was not Ashley Pope's strength.

She wanted him. She wanted his sex, his strength, his manliness. He thought his purity was what she wanted and he gave it to her. In the white room under the white light of God he gave her his white liquid.

And then redemption. She made it so easy, so very easy. First the pillow over her face. The knife would come later. A stifled scream. He thought it beautiful the way the color of the pillow matched her throat. Both so creamy white. Like the light. Yes, she was redeemed. Saved.

How does the world end? Not with a bang but a whimper.

Charles announced himself to the doorman who immediately rang up to Ashley's apartment. Naturally he didn't get a response.

"Do you think she's in the shower?" Charles asked, uncomfortable about standing around a lobby, even if it was after midnight.

The doorman was not at all sure she was in the shower. Intuition told him something was wrong. Something about that guy who'd just left gave him the creeps.

"Let me go up with you," Tony said, taking the housekeys. "Gene," he said to the other nightman, "I'll be down in a second."

It took a little more than a second actually. Once they were inside Ashley's apartment and saw her lying naked on her bed, her arms folded and a cross around her neck, Charles had to convince Tony that he'd never been there. He did it with the help of a hundred-dollar bill. Only then, when the way was clear, did Tony call the cops.

• XXXI •

As far as Vince was concerned, Gilbert's version of the film corroborated Charles's story. That didn't make him happy at all. Angelique's killer was still on the loose.

So Vince decided to go home, waiting for O'Rourke to track down the porno director and contact him when he was found. He took the red-eye back and called Olive.

"Vince, where are you?" Her anger had turned to worry and concern. The last she'd seen of Vince was two days before when he'd escorted Charles out the door of Sardi's. Charles had made it back home safely, but what had happened to Vince?

"I'm at the airport, sweetheart. Listen, I'm really sorry. It's just that the past few days have been a mass of confusion."

"I was worried about you, Vince. Where were you?"

"California. It's been a very long night, but I really want to talk to you."

"Coffee?"

"If you could."

It felt so good just to be speaking to him. "Vince?"

"Yes?" he said in a yawn.

"Did your going out there have something to do with Charles?"

He took a deep breath. "Can I come by? We'll talk then."

"Certainly, Vince." He heard coolness now mixed with the concern.

"Olive?"

"Yes?"

"Is Karla with you?"

"No. As a matter of fact, *she's* in California."

"California? Why?"

"Her friend Becky's father died and . . . I don't know, I think it was some sort of accident. So Karla flew out there with her."

"And who's on duty? Outside your door."

"I told the police I'm fine. Really I am. I don't think there's anything to worry about. The play opened and nothing happened."

"You're alone?"

"Well, yes."

"I'll be right over."

Even Olive couldn't maintain the formality she would have hoped for when she saw Vince. As if he were a comfortable coat, she bundled herself up in his arms.

"I'm sorry. I'm so sorry." He kept repeating himself, as if there was nothing else to say. As if there was nothing else he could say.

"Vince."

"Don't speak," he said, holding her tightly, leading her to the couch. He kissed her forehead, lips, cheeks, and then her lips again. "Please let me explain."

"Vince."

He hushed her with his finger. "I love you." He said it with passion, commitment. The thought that he might have lost her was unbearable. "I have always loved you.

But I had made a promise to Janice, and then when I saw you again I didn't know what to do."

"But why didn't you just explain it to me?"

"Why? Haven't you learned that questions of why never have answers? I didn't want to hurt her. We were together." The phone interrupted his kisses as well as his thought. "Don't get it," he said. He kissed her once more and this time she lost herself to him. To the kiss, the embrace.

"Vince."

"Don't get it."

"I must," she said, laughing. "It might be Karla."

"Before you pick it up," he said, stopping her.

"Yes?"

"Will you marry me, Olive?" He had been wanting to ask her since they went skating. "Will you?"

The question took her breath away. No, it wasn't the question. It was the joy, the indescribable joy at the goodness that was entering her life.

"Yes, Vince. Yes, I will." Then back to reality. "Hello?"

"Is he there?" a gruff, unfriendly voice asked.

"Captain O'Connor?"

"Is he there, Miss Kingsley?"

"Why, yes, he is."

"Well, get him on this phone. Now."

"Whew!" she said, covering the mouthpiece. "This is not a happy person." Vince took the phone from her.

"Where the fuck have you been?" O'Connor screamed into the phone.

"I missed you too," Vince said, taking a deep drag on a Marlboro.

"The Pope's been killed, you moron."

"The Pope. What the hell are you talking about? The Pope as in Vatican?"

"No, the Pope as in East Fifty-seventh Street."

The Pope. "What happened?"

"Someone got to her last night."

"Shit."

"Look, Luscardi." He only called Vince by his last name

when he was really pissed. "What the hell were we supposed to do, have the whole cast covered?"

"The tiptoe killer?"

"Looks that way, but no toes were missing. Just the cross on the inner thigh and the arms across the chest."

"That's it?"

"No." Even O'Connor didn't really want to talk about it. "He circumcised her."

"He *what?*"

The expression of shock on Vince's face told Olive something was very wrong. "Vince, tell me."

He shook his head.

"A pretty clean job," O'Connor said. "Just sliced it off."

"Where is she now?"

"Where do you think? The morgue."

The morgue. You come in from someplace real soft and if you're not careful...

"The doorman says she had two visitors. God and the mayor of New York."

"God?"

"Yeah. Apparently a regular boyfriend of hers."

"Tell me, Vince," Olive said, touching his hand.

"Haskins?"

"Could be. Whoever it was, either there was a party or the guy was on something."

"Why?"

"Looked weird. Had on makeup."

"I'll check it out," Vince said, knowing where he was heading first.

He hung up the phone, took Olive's hand, and led her over to the couch. The question was, who had done it? It was either Haskins or Long. Unless someone had made their way in through the window. Vince would bet it was Long. That bastard. He really hoped it was Long. Now he'd put him away for life.

"Olive."

"Vince, don't look at me that way. Please tell me."

He held onto both of her hands. "Ashley's dead."

"No!" Oh, God, no. Again. Anything she touched seemed to die. Anything she loved. How was it possible? "But she's starring... Dead?"

"Olive, listen. There are going to be some policemen coming up here to stay with you."

"But you..."

"I'll wait until they come and give them instructions. I don't want anyone here. You understand that. And you are not to go out." He smoothed back her hair in much the same fashion that a loving parent might.

"Does Richard know?"

"Richard who?"

"Dixon. Vince, I can't believe it." She tried to understand. "What about the show?" she murmured vaguely.

"Olive darling. Please just wait here. There will be men stationed in the hallway." He kissed her forehead. "Promise you won't go out."

"I'd like to ask Richard over and tell him in person."

"All right. I don't see why that's not possible. Just tell the doorman who you're expecting."

"This is beginning to bore me," Charles said. He had graciously allowed Luscardi into his study, expecting an apology for being wrongly accused of killing that girl. But no, Luscardi was back on the beat with new accusations.

"Listen, wiseguy," Vince said, trying to keep cool. "If you think this is boring you don't know what sitting in the slammer for the next twenty years could do. You were up to see Ashley Pope last night and I want to know why."

"Why?" Charles got up from his comfortable chair and walked over to the window. Outside, the wind was doing a twirling dance with the litter while the nannies strolled the children up John Finley Walk, behind Gracie Mansion. Charles thought of Ashley, twirling and twirling, then falling to the stage. For some reason it just hit him that she was dead.

"You're not going to believe me but I liked her." He turned around and faced the detective. "I mean really liked her. In an odd sort of way we were comrades. Orphans of sorts."

"Look," Vince said, impatiently stabbing out his cigarette. "Skip the romance. Why were you there?"

Charles may have acquired polish, but his roots were crude and he could call on them any time he wanted. When he spoke his voice was hard. "Will it make you feel better if I say I was there to screw her? Is that what you want to hear, Mr. High-and-Mighty?"

Vince was up bullet-fast. "Look, buddy. Don't call me names because I don't like it. You're just a fuckin' whore who made it big. Sold your body sixteen years ago and you're still doing the same thing. Why were you there?"

"To screw her."

"And."

"She was dead. Or damn well near it."

"And how do I know you didn't do it?"

"You don't."

"Careful, boy."

"Check the prints."

"Oh, so you're so familiar with all this that you know about prints. Well, we found some of yours up there."

"It wasn't the first time."

"Do you know what would happen to you if we let this out?"

"Yes," Charles said, dropping all arrogance. "I'd go back to my law practice. Hide out for a couple of years. Repair my marriage and then run for president."

Vince knew that the sad truth was that he could be elected.

"Were there any other prints?" Charles asked.

"Yes." Vince was bluffing. Sure there were other prints. But none that could be identified. "You weren't the only one she was screwing."

"Robbie Haskins?"

"Haskins. Oh, shit."

"I told you. She wasn't just a fuck to me," Charles said, but Vince was already out the door.

* * *

Robbie Haskins. They had run a check on him before and his record was as clean as Vince's. But it could have been Haskins. There was no answer so the doorman took him up.

"When did he leave?" Vince asked.

"Not too long ago," the doorman said as he turned the key to open the door.

"Was he in last night?"

"No. As a matter of fact he came in real late. That must have been some party he went to."

"Why?" The door opened into an apartment that glowed from Top Job and smelled from Pine Sol. But immediately Vince felt something strange. Death. The apartment stank from death. All the plants were dead. Then he saw the blood.

"Had on some wild makeup," the doorman said. "He'd painted himself black."

Vince was already doing a survey of the apartment.

"Need me?" the doorman asked.

"Uh-uh," Vince said, heading for the phone. "I'm calling for a backup. They'll be here in a few minutes."

It was Haskins. As soon as he walked in he sensed the sickness. It was all around him. In the corner of the bedroom by the small waterfall. Over the bed in the crucifixes. In the bottles and bottles of cleansers. In the cheap imitation of Michelangelo's *Pieta* covered in honey and rose petals.

And the movie projector. Vince turned it on. He smelled a setup, as if the film had been planted there. As if Haskins would jump from the closet and blow his brains out. It was the same film as the one Don had received. Looked like his detective days were over.

The stink in Olive's lobby ran up Robbie's nostrils, almost asphyxiating him. It didn't stop him, just asphyxiated him.

"I'm going to the Kingsley residence," he said to the doorman, beaming a charming smile.

"Name?" The doorman stood there with a piece of paper. Dixon's name was on it.

"Richard Dixon."

Naturally he was let up.

"Robbie!" Olive was a little surprised when she opened the door and saw Robbie instead of Richard, but she didn't think twice about it. Obviously he had come there to commiserate. She nodded to the policemen that it was all right as Robbie stepped into her apartment. "You poor thing," she said. "You know, of course."

"Yes, Olive. I do." He spoke slowly, distinctly. Yes, he thought, it was horrible. Awful. He knew Ashley had suffered and had wanted to make it as easy on her as possible.

"I know how much you cared for her," Olive said with genuine compassion.

Robbie was surprised by her concern. It made him reconsider his edict. But no. He had to be strong.

"That's not why I came," he said, drawing himself away.

Now it was her turn to be surprised. First by his lack of emotion, and secondly by his abruptness. But perhaps he was in a state of shock, she thought. Yes, that was it. Shock. "Let me get you a cup of coffee."

He watched her cautiously. Did she know? How could she not know? As if the thoughts were transmitted from his mind to hers, she realized his head was shaved.

"Robbie?"

"Yes, you can make me a cup of coffee," he said, entering the kitchen with her.

She turned the lights on. "What happened to your hair?"

He didn't answer.

"Do you like sugar and milk in it?" she asked, taking a coffee mug down from the cabinet. Just as she was about to pour the coffee the doorbell rang.

"That must be Richard," Robbie said.

"Yes, of course." She walked into the living room. "Who is it?" she asked the doorman over the phone. "She turned to Robbie. "It's my mother."

* * *

"Did you see these headlines?" Karen asked as soon as Olive opened the door. "Ashley's been murdered, darling. What happened?" Karen was almost as dazed as Olive. Then noticing Robbie, she greeted him warmly. She hadn't quite absorbed the reality of the situation, but she'd sensed her daughter would be upset, possibly in trouble, so she'd come to see her.

"Mother. Robbie was very close to Ashley and I think he's upset."

"I'm not upset, Olive," Robbie said, correcting her. He leaned over as if to scratch his ankle. Yes, the blade was still there. Inside his boot.

"But you must be," Olive said, leading the way back to the kitchen. "What happened? Does it say, Mother?"

"No, it's the typical *Post* headline without any story. They must have just heard and printed it before they could get more details." Karen began to skim the article while Olive lifted down another coffee cup.

"Coppers are floppers." Robbie said it slowly, methodically, like a metronome.

Olive stopped, not fully absorbing the line. "What did you say?"

"Coppers are floppers."

"What an amusing statement," Karen said, taking off her coat. "What does that mean?"

"Robbie!" Olive froze, leaning against the cold, gleaming stainless-steel kitchen cabinets. "He's coming back," she said. "Vince is coming back. There are policemen just outside."

"They stink, don't they?" He would have to reach down to get her. He'd have to alter his position to see her clearly, so strong was the light coming from her. But it was the light of evil, of black magic. Black magic always kills white magic. Except now. Now he would kill the black magic and resurrect Ashley. Yes, that's how it would be done. The blade stunned the early morning light. "I will work quickly."

"What's going on?" Karen asked, her voice reaching a high pitch.

"He killed her!" Olive yelled. "He killed Ashley!"

"Never," Robbie said, offended. "I let her live." Then with the swiftness of a deer he leaped across the room to kill the black magic.

"Olive! No!" Karen shouted. Quickly, without thinking, she threw herself over her daughter. He would not snuff out this light.

Robbie drew his hand high as Cain had with Abel. The gleam of the knife married the gleam of the morning. The sun shone brightly on the blade and he knew God approved. He drew it up high and plunged it deep, deep into Karen's heart.

"Olive!" Vince shouted through the door.

"Vince!" She screamed his name over and over again, until the walls, the air, the building, the city heard it. Robbie was turning toward her, stepping over Karen's body. She was next. This time he wouldn't miss.

Vince tore into the kitchen and Robbie screamed curses at him, this intruder. They always came in at the last minute to corrupt, to stop salvation. "Get thee back, Satan."

No, he wouldn't allow this copper, this flopper, to take away the purity. "You—" But before he could get out the next curse he was silenced by the bullet from Vince's gun. Then another. And another. And another.

"Stop! Stop!" Olive yelled after each shot. "Oh, please stop."

Her voice penetrated at last and Vince lowered his arm. Robbie was dead. "Olive." He reached for her, but she slipped out of his grasp. Like someone drugged, she walked over to her mother. They were no longer carbon copies. She threw herself over her mother's body. They all witnessed it, the cops, the neighbors en route to work. How proud Robbie would have been for the witnessing.

"Oh, Mother. Oh, Mother. Please don't be dead. I—I was just beginning to . . . love you. Please, Mom. Please."

Vince went to her, held her. One of the rookies took Karen's wrist. It was cold, there was no pulse. The rookie shook his head and Vince knew it was over.

Olive pulled away from him and embraced the limp

figure. "She's . . . is she . . ." She let go and stood up, once again a Kingsley. "Tell me, Vince." There was no stutter, no emotion. Her jaw was set. "Is she dead?"

He wrapped his arms around her. "Yes, Olive," he said, stroking her hair. "Yes, she's dead."

The last thing Olive heard before fainting was the sound of her own voice screaming.

• XXXII •

***ISADORA, ISADORA* JINXED**
Karen Kingsley, mother of Broadway choreographer and Balanchine prima ballerina Olive Kingsley, was brutally knifed to death in her daughter's apartment just hours after *Isadora*'s star, Ashley Pope, was killed. Robbie Haskins, lighting designer for the new show, stabbed the woman and was turning on Ms. Kingsley when Detective Vincent Luscardi shot him. A motive is not yet known. Mrs. Karen Kingsley had only recently returned from France to be with her daughter at the opening of the show.
Miss Pope, star of the hit *Isadora, Isadora,* had been Haskins's lover. There is no word yet as to the possible connection between the two murders.

Karen Kingsley was laid out in one of her Chanel suits. It wasn't a new one, but one that she favored nonetheless.

Why do people give the dead flowers? They can't smell, can't see. Why, Mother?

"Now, now, Olive darling. Flowers make the living feel more cheerful."

Olive looked at her mother and at the flowers and didn't feel cheerful. She didn't feel anything. She was numb. A merciful numbness had taken over from the first moment she had seen her mother in the coffin, and it hadn't left.

Her peripheral vision caught Elizabeth Anne standing in the doorway, looking as inconspicuous as Karen might have. Elizabeth Anne, dressed tidily in a gray wool dress with shoes to match, was in shock too.

God bless her, Olive thought. Her teenage friend had never left her side since she heard of the murder. She even slept at the apartment. Yet, at the same time, she managed to give Olive the space to be alone.

Then Karla. She'd flown back immediately, leaving Becky alone to deal with the grief of having lost a father.

Liz walked over to Olive and placed a hand on her shoulder. "How are you doing today?"

"I don't know," Olive said. "I'll tell you as soon as I know."

"Will Vince be here?"

"Of course, Liz," she said, holding her friend's hand. "Of course." Something about Liz suddenly looked old to Olive, and she knew it was a reflection of herself, of her own age catching up with her.

Then Karla approached them, removing the sadness, the feeling of aloneness.

"How's my Karla today?" Elizabeth Anne asked.

"Okay, Aunt Liz. But I miss Grandma. I wish she'd been around when I was a kid."

"Why is it that people look smaller when they're dead than when they're alive?" Olive asked no one in particular. "She was always so large to me. Looming. Frightening. Now she's just a little lady lying in a coffin. Totally helpless. You didn't deserve this," she said to her mother. "You really didn't."

"Pardon me, Miss Kingsley," an unfamiliar voice said.

"The minister is here and we're ready to begin the service."

Olive looked at him as if he were a Martian. Obviously familiar with the look, he told her she had a few minutes.

"We'll come back shortly to remove the casket." His voice was somber, nonthreatening. "At that time we would appreciate your following behind the coffin. Please say your final farewells now."

Obediently Olive bent over and kissed her mother good-bye. "I love you," she said as the tears flowed. "Say hello to Daddy for me."

Karla, dear sweet Karla, wiped the tears from her mother's eyes. "Can I kiss Grandma good-bye, too?"

"Of course, darling."

Liz, ashen and shaken, watched them hover over the body until two men came in and wheeled the coffin away.

Then, as instructed, they followed the coffin into the almost-empty chapel. Vince and Charles were the only ones present.

Oh, Mother.

Babs says: The unfortunate hex on our prima ballerina's pet project hasn't hurt sales a bit. Rumors are flying that Balanchine's beauty just might get back to the barre and play the role herself. Speaking of which. Not rumor but fact, three major publishing houses have asked Olive if they can do her biography. In any case, the tickets to *Isadora, Isadora* are sold out through July 4. Well, every cloud does have its silver lining.

Silver linings aside, Karla was not the lucky one. She had tried speaking to Charles at the funeral but he wouldn't have it. So she was back to calling him at the office. She rang him at least two dozen times and two dozen times his secretary told her the same thing. "He'll get back to you as soon as he can."

Not only that, but she was totally alone with this. Becky was still in California. Her mother was a mess. Certainly she couldn't speak to Vince. So instead of examining the situation she examined herself.

She stood naked before her long mirror, looking at the perfect body reflected before her. Behind her was the residue of childhood, objects she would soon discard. Objects like stuffed animals, favorite books, seashells, and report cards that she would find too childish, only to miss them and regret their loss years from now.

She was a centaur of sorts. Half human, half beast. Complete fantasy. She was neither beast nor fowl. The fantasy was that she would always remain this svelte, youthful, firm, demanding, yet somewhere deep inside she knew it was untrue. If she had this child she would get fat and lumpy like other preggies. Maybe she'd even stay that way. Maybe she'd get ugly stretch marks. Maybe even sag.

She thought of Charles and how he had been behaving lately and didn't know if he deserved to have her have his baby.

Charles? He had finally gotten back his own silver lining. His fear of sixteen years was over with. He was saved and forever grateful he had never been linked publicly with Ashley Pope. He was lucky and he knew it. Lucky politically. Personally he was on the edge. It was two nights before the big event, the anniversary bash, and he couldn't afford to be on the edge.

When Elizabeth Anne came home to him that night, supporting him, loving him, telling him she forgave him, he told her how much he loved her and that after the election they would go away. She felt sad, tired, thrilled that he was with her.

"Where?" she asked, willing to accept any crumb of affection. "Mykonos?"

He ran the back of his hand over her cheek and kissed her eyelids. Then his mouth met hers and he whispered, "Yes, yes, yes. Mykonos."

"She's at it again," Karla said, grateful for Aunt Liz's visit.

"The barre?" Elizabeth Anne knew each and every one

of Olive's bad habits. In reality there was only one. Similar to hers but spelled differently.

"Yes, Aunt Liz," Karla said, walking over to the bar. "Martini?"

Elizabeth Anne nodded. "Extra dry."

For Karla, Elizabeth Anne was once again becoming Aunt Liz. It seemed as if old relationships were being reestablished. Or almost. "Uncle Charlie's not coming?" Karla asked, handing the drink to Elizabeth Anne.

"He has so much work." She sipped the clear poison. "What did they do before these were invented?"

"I beg your pardon?"

"Nothing, darling. Has Vince arrived?"

"Not yet." Karla suddenly remembered he was coming for dinner. "I better get the spaghetti sauce going."

Karla thought of how amazing it was that over the past two days just the simple act of preparing a meal took away a lot of the pain. The pain of losing Grandma, the pain of not seeing Uncle Charlie. "It's hard to believe she's dead," Karla said, walking into the kitchen. "She was really a strong person. And I remember how she made me call her Karen, but then once she decided I should call her Grandma, that's what I had to call her. There were no two ways about it. If I forgot and called her Karen, she'd get really p.o.'d."

"You should have known her way back when," Elizabeth Anne said remembering Olive's teenage years. "Do you think I should go to her? Olive, I mean."

"Wait till Vince—oops, that's the bell. I'll bet that's him."

"What's she dancing to now?" Vince asked. He kissed Karla on the cheek, then handed her a bouquet. "These are for you."

"Flowers! I love flowers." She unwrapped them. "Baby glads. I love them. And birds of paradise. Far out. Mom's doing *Nutcracker*."

"Maybe that's a hint about what kind of mood she's in. Should I go in?"

Karla and Elizabeth Anne looked at each other. "Yes."

* * *

"Olive?" The room was dark. She wasn't dancing. "Olive?" He heard a rasp, a sharp pain that ripped through the throat, as if whoever had let it out didn't want to. He traced his way over to the sound and took her in his arms.

"Vince, how can she be dead? I . . ." The words wouldn't come out. She waited, and as before, the pain left as abruptly as it had come, numbed by the sweet anesthesia of shock.

"Olive, shhh, my darling. You must stop this exercising and eat. Karla's cooking her best tomato sauce." He held her for a few minutes more, then asked if he could turn on the light.

"Yes," she said. Just having him there made her feel better, much better.

"Can we come in?" Karla asked, knocking lightly on the door.

"Yes." Olive looked at herself in the mirror. Her mascara was all over her face, her hair was a wild tangle, and she didn't care. "Karla, will you braid my hair?" She craved the touching more than anything.

"Sure, Mom." It was the first request Olive had made in two days and Karla was grateful for it. She knelt behind her mother, and Vince and Elizabeth Anne sat on either side of Olive, each taking a hand.

"You're looking much better today, love," Elizabeth Anne said. "This has been quite an ordeal, hasn't it, Olive?"

"I don't know why she was given to me only to be taken." Olive's voice held the simple confusion of a child. "If she'd remained in Europe and died, perhaps I would have experienced grief, but it would have been mostly shock. But this . . . I really had grown to love her." She let out a deep, heavy sigh. "This is almost unbearable." Turning to Elizabeth Anne, she asked, "Do you think she knew?"

"What, Mom?" Karla asked, continuing to work her mother's hair into dozens of braids.

"Are you cornrowing my hair?"

"Sure, why not? Do you think she knew what?"

"That I . . . that I . . ." Her lip quivered. She had to say the words. Had to. "Loved her."

"Oh, Mom." Karla hugged her from behind. "Of course she did."

Olive turned around. "Karla, do you know how much I love you?"

"Mom."

"Do you?" She demanded an answer. No games. What if she died now? "Do you know that I would—that I would die for you? As she died for me."

"Mom, please." But it was too late. Karla was a part of the tears. And then so was Elizabeth Anne.

"Is a man allowed to cry, too?" Vince asked.

"Yes, darling," Olive said, taking his hand. She looked at Karla again. "Tell me you know."

"I know, Mom. I know."

"It's just that it's so final," Olive said, feeling very sober, very dry. She turned to Vince. "You know, I thought I'd never see you again. It was sixteen years, wasn't it?"

"Indeed it has been sixteen years."

"Yet, when there's life there's hope. We can change in life, can't we? God, I never really thought about it."

"Keep your head straight," Karla said, resuming the cornrowing.

"If you knew you were going to die tomorrow," Olive asked Elizabeth Anne, "what would you want? What would you say?"

"I need a refill to touch that one." Elizabeth Anne splashed more gin into her glass and sat back down on the floor. She paused, then said thoughtfully, "I'd tell Charles I love him. And then I'd ask if I could have him back. The way I used to have him. When we were first married." In afterthought she smiled and held Olive's hand. "And I'd tell you and Karla how very much you've meant to me."

"Oh, Liz." Olive looked at Vince and asked him the same question. Without any hesitation he answered, "I'd ask for one last moment with Angelique. I'd want one last time with my daughter."

The word *daughter* touched something very deep inside Olive, and she started to cry again.

"And you, my darling Karla?"

Karla stopped the braiding and took a moment to answer. "I'd ask you who my dad was. And then I'd try to find him."

Olive gasped at the ingenuousness of the request. "Oh, Karla." She took her daughter's hand and kissed it, realizing for the first time what a precious secret she held. If it had been she who was killed instead of Karen, these two people, this father and daughter, would never find each other. She took a deep breath, for courage, for truth.

She held on very tightly to Karla's hand, then took Vince's. "This is your father, Karla," she said, joining their hands. "This is the man who gave me an afternoon of pleasure and left me with a lifetime of joy."

At first no one got it, no one except Elizabeth Anne. She remembered. She had known Olive back when. She remembered how close Vince and Olive had been. What she couldn't understand was why she had never suspected.

"Olive?" Vince said, not really believing her.

She shook her head. "I was meaning to tell you. Oh, Vince. I just didn't know how. I didn't know how you'd respond. I thought... I thought maybe you'd be angry. Maybe Karla would be upset. I thought if you found out you could take her away. Maybe Karen could take her, but now I realize Karla's all I have. And you. You're all I have left too, Vince."

"She's my daughter?" It was still unbelievable. "This beautiful young lady, this perfect child, is mine? Olive? Tell me it's true."

"It's true."

Karla was in shock. As for Vince, he answered his own question. Can a man cry? Yes. Like a baby.

• XXXIII •

The black limousines started arriving at eight. The unfashionables were the most punctual. Elizabeth Anne didn't care. Important or unimportant, it didn't matter. Charles and she were going to have a baby. She knew it. Yes, it would be all right. And they were going to Mykonos. He had promised.

Caught in the flush of renewed love she mingled, smiled, overheard gossip. She was the perfect hostess.

Olive hadn't wanted to come to the party. She felt it wasn't right, was disrespectful. She felt she couldn't socialize properly. But Vince and Karla and Liz had talked her into it. Karla had been the worst, absolutely impossible. She had insisted Olive come. She said she wanted to show up with her dad and mom together, holding hands. Like a family.

Naturally, Olive complied.

"Uncle Charlie?"

"Karla dear. You look exceptionally dazzling tonight."

"Uncle Charlie, may I speak to you?"

He had that political smile plastered on his mouth. It

didn't touch his eyes. "Of course." Then noticing the Governor and Mrs. Cuomo's entrance he had an excuse to avoid her. Funny, he had never noticed how annoying she could be. A pest actually.

A servant presented a tray of champagne glasses. Karla took one and sipped it slowly. "Yuk. How can people drink this stuff? Hi," Karla said to the tall woman standing beside her. Vince and Olive were mingling, leaving Karla to roam about on her own. "I'm Olive Kingsley's daughter. We met at one of my mom's performances."

The tall, intimidating-looking woman smiled when she heard Olive's name. "I would have never recognized you, dear. You've grown so. I believe it was when your mother was dancing Giselle. She was exquisite."

Karla remembered it, too, and for a moment felt nostalgic. Life seemed so simple then, so easily organized.

"I threw an orchid onto the stage," Verushka added.

Ah, he'd left the Cuomos.

"Charles." She never called him Charles. Karla used the same voice she heard adults use when they were trying to show who was boss. "I must speak to you. Right now." Charles would have once again refused, but Vince joined them. Charles knew that one small leak from Vince Luscardi's lips could ruin him forever.

"Certainly, Karla."

"Is something wrong, Karla?" Vince asked, placing a strong arm around the girl's shoulders.

"No, Vince. I just wanted to talk to Charles for a minute." Cautiously she added, "Alone."

"Certainly, Karla," Charles said. "In my office?"

Why wasn't he excited? Karla wondered. Why wasn't he happy to see her? It had been almost two weeks. No, it had been more than that. Well, he'd be excited as soon as he heard. Then she'd make him suffer. Maybe she'd threaten to kill his baby. Yes, maybe that's what she'd do.

Elizabeth Anne watched as they walked off to his office together and was pleased that their relationship was still intact. Now Karla had two daddies.

"Now what is this big surprise you're talking about?" Charles asked, sitting on the couch.

"Are you angry with me?" Karla asked. "What have I done?"

He softened. She was a child. No. She wasn't a child. Perhaps she'd resembled one when they first became lovers, but now she was a full-blown woman without any of the grace. Without any knowledge of the rules. Still, she was practically his niece.

"Karla, honey, I don't want to upset you and you haven't done anything wrong, but we must stop our meetings."

"Why?" Her eyes were bright with tears.

"Because, Karla. The press. Certainly..."

"Charles, I'm pregnant. That's the surprise. I'm going to have your baby. Isn't that the most wonderful news you've ever heard?"

No, it wasn't. Not at all. Pregnant. He had never made a girl pregnant in his entire life.

"Are you sure?"

"Yes, the rabbit died." She said it with pride.

"I thought you were on the pill." He got up. He was perspiring. His hands were cold and clammy. He paced the room, then sat down again. For the first time in his life, Charles felt faint.

"Are you all right?" Karla asked, rushing to him, touching his moist face.

He pushed her away. He was enraged. "Are you sure?"

"Yes, why do you keep asking me that?"

"It can't be. That's why. I thought you were on the pill."

"You can call Dr. Nathanson if you want to confirm it," she said, choking down the tears.

He saw how upset she was and put his arms around her. "Karla honey, I'm sorry, but I just never expected anything like this to happen, angel."

"But I thought you loved me."

"What made you think I'd leave your Aunt Liz, Karla? We never discussed marriage, did we?"

"But I thought you loved me."

"Karla." He turned her face toward his. "Look at me, angel. I'm very fond of you, but..."

She couldn't hear any more. She covered her face with her hands and sobbed.

"Don't cry," he said, feeling very paternal now. "I'll take care of you. We'll get you to the best gynecologist. The best. You'll be fine in a day or two. We can do it here or in California. I have friends there. Please, babes, don't cry."

Becky was right, Karla thought. He wasn't going to marry her. He didn't love her. He didn't want their baby. He was just fooling around with her, using her. The pain cut through her, and she wanted to kill him. She knew that would make the pain stop. It would make her feel better to get back at him.

He kissed her on the cheek. "Okay?"

She nodded. After taking a few minutes to dry her face, they returned to the buzz of the party.

Peter Duchin was playing "Feelings." Charles had none, Karla thought. None. Least of all for her.

"Did you get to speak to him, darling?" Olive asked Karla as she emerged from the study.

"He's a prick," she said. She turned to Vince. "Daddy, will you come on stage with me?"

"Of course." He looked at Olive and Olive looked back. They both shrugged.

"Is there a song you'd like to sing?" the conductor asked the young beauty who walked up to the microphone.

"No, sir. I just want the mike."

Karla tried smiling at the crowd, but everyone looked too scary. Thank God Vince was with her. But it was Charles who inspired her, Charles who was walking toward her, ready to take the microphone away from her. Swallowing her tears she said, "I want all of you to know that Charles and I are going to have a baby." That was easy.

Laughter.

Silence.

Laughter.

"I'm sorry, Aunt Liz, but I thought he was in love with me. Whenever we made love he always—"

Vince started to say something, but Charles stopped him. He stopped them both by taking the microphone away.

"Thank you, Karla, honey. That's the nicest compliment I've had all year." He turned to the crowd, played them. "Isn't it wonderful what active imaginations fifteen-year-olds have?"

"Yes, it is amusing, isn't it?" someone said.

No, it wasn't amusing at all. Not to Vince, newfound father. He wasn't amused because he knew it was the truth. So he belted Charles, first in the gut, then in the eye.

He took Karla's hand and they left the stage.

"I thought he loved me," was all Karla could say. "I thought he loved me."

Vince held onto Karla tightly until they found Olive, who was looking for Elizabeth Anne.

"Let's leave," he said.

"But Liz..."

"Right now."

More than anyone else, Elizabeth Anne knew it wasn't Karla's imagination. She knew it was the truth, the whole truth, and nothing but the truth. She walked into the study and wheeled out the television and VCR, turned them on, and announced the premier showing of a new film. For the fourth and final time Vince got to watch the young Charles Andrew Long screw his Angelique.

"What are you going to do, baby?" Olive asked, trying to soothe her daughter. They were home and Vince stood behind Karla, his hand on her shoulder.

"He doesn't deserve to have my baby. I thought he loved me, Mom. How could Uncle Charlie lie like that? I thought he was my friend. Mom?"

"What, baby?"

"Do you think I'm terrible? Does Aunt Liz hate me?"

It was Vince's turn to speak. He had to, for Angelique's

sake. "No, Karla, you're not terrible. Please understand that." Oh, those swollen eyes. He hated to see her cry like that, but then he remembered Angelique. She never cried. She was just like him. Maybe this was better. With his thumb he rubbed away a tear that had caught itself on her lower lashes. "You're young, darling. Just young. Fifteen is still childhood."

"I'm not a child," she said, stamping her foot.

"Maybe not physically," he said. "But you are a child emotionally. If you weren't you wouldn't have gotten involved with him, or if you did you would have known."

"Known what?" she asked with a sob.

"That it wasn't love."

Babs says: Apparently our beloved mayor sowed a few wild oats in his youth. One was a lovely young thing immortalized on celluloid. Still quick on the draw, Charles did manage to have the showing stopped within minutes of it being turned on.

Yes, the evening was chock full of surprises. While the guest list could have filled a year's worth of *WWD*, the star-studded cast was still shocked and amused when Olive Kingsley's gorgeous daughter Karla announced that she was bearing the mayor's child. Obviously too much Dom. But still it was fun.

There was one poor sport. That brute of a detective who's been guarding Olive Kingsley's body with his life. He didn't like Charles's denial of fatherhood and smashed him in the eye. Well, thank heaven the price of sirloin has come down. Things could be worse.

Elizabeth Anne sat with the early morning edition of the paper and chuckled over Babs's piece. This time the golden boy was getting it. She liked that. She would have liked it better if she could get that click, that fine buzz, but she couldn't. First wine, then whiskey, then vodka. Nothing. Nothing. Nothing. So she went to a bar and drank until seven, and nothing. Nothing to do but return home.

Home to Charles. But she needed to make things right with Karla first.

My dear Karla,

I am sure you're going through hell, darling, and I just want you to know that when this horrible nightmare has ended I will still be your aunt Liz. I have always loved you and your mother. You know that. It's not been an easy time for any of us, but that's no excuse. Perhaps I should have seen certain signs. Perhaps if I was more awake you might have been able to come to me to discuss this situation.

Please know that I love you and if there's any way I can be an auntie again I will try. Just remember that I will always be your aunt Liz, that I will always love you, and you shall always remain precious to me.

You have all my love,
Aunt Liz

The tables were reversed. Charles was on guard, sitting in the rocker in the living room while he waited for Elizabeth Anne's arrival. All that was missing was the shotgun.

When she entered it wasn't peevishly or solicitously. She walked into the mansion, regarded him for a moment, and went upstairs.

"Don't you have anything to say?" he asked, following her.

"Yes." She wasn't a bit drunk.

"What is it?"

"I hope I'm not pregnant too."

"You don't believe that story, do you?"

She turned around. She was no longer a Manchester, no longer controlled. Thirty-seven years of rage came out. "She's my friend, goddamn it. My goddamn friend. Karla's our godchild, you—you filthy lecher." She couldn't get the words out. "You pig." She spat it at him.

"It's a lie," he said. "It's a lie."

"Like the movie?"

"She's not pregnant."

"Why don't I call Olive and ask her?"

"Sunshine." He reached for her, hoping to placate her.

She stepped back. "Don't you Sunshine me! It's over. Do you hear me? *Over!*" She began wildly pulling things out of the closet. "It's over."

"Where are you going?"

"I'm going to dry out. To get the gray part working in my brain."

"But the election."

"Fuck the election."

"Elizabeth Anne, I'm surprised at you."

"Fuck the election. Do you hear me?"

"Darling. Please. The help can hear."

"And so will the neighbors if I have my way. Who do you think you are? You sleep with my best friend's daughter. Shack up with Ashley Pope. Make porno movies, and you want it all kept quiet. Just who do you think you are?"

"Liz, you're being irrational."

"No." Her blue eyes were frightening in her rage. "I was irrational all these years. Loving you. Waiting for you. Begging to be loved back." She bit her lip to keep the words in, but then let them fly. "They were right. You are a mutt. I'm leaving you, Charles Andrew Long." Tears flooded from her eyes. "I'm leaving you, Charles." Her body shuddered with wracking sobs, and he held her. He was frightened, very frightened. "And if you really expect me not to," she added brokenly, "then *you're* irrational."

The phone rang, breaking them apart.

"Answer it!" she yelled. "It's probably one of your women."

Charles answered it sheepishly. "It's for you. Olive."

"Will you please leave me alone?" she asked him. "Olive."

"Elizabeth Anne—"

"I'm going away for a while, darling."

"Where?"

Elizabeth Anne sighed. She couldn't believe it herself. "The Betty Ford Clinic. How is Karla?"

"Liz. I'm so sorry about this."

"Karla?"

"Karla's fine. She'll be all right. What about you and Charles?"

"I've written Karla a letter."

"But Charles . . . ?"

"Are you angry, Olive?"

Olive wanted to lie but couldn't. "Yes."

"At me?"

"No Liz, not at you. I love you."

Tuesday night Olive turned on the TV, interrupting Karla and Vince's game of backgammon.

"Hey, turn that off."

"I just want to hear . . ."

"It's still early," the newscaster said, "but there are a fair number of projections in. The incumbent, Charles Andrew Long, once a runaway is now just a favorite. He is expected to win, but we can't be sure. It looks like he's taking Manhattan but Brooklyn, which was his before, is not his now. Monroe has picked up a lot of votes. The Bronx . . ."

The phone rang and Olive answered it. "It's for you, Karla. Rebecca."

"Becky!" Karla hadn't spoken to her friend since her grandma's funeral. It would be so good to hear her voice. "Let me take this in my bedroom."

Walking more slowly than usual, Karla left Vince and Olive to discuss the election.

"What took you so long?" Becky asked.

"Oh, Becky, so much has happened. I can't believe it. First, how are you feeling?"

Becky sighed one of her deep, deep sighs. "Karla, it's horrible. I have no one. No family. Do you realize that? No one."

"I'm really sorry. Becky, we're just kids. How come all these horrible things happened to us?"

"It was some gangsters who killed my dad."

"What?"

"I don't know, but the police are looking into it. I don't want to talk about it."

"When are you coming back?"

"Soon. Maybe two weeks. I'll stay in school 'til June."

"And afterwards?"

"Then I'm going to Israel."

"Why Israel? Isn't there a war going on?"

Becky laughed. "Yes, but in case you hadn't heard, there's one going on here too. It's just that no one calls it that." She paused. "So what happened? With Charles."

It was Karla's turn to sigh. "I lost it."

"What?"

Karla told Becky about the party. About what Charles said and how she realized that Becky was right after all and he had never loved her, and about how she made that announcement and came home and cried and cried and cried.

"And then what happened?"

"I went to sleep, but in the middle of the night I woke up with these cramps. The worst cramps in the world. Like the ones you get in your leg, except in your stomach. Worse than the worst period cramps."

"And?"

"And I had blood all over me. Mom took me to the hospital and they said I'd miscarried. Oh, Becky, it was horrible, but it was good. I—I guess I would have had to have an abortion."

"How long were you in the hospital?"

"I got out yesterday. But Becky, listen to this. I saved the best thing for last." Her voice was excited, young again.

"What?" Becky asked. "Tell all."

"I found my father."

"What!"

"I mean he found me. I mean Mom brought us together."

"How? My gosh, Karla. How is that possible?"

Karla told her that story, too, and they both cried.

"You're coming back, right?" Karla said.

"Sure am."

"Well, I'm going to try to talk you out of going to Israel."

"I'll tell you what. I'll bring you all over next year. You guys might like it."

"Maybe. Maybe."

"Where's Mom?" Karla asked, emerging from the bedroom.

"She's in her room, sulking," Vince said, hiding his smile.

"Funny." Karla studied him, trying to search him out. He was still new to her.

"Come on. It's your move."

"Is she okay?" Karla asked.

"Yes," Vince said, finally smiling, showing his joy. "She's just arranging things. She says she's making room for me in her life."

Karla inhaled deeply and asked the question she'd been wanting to ask for days now. "You guys are getting married soon, right?"

"Right." His voice was serious but his smile was radiant. Then he let go, holding open his arms and inviting her in, his love child, his daughter.

"Oh, Dad, I'm so glad," Karla said, going to him.

So was Olive. She had retreated to her bedroom, to seek out the past—as well as the future. She stood on her toes and reached up into the closet. The first thing she pulled out were the two boxes of black flats she hadn't worn in a couple of years. Then she took down the Erica Wilson needlepoint she'd never finished. Behind that she found what she was looking for.

The ice skates. Slowly, reverently, as if they were a treasure from some ancient time, she lifted them down. As she had so many years ago, twenty-six to be exact, she sat on the floor and held them close to her nose. To smell the leather. To remember the love with which they were purchased.

Olive closed her eyes and felt a powerful energy surge through her. She felt as if she were involved in a deep inner dialogue with her father. He was there with her, right beside her.

"Daddy, you were right. You said one day I'd have it all. You said no one had it better than me. You were right. I have it. Took long enough, don't you think?" She looked over her shoulder, also as she had so many years ago, but no one was there. No one to disturb her, just easy chatter coming from the living room.

"It took long enough, Dad, but it was worth waiting for. It was worth every second."

Was it her imagination or did she really hear a voice whisper softly, *Everything will work out perfectly, pumpkin. You'll see.*

"Thank you, Daddy. Thank you. And Dad, please take care of Mom. She needs you now. Very much."